A self-confessed bookworm, at university and then went on to become a science teacher and, later, headteacher of a secondary school in Oxfordshire. After retiring, she turned to crime writing and hasn't looked back since. *The Great Shroud* is the fifth book in her much-loved Anglian Detective Agency series.

Also by Vera Morris and available from Headline Accent

THE GREAT SHROUD

VERA MORRIS

ACCENT

First published in 2021 by Headline Accent
An imprint of HEADLINE PUBLISHING GROUP

5

Cataloguing in Publication Data is available from the British Library

ISBN 978 1 4722 8366 5

Typeset in 10.5/13pt Bembo Std by Jouve (UK), Milton Keynes

Printed and bound in Great Britain by Clays Ltd, Elcograf S.p.A.

HEADLINE PUBLISHING GROUP
An Hachette UK Company
Carmelite House
50 Victoria Embankment
London EC4Y 0DZ

www.headline.co.uk
www.hachette.co.uk

For four dear friends
Liz and Graham, and Kath and Bob

For all the people who work for, and support,
one of our greatest charities:
The Royal National Lifeboat Institution, and especially
to those who risk their lives to save others

A sullen white surf beat against its steep sides; then all collapsed, and the great shroud of the sea rolled on as it rolled five thousand years ago.

Herman Melville, *Moby Dick*

Chapter One

The Aldeburgh fish and chip shop was closed for the day, and the sun had set. In the flat above the shop Matthew Grill was alone. In the bathroom he splashed water over his face, and pulled a comb through his thick brown hair. He'd had a bath as soon as he got home after he'd finished selling the rest of the day's catch from his hut facing Market Cross Place. He'd scrubbed himself hard, trying to scour away mucus, scales and the smell of fish, then splashed on the Old Spice Musk aftershave he'd bought from the chemist in the High Street.

The girl behind the counter had smirked at him. 'Not like you, Matt. Your Sarah turning you into one of them new men?' The pharmacist coughed and gave her a stern look. He'd paid, grabbed the bottle and left without replying. She was close to the mark. Sarah had started pushing him away. 'You stink of fish. I have to smell it all day long, and then you come home smelling ten times worse than the shop.' She hadn't been like that when they were first married. Sometimes he'd taken her when he came back from the hut, before they opened the shop for the evening.

Married nine years. She was as beautiful as then: blonde shoulder-length hair and a good figure – but it was her irresistible face, and the way she looked at you, her large blue eyes seductive behind half-closed eyelids. She still flipped his stomach over.

*

1

The day had started well. He'd opened the prep room door of his fish and chip shop, and heaved in a loaded container of glistening cod and haddock. No sign of Sarah. 'Morning, Ethel.'

'Morning, Matt. Want a cuppa before you go back to the hut?' She didn't wait for an answer. 'Lily,' she shouted to the girl scrubbing down a draining board, 'tea for Mr Grill. Nice and strong, not like that weasel's piss you gave me yesterday.' She seized a large cod and with a few swift movements of her knife chopped off its head, ripped out its guts, and cut it into fillets. 'That's a good, big 'un.'

'Seen Sarah?'

'Yes, she's up and out. Said she had some shopping to do.' She didn't look up from her work.

He drained his mug. 'Good cuppa, Lily.'

Lily Varley blushed and smiled. Ethel sniffed.

'How's your mum, Lily?'

The smile disappeared. 'No better; doctor's coming this morning.'

'Do you need to go home?'

She went back to her scrubbing. 'No. Dad'll be there.'

'Give her my regards.'

She turned and smiled. 'Thank you, Mr Grill.'

'Right, Ethel, I'll bring the next load in, then me and your Tom'll be busy all morning.'

'Good catch?'

'Not bad at all. Besides this lot,' he pointed to the container, 'some good-sized Dovers, bass and five lobsters. Tom's boiling them up. Chef at the White Lion Hotel, he's ordered three, already.'

'See you later, then.' She continued her massacre.

'You on this evening?'

'No, but I'll have prepared everything.' She turned to Lily and pointed to a bulging sack. 'Time to get those spuds peeled so I can chip 'em.'

'I'll move them to the yard for you, Lily. Are you working this evening?'

She nodded. 'Yes, I'm serving with Betty, Wilf's frying.'

'Lily.'

2

'Yes, Mr Grill?'

'Don't walk home by yourself. That's an order.' He turned to Ethel. 'Can you make sure someone will walk Lily home before you leave? What about Wilf?'

'There's no need, Mr Grill. It's not far to home, and people will still be around,' Lily said.

She sounded cross. Good to be strong-minded, but not now. 'While you're working here, you'll do as you're told.' He tempered his words with a smile.

Her lips quivered. 'If you say so, Mr Grill.'

'I'll make sure she's OK,' Ethel said. She slashed at the air with her filleting knife. 'I'd like to catch the bugger – I'd settle his hash if he attacked me.'

Lily giggled. 'I think you're too old for him, Ethel.'

Ethel waggled the knife in Lily's direction. 'And you're too tall, from what I've heard he seems to like little ones, you cheeky sod.'

He left them to it.

Matt ran down the stairs and opened the door that led directly into the High Street. He stood back and looked up at his home. It dominated this part of the town; three stories high, with a grand door to the shop on the corner, and above it, against blue paint, the sign, Aldeburgh Fish and Chips. It was exactly as it had been when his mother ran the shop. He hadn't changed a thing. *He* hadn't wanted, or needed, to.

He grimaced; he should have checked everything was ship-shape before he left. He felt in his jacket pocket; he had the keys. He turned right and came to the gate leading into the yard. It was never locked. He took a key, opened the prep-room door and flipped down two switches. The yard and prep room were flooded with light. First, he checked the smokery. There were some bloaters hanging up. No other fish. That was one thing he would like to get rid of. It didn't seem worth the effort, but his mother didn't like to waste fish and she said kippers and bloaters still sold, especially to the older folk, but also to hotels. He hated dealing with the smoked salmon:

3

they had to buy in the fish and he couldn't persuade Ethel to slice it up. 'You do it better than anyone else,' she said. It was a real fiddle pulling out all the pin bones.

He walked round the yard; the potato peeler was clean and the stone floor had been swabbed down. He didn't know why he bothered checking; Ethel, or whoever was in charge of the preparation, was trustworthy. The prep room was just as clean and tidy; the chip-cutting machine immaculate. But there was still that lingering gluey smell, even though the wooden boards used for cutting up the fish were scrubbed clean. It hadn't bothered him until Sarah kept going on about it.

He sighed. If only his mum hadn't decided, after his dad died, she didn't want to run the chip shop any more, and had taken a job as a school cook. If she'd been here, Sarah wouldn't have got all those big ideas.

It was ten years since Dad had drowned. Matt had been twenty-one, courting Sarah, and amazed she'd agreed to be his girlfriend. They'd married a year later; she'd given up her job in an office in Ipswich to help Mum in the shop. She was a hard, quick worker, and used her bookkeeping skills to take over the accounts and tax returns. Mum said she'd got a good brain; she was happy to leave the business *and* the profits to them when she'd moved to Blackfriars School.

Then, after the murders, the school closed down, and Mum became a member of The Anglian Detective Agency, looking after the three detectives, working and living in Miss Piff's house in Dunwich. And she wasn't Mabel Grill any more, she'd married Stuart Elderkin, one of the detectives. Matt liked him, but he didn't like the thought of his mum in bed with another man.

He puffed out a stream of air and went into the shop. It was also clean and tidy; smells of beef dripping and vinegar lingered in the air. He grimaced and rubbed his chest; he needed to take some bicarb. It was the third time in as many days Sarah had plonked battered cod and some tired chips in front of him for his supper. 'Sorry, haven't had time to go to the butchers. I'm meeting Mandy at seven. I expect you'll be fast away when I get back. I'll sleep in the other bedroom. Don't wake me when you get up, too early for me.' She pecked at his cheek, then sniffed. 'That's nice. Old Spice?' She paused. 'Why don't you try Brut? I like that better.' He'd reached out to pull her to him, but she had slipped away as sinuous and as quick as a silver eel. Who'd she smelt Brut on?

He opened the front door of the shop, locked it and stepped out into the narrow street dividing the shop from the White Hart Inn. He walked towards the sea, pausing under a street light on Crag Path to glance at his watch. Half-nine. He wasn't meeting him until ten-fifteen. God knows why it had to be so late. He needed to be up at four and out in the boat by half-past. Sun didn't rise 'til half-six, but they must be at the fishing grounds before the rest of the boats got there. His dad had trained him to be up and about early. 'Soonest out there, soonest home, soonest money in your pocket.' If he'd heard it once he'd heard it a thousand times. Now, he wished he could hear it again.

A north-westerly wind was blowing over the Suffolk fields. It had been a poor summer weather-wise: cool, below average temperatures, with only a few brief spells of sunny weather. There hadn't been so many day trippers this year, but the shop had done well and the catches were still good. His stomach clenched. He didn't want to think about it. He still hoped his suspicions were wrong.

He'd stopped checking the monthly statement from the bank; Sarah did all the bookkeeping and tax returns. She used to show him the statements and explain the details. He was grateful, figures bored him, apart from the weight of catches and the price per pound of different fish. A few days ago, an envelope, embossed 'Midland Bank' on the back, shot through the letter box as he was about to go out. He had torn it open, wanting to see the total for August. It was always their best month: a peak month for visitors, the bank holiday an extra boost. He'd stared at the figure. That couldn't be right. He didn't understand it. It should have been much more than that. Where had the money gone? No! He felt cold and sick as he thought of the obvious, perhaps the only, plausible reason.

He walked north along Crag Path, oblivious to the off-shore

breeze bringing with it smells of the land, oblivious to the dark, sighing sea and the sickle moon high in the sky, clouds racing over it. Now he had to sort out *another* problem. He didn't want to do this, but he'd promised her he would. He blew out his cheeks. He'd sort this one out tonight. It shouldn't take long. He was probably a bloody fool, but it niggled at him. He had to make sure. Should he have talked it over with someone? But, if he was off the beaten track, which he probably was, he'd look a fool, and it wouldn't be fair to put his thoughts into someone else's head if he was wrong. Was there time to nip into the Cross Keys for a pint?

'Hello, Matt.' There were several of the lifeboat crew propping up the bar, including Tom, Ethel's son, his first mate on the boat and second cox'n of the lifeboat crew. Matt had been proud when he'd been made cox'n, the boat's commander; carrying on his family's tradition. He wished his dad had lived to see him take up the post.

He waved to them, then moved to the far end and ordered a pint of Adnams bitter and took it to a vacant table near a window looking out onto Crabbe Street. Tom said something to the rest and made his way over.

'Heard about that German coaster that exploded off Folkstone?' Tom asked, sitting down opposite him, his clown's face smiling below a mass of curly brown hair. However down you felt, Tom's face made you smile.

'No, missed that one. Anyone hurt?'

'Two injured, one had to be winched up by coastguard helicopter. She was five miles south of the town. Could have been much worse.'

He took a deep swallow.

'That was a good catch today, Matt; let's hope tomorrow'll be as good.'

'Ay, it was.'

Tom shifted in his chair. 'You all right, Matt? You've not seemed yourself lately.'

He didn't reply. What could he say? He was worried his wife was two-timing him and taking money from the shop for herself? He

6

was worried someone he knew had done something dreadful? He finished his beer. Tom looked puzzled; he was waiting for an answer. 'I'm fine, Tom, don't worry about me. I'm off, need my beauty sleep. See you tomorrow.'

'Good night, Matt. Don't forget, I'm always here for you.'

He smiled at him and slapped him on the back. It was true, they'd always looked out for each other, right from their first day at school. His best friend – he decided he'd talk to him, and his mum, but he needed to have it out with Sarah first.

'Night, Tom. Don't stay too long, don't want you half-drunk tomorrow, falling overboard.' He waved to the others and stepped out into the night.

Chapter Two

Wednesday, 13 September, 1972

Tom Blower, half-asleep, half-awake, moved uneasily under the bedding. He turned and slipped his arm over Betty's body, easing himself close to her, his chest against her back, cupping a breast with his hand, tucking his knees into the back of hers, forming the spoon. He slid his hand inside her nightdress, her skin soft against his rough palm. He sighed, and buried his face in her hair. She made a soft, moaning sound. His worries about Matt eased and he drifted into sleep.

There was a great crack of noise. He jerked up. A maroon. Then the second. He leapt out of bed and dashed to the window. Two white flashes, high in the air. Explosive signals fired from the mortars at the Coastguard Station at Fort Green. He ripped off his pyjamas, groped for his clothes and pulled on his pants. Betty was up, switching on the light, throwing him his other clothes. The alarm clock by the side of the bed showed ten past two.

She hugged him. 'Take care, my boy. We need you.'

A quick kiss, a fleeting look at Mary and Joshua, still asleep in their rooms.

'I might beat Matt to the lifeboat,' he shouted as he ran down the stairs, unbolted the door and burst into Slaughden Road. Matt had an advantage, he lived closer to the lifeboat; if Tom got there before him it would be the first time. The streets were deserted, dark, the sound of his pounding footsteps echoing from walls as he cut through

Hertford Place onto Crag Path. In the distance he could hear other men running. His heart raced, adrenalin surging through his body. This was what they loved, all the crew, every one of them. Someone out there needed you, prayed you'd come to them. When they were ready to launch, the *Charles Dibdin*, with everyone on board, was tipped forward, the securing chain knocked off and the boat started off down the slipway, gathering speed, hitting the sea in a burst of spray and a gut-retching thud, as it met solid water.

The wind had changed since he went to bed. It was blowing off the sea and he could make out the white caps of waves. Where would they be needed tonight? There were lights on in some of the houses on Crag Path. Those maroons would wake the dead. His feet pounded the promenade, every cell of his body energised. He was ready and eager to be part of the launch into the dark waves.

He hoped Matt was all right, and he'd had some sleep. He was sure Sarah must have upset him. It wouldn't be the first time. Matt had told him a few months ago she'd wanted to close the fish and chip shop, and turn it into a restaurant. Aldeburgh without its chippy? Matt said they had had terrible rows as he'd refused to even think about it. 'She seems to have forgotten it isn't even our shop, although it will be one day, it's my mum's,' he'd said.

As Tom neared the car park, there was the thump, thump, thump of heavy machinery – a light on in the lifeboat shed. What the hell was Matt doing? Why'd he turned the tractor on? It wasn't needed until they came back, when it hauled the lifeboat back onto its landing slide.

He raced towards the noise. A slit of light shone onto the pebbles of the beach. The door was ajar. The sound wasn't right. There was something wrong with the tractor. A wave of diesel fumes seared his nostrils as he pulled the door fully open. The room seemed empty; the row of orange life jackets hung on pegs, the table and sink, the electric kettle – everything was normal. Where was Matt? He turned towards the tractor, on the south side of the shed. Then he saw him.

'No!' Matt was caught in the chain that hauled the boat back up the slipway. His head banging against the tractor, his body flopping like a dead rabbit, arms and legs jerking. Tom froze in horror, his legs turned to jelly. This couldn't be happening. He staggered to the tractor and turned off the ignition. The reverberations of the engine spluttered and died.

He knelt down beside him. 'Matt, Matt.' Tears rolled down his cheeks. There was no need to search for a pulse. Matt's head was a bloody mass. Tom tried to ease him away from the machinery, but something was gripping him round his neck. He laid his hand on Matt's hair, rocking backwards and forwards, calling his name.

The sound of running footsteps.

'My God, what's happened, Tom?'

Clasping Matt's body to him, he turned.

Alan Varley, the boat's engineer, face white, eyes staring in disbelief, was standing petrified in the doorway.

Tears streaming down his face, Tom groaned, 'It's Matt – he's dead.'

Chapter Three

It was a bright morning as Frank Diamond, the founder of The Anglian Detective Agency, drove to a new case. He turned to Stuart Elderkin. 'What's the name of this place we're going to?'

'I've told you twice already. You're slipping back into that bad habit you had when we were in the police. Always wanting things repeated. If I didn't know you better, I'd think you were losing your marbles.' Frank was formerly a detective inspector in the Suffolk Police Force and Stuart his sergeant.

Frank glanced at the dashboard; eight forty, their appointment was for nine. He floored the accelerator of the Avenger GT and overtook a tractor. 'You hadn't said anything for at least ten minutes. It was a way of checking if you were still alive.'

Stuart sighed. 'It's Gladham Hall, and don't forget what Dorothy said, address him as Sir George.' Dorothy Piff was the Agency's administrator, her house being their base. 'Think I'll have a few puffs before we get there, don't think I'll be allowed a smoke once we get inside.' He fumbled in his jacket pocket and took out a briar pipe, a tin of shag tobacco and a box of matches.

Frank groaned. 'In that case, open your window.' He turned off the A12 for Wickham Market, then took the B1078 for Needham Market.

Several puffs later, 'We're coming up to it,' Stuart said. 'There, on the right. See the gates?'

'You can hardly miss them,' Frank replied. He waited for two cars to pass then turned between impressive wrought-iron gates onto

11

a wide gravelled drive. No sign of a house, just acres of parkland. 'I'm more interested in the case, whatever it is, now I've seen this. I hope the house lives up to its surroundings.'

'See your team did well last night. Two nil, not a bad result.'

Frank nodded. 'I think the Anfield crowd expected more, it might not be enough. Eintracht Frankfurt are a good team; we might go down when we get to West Germany.'

'You ought to support our local team,' Stuart said. 'Ipswich did well in the Texaco Cup. Good win, four-two.'

Frank laughed. 'Stuart, they were playing St Johnstone!'

'A win's a win.' The parkland merged into wide lawns, bordered by yew hedges. 'Dorothy said there's three hundred acres of land,' he muttered, taking a last suck at his pipe.

'What a pile!' Frank exclaimed as they turned a bend in the drive. The hall was impressive, four-storied with tall chimneys, built of once-red brick which had faded to pale pink. He parked the car in front of a wide flight of stone steps, leading up to a massive oak door.

Stuart turned to him. 'Dorothy was right, you should have worn something a bit more formal.'

Frank shook his head. 'Apart from the suit I take out exclusively for all the funerals we keep having to go to, this is as formal as I get. They're lucky it wasn't a T-shirt and jeans.' What was wrong with a black leather jacket and white polo? He was wearing proper trousers; they even had a vague crease in them. Stuart as ever was the essence of respectability in a three-piece suit, white shirt and sombre tie. Mabel, his wife, and the Agency's cook and housekeeper, had fussed over him before they left. 'Not every day you meet one of the nobility,' she'd said.

Dorothy had sniffed. 'He's only a Knight Bachelor, made his fortune making sweets.'

Mabel brushed an invisible hair from Stuart's lapel. 'Trubshaw's Truffles, they're my favourite, but I wouldn't mind a box of Trubshaw's Trios, if Sir George is giving away free samples.'

Dorothy rolled her eyes. 'The only thing he's free with is his morals, so I hear. He embarked on his third marriage about ten years

12

ago; she was a finalist in Miss Great Britain . . . 1952? No doubt he'll be trading her in for a new model before long.'

Frank smiled at the memory of the exchanges and the look on Dorothy's face.

The front door silently swung open and 'a lackey' in a dark suit stared at them.

Frank thought his left eyebrow moved a millimetre upwards as he cast a glance over his dress. 'Mr Diamond and Mr Elderkin to see Sir George,' he said, trying to keep a straight face.

The man stepped aside and waved them in. 'I will let Sir George know you are here.' He glided away, leaving them, no doubt, with time to be impressed by the palatial hall and a wide staircase sweeping upwards, curving to the left, its barley-twist oak balustrade gleaming from centuries of wax polish and elbow grease.

The man glided back. 'Please follow me, gentlemen. Sir George is in the sitting room.'

He opened the door to a vast room panelled in pale oak, its walls festooned with portraits of bewigged men and unsmiling ladies in various period dresses. A man rose from a cluster of ornate furniture grouped round a marble fireplace.

'Welcome, welcome.' He was a few inches taller than Frank's five eleven, with an avuncular face, light brown wavy hair dusting his collar, a large bony nose and a no-lips mouth.

After introductions he waved them towards the fireplace and two settees plus two tub chairs, all covered in the same patterned red satin.

'No fire, I'm afraid, not ready for that yet, are we?' He laughed heartily.

Frank couldn't see the joke, but smiled politely.

'Do sit down. I hope you didn't have any problems getting here?'

Where does he think we came from? Outer Mongolia?

'No, indeed, we had a trouble-free journey,' Stuart replied, sounding like an undertaker about to move the corpse from the funeral parlour to the grave.

'Good. Good,' Sir George said. 'Can I offer you refreshment?

Coffee? Or something stronger?' He raised his eyebrows and twinkled at them.

'Coffee would be fine,' Frank said. Drinking at nine in the morning?

Trubshaw pressed a bell. The front-door man – was he the butler? – glided in.

'Coffee for three, Giddings, and perhaps a few buns . . . or whatever Cook has made.'

Stuart beamed.

Frank decided he'd inherited some of his father's rabid left-wing views as he was starting to dislike Trubshaw and his gilded life. 'Sir George, you didn't make it clear when you phoned, exactly what you wanted us to do for you. Perhaps, before the coffee comes, you might enlighten us.'

Trubshaw moved uneasily in his chair, the friction between satin and the expensive cloth of his trousers making a slithery sound like a snake moving over dry grass. 'Oh, yes, of course.' He grimaced, the lines running from his nose to his mouth deepening, making him look older than his fifty-nine years. 'Before I tell you, I must be reassured you won't discuss this with anyone else.'

Frank explained that before they accepted a case it was discussed with all members of the Agency and they only accepted it on a majority decision, although usually there was no problem.

'Can you rely on the discretion of all of your partners?'

'Completely.'

'Very well. I want you to investigate the theft of some very expensive jewellery.'

'You've informed the police?' Stuart asked. 'You'll need to do that for the insurance, won't you?'

More snake-like noises.

'No, er, no, I haven't. The items were not insured, and I don't want a load of country bumpkin flat-feet tramping all over my property. I've had excellent reports of your successes and I'd like you to take on this case. I'll pay above whatever your rates are, I'm a generous man, don't worry about not getting your money.'

14

Up until that moment, Frank hadn't been worried about non-payment. 'If we take the case, the usual terms will apply and you'll be asked to sign an agreement, so I'm afraid there's no chance of non-payment.'

Trubshaw looked flustered. 'My word's usually been enough when I make a deal. However, I suppose this is the modern way.'

Stuart's back had straightened at the mention of flat-footed coppers. 'I presume you know Mr Diamond and myself are former detectives in the Suffolk Police Force? We still have many colleagues and friends there.'

Trubshaw's already choleric complexion deepened. 'Oh, of course. I'd forgotten. Do forgive the faux pas.'

'What items were stolen and when did this happen?' Frank asked.

Trubshaw leant towards them. 'Three very beautiful pieces of jewellery: two rings and a bracelet. I've photos of them – in colour,' he said, cocking his head and smiling as though this was an achievement equal to the production of an old masterpiece. He passed the photos to Frank, who glanced at them and handed them to Stuart.

When the photos were back in Trubshaw's hands, he rapped his fingers against them. 'There's too much of this going on. I read in the paper only this morning, Bernard Lee.' He paused, obviously feeling he hadn't grabbed their attention, and rapped the photos again. 'You know, the actor. He was robbed in a hotel room by two young thugs. Disgusting.'

'Shall we get back to the jewellery?' Frank asked.

Trubshaw frowned and pointed to the first photo. 'Flawless emerald-cut diamond ring. Nearly four carats. Worth forty thousand pounds. The next one, French handmade platinum bracelet with a Ceylon sapphire and a diamond-cluster strap, forty thousand five hundred, and lastly, my favourite, a 1930s' Art Deco diamond-cluster ring, with a central three-carat diamond, all set in platinum, at least another forty-five thousand.'

Stuart pursed his lips. 'I can't believe you didn't insure them, sir. One hundred and thirty thousand grand's a lot of money. Can I ask why you didn't insure them?'

Trubshaw's nostrils flared. 'That's my business, not yours.'

Frank gave him the fish eye.

Trubshaw shrugged his shoulders. 'If you must know, it was Lady Trubshaw, she forgot to remind me those particular pieces were due for renewal. She's terribly upset about the whole matter, so when you meet her, please don't ask her about any of this. Only deal with me.'

The door opened and Giddings entered, carrying a loaded tray. A petite, voluptuous platinum blonde bounced after him. 'Oh, do hurry up, Giddings. I've seen stiffs move faster than you. That coffee will be stone cold if you don't get a shift on.'

Giddings' pace increased from glide to stride, his face turning from alabaster to rosy marble.

'There you are, Georgie. Trying to keep me away from these handsome men.'

Frank and Stuart stood up.

She pranced towards them, holding out her hand, her large breasts moving in unison. 'Oooh, real detectives. I've read about you two.' She turned her come-hither eyes onto Frank. 'You remind me of The Saint. Are you Diamond or Elderkin?' She turned to face her husband. 'See, I can remember names when I want to.'

Frank shook her hand; it was dry, warm and lingering. 'I'm Frank Diamond, Lady Trubshaw.'

Her happy, moon-shaped face creased with laughter. 'Call me Hazel, dear. Can't be doing with all that formality. Georgie likes it, but it's never cut any ice with me. I didn't marry him for his title, you know.'

Frank longed to ask if free Trubshaw's Trios had seduced her. He smiled politely.

'You must be Mr Elderkin?'

Stuart tentatively stretched out his hand, as though afraid she might start nibbling it. 'Pleased to meet you, Lady Trubshaw.'

She pumped it up and down. 'I've told you, it's Hazel.'

While this was going on, Frank was observing Sir George. He was surprised; instead of the expected expression of annoyance or even anger, a smile played over those thin lips and a look of fondness

16

and indulgence softened his face. Sir George was enamoured by Hazel's antics.

She moved to the coffee tray. 'How do you like your coffee, Frank? Black, hot and strong? Or creamy and sweet?' She dimpled at him.

'Black, please.'

'And what about you, Mr Elderkin?'

'Cream and three sugars, please.'

'Ooh, same as me. Georgie likes it hot and strong, don't you, darling?' She took a cup to him and kissed his cheek. 'That's how I like my men, hot and strong, and I've never found a hotter or stronger one than Georgie.'

'Steady on, Hazel. You'll be getting me a reputation.' His expression indicated it was one he liked.

'You deserve it, my darling.'

So, Trubshaw's Trios didn't feature in Hazel's passion for Sir George. The coffee was excellent, but he'd had enough of Georgie and Hazel's mutual admiration society.

The door opened. 'There's a telephone call for Mr Diamond, Sir George,' bleated Giddings. 'In the hall.'

Frank frowned. Must be from Greyfriars, no one else knew they were here. Stuart frowned. Frank stood up. 'Sorry about this, Sir George.'

'Nonsense. Giddings, show Mr Diamond to the phone.'

He followed Giddings out to the hall. From a marble side table Giddings handed him a gold-plated, he presumed it was plated, receiver. Frank gave Giddings a hard look; he moved away.

'Hello. Frank Diamond here.'

'Frank! Thank God.'

It was Laurel, sounding anxious.

'Laurel, are you all right?' What was he thinking, she was obviously not all right?

'Frank, you must come back immediately.'

'What's happened?'

'Oh, Frank. Mabel's in pieces. You must get Stuart back as soon as you can.'

17

He waited.

'It's Mabel's son, Matt; he's dead.'

His stomach dropped. 'Christ! What happened?'

'Nick Revie came to tell her. It seems there's been an accident.'

'A car accident?'

'No. From what Revie said it was a freak accident. I didn't take it all in. Mabel collapsed. Oh, Frank, this is awful. She needs Stuart.'

'Is Revie still there?'

'No, he's gone.'

'Right, be with you as soon as we can. Hold the fort.'

'Dorothy's doing that. Please hurry. We need you.' The phone went dead.

He took a slow, deep breath. No time to waste. He half-ran back to the sitting room.

'Sorry, Sir George, we have to leave now. Emergency back at the Agency.'

Stuart froze.

'What's happened?' Sir George asked.

'I'll contact you later. Stuart – let's go.'

Stuart's face paled. 'Is it Mabel? Is she all right?'

'She's OK. I'll explain in the car.'

'Is there anything we can do?' Hazel Trubshaw looked genuinely worried. 'Let us know, won't you?'

He nodded and, grasping Stuart's arm, they hurried from the room.

Chapter Four

Laurel hugged Bumper, her black Labrador; his solid body and thick fur were a comfort. He looked up at her, seemingly puzzled, his liquid brown eyes searching her face, as if for clues.

Dorothy came into the sitting room, sat down, took her cigarette case and lighter from a table and lit up.

'How is Mabel?' Laurel asked. 'Shall I go in?'

'No, she said she wanted to be alone. I don't think she believes Matt is dead. I'm not sure I do. You didn't know him, did you?'

'I met him a few times, but you're right, I didn't *know* him. I liked him; he seemed a good man, and from what Mabel has said he worked hard, and was well thought of in Aldeburgh.' She pulled Bumper tighter. He gave a whine. 'Sorry.' She kissed his nose. 'Nice-looking man.' She paused. 'I'm not sure I took in everything Revie said – about how he died.'

Dorothy nodded. 'Freak accident, from the sound of it. Mabel says Matt wouldn't be so careless. One minute she's saying he can't be dead, then the next she's swearing at him for being slapdash. She's not making much sense.'

Laurel sighed. 'I'm not surprised. I do wish they'd hurry up. She needs Stuart.'

Dorothy's head went up. 'I think I can hear Frank's car.'

Laurel ran into the hall and opened the front door. Stuart shot out of the car; she'd never seen him move so fast, he was by her side before Frank had closed his car door.

'Where is she?'

'She's in your rooms.' Mabel and Stuart, like Laurel, lived at Greyfriars, Frank remaining in his cottage on the Minsmere cliffs.

Stuart hurried away.

Frank took hold of her shoulders and studied her face. He pulled her to his chest, his shoulder-length curls caressing her cheek. Relief surged through her. Frank being here made it more bearable. He pressed her close, hugged her tight, then holding her shoulders, gently pushed her away.

'OK? This *is* bad. We'll all have to do whatever we can for her. She's been worrying about Matt and Sarah for months. I thought she was perking up lately, but this is terrible. Would you like some coffee?'

She nodded.

'Let's go into the kitchen. I'll see if Dorothy would like one.'

He came back with her, and busied himself filling the percolator. Dorothy sat opposite her, puffing on a cigarette, probably lit from the last one. They looked at each other and Laurel stretched out her hand and Dorothy grasped it. They didn't say anything.

Frank placed three mugs on the table. The smell of the coffee was strong, aromatic, comforting.

'I didn't disturb Mabel and Stuart,' he said. 'Mabel's having a good cry.'

Dorothy let out a long exhalation. 'At least she's got a good broad shoulder to lean on, someone who loves her. I'm glad of that.' Her face showed her understanding of the hurt Mabel was going through. Both Dorothy and Laurel had lost a sister in the near past, both killed before their time. Laurel had had her parents to share her grief, but Dorothy had no close family, only her many friends. Friends were wonderful, Laurel thought, but at a time like this you needed your family.

Frank brought the percolator to the table. 'Top ups?' He shared out the remains of the coffee. 'Laurel, when you phoned, I couldn't make much sense of what had happened to Matt. Can you fill me in?'

'Sorry, I can't. I was desperate to get you both back to Greyfriars, especially Stuart.'

He turned to Dorothy. 'Can *you* remember what Revie said?'

Dorothy stubbed out her cigarette and took a sip of coffee. 'Revie turned up just after the two of you left to see Sir George. About eight thirty. Mabel answered the door.'

Dorothy had been in the office sorting out some filing when she heard the front doorbell.

'I'll get it,' shouted Mabel. 'Hello, Nick, this is a pleasant surprise. Bit early for you, I hope you haven't come for a bacon butty, I'm right out of backside.' There was a pause. 'What's the matter?' Her voice changed.

'Mabel. Can we go and sit down somewhere?'

Dorothy stiffened. Revie's tone was sombre, not his usual bluster. She hurried into the hall.

'Ah, Dorothy, good. Can we all go into the sitting room?' His face was worried, tired, grey, one arm round Mabel's shoulders as he steered her out of the hall.

'What's happened? Is it Stuart?' Her voice was breaking. 'Has there been an accident?'

'No. No. Stuart's fine,' he said as he guided her to the settee. 'You sit there, Mabel.' He jerked his head at Dorothy, indicating she should sit next to her.

Mabel was staring at him with wide, glazed eyes.

'I'm very sorry to tell you, Mabel, your son, Matthew, has had an accident.'

She started up from the chair. Dorothy grasped her arm, pulling her back.

'An accident? You mean at sea? Don't tell me he's been drowned like his father!' she wailed.

'No, not like that, but he's dead, Mabel. I'm really sorry to tell you, he's dead.'

'No!' Mabel screamed. 'No, not my Matt. Not my Matt.' She collapsed against Dorothy, her body crumpling, her face a ghastly white.

Revie shot up. 'Put her head between her knees, Dorothy.'

The door opened and Bumper shot in, stopped, and growled at Revie who was helping Dorothy with Mabel.

21

'Bumper! Stop that!' Laurel said, as she came into the room. 'Nick? What's happened?'

Dorothy looked up. Laurel was standing holding Bumper back by his collar, her mouth open. 'It's Matt, he's dead. Nick's just broken the news to Mabel.'

Laurel's face blanched. 'I'll get some water,' she whispered.

'Make it something stiffer,' Revie growled.

'We moved her to her bedroom, she couldn't stand, I wanted to get the doctor, but Dorothy persuaded me it was best to get Stuart back as quickly as possible. We took it in turns to stay with her, but then she wanted to be by herself,' Laurel said.

'Did Revie explain what happened?'

'Only briefly. It was obvious Mabel wasn't up to hearing the details, and he couldn't say too much to us,' Dorothy said. 'Matt died in the lifeboat shed.'

'The one on Aldeburgh's front?' Frank asked.

'Yes. All Revie would say was there'd been a freak accident and somehow part of Matt's clothing had got caught up in the tractor engine they keep in the shed. They use it for hauling the boat back onto its launching slide,' Dorothy said.

'When did this happen?' Frank asked.

'Early hours of this morning. Maroons had gone up and Tom Blower, Matt's best friend, found him. That's all Revie told us. He said he'd come back when Mabel was able to take in the details.'

'Was he dead when his friend found him?'

'We don't know.'

'What about Matt's wife? She must be in a state.'

'Revie didn't mention her. He said he had to get back to Ipswich. It seems the search for the man who's responsible for the deaths of the three young women isn't going too well,' Dorothy said.

Frank nodded. 'Let's hope the bastard, whoever he is, doesn't kill again before they catch him. It's times like this when I wish I was back in the force.'

Laurel's stomach contracted: three young women murdered.

22

Another mass murderer. She thought of Nicholson, the headmaster of Blackfriars School, and his obsession with red-haired girls, and her own near death. She shuddered. She shouldn't be thinking about herself; she and the rest of the team must try and help Mabel and Stuart. Thank God Frank was here.

Dorothy slowly got up. 'I'll knock on their door. See if there's anything they need.'

'Frank, let's take Bumper in the garden for a few minutes.'

The sun was shining, but a north-westerly breeze was keeping the temperature down. The garden was vivid with autumn colours: bright dahlias, yellow rudbeckias waving their giant daisy heads, and the first autumn crocuses and cyclamen were flowering under the apple tree. Frank sat on the bench and patted the space next to him. She sat down; Bumper flopped at her feet.

They sat in silence. A flock of lapwings passed overhead, no doubt on their way to Minsmere, their sad calls like cries for help.

'I'll phone Revie, see if he'll tell me a few more details. She'll want to know what happened when she's recovered. It might be better if I talked to Mabel rather than Revie coming over again. What do you think?'

She nodded. 'Yes, that's thoughtful of you.' Or did he want to satisfy his own curiosity? She could understand that. There was always the need to know. The how. The why. And who had done it. But this time there wasn't anyone else. Somehow Matt had caused his own death. A terrible thought shafted through her brain. 'Frank, he couldn't have committed suicide, could he? That would be too awful. Mabel would take all the blame onto herself. She's been so worried about Matt's marriage.'

Frank nodded. 'Yes, it did occur to me, but I can't see, from what we know of him, how it could be suicide. I don't think he was the type. But you never know, do you? I suspect he'd have chosen The Great Shroud, if he wanted to do away with himself.'

'The great shroud?'

'The sea. Herman Melville's name for it.'

She shivered. 'That's a terrible name.' She loved the sea, couldn't

23

imagine not living by it. It had been part of her life since she'd been a toddler, fascinated by the waves, running fearlessly into them, hauled back by her parents. Learning to swim by herself; filled with joy when she realised she was free of the sea bed and was doggy-paddling through the water. And the sea had refused to claim her when she fought for her life off Minsmere beach last March.

Frank got up. 'It's an apposite name, especially in these parts. Right, I'll see if I can get hold of Revie. Once Mabel's back on her feet, she won't rest until she knows what happened to Matt.'

Laurel lit a fire in the sitting room. Although they didn't really need one, she'd decided flames and warmth would be a comfort, not just to Mabel, but to all of them.

Dorothy was sitting close to the fire, her hands stretched out, fingers wide, as if she could draw the heat of the flames into her body.

Frank moved to the sideboard. 'I'm having a Scotch, in fact I'm having a single malt.' He looked at them. They both nodded. He brought generous measures in cut-glass tumblers, and came back with a glass jug of water. Dorothy shook her head, but Laurel placed a finger against her glass to show the amount she wanted. They sat round the fire in silence. Bumper was stretched out on a rug in front of the dancing flames, revelling in the first fire of the autumn.

The sitting-room door opened. Laurel's back stiffened and her stomach knotted. They came in, Stuart with his arm round Mabel. He met their eyes, his face was grim. She'd never seen him so down, so sad, so despairing. Mabel's head was bowed, she couldn't see her face. She got up from the settee so they could sit together.

Laurel bit her lip. The air was charged with uncertainty and the fear of saying something that made the situation worse. She went to Mabel, knelt down and put her arms round her. 'Mabel. I'm so very, very sorry. You know we, Frank, Dorothy and myself, will do anything you want.'

Mabel looked up. Her normally round and cheerful face seemed to have collapsed into itself, her reddened eyes full of pain, fresh tears welling up at Laurel's words. 'I want to know what happened and I want to see my boy.'

Laurel looked at Frank. He joined her. 'I phoned Nick Revie and he gave me a few more details. Do you want me to tell you what he said?'

She put out her hand and he held it tight. 'First of all, when can I see my boy? I need to see Matt,' Mabel said.

Frank bit his lip. 'I'll ring Revie up again. I'll find out when . . .' His voice trailed off.

Mabel shook her head, a stream of fresh tears trickling down her cheeks. 'I know what has to happen. I'd stop it if I could, but I can't, can I?' She turned to Stuart for confirmation.

'No, my love, you can't. But if it's Martin Ansell he'll treat Matt with great respect.' He hugged Mabel to him. 'Frank, do you know if it's Ansell?'

Frank pulled the lobe of his right ear. 'No. I'll ring Revie and ask if he can make sure Martin does the . . .'

'You can say it, Frank – the autopsy. I know it has to happen. Would you ask Nick Revie if you can be there? As a special favour to me? It would be a great comfort if you would,' Mabel said, wiping her eyes and regaining her composure.

Laurel knew Frank was fascinated by post-mortems; part of his degree was zoology and he'd told her he loved dissecting different animals. The only part he wasn't keen on was the smell coming from the newly slit-open abdomen. She was glad Mabel hadn't asked her to go with him, though if she'd asked, she would have gone.

'Yes, I'm honoured you've asked me, Mabel,' Frank said. 'Are you up to hearing what Revie's told me so far?' She nodded. 'Tom Blower was woken up by maroons going off. It was just past two. When he got near the lifeboat shed, he heard the noise of the tractor engine. The shed door was open and he saw Matt had somehow been caught up in the tractor engine. He was dead. Alan Varley was next and Tom got him to call for an ambulance and the police. But it was too late, Mabel. Nick said Matt's scarf had caught in the machinery and,' he hesitated, 'and it had twisted round his neck and . . . choked him.'

Mabel's mouth was open and she was violently shaking her head. 'No. No, that can't be true. It can't have happened like that. A scarf? Matt never wore a scarf. His father wouldn't wear a scarf. Matt was like him. Never, never. Not in the whole of his life. He never wore one. Not at sea, not on the land. Someone's killed my boy, my Matt.'

Chapter Five

Thursday, 14 September, 1972

Frank looked at the dashboard clock of his Avenger GT. Twenty-five to nine. The post-mortem was due to start at nine; he might be a bit late as the traffic from Dunwich to Ipswich down the A12 was busy, and several tractors moving from farm to farm had held him up. It certainly wasn't an Indian summer, a cool north-easterly breeze bringing clouds and showers. Gloomy weather, suitable for the task ahead.

He pushed open the door of the mortuary, and made his way to the autopsy room.

'Good morning, Mr Diamond,' Detective Inspector Nicholas Revie said, looking at his watch. 'Five minutes late. If you were still in the force, I'd give you an official reprimand.'

They shook hands. Revie's short, squat body was dressed in a smart navy suit. Frank wondered where the raincoat and trilby had been slung. He remembered their first meeting; Revie had barrelled into the newly deceased Sam and Clara Harrop's house, a lookalike James Cagney, his small, bright blue eyes fixed suspiciously on Frank, hoping, no doubt, to find he was responsible for the still-warm corpses.

'At the moment, I wish I was a detective inspector, Nicholas. I'd like to help catch the sick bastard who killed those young women. Are you making any progress?'

Revie pulled a face. 'Off the record, and I mean completely off, not a word, even to your mates back in Dunwich, we haven't made much progress at all. The only thing we are sure of is it's the same person.'

His nerve endings bristled. 'Really? That's something, nothing worse than having more than one killer on the loose. What's the connection?'

Revie pulled a face. ''Fraid I can't tell you, but apart from that one common factor, there's nothing else that is consistent. All the women were young, ages vary from seventeen to twenty-four, they don't look alike, one was a blonde, another had long brown hair, the last had curly mousy hair; they were all small women, I'm not sure if that is significant. All raped, but different locations, seemingly random.' He shook his head. 'I can't sleep thinking he may soon kill again. We've warned the public, I think most families are making sure their wives, daughters and sweethearts don't go out at night alone, but you know what some young women are like: they think they're immortal, it won't happen to me. Off they go to a dance, or the flicks, perhaps in a group, they walk home together, but one of them has to walk the last part alone. He might be waiting for her.'

Frank thought of his last case as a detective inspector and the man who had been secretly killing over many years. Laurel had nearly been his last victim. That case had brought them together, and after the murders were solved, he'd persuaded her to become his partner and set up the Agency. A decision he didn't regret.

Mass killers were not always men, something to be remembered. Myra Hindley. The public were disgusted when the Governor of Holloway Prison had recently given her permission to go out for walks after only six years inside.

It was always, he thought, the most difficult and heinous crime to solve, the murderer who had to satisfy some strange sexual desire, the need to slake their lust by overpowering, dominating and eventually killing the person they longed for. He'd found it almost impossible to think himself into the mind of such a person; but sometimes it was necessary to try and do it if they were to be caught. He shook his head and sighed.

Revie was staring at him, rubbing his chin.

Frank raised his eyebrows. 'Something the matter?'

'You said you'd like to help?'

'Yes, of course. Anything.'

'I need to talk to someone who isn't close to the case, someone who won't make a judgement. Would you be willing to meet me for a drink and a chat? Better still, ask Laurel if she'll come with you. She'll see it from the woman's perspective. I know I can rely on you two not to talk to anyone else.'

It had cost Revie a lot to ask for help. Frank was touched and proud to think he valued his and Laurel's opinions. 'I'm sure she'll be as chuffed as me. If it's going to help to talk over the case, we'll be pleased to do that.'

'Thanks, mate. How about this Saturday night?' He grimaced. ''Fraid we'll have to meet in Ipswich. I'm off duty, but I've got to be on the end of a phone in case . . .'

'That's no problem. Any idea where to meet?'

'The Seahorse, Bank Street – sorry, they've changed the street's name, it's now Foundation Street, but most of the locals still give it its old name. Big pub, I know the landlord, he'll give us a quiet spot and I can have any phone calls put through to his number.'

'Time?'

'Say eight thirty? Make sure you eat before you come, all you'll get are crisps and the odd pork pie and if you're lucky, pickled eggs.'

'I'll ring to confirm Laurel's coming.'

'No need, I know she will. Don't tell the others we're meeting.'

Martin Ansell, the pathologist, came in from his office. 'Frank – Mr Diamond. I'm glad to see you.' He pointed to the autopsy table. 'I'm so sorry to have Mabel's son here. Please tell her she can come tomorrow to see Matt.' He looked at Revie. 'I'm pleased you allowed Frank to be present.'

'It's the least I could do for the poor woman. I'm very fond of Mabel,' Revie looked at Frank, 'and not just because she's a first-class cook and indulges my love of bacon butties. However, this visit is off the record, don't go spreading news of my largesse round the neighbourhood. The Chief Inspector would come down on me like a ton of bricks if he heard.' He whipped round. 'That goes for you as well, Ansell.'

Ansell's tall, thin figure straightened. 'Of course, no need to mention it.' As he put on his gown and gloves his diffident appearance morphed into one of authority, competence and knowledge. He loved his work and took great pride in discovering all he could to establish the cause of death and if it was murder, helping the police to catch the killer.

Frank looked round the mortuary. It seemed slightly different to the last time he'd been here. 'Have you made some changes, Martin? It looks less, er, grubby?'

Ansell's hands were grasping the white sheet covering Matt Grill's body; he paused and smiled. 'I persuaded the authorities to re-grout the tiles and to lay a new floor covering. It's a start, but when I think of the autopsy suites in the States, we've a long way to go.'

'Right, let's get cracking,' Revie said. 'I've a lot on my plate at the moment.'

Frank thought his choice of words was not the best. On a stainless-steel trolley, close to the body, were a sternal saw, skull key, rib shears and numerous scalpels lined up for Ansell's use. Ansell pulled the sheet away and Matt Grill's body lay exposed. Frank tried to push out of his mind the thought that this was Mabel's boy, her only child, dead in his prime, his muscled but lean body stilled for ever.

Ansell pointed to Matt's neck, livid with purple welts, and above, his blackened and cut face. 'The scarf had been twisted by the machinery round his neck.' He pointed to a piece of material laid out on a side bench.

Frank looked at it. 'I might as well tell you now, Mabel is adamant Matt never wore a scarf. She says he didn't own one. She's sure this was not an accident.'

Revie puffed out his cheeks and joined Frank. He picked up the scarf. It was in two pieces. 'Looks like a woman's scarf to me. Can't see a bloke wearing this, unless, you know . . .' He put one hand on a hip and patted his waved, brilliantined hair. 'Matt Grill wasn't that way inclined, was he?'

Frank shook his head, more in condemnation than denial.

Ansell joined them, frowning. Although creased and dirty, smeared with engine oil, and torn, the cream abstract design on the maroon background was clear.

'What's it made of? It's quite light, the material's almost sheer,' Revie asked.

'It's polyester; there's a label.' Ansell pointed to the edge of the long scarf. 'Baar and Beards, Italian.'

Revie scrutinised Ansell's face. 'I didn't know you were an haute couture expert, Mr Ansell.'

Ansell's face reddened. 'I'm thorough in my research. I certainly thought the scarf didn't match the rest of Mr Grill's clothing.'

'Is there any possibility this was not an accident?' Frank asked him.

Revie groaned.

Ansell moved back to the autopsy table. 'What are you suggesting?' he asked.

'Could he have been knocked unconscious and then someone wraps the scarf round his neck, attaches him to the tractor chain, switches on the engine and the scarf chokes the life from him?'

Ansell frowned. 'Or, I suppose he could have been strangled to death with the scarf and then attached to the engine.'

'Could you make out how the scarf was tied?' Frank asked.

'No, they'd cut it before I got there. Perfectly understandable as they wanted to release Matt from the machinery.'

Revie leant over the body and eye-balled Ansell. 'Can you prove either of these theories? At the inquest are you prepared to say you think Matt Grill was murdered?'

Ansell recoiled, his anxious spaniel-like eyes widening. 'No need to be so aggressive, Inspector Revie. No, at the moment, I can't see any evidence of foul play. It appears to be a freak accident. However, Mr Diamond's remarks about the scarf do suggest we shouldn't rule it out just yet.' He pointed to the corpse's eyes. 'He died of strangulation, note the petechias, burst blood vessels in the whites. I've taken blood samples. When we have the results of oxygen levels and also with further dissection, I'm sure my verdict will be qualified.' He pointed to the neck. 'You can see how deep the scarf has bitten into the flesh. The blood supply to the brain will have been cut off, I expect to find the coronary arteries to have been completely compressed.' Taking up a scalpel, his hand moved to a point below the end of the sternum.

Frank searched in his jacket pocket for his silver vinaigrette, ready to block the sweet and sickly smell of the abdominal gases Ansell would release from the body. He brought the vinaigrette to his nose, the metal cool and smooth against his skin; he took a deep breath. Ugh. He wasn't sure which he preferred, the scent of death or the perfume Laurel had given him to soak the sponge in – Tabu – an exotic Spanish perfume someone had brought back from a package holiday as a present for her. 'Not to my taste,' she said. 'However, it may turn you on. Let me know, I might ask for it back.' He wished he believed her.

'Nick,' Frank asked, 'is it all right if I describe the scarf to Mabel? It may jog her memory.'

Revie rubbed his chin. 'Don't see why not, but make it clear to all the team, this detail and any others you may tell them must not go beyond Greyfriars House.'

Ansell skilfully inserted the tip of the scalpel below the breastbone and sliced through the skin and muscle to reveal the shining intestines.

Frank decided Tabu was preferable to the smell penetrating the room. But only just.

Chapter Six

Friday, 15 September, 1972

Mabel steeled herself as she, Stuart and Frank stood outside the door to the mortuary. She must stay strong. She so desperately wanted to see Matt, to be able to touch his face, kiss him, to hope, like the prince in *Sleeping Beauty*, that her touch and kiss would bring him back to life. She knew that was stupid. She glanced up at Stuart, who was holding her tight; from the expression on his face, she knew what he was thinking: she wouldn't be able to hold it together, she would collapse, a weeping mass of blubber, as she'd been when she heard the news. No, she wouldn't do that again. She must see everything, ask questions of Inspector Revie and Mr Ansell. Make them see it couldn't have been an accident; her Matt wouldn't have done something so silly. He was a steady man, like his dad, Bill. But Bill had drowned at sea; he'd been one of the most skilful and experienced fishermen for miles around, but the sea had taken him.

'Ready to go in, Mabel?' Frank asked.

She nodded. He'd driven them, so Stuart could sit in the back with her. When Revie had told her of Matt's death a great feeling of loneliness swept over her. Her only child dead. No other near family. But the love of Stuart, his deep sorrow for her and the suffering etched on his face had somehow given her strength to bear the tearing pain.

She wasn't alone. She had Laurel, Frank and Dorothy's love and support; she hoped she might be able to somehow survive Matt's death, but last night, unable to sleep, she'd wished she could lose consciousness and never wake up.

Frank pushed the mortuary door open.

Cold air hit her face. A sickening smell of disinfectant mixed with an artificial floral scent made her stomach heave. The room was like something out of a horror film, icy white walls, grey stainless-steel sinks and work tops; it partly reminded her of the kitchen in Blackfriars School. She shuddered. Joints of red meat sitting on boards, strings of sausages waiting to be grilled, dark gravy swirling in deep pans flashed through her mind. She put a hand over her mouth. In the centre of the room was a table, on it a shape covered with a white sheet. A body. Matt's body?

Frank went to a glass door, knocked and opened it. 'Mabel's here.' He stepped back and Inspector Revie and Mr Ansell came out of the room.

'Mabel,' Revie said, taking her hands, 'I'm truly sorry you had to come and see your son like this.'

His face was grey, worry lines she hadn't seen before etched on his face, his small blue eyes looking into hers with understanding.

'Thank you, Nick.'

He looked relieved.

Martin Ansell, looking as though he wished the floor would open beneath him, mumbled, 'My deepest condolences, Mrs Elderkin.'

She nodded. She wished he'd called her Mrs Grill, today she wanted to be Matt's mum, Mabel Grill, married to the cox'n of the Aldeburgh Lifeboat, a successful business woman, running their fish and chip shop, proud of her husband, and her son, Matthew. 'He's a chip off the old block,' people would say. 'Nearly as good as his dad on the boat, I hear.' Or, 'It's a fine-looking boy, you've got there, Mabel.'

Revie touched her shoulder. 'Do you want to see Matt now? Or would you like a cup of tea first? Martin's got everything set up in his office.'

'Thank you, but I want to see Matt.'

Ansell walked over to the central table and stood at one end. He

34

stretched out an arm, inviting her to join him. She took a deep breath, and unsteadily walked towards him, Stuart firmly holding her left arm. She wanted to see him – she didn't want to see him. What she wanted was to see him alive. She wanted him to smile at her, to say, 'Hello, Mum. You look good today.' She didn't want to see him cold and dead, never to speak to her again, never to give her a hug, never to say to anyone who'd listen, 'My mum's the best cook in Suffolk,' and she'd say, 'Only Suffolk?' and he'd reply, 'I expect you're better than anyone anywhere, but I haven't travelled much, apart from out to sea.'

Ansell gripped the edge of the white sheet. He looked at her. She nodded. Stuart's grip on her arm tightened. There was Matt's thick brown hair, with the short quiff at the front, his eyes were closed, his neat ears and weather-beaten skin. She leant over him, the left side of his face was marked and covered in – what – make-up? She reached out and wiped a finger over his skin, lifting a greasy brown cream from his face. Below were purple bruises. 'What's this?' She waved her finger at Ansell.

He gulped, his skin reddening. 'I'm sorry, Mabel. I did that so . . .' He couldn't get the words out.

'So he wouldn't look bad for me? I want to see what was done to him. I've a right to see how he was found. Wipe it off.' She felt Stuart's body turn towards Revie. She looked up at him, he looked shocked and worried.

'I'm all right, Stuart. I want to know the truth.'

Stuart and Frank were certain it was an accident. When she'd cried out someone had killed Matt, she could see from their expressions they didn't believe her. When she'd calmed down, Frank had asked her if she knew anyone who would want Matt dead.

'Sarah,' she'd said. 'It has to be her.'

'Just because your marriage is going through a bad patch, doesn't mean you kill your spouse,' Frank said.

'What would Sarah gain from killing Matt, love?' Stuart asked. 'And, let's face it, Matt was a strong young man; she'd couldn't have overpowered him.'

35

She glowered at them.

'Sarah isn't going to gain financially, is she?' Stuart persisted. 'The shop and flat belong to you, so does the boat.'

She'd refused to answer.

Ansell wiped Matt's face with a damp cloth. 'I'm sorry, Mabel. I tried to . . .'

'I know,' she said, 'you did your best. If it was a normal death, I wouldn't have made such a fuss.' Matt's face was stern, unsmiling, she could see the livid cuts and bruises on his face. She touched his nose. It wobbled.

'It was broken,' Ansell said. 'I tried to make it straight.'

He'd rolled the cloth down to his chin. She waved her hand, indicating he should take it down further. Ansell looked at Stuart. He grimaced and nodded.

His poor throat was black, purple and blue; there were deep grooves where the flesh had been squeezed into folds. She gasped. 'My poor boy. What did they do to you?' She bent over him and caressed his damaged face, laying her cheek against his. 'Matt, Matt, my baby boy.' How proud they'd been of him. How much they'd both loved him. A son. Bill had been ecstatic when he was born. Another Grill to carry on the name. A boy who'd learn to love the sea as he did; who became his first mate on the boat, part of the lifeboat crew, who'd inherit the business when he and Mabel had retired. Who'd one day marry and they'd have grandchildren.

All the way through Matt's life, they'd been proud of him, even his stupid teenage mistakes. 'Boys will be boys,' Bill would say to her after he'd sent Matt off to bed for some misbehaviour. The one mistake he'd made was to fall in love with that Sarah. Mabel had never liked her. Did she really love her Matt? Or had she seen the money that came in to the business? But he'd been angry when she'd asked him to wait a few years before marrying the girl. It was losing Bill. If Bill had been alive, he'd have persuaded Matt to wait. She was sure, given time, he'd have got over his lust, and common sense would have set in. She hadn't the will or strength after Bill drowned, she wanted to get away from the shop, from the people of Aldeburgh and their sympathy and questions. She should have been stronger, stood up to him, made him wait.

'Mabel. That's enough for now. You can see him again soon,' Stuart said, as he tried to prise her away.

Skin so cold, no smell of the sea in his hair, no stink of fish when he'd been gutting them for customers at the hut, only the harsh smell of chemicals and death. She slowly pulled back, then kissed his lips. No warm response. They were cold and stiff. Ansell looked at her and she nodded. He gently pulled the cloth over Matt's face. Behind his glasses, his eyes were tearful. It made her own eyes well up.

'Let's all have a cup of tea,' Revie said, leading the way to Ansell's office. She didn't want to drink here, so near to Matt, but they'd all been so kind. Frank was already in there, pouring boiling water into mugs.

'I'm afraid I've only got tea bags,' Ansell said.

She sat on one of three chairs. Frank put a mug of milky tea in front of her. Stuart sat next to her, Revie sat opposite, Frank and Ansell hovering behind her. She sipped the tea. Horrible – weak and too milky. 'Thanks, Frank.' There was a long silence, everyone drinking, avoiding each other's eyes.

She looked at Revie. 'What are you going to do?'

Stuart wriggled on his chair.

Revie frowned. 'What do you mean, Mabel?'

'When will you start the investigation?'

He pursed his lips. 'Now, you know we only investigate if there are suspicious circumstances, don't you?'

Her blood quickened. 'You're telling me how Matt was killed wasn't suspicious?'

'Do you want to talk about this now, Mabel? I'll come and see you in a few days and tell you everything we know about Matt's death. You'll be able to take it all in more easily, then.'

She glared at him. 'Don't you pussy-foot me. I want to know now. I want to know about this scarf. I've told you, I've told them,' she waved at Stuart and Frank, 'Matt never wore a scarf; his dad never wore one, thought a man had to be a pansy to need a scarf. You see them Londoners, mincing round our town, with their silly scarves, or their jumpers draped over their shoulders. Pretentious ne'er do wells.' Stuart stiffened. 'Sorry, dear, I'd forgotten you wear scarves, but yours are nice, sensible, woollen ones.'

Revie sighed. 'All right, Mabel. I'll pass over to Martin as he performed the post-mortem; if I tell you, I'm bound to miss out details, and then he'd have to chip in.' He turned to Ansell. 'Go ahead.'

Ansell faced her, his eyes, behind his spectacles, widened and his lips twisted, as though unwilling to form the words.

Mabel patted his arm. 'It's all right, Martin, I know it's hard for you, you don't usually do this, do you? Speak to someone who's lost a loved one?'

His face relaxed. 'I usually speak at the inquest, or as a witness in a trial.'

'You may have to do both again,' she said.

Stuart shot a look at Frank. He didn't think Matt's death was suspicious. None of them did.

'Mabel,' Frank said, 'I know what Ansell's going to say. The police can only go on the evidence put before them; they can't investigate a death just because a relative thinks it's suspicious. Try and be prepared to be disappointed.'

Her jaw tightened, she looked at Ansell. 'Get on with it.'

'As you know, Mr Blower found Matt in the lifeboat shed. The light was on and the tractor motor was running. Matt's scarf had caught in the tractor chain and the scarf had tightened round his neck, cutting off the air to his lungs and completely constricting not only the windpipe and veins of the neck, but his arteries as well. He was strangled to death.'

She groaned, images in her mind of Matt fighting to free himself, his hands trying to pull the scarf loose, panic setting in as he realised he couldn't and then the terrible gasping for breath. What passed through his mind before he lost consciousness? 'Do you know when he died?' Mabel asked.

'Matt left the pub just after ten,' Revie chipped in.

'I estimate the time of death to have been between eleven and one,' Ansell said.

'How long do you think it took for him to . . .?'

Ansell avoided her eyes. 'A few minutes.'

'How many minutes?'

'That's enough, Mabel. Stop torturing yourself,' Stuart said.

Torturing herself? It was the not knowing that was torture. The certainty Matt couldn't have been so careless. She turned to Revie. 'And what have you got to say? Have you questioned anyone?'

Revie's face flushed. 'I haven't done that myself, but we've talked to Sarah, to Mr Blower and to the other members of the lifeboat crew. It wasn't unknown for Matt to test the tractor engine if he got to the shed before anyone else. As you know, the engine's used to pull the boat back to her launch pad after she comes back.'

'That's the engineer's job, not the cox'n, to make sure the boat's engine and the tractor engines are in top condition. I don't think Matt would do that before an emergency launch.'

'We've been told he's done this in the past and he did this time,' Revie snapped.

'I haven't seen Sarah yet. I've talked to her on the phone. What's she got to say? I wasn't thinking straight when we talked.'

'Sarah was in bed when I went round to their flat. She hadn't realised Matt wasn't at home. She'd heard the maroons, knew he'd be out at sea, and thought he'd come back and gone to bed. She was sleeping in the spare room, so he wouldn't wake her when he came back.'

A dark fog seemed to cloud her mind, like the worst conditions at sea, when streams of black sea-clouds masked shallow sandbanks, jagged rocks and approaching vessels. When her Bill had leapt from his bed when the booming maroons exploded, she'd got up with him and never returned to their bed. She'd get dressed and go to the lifeboat station, waiting until he and all the others were safely back. She wouldn't be the only one, other wives, mothers and sweethearts gathered in a huddle, summer or winter, until their men were back safe. That Sarah – did she care if Matt came back? Was she glad he was dead? What did she know about how he died?

'What about the scarf? Can I see it?'

39

Revie let out a long, hard breath. He nodded to Ansell. 'Yes, it's still here.'

Ansell moved to his desk, Revie shifted, and Ansell opened a drawer and took out a plastic bag. He laid it before her and slowly pulled out the two pieces of a long, fine scarf and placed it on the desk.

She reared back, gasping, her hand at her throat. She imagined it wrapped round her boy's neck, choking the life out of him. She leant forward. It couldn't be. Yes, it was. She was sure it was the same one. Maroon with a cream pattern of squiggles and lines. She wouldn't have chosen it for herself, she'd thought it too modern, but she thought *she'd* like it. 'That's Sarah's scarf. I bought it for her Christmas present last year.' She looked at them triumphantly. 'There, what did I tell you? How did Sarah's scarf come to be round my Matt's neck?'

Back at Greyfriars, Laurel was restless, even a walk along the beach with Bumper hadn't calmed her. The sky had clouded over, the weather matching her thoughts. The world seemed to be becoming a more violent place: another IRA bomb exploded at the Imperial Hotel in Belfast. Even in sport there was hate and savagery. On the football terraces, on the pitch. She shook her head. That dreadful day at the Munich Olympic Games: eleven Israeli athletes slaughtered by Palestinian guerrillas. She was glad they'd decided to start the games again.

She'd tried several times to push from her mind the thought of Mabel going to the mortuary to see her dead son. The first time she'd entered that white-tiled room, with its odours of death and disinfectant, had been to see her younger sister, Angela, lying on the dissecting table, already cut up and despoiled, brain weighed, abdomen slit open, stitched up like an eviscerated turkey at Christmas. Since then, she'd had to return several times to view bodies, and each time the feeling of dread returned. It was where she'd first met Frank, then a detective sergeant in the Suffolk Police Force. Just over three years ago. Too many things had happened since then, too many violent and horrible deaths.

But this was truly awful, although it was an accident, robbing

Mabel of her only child. It sounded like a careless accident, an unnecessary death. Three people robbed of someone they deeply loved, all by violent deaths – she of her sister; Dorothy of her twin sister; and now Mabel robbed of her beloved son, Matt. At least there was no one else involved in his death, although Mabel couldn't, at the moment, accept his death was an accident. She hoped after seeing his body and hearing from Inspector Revie and Martin Ansell, she would begin to realise no one else was involved. Bumper butted her knee and looked up at her, his brown eyes pleading. For a walk? A biscuit? Both?

Dorothy came into the sitting room. 'They're back. I'll put the kettle on. Cake? Biscuits?'

Bumper cocked his head and rushed to Dorothy, wagging his tail.

'Sorry, I forgot to spell it out,' she said, patting his head.

'I think he's learnt to spell that word as well as w-a-l-k and d-i-n-n-e-r.'

Bumper's tail-lashing per minute increased.

'Perhaps just tea to begin with, food might look a bit insensitive; don't forget, Frank will want coffee.'

Dorothy sighed. 'Why won't he put up with instant? The rest of us do.'

Laurel smiled. 'We can't change Frank.'

Dorothy looked at her over her blue-rimmed spectacles. 'I'm sure if you put your mind to it, *you* could.'

'I don't think I want to.'

Dorothy left the room, followed by Bumper. A door opened.

'Mabel, you look all in. I'm making some tea, we're having it in the sitting room; would you like a biscuit? Or do you want to go and lie down?'

'No, I don't, I want to talk to all of you.'

Laurel bit her lip. Mabel's voice was raised and aggressive. It didn't bode well.

The door opened and she came in, her face drawn, lined, looking older than a few days before. Behind her was Stuart, his face grey and haggard with worry.

'Mabel.' She held out her arms and hugged her.

41

'You won't let me down, Laurel, will you? They won't see it, they all think it was an accident, but I know my Matt. Someone killed him. They did, I know they did.' At each word, her voice heightened, until the last words were screeched and she burst into hysterical tears and collapsed against Laurel.

Laurel guided her to the settee. Stuart turned and left the room. Laurel let her sob, saying nothing. How could she help her? It was impossible. Where was the tea? She suspected Dorothy and Stuart were waiting until they thought it was the right time to bring it in. Where was Frank? Had he gone back to his cottage? She hoped not, she needed his support. Mabel was looking to her for help, but what could she do?

It seemed an eon before the door opened and Dorothy came in carrying a tea tray, followed by Stuart carrying a plate of biscuits.

'Where's Frank?'

'He's taken Bumper for a walk, he should be back any minute,' Stuart said. He sat next to Mabel and Laurel released hold of her.

A few minutes later Frank and Bumper slipped into the room, Frank with a mug of coffee, Bumper with his blue ball firmly between his teeth.

'Wouldn't be parted from it,' Frank said.

For once Dorothy didn't object to the slimy ball being brought into the house, even though it would soon be dropped onto the carpet when the biscuits were passed round. 'Here's your tea, Mabel.'

She took the cup and saucer, after wiping her swollen eyes.

The room was silent, apart from slurps and sips. Laurel's stomach knotted; the tea tasted bitter. She put down her half-finished drink on the floor then, as Bumper showed interest, she got up and took it to the kitchen. She poured the stale tea down the sink. God in heaven, what was going to happen? What would Mabel do? Voices, raised voices, drew her back to the sitting room.

When she entered it, Mabel, her face flushed, was talking. 'I don't care what Revie said, and I won't care if the inquest decides it was an accident. I know it wasn't and I want you to find out the truth. I deserve to have your help. You can't refuse me.'

42

Stuart was shaking his head. 'We can't start an investigation, love. We need to wait and see what the coroner says. We'll have to accept his verdict. If there's been foul play, then the police will investigate.'

'We all know what the verdict will be; Revie as good as told me, and that Mr Ansell, he said he couldn't find any evidence that some-one else was involved. They're not going to listen to me, are they? It's up to you.' She glared at Stuart, and then at Frank. 'But you won't help me, will you?'

Frank took a deep breath. 'Even if I thought it was the right thing to do, Stuart can't be involved, he's too close to the . . . er, case. I've got to continue with Sir George's stolen jewels. We need to keep the Agency ticking over. I'll deal with that, Stuart can be with you, until you are . . . er.' For once, he couldn't find the words.

Mabel turned to Laurel. 'I expect you're going to side with them?' Her shoulders collapsed, the fight seeping from her. 'Will no one help me?'

Laurel's heart twisted. She remembered how she'd felt when the police, apart from Frank, had botched the investigation into her sister's death, and had driven her into making her own search for the murderer. Her rash behaviour had nearly lead her to ruin her life. She went to Mabel. Crouched down and took hold of her arms. 'If Frank, Stuart and Dorothy agree, I'll try to help. I'll ask Revie if I can talk to the people close to Matt. I may be able to throw some light onto Matt's death.' She looked at the others. Stuart looked hor-rified, Frank angry and Dorothy distressed.

'Are you agreeable? It will depend on Revie, of course,' she asked them.

Mabel hugged her. 'Bless you, bless you.'

She looked at Frank.

'We haven't got much option, have we?' he said. 'It looks like a fait accompli. Excuse me, I'm going back to the cottage. See you all tomorrow.'

Laurel closed her eyes, leaning against Mabel. She'd split the Agency in two.

Chapter Seven

Saturday, 16 September, 1972

As Frank pulled into the car park of The Seahorse, his heart sank; on the way he'd decided to make do with a couple of pints of bitter. He pointed to the sign below that of The Seahorse.

'Tolly Cobbold,' he moaned. 'Just my luck.'

'What's wrong with Tolly Cobbold beer?' Laurel asked.

'They changed to kegs, full of fake bubbles – weak carbonic acid – it gives you gut ache.'

'Never mind, you can have a bitter lemon.'

He mimed being sick.

'Behave, Frank. Surely you can manage one evening without alcohol.'

'Are you going to join me on the wagon?'

'I don't think twenty-four hours without booze will entitle you to declare you're a non-drinker. I'm looking forward to a few glasses of whisky. Especially if Nick is paying.'

It wasn't his kind of pub: a large, brick edifice with several chimneys, built he guessed in the 1930s. No history, no romance. Why on earth did Revie choose this as his watering hole?

'Don't be so childish, Frank. We're here to help Nick, and possibly ourselves, so don't go mardy on me.'

'When did we get married? I seem to have forgotten.'

'What?'

'Well, you're nagging me like a wife of several years.'

Laurel dug him in the ribs. 'Thank you. Let's get out of this car and get on with the job.'

There were times when he was glad their relationship hadn't progressed from working partners – this evening was one of them. He hadn't recovered from Laurel agreeing to help Mabel.

He pushed open the door to the main bar and stepped back to allow her to enter. A wave of tobacco smoke hit him. Sometimes, when smoke drifted from Stuart's pipe, or one of Dorothy's cigarettes, he vicariously enjoyed the smell of the different tobaccos and the slight tingle of nicotine in his nostrils, but this was too much.

Laurel was wrinkling her nose. 'I'll have to wash my hair tomorrow morning.'

The room was large with a long bar running down the left. Nick was leaning on it, chatting to a woman behind the bar. He was casually dressed in an open-necked shirt, brown cardigan and beige trousers; they made him look older and less important. He seemed relaxed, smiling as the barmaid related a story, waving her arms and rolling her eyes as she came to the end. Nick laughed. Frank hadn't realised Nick had so many teeth.

He tapped him on the shoulder. 'Good evening, Inspector Revie.'

Revie whipped round. 'For God's sake, stow the title. In here, I'm Nick – this is one place where the man next to me at the bar doesn't automatically move two yards away. I'd like to keep it that way.'

'Sorry, didn't realise you were so touchy.'

Revie thumped his chest. 'Beneath this steel exterior is a sensitive man.'

'I didn't doubt that for a second,' Laurel said.

She was buttering him up. Hoping he'd let her interview Matt's relatives and friends.

'Evening, Laurel. Good to find someone who understands me. What can I get you?'

Laurel surveyed the optics. 'I'll have a Bells with a splash of water.'

'Double?'

'Why not? Frank, stop scowling at me.' She pointed to him. 'He's upset as he'll have to have keg beer or a bitter lemon.'

'No need for that. The landlord keeps one beer on a gravity dispense,' Nick said.

'Thank God for that,' Frank said. 'What is it?'

'Tolly Bitter.'

'Perfect, I'll have a pint.'

'I can't remember asking you,' Nick said.

'Grow up, boys,' Laurel exclaimed. 'And what's a gravity dispense?'

'Ignoramus! Tapped from the barrel,' Frank replied.

Revie pointed to a door at the far end of the bar. 'Go through there, take the first door on the right. There's a small room where we can have a bit of privacy. I've squared it with the landlord.' He waved to a man behind the bar. 'I'll bring the drinks. Crisps? Peanuts?'

They both declined and pushed their way through the crowd. Frank decided it wasn't such a bad pub: lively, clientele all having a good time, mostly men, but a fair sprinkling of husband and wives, dressed up for a Saturday night out, hair permed or brilliantined according to sex, and a few older teenagers, boys with kipper ties and tight trousers, girls in short dresses and Mary Quant hairdos.

It was an intimate, cosy room, with two tables, and chairs to match, a small sideboard and a redundant fruit machine. Thankfully there were no flashing lights or rotating rows of pears, oranges and apples.

'I've never seen Nick so relaxed,' Laurel said. 'He's like a different man.'

'It makes me wonder if what he said is true, and that tough exterior is just a shell hiding the true Nick Revie,' Frank mused.

Laurel put a finger to her lips and pointed to the door.

Revie barged in carrying a tray of drinks. He plonked it down on the table they'd chosen to sit at. 'I got the landlord to make sure your pint was nice and clear. He said it was the middle of the barrel.'

Frank lifted up the pint mug to the light. 'Looks good. Thank you, Nick.' He eyed Revie's and Laurel's drinks. 'Doubles?'

'They are. Laurel and I are going to match each other, tot for tot.'

'This is the first I knew it was a drinking competition,' Laurel said.

Revie emitted a deep sigh of satisfaction as he sat down and took a sip from his glass. 'And it's not the first tonight, you two better drink up, you're well behind.'

'I hope you're not driving home,' Laurel said.

'Ignore her, Nick, she's in a disapproving mood tonight.'

'No, I'm not. It wouldn't do for an inspector to get caught for drink driving.'

'Thank you, Laurel, nice to have someone worrying about me. All is in order. Young Cottam dropped me off and he's picking me up at ten thirty.'

Frank shook his head. 'Police corruption – it's a wonderful thing.'

'I see Myra Hindley's walks have been cancelled. She came back drunk and beat up a prison officer,' Revie said. 'Bloody do-gooders.'

'Showing your sensitive side again, Nick?' Frank said.

Revie grinned, then his face took on a serious mien. 'Thanks for coming tonight.' He sighed, this time a worried sigh. 'Do you want to relax with your drinks before I start?'

'No, Nick, you go ahead. Do you want us to interrupt with questions, or shall we wait until you've finished?' Frank asked.

'No, let's have a free for all. I'm just hoping by talking it over, something might click. I know I don't need to say this, but the contents of this conversation mustn't be repeated, except between the two of you. You never know, something might occur to you later.'

They both nodded.

'You know the main facts: three young women strangled and raped.'

'Strangled? The method hasn't been in the papers or on the telly,' Frank said.

'Correct. I'll come back to that later. It ties, if you'll pardon the expression, the three murders together.'

The skin at the back of Frank's neck tightened. He wanted to know everything – now, but he must let Revie tell the story in his own time.

'Three young women, one seventeen, one twenty and one twenty-four. The teenager worked in a shop in Ipswich, travelling by bus to

47

her home in Nacton. Never got home one Thursday evening. Parents phoned the police when she wasn't back by eight, after they got in touch with the shop management, who confirmed she'd left at the usual time. Friends said she'd missed the bus she normally caught and said she'd walk a few stops up the road to pass the time. The conductor of the next bus can't remember her boarding. She was found three days later in Nacton Woods. Strangled and raped.'

'Raped before or after?' Frank asked.

Laurel pulled a face.

'Shortly after, Ansell said, she'd have been unconscious if not already dead.'

'That's a small mercy, if you can call it that,' Laurel said. 'Bastard!'

'Next the twenty-four-year-old, a teacher, again working in Ipswich.'

'I know,' Laurel said. 'My old school. I didn't know her, she started after I left.'

'Yes, married, but no children, thank God.'

'I don't know why you say that, it might have been a comfort to her husband if there'd been a child. Part of her would still be with him,' Laurel said.

Revie tilted his head and smiled at her. 'You're a good girl.'

She blushed.

That was better, Frank thought, his Laurel had returned.

'Again, she caught a bus from the school to Martlesham, her husband works at the airport. There's no evidence she missed the bus. It was raining heavily that day. Her body was found on Martlesham Heath two days later. Same cause of death.'

'No chance the husband was involved?' Frank asked.

'He had an alibi for that evening, he was working. Ansell put the time of death between six and ten the day she went missing, so he's in the clear. Also, it looks like the same killer.'

'That's definite?' Frank asked, his fingers twitching at the thought of the chase. But it wasn't his chase.

'As sure as we can be. The third victim, twenty-year-old, worked in Saxmundham in a shoe shop and lived in the town, so no bus to catch home. She went out without her parents' knowing to walk a few miles to see a friend. Boyfriend. Never got there. Found in the fields near Leiston Abbey the next day. Same scenario.'

'It's extremely unlikely you're going to have three killers working in such a small area, so, what links these murders?'

Revie leant towards them, his eyes narrowed, skin taut, the day's bristles standing out dark against his sallow skin. 'It's the only important fact we have; how important it is, I'm not sure.'

Frank's chest felt as though it would burst; he realised he was holding his breath in anticipation of Revie's words. 'Yes?'

'The murderer used the same kind of material to strangle all three victims: a hemp rope. Twelve millimetres in thickness, common as chips, especially in this part of the world.'

'So, not much help?' Laurel said.

'Correct, but he used a particular knot to tighten the rope.'

Frank's breathing stopped.

'Ansell noticed it and connected the first and second victims.'

'He's a brilliant pathologist,' Laurel said.

'We're lucky to have him, and when you think of the impression he first made when working on Susan Nicholson's case . . .' Revie mused. 'I must admit, I thought he'd got the time of her death wrong. What do I know?'

Frank rapped the table with his fingertips. 'Get on with the knot.'

Revie raised his glass and took a sip of his drink; he winked at Laurel. 'I do enjoy riling him.'

She raised her glass. 'Ditto.'

'You're not going about this in the right way, Inspector Revie,' Frank said.

'I'm sorry, you're right, but I'm enjoying being with you two, I feel better than I have for weeks.'

Frank let go of his impatience. 'Take your time, Nick.'

Revie resumed his tense position and whispered to them, 'It's called a strangle knot. We called in an expert and he said it's also known as a binding knot, similar to a constrictor knot. Simply put, you wind the rope twice round whatever you want to tie up and loop the end under the two turns and pull.'

Laurel grimaced.

'What does that suggest?' Frank asked.

'The expert said whoever he is, he must be practised in using knots, this wouldn't be the way most people would go about strangling someone.'

'You're looking among the fishing and boating communities?' Frank asked.

Revie's face was glum. 'We are, but in this part of the world it isn't just the fishermen and the yacht wallahs who know how to tie a knot, every other bugger round here owns a small boat, or uses knots to tie up sacks and meal bags, so add the farmers and farm labourers as well.'

'And don't forget every Boy Scout will grow up into a man who knows how to tie several different kinds of knot.'

Revie groaned.

'And what about the Guides and Brownies?' Laurel said.

'Laurel, be serious,' Frank said.

'I am. I learnt quite a few knots in the Brownies.'

Frank laughed. 'Did they have a uniform big enough?'

'I loved being in the Brownies, I was a sixer, leader of the Gnomes, I loved dancing round the giant toadstool.'

'Really?' Frank said. 'I'd call that corrupting young girls – worshipping a phallic symbol. I'm surprised at you.'

Her face coloured and she glared at him.

He laughed. 'Sorry, Nick. Go on.'

'This murderer must be able to tie this knot quickly, probably unthinkingly. You'd need extreme skill to whip a rope twice round someone's throat and slip the end under the loops. Surely that would give the victims time to fight back?' Laurel said.

'You'd think so,' Revie replied. 'But if you were a strong, well-built man and the victim trusted you, plus you're a small, petite woman, it's possible. Well, it's not only possible, it's happened.'

'When you say petite, can you be more specific?' Frank asked.

'The victims were not only short, ranging from four foot eleven to five foot one, but they were delicately built, almost child-like, weighed between six and a half stone and seven and a half. Bones like birds.'

'There is a resemblance then. Does this mean he chooses his victims because he can easily overpower them?' Frank asked.

'Or, he may be attracted to tiny females,' Laurel said.

'In that case, you're safe,' Frank riposted.

She glanced at him sideways and frowned. 'When will you stop being a motor mouth?'

He winked at her. 'Sorry. To sum up, because of the skill needed to tie the strangler knot, he must be a fisherman, or boatman, of some experience, he's possibly a small but powerful man, choosing only those victims he can cope with, or he could be of any build, possessing a certain strength, who's turned on by tiny women,' Frank said.

'Yep, that sums it up,' Revie said. 'Any other ideas? Throw in anything, the weirder the better. I need something I haven't thought of already.'

Laurel frowned. 'The murders are all within a certain area, east of Ipswich. The theory is a criminal usually operates within the area he knows.'

'Agreed. We're concentrating on a line from Ipswich to the coast and north to Saxmundham, at the moment. We're tracing the routes the girls took, contacting all their known friends and workmates, trying to build a picture, asking about any strange men seen in the area, door to door, all the usual channels of investigation,' Revie said, his face downcast.

'I think we need another drink,' Frank said, getting up.

Revie placed his hand over Frank's. 'No, this night's on me. While I get them in, you two see if you can think of anything different we can do, or any other line of enquiry we can take. Same again?'

Laurel nodded. 'Thanks, Nick.'

He looked at Frank. 'Bitter all right? Or do you want something different?'

'No, thanks, surprisingly quaffable.'

'Good.' He piled the glasses on the tray and marched off to the bar.

'It's horrific, isn't it?' Laurel said, looking upset. 'Those poor women, they didn't stand a chance.'

'It's times like this I wish I was still in the police,' Frank said.

'I can understand that, but I'm glad you aren't. I might still be in jail.' If Frank hadn't resigned from the police force, he'd have had to arrest her for her reckless actions when she tried to uncover her sister's killer. She'd never be able to repay him for that.

Frank smiled and took hold of her hand. 'You'd be no good to me there. I don't regret leaving the force, but when you hear of bastards like this guy, you wish you were helping to catch him.'

Revie returned and doled out the drinks. 'I hope you've come up with something?'

'Sorry, Nick, we've been chatting.'

'About the murders,' Laurel chipped in.

'Cheers.' Revie raised his glass, which looked like another double.

'Nick, do you think the killer mistook these women for young girls, eleven-or twelve-year-olds? Some kids of that age are as tall, or even taller, than the women who were strangled,' Laurel asked.

'What are you implying?' he replied.

'Could he be a paedophile? Would it be worth checking on any known men who target children?'

Revie nodded, twisting his mouth. 'It could be worth checking, bit of a long shot. Good thinking, Laurel. It's something new to take to the table. The team are getting tired and jaded, some of them are starting to think we'll never catch him. If something doesn't break soon, the top brass will bring in the big guns.'

Revie wouldn't like that; he was a proud man with a good record for getting his man or woman. 'I'm wondering why he's started killing? What's triggered it? If we think he's got an obsession with petite women, not just young girls, where did that begin? Perhaps he had a sister and something happened in their childhoods.' Frank raised a finger. 'Do you think it might be worthwhile talking to any local prostitutes of a similar build, and finding out if they have any regular clients who liked them because they were small? And, if so, were they violent, and liked to simulate choking them?'

Revie thumped the table. 'I like that one. I've got a couple of officers who've got good relationships with the Ipswich prossies.' He looked at Laurel. 'One's a female officer. I've got high hopes for her. I hope she can stick all the comments she gets from some of the old lags. You'd like her, she's a good girl.'

'What about prostitutes outside Ipswich?' Laurel asked.

'There's always a few in every town. I'll get the local bobbies to question them if they have a small build.'

'Are there any in Aldeburgh?' Laurel asked, her eyes wide.

Revie laughed. 'There are a few posh tarts . . . and a few rough ones.'

'How do you know that?' Laurel asked, looking intrigued.

Revie tapped his nose. 'That's a leading question, Laurel, not one a polite young lady should ask.'

'She's not young and she's certainly no lady.'

Laurel sighed and shook her head.

'But absolutely adorable.'

She kicked Frank viciously in the shin.

Revie looked at his watch. 'Now, children, stop messing about. Time you went home and put on your jimjams and nightie.' He sniggered. 'Of your own choice, obviously.'

Laurel's cheeks were flaming, but she couldn't suppress a smile. 'Before we go, Nick, I need to ask you a favour.'

'I can't refuse, can I? You've both come up with new ideas and the craic has done me good, I feel a tad more positive than I did when I came in. I need to get that positivity to the team, get some fresh energy into the inquiry. Ask away.'

'You know Mabel is sure Matt's death wasn't an accident?'

'She's not come round to the obvious verdict – accidental death?'

'No. She's asked me to talk to everyone who knew or had dealings with Matt, including his wife and his best friend, Tom Blower. Would I be stepping over your line if I did that? Do you object?'

Revie rubbed his chin. 'We aren't doing any further investigations into Matt Grill's death. If it will help to calm Mabel down and reassure her it was an accident, I can't see any problems.'

'Thank you, Nick. Supposing I do find something suspicious? I know it's not likely, but you never know what comes up once you start digging.'

'Too true, and if anyone can winkle out people's secrets, it's you, Laurel.' He looked at both of them. 'As I've said before, I wouldn't mind both of you on my team. Yes, you go ahead, but contact me if anything suspicious appears. If it wasn't an accident, I want to know.' He gathered the empty glasses onto the tray. 'Thanks for coming tonight.' He pursed his lips. 'And if you come across anything you think might be linked to the murder of the three women, get in contact straight away. You never know, you might bump into a pervert or two on your daily rounds.'

'You'll be the first to know,' Frank said. 'But don't hold your breath, and good hunting. If we can help in any way, just ask.'

The landlord poked his head round the door. 'Inspector Revie, it's your sidekick, Cottam, asking for you.'

Revie's face paled. 'I hope he's calling to tell me he's picking me up in five minutes.' He put down the tray and darted from the room.

Chapter Eight

Monday, 18 September, 1972

Frank wasn't in a hurry as he drove up the A12 on his way to Gladham Hall. The past few days had left him feeling sad, frustrated and indecisive. He could understand Mabel's need to place the blame for her son's death onto a person unknown; to deny Matt's carelessness. The scarf was puzzling, especially as it belonged to Matt's wife, Sarah. Mabel had challenged her when she'd phoned over the weekend. Sarah said she'd lost it several months ago; Matt must have found it, even taken it himself. If the marriage was coming to an end, if Sarah had threatened to leave him, sometimes a garment, or belonging, of the person you loved and lost, or were about to lose, took on a new meaning and became precious.

Everything seemed a mess: no interesting cases for the Agency lately, and now Mabel persuading Laurel to question people about Matt's death, and Revie playing ball. He'd hoped Revie would have said no to Laurel, but she'd charmed him. He smiled, wishing she'd focus those skills on him.

It didn't help that the country was in a mess too: prices out of control and unemployment soaring towards a million. Plus, that crazy bastard Amin kicking the Asians out of their country. He needed a pick-me-up; after he'd seen the Trubshaws he'd drive to Orford and have lunch at the Oysterage. He pulled a face. Were they open on a Monday? He passed through Wickham Market; perhaps he'd stop there on the way back, have a look in the secondhand bookshop; he'd picked up some interesting things in the past.

Was it possible the Agency had reached a point when it might disintegrate? At the moment he was the only partner working, and he couldn't see Stuart joining him in the near future; Mabel was going to need a lot of support and obviously she wouldn't be able to feed and water the rest of the team.

And then there was Laurel. He wasn't sure how he felt about her. No, that wasn't true, he wanted her, and if she'd have felt as he did, then they'd be lovers by now. But would it have lasted? Would he have at last found the one? Or would she have tired of his lack of commitment and looked elsewhere? Last June it looked as though it would happen, the night he'd invited her over for dinner. He remembered her smile and the seductive look in her eyes as she'd agreed to come, and then the touch of her lips as she leant through his car window and kissed him. But the night had ended in disappointment. When she came to his cottage, her mood had changed, she said she couldn't stay long and kept a safe distance from him. He hadn't pushed it; he had some pride.

The members of the Agency had formed such a strong team, complementing each other with their different strengths, working their way through some exciting and fascinating cases, with great successes: finding David Pemberton and seeing the joy of his father when they were reunited, solving the disappearance of the two girls from the holiday camp, and the last big case when he nearly lost Laurel to the sea. That had been the turning point for him as far as Laurel was concerned. Perhaps it was time for the Agency to split. Could he continue to work with Laurel and not make some crass move that would scupper their working relationship? Would he be better to move out of the area and set up on his own? Go back home, to Liverpool? He shook his head. Within his mother's reach? To hear the triumphant voice of his father at the rise of trade union power? He loved them – but at a distance.

Gladham Hall's drive was as impressive as last time. He'd phoned Sir George after their sudden departure last Wednesday and explained

Mr Elderkin wouldn't be coming. Sir George said he understood, but the tone of his voice suggested he wasn't too pleased. But perhaps the thought of only paying for one detective instead of two would ameliorate his feelings.

A different man in a dark suit opened the front door. Perhaps Sir George had a man for each day of the week. He was once again shown to the sitting room. Sir George was reading *The Times*, his lower lip protruding, making him look like a prematurely aged, sulky schoolboy.

'Ah, Mr Diamond. Good of you to come. Where is Mr Elderkin?'

Frank tried to keep a straight face. He'd already explained when he rang to make this appointment. 'Mr Elderkin was unable to be here as I told you; his wife's son suddenly died, and she needs his support. However, I'm sure I can manage your problem by myself.'

Trubshaw shrugged. 'Very well. Shall we proceed? I'm a busy man, Mr Diamond. When you're the head of a big business –' as opposed to a tiny detective agency – 'you have to look ahead. How will the new Value Added Tax affect my firm? Will the rate of price increases put the Great British Public off buying Trubshaw's Toffees? Inflation is running between eight and ten per cent! This can't go on.'

Frank hoped not, and took the seat Trubshaw indicated. No offer of coffee. He put his briefcase on the floor and took out a notepad and biro. 'I'd like to take a few details. I know you said you hadn't insured the jewellery because Lady Trubshaw didn't remind you it needed renewing, but as I understand, insurance firms remind clients when it's time to renew. They're keen on taking our money. Didn't that happen?'

Trubshaw's chest visibly increased in girth and his face flushed. 'That's a very personal question. Surely it doesn't have a bearing on the case? I don't wish to discuss such details with you.'

Frank was beginning to wish they hadn't taken the case. 'No, at the moment it doesn't appear relevant, but it seems strange.'

'I've told you. Hazel forgot about it, you know what women are like, no head for finances.'

He didn't think Dorothy would be pleased to hear that one. Possibly Lady Trubshaw wouldn't either, especially if it wasn't true. Insurance companies didn't send out just one reminder.

'So, all your other valuables *are* insured?'

'Yes, of course.'

'Thank you.' There, that wasn't so painful, was it? Something fishy here. He wondered if he could find out the name of the insurance company, and if he did, would they play ball and give him details? He'd get Dorothy to chase that one up.

'Would it be possible to see where the rings and bracelet were kept? I presume they weren't in a safe?'

Trubshaw rose. 'No, they were taken from Lady Trubshaw's bedroom. Please follow me.'

Separate rooms? So, it wasn't only the Queen and the Duke of Edinburgh, even minor members of the aristocracy had to make midnight trips if they were feeling randy. He bet there was a groove in the carpet between Sir George's and Lady Trubshaw's bedrooms. He wondered which way the carpet pile was worn?

Trubshaw led him from the hall up the wide oak staircase, then down an equally wide corridor, lined with portraits of bewigged gentlemen who looked as though they'd smelt something nasty, to a panelled door on the right. He knocked and opened the door.

'Ah, you're here, Hazel. Mr Diamond wants to see where you kept the jewels.' He turned. 'She's just, er . . . making herself presentable.'

'You can come on in,' Hazel shouted. 'I'm decent.'

Frank hoped this wasn't true, he needed cheering up.

The room was spacious and gave the impression of a French boudoir, as seen in films, not personally. Lots of pink, cream frills, satin and lace, with a vast four-poster double bed covered with a pink satin quilt. Lady Trubshaw was seated at her dressing table, its legs discreetly covered in more pink satin. She wore a matching dressing gown, her blonde hair loose, a cigarette between the fingers of her right hand. Waves of a heady scent flowed towards him.

'Good morning, Lady Trubshaw.'

'Don't be so formal. Call me Hazel.'

She obviously wouldn't take no for an answer. He hadn't changed his mind, he didn't want to be on first-name terms with her or Sir George.

He glanced at Sir George. He didn't seem to mind, there was a softening of his face as he looked at his wife. Frank decided he knew which way the carpet pile was worn, except there wasn't any carpet, he'd have to change that to a groove in the floorboards.

'Thank you, but I think we must keep our relationship on a business footing.'

She gurgled. 'OK, love, as you like.'

Sir George went over to her and kissed her cheek. 'Good morning, darling. Did you have a good sleep?'

She playfully punched his shoulder. 'Like a log,' she said, 'always sleep well after a bit of exercise.' She winked at Frank.

There was something about Hazel Trubshaw he liked, and it wasn't just the impressive cleavage revealed by her gaping gown; her raw earthiness and lack of pomposity endeared her to him. 'Where did you keep the rings and bracelet?'

She got up and waved him over to the dressing table. 'I put them in here.' She pointed to an antique box made of some exotic wood, its top inlaid with a jade medallion.

'Was it locked?'

'No, we'd come in from a late night.' She raised her eyebrows suggestively. 'I just put them in the box. The next day I forgot to give them to George to put in the safe. We went to Newmarket races and in all the excitement I completely forgot about them. When we got back – we stayed two nights in Newmarket – I noticed the box was open. I was really upset; they were some of my favourite pieces.' She went over to Sir George. 'You were ever so good, love.' She looked back at Frank. 'Most men would have gone berserk, but my husband's a real gentleman.' She winked again. 'Only thing he hasn't done is bought some replacements.'

Trubshaw pinched his wife's cheek. 'I might not need to if Mr Diamond can recover them for us.'

Frank didn't hold out much hope. It was ten days since the jewels had been stolen; by now they'd have passed through a fence's hands, and possibly been broken up, although he doubted that, as a great deal of the worth was in the design and setting, especially the bracelet. He hoped the burglar was a connoisseur.

'Did you notice if any of the windows had been forced? Or doors broken open?'

'No, nothing like that,' Sir George said.

'What about the staff? I'd like a list of their names and the duty rota, say a few days before the jewels were taken, to a few days after. It'll help me to get a better picture of the comings and goings.'

Sir George sighed and Lady Trubshaw looked at him with narrowed eyes, her jolly mood evaporating. She looked as though she was weighing something up. Why didn't they like this line of questioning?

'Shall we go downstairs?' Trubshaw asked.

Frank nodded. 'Would you object if I walked round the house and grounds by myself? Perhaps some time tomorrow?'

The Trubshaws exchanged glances.

'Why do you feel you need to do that? I can't see it will help you,' Sir George said.

'I like to have a feel of the place. Also, I'd like to talk to any of the staff I meet. An informal chat is often more productive than a formal interview.'

Trubshaw opened the bedroom door. 'Let's go back to the sitting room.' He hadn't given permission. Does he want his stolen jewellery returned? Any other person who'd been robbed was usually willing and eager to help.

'I'll be down as soon as I've dressed,' Lady Trubshaw said, a note of panic in her voice.

As they traversed the corridor and staircase, he decided to needle Sir George into an answer. 'From your silence I gather you aren't happy with my requests.'

Sir George pivoted on his toes on the bottom stair, putting himself at a disadvantage, as now Frank was taller than him. 'No. Not at all. But I must tell you I have complete trust in all my employees, at least those who work in the house. I couldn't say that about the gardeners and groundsmen. I don't know them as well as the house staff.'

They resumed their former seats in the sitting room.

'Sir George, have you any suspicions about anyone? Did a visitor, or even an acquaintance, express an interest in your wife's jewellery? Perhaps admired it, or asked questions about it? The bracelet is especially interesting and unusual.' He paused.

Sir George bent his head, frowned and twisted his lips. He did seem to be mulling over the question. 'I can't think of anyone, but I will give it some thought. No, I haven't got any suspicions.'

The last words didn't ring true. If he had doubts, why wasn't he willing to share them? 'I need to ask Lady Trubshaw the same questions.'

As if called by her name, Hazel Trubshaw marched into the room. She shot a worried glance at her husband, as though she was wondering what he'd said.

'Hazel, can you help us?'

She sat beside him and he placed an arm round her waist and drew her close, as though he was using her as a shield. Frank repeated the questions.

She sat down on the arm of his chair. 'The circle we move in are too polite, or too tight-arsed, to ask questions about my clothes or jewellery, although they might be dying to know. It's thought rude to ask questions like that. Me, if I want to know something, I ask. It's non-U to talk about money. Silly, I call it. First thing I asked George was how much he was worth.'

Sir George reddened. 'Really, Hazel, Mr Diamond will get the wrong impression.'

Frank didn't think so.

She grinned at him, her ebullient mood restored. She pinched Sir George's cheek. 'I fancied you on sight, and when I found out you were Trubshaw's Toffees, I fancied you even more!' She leant back, gurgling with laughter.

61

Sir George's face was a mixture of embarrassment and pride.

This case looked messy; Frank would have to get some order into it. 'I'd like to start by interviewing all the staff. Could you give me a list of their names, how long they've worked for you and any personal details that might be relevant?'

Trubshaw frowned. 'Such as?'

'Their last employment before they came to work for you, with details of names and addresses of employers. Also, if you have files with details such as references, I'd like to see them.'

Trubshaw leant back, his shoulders drooping. 'When do you want all this?'

'Tomorrow. I can read it through and then start interviewing them, possibly in the afternoon. I presume they know about the theft?'

'Only Anne, she looks after my clothes. She may have told some of the others, I didn't tell her not to,' Hazel said.

Trubshaw shot a look at his wife. 'Hazel,' he hissed, 'I thought we agreed not to mention this to the staff.'

She shrugged. 'Anne's like a friend, I couldn't help having a moan about it. She was ever so upset.'

Frank got up. He'd had enough and wanted to get back to Greyfriars and see if he could do anything for Mabel and Stuart. Mabel was going to the fish and chip shop today and Laurel was going with her. He hoped he might be able to throw in a few words of caution before she left. If he'd missed them, at least he could have a talk with Stuart; see what he really felt about the situation.

'I'll be back tomorrow morning, say nine thirty? You'll have the list and details ready for me? Also, if I could have the use of a room, with a telephone if possible, that would be great.' He smiled expectantly.

Trubshaw sighed. 'I'll get my secretary on to it this afternoon.'

'Before I leave,' Frank said, his hand on the door knob, 'I think you ought to reconsider informing the police. Over the past two years there've been several burglaries from large houses and stately homes. The police believe several of them may be connected. The items stolen are, in many cases, small items of great value, like your own stolen jewellery. It may be worthwhile even if you still want to retain the services of our Agency. It will help them to build up a picture. It might even help them to solve the cases.'

Trubshaw reddened. 'Don't you want this case? Have you so much work you can afford to turn me down?'

He shouldn't have bothered. 'No, not at all, Sir George. I felt I should mention it.'

Lady Trubshaw pulled at Sir George's sleeve. 'Mr Diamond's only trying to help, love.'

Trubshaw got up. 'Very well, I'll think about what you've said.'

Sir George didn't sound keen.

He definitely needed a break; he didn't like working for the Trubshaws, Sir George was evasive – something wasn't right with the case. And he didn't fancy going straight back to Greyfriars, the atmosphere wasn't good. If only Mabel could accept Matthew's death was an accident. He was very fond of her, but her intransigence was causing friction between members of the Agency.

Chapter Nine

Laurel glanced at Mabel, who was sitting like a wooden effigy in the passenger seat of her Cortina. 'I think Stuart was upset you didn't want him to come with you,' she said. They were on their way to Aldeburgh, to the fish and chip shop, to see Sarah, and also Ethel Blower; first stopping at the hut on the promenade to meet Tom Blower.

'I know,' Mabel said, 'but I think you'll have an open mind about how Matt died. Stuart thinks I should wait for the coroner's verdict and abide by that.'

'It's sensible advice, Mabel.'

'I know what the coroner will say. I've listened to Nick Revie; it'll be death by misadventure. I don't want us to waste weeks while we wait for that. After a murder you need to start investigating as soon as possible. The longer we leave it the more likely clues will go stale. I've learnt that much working for a detective agency.'

Her voice was grim, but she was in control of her emotions – at the moment.

Laurel glanced at Mabel again. 'Nick's been helpful, he's allowing me to ask questions – I presume you still want me to go ahead?'

Mabel looked at her, her face softening. 'I know you don't want to do it, but I know you will for me, won't you?'

Laurel smiled at her. 'Yes. I'll do it.'

They were approaching the fork in the road that led to Thorpeness. 'Do you want to go to Aldeburgh direct or via the sea?'

Mabel pointed east. 'By the sea, then we can stop at the hut and talk to Tom before I see Sarah.'

The sun shone fitfully between patches of cloud, lighting up the yellow flowers of the heath's gorse bushes as they drove along the narrow road. The false windmill on the right came into view; like all the rest of the fantasy holiday village, with its mock Tudor and Jacobean houses built in the 1920s by a Scottish barrister, it was not what it seemed.

'I love this place,' Mabel said. 'When Bill was alive, we'd often walk here of an evening, when I'd closed the shop, and have a pint at the pub.' She smiled. 'Only when the weather was fair; it can blow hard and there's no shelter along the shore line.'

Laurel remembered the day she met Oliver, and went with him to check on the health of Dr Luxton. They'd walked together through a howling gale to Luxton's bungalow, a short way from the village along the road to Aldeburgh. She shuddered as she remembered finding Luxton's body.

Thorpeness awakened so many different emotions in her, mostly to do with family holidays and her dead sister, Angela. There were many happy memories, but it also stirred up feelings of deep loss, and regrets for her own stupidity in trying to bring Angela's murderer to book. If it hadn't been for Frank . . .

She found a parking space near the Moot Hall. 'Do you want me to come with you? Would you rather see Tom by yourself?'

Mabel shook her head. 'I want you to hear what he has to say. I may have to talk a bit of business as well. The boat's got to keep fishing; he's got to make a living. Matt wouldn't have wanted Tom to go short; they've been best friends since they went to primary school. You'll like Tom, *he's* got a good wife and a couple of lovely kids.' Her mouth turned down. 'No prospects of my having any grandchildren now. Sarah, she didn't want children, Matt did tell me that, it was one of the reasons they weren't getting on. Matt said he thought she'd change her mind, but I didn't think she would, and I was right.' Her voice was bitter.

They walked over a strip of grass to the promenade and a hut set on the shingle beach. Unlike the others there wasn't a blackboard outside, with a list of the day's catch chalked up. A fishing boat was beached nearby; there were gulls sitting on the roof of the hut, some wheeling round, crying, hoping fish skins would be thrown to them. Concrete steps led up to a closed door. Mabel knocked and the door jerked open. Whoever was on the other side had been waiting for them.

A worried face surrounded by wild curly hair gazed at Mabel. 'Auntie Mabel – Mrs Gri – sorry, Mrs Elderkin, I don't know what to say to you. I'm so sorry.' The man paused, there were tears in his eyes and shadows under them. He looked grief-stricken.

Mabel held out her arms. 'Why, Tom, I know you are. You were his true friend. I'm still your Auntie Mabel, nothing's changed there.' They held each other close, both sobbing. Laurel wished she could disappear. How would Tom Blower react to her, to a stranger who'd seen him break down? Most men thought crying was a weakness, something women could do, but not men, especially strong, silent seamen. Mabel extricated herself, wiping her eyes, then Tom's, with a tissue she took from her handbag. Laurel had brought a box of Kleenex with her but left it in the car. Mabel was always well prepared.

The inside of the hut smelt of a mixture of fish and bleach. On a shelf was an Avery scale, round the edge of the room were wooden-topped cupboards, and in the centre, a small table and two stools.

Tom pointed to these. 'Please sit down.' He held out his hand, a faint smile on his lips. 'Pleased to meet you, Miss Bowman, Auntie Mabel told me she was bringing you.'

She shook his hand, which was rough and calloused; she liked the look of him, and could imagine he would be a good friend, with his homely, but not unattractive face, his gaze open and honest. But, could he have more to do with Matt's death than just finding his body? Did he have anything to gain from his death?

'Shall I make us some tea?' he asked.

Mabel nodded. 'That's kind of you, Tom. Then I want you to tell me, although I know it will be hard, how you found my boy.'

He gulped. 'Haven't the police told you?'

She pursed her lips. 'They have, but I want to hear it first hand, and I want Miss Bowman to hear it, too.'

He took the kettle from a gas ring and poured boiling water into

66

a metal teapot. He opened the door of a large fridge, a strong whiff of fish shooting into the room, but as far as she could see, milk was the only occupant. He remained silent until the tea had been brewed and poured. He upended a crate and sat on it, holding his full mug close to his chest, as though he needed the warmth. The tea was strong, brown and slightly salty.

'I know it's difficult, but start from when you heard the maroons,' Mabel said.

He closed his eyes, as though he couldn't bear to look at the pain on Mabel's face. When he reached the point of finding Matt's body in the tractor shed, his voice faltered, blood draining from his face.

'Go on, Tom, it has to be told,' Mabel said, her voice surprisingly calm, as though she was holding back her own feelings for Tom's sake.

When he'd finished the dreadful story, he opened his eyes and looked at Mabel.

'You did well, Tom, thank you.'

'Tom, is it all right if I call you Tom?'

He nodded.

'I'm Laurel, by the way.' She smiled encouragingly. 'Was it usual for Matt to start the tractor motor before the lifeboat was launched?'

He shook his head. 'No, but he did do it occasionally. When the maroons go up, all we're concentrating on is finding out where we're going, what's happened and getting the launch off as quickly as possible. The tractor's used to pull the boat back up onto its launch pad after we come back.'

'See,' Mabel hissed. 'What did I tell you?'

Tom shot her a worried look. 'But it happened.' He stopped. 'It could be Matt got down there early, I think he may have been in the tractor shed before the maroons went up. I'm not sure he went home. He was wearing the same clothes as when I saw him in the Cross Keys earlier that night.'

'Really?' Laurel said. 'Was he wearing the scarf when you saw him?'

Tom frowned. 'The police asked me that. I had to say I didn't know.' Mabel sniffed. 'I'm sorry, Auntie Mabel; it might have been inside his jacket. I know Matt sometimes did go into the hut by himself to check on the equipment; he was a real stickler, always checking all the gear was there, in good order. I thought maybe after leaving the pub, he decided to go to the shed.'

'But why would he start the tractor engine?' Laurel asked.

'It *has* been playing up. He'd been on at Alan Varley, he's the engineer, to give it an overhaul, but Alan's been taken up with his wife lately. You can't blame him for that.'

She turned to Mabel. 'Is Mrs Varley ill?'

Mabel nodded. 'Cancer, very bad. Their daughter, Lily, she works in my fish and chip shop. Lovely girl, should be working somewhere better. She could have stayed on for A levels, but Alan wouldn't let her. He's got old-fashioned values as far as women are concerned. You might meet Lily later. I've asked Ethel, Tom's mum, and Lily, to be at the shop. How is your mum, Tom?'

His face became even more sombre. 'She's really upset, all the staff are. Matt was like a brother to me, and Mum, although she doesn't usually show her feelings, has been . . .' He sighed. 'She'll do anything to help you, so will I, Auntie Mabel. Anything at all, you've only got to ask.'

Mabel patted his hand, sniffing, trying to hold back tears. 'Dear boy, thank you.' She looked at Laurel.

'Tom, Mabel has asked me to talk to all the people who knew Matt, but I won't ask you any more questions today. Mabel wants me to see if I can discover why and how Matt met his death in such a strange way.'

Tom's eyes widened and his mouth fell open. 'Auntie Mabel, you surely don't think someone was mixed up in this?'

The ram-rod back emerged. 'Yes, I do. I'm sure Matt was murdered.'

Laurel drove to Mabel's fish and chip shop. A large sign in the main window, edged in black, read:

WE ARE CLOSED AND WILL BE
UNTIL FURTHER NOTICE

Mabel opened a side gate which led into a yard. 'That's the smokery over there, and that machine peels the potatoes.' She opened a door to the inside. 'The prep room,' she said. Two women, one middle-aged, the other a teenager, were seated on stools at a table. They got up, their faces anxious.

The older woman tentatively held out her arms. 'Mabel, my dear, my poor dear. I am so sorry, he was such a lovely man. We're all devastated. My Tom, he'll never get over it, nor will I.' She hugged Mabel to her. They were the same height and age. They must have been young mothers together, knowing each other because of the sons' friendship. Friends and workmates. The teenage girl had sat down on her stool, crying, a handkerchief held to her eyes. They must be Ethel and Lily. Mabel had told her about both of them as they drove over from Dunwich. She said Ethel did most of the work in the shop, it seemed her daughter-in-law, Sarah, hadn't been pulling her weight these last few months, and was often out, seeing her friends, or going to Ipswich shopping. Mabel said Ethel hadn't wanted to talk about it, but Mabel, worried about the weakening marriage, had tackled her several weeks ago and squeezed the truth from her. Laurel wished Mabel had been more willing to talk about this to her, or Dorothy; she wasn't sure how much Stuart knew.

'Laurel – Ethel and me, we're going up to the flat for a bit. We need to sort some things out.'

Laurel smiled and nodded, and went over to the girl and moved a stool close to her. 'Hello, you must be Lily,' she said. 'I'm Laurel.'

Lily wiped her eyes and gave her a weak smile. She was a bonny girl, about five feet four, she guessed, with thick brunette hair swept back from a high forehead, large brown eyes, a strong straight nose and a wide, full-lipped mouth. A budding beauty with her creamy skin and a womanly figure for her age. Mabel said she was a much more robust version of her mother.

'I'm a member of The Anglian Detective Agency, I work with Mabel, Mrs Elderkin, and the other detectives.'

Her eyes widened. 'I know who you are, I've seen you in the town. I think you're very brave, tackling all those bad men.'

'Thank you, Lily. You obviously knew Matt well.'

Her eyes welled up with tears. 'I can't believe he's gone,' she sobbed, wiping her nose and patting her cheeks with the hankie. 'I thought Mr Grill was one of the nicest men I've ever met. He was always so kind to me. Always smiled and had a cheery word. I thought Mrs Grill, the young Mrs Grill, was so lucky to be married to him. He was real handsome.' She blushed, looking as though she wished she hadn't said that.

A girlhood crush? The way she described his kindness suggested not all the men she was in contact with were so charming.

'Lily, I hope in a few days I may be able to come back and have another chat with you about Mr Grill. Would that be all right?'

She looked puzzled. 'Why would you want to do that?'

This was difficult, perhaps she shouldn't have spoken so soon.

'Mrs Elderkin,' she pointed to the ceiling. Lily nodded in understanding. 'She wants me to talk to people, to see if . . .' This was difficult, she didn't want to frighten the girl.

The expression on Lily's face changed, no more tears and her eyes flashed. With anger?

Lily leant towards her. 'Does she think there was something funny going on?'

There was more to Lily than just a typical teenage girl. Her face showed character and fire. 'Yes, she thinks Mr Grill's death is not as straightforward as it appears.'

Lily's back straightened. 'I couldn't believe it when I heard how he died. He was the cox'n of the lifeboat, you know; he risked his life for others. My dad said he was a first-rate cox'n, brave but not reckless, you could depend on him to keep his head, even in the most dangerous circumstances, that's what my dad said.'

'You won't mind if I come back and talk to you again?'

'No, I won't,' she said stoutly. 'Although I'm not sure what I can tell you that will be of any help.'

Laurel touched her arm. 'You work here, I'm sure you know lots of people who knew Mr Grill. It's surprising, it may seem like a

70

small detail to you, but when it's put with others, it can help to form vital evidence.'

Lily's face expressed interest. 'I hadn't thought of that. You can count on me. I'll help in any way I can. Where would we talk?'

'I can come to your house if you don't want to talk to me here.'

'No. No.' She shook her head violently. 'You mustn't come to my house.'

Her mother? She wanted to shield her mother from any unpleasantness? 'We can meet for a tea or coffee somewhere. I'll contact you through the shop.'

'Let Ethel know. She'll tell me.'

The side door opened and a woman with shoulder-length blonde hair stood in the doorway glaring at them.

Chapter Ten

This must be Sarah, Matt's wife; she was more attractive than the description Mabel had given. She reminded Laurel of a modern version of a fifties film star, with shoulder-length blonde hair, cascading from a high forehead and skimming her right eye, very femme fatale. She certainly didn't look pleased to see them, her full, sensuous lips in a definite pout.

'Who's this, Lily?' she said. 'And what are you doing here? The shop's closed.'

Lily's cheeks flamed. She started up, knocking her stool against the table.

Laurel got up. 'I presume you must be Mrs Grill?'

Sarah Grill ignored the proffered handshake. 'I am. Who are you? And what are you doing in my shop?'

Laurel decided to ignore the last question. 'I'm Laurel Bowman, I work with your mother-in-law, Mrs Elderkin, at The Anglian Detective Agency. I'm very sorry for your loss. I didn't know your husband very well, but Mabel's told me so much about him. He was liked and well respected in Aldeburgh.'

At the mention of the Agency, Sarah's already pale face lost what little colour it had. 'Why are you here? You've no right to be snooping round, talking to my staff.' She turned to Lily, who was trying to make her way out of the room. 'Lily! I'll speak to you later.'

Sarah turned to Laurel and pointed to the door. 'Get out, whatever your name is, or I'll call the police.'

Laurel bit her lip. Keep calm, she told herself. No wonder Mabel wanted to plant Matt's death onto Sarah – quite understandable. 'I'm afraid you misunderstand, Mrs Grill, I'm here at the request of—'

She didn't have time to finish the sentence as Mabel burst into the room, closely followed by Ethel.

Sarah whirled round. Laurel wouldn't have been surprised if there'd been a flash of lightning between the two women, as the air was charged with electricity.

'Sarah! Miss Bowman is here at my request and I don't think I have to remind you that this is not your premises – this shop and flat are in my name. Not yours!'

This was a side of Mabel she hadn't seen before. She was usually a tolerant woman, always ready to help others, with a soft edge to her. But this Mabel was a virago, her eyes blazing, breasts heaving, her voice full of dislike and venom. Good job Stuart wasn't here, all his illusions would have been shattered.

Mabel pointed to the table. 'We'll all sit down. I need to ask you some questions, Sarah.'

Sarah had retreated, her back against the wall, but her chin was tilted up and those large, blue eyes were as hard as bullets. Had Mabel met her match?

'What do you mean, ask me questions? That's the job of the police; I thought you'd know that being as you married an ex-copper. Didn't he tell you?' She didn't move.

Laurel was afraid this was going to turn into a very nasty scene; it was well on the way. She got up. 'Please take my seat, Mrs Grill. Can we get more chairs?' She looked enquiringly at Ethel. Grim-faced, Ethel nodded, and went out of the room.

'Mabel,' Laurel asked, 'would it be a good idea to ask Lily to make some tea for all of us? I could certainly do with a cup.'

Mabel stared at her, as though she'd just realised she was in the room. Laurel gestured with her hand, making calming movements. Mabel continued staring, then the message seemed to penetrate. She took a deep breath and nodded. 'Lily, would you do that? Anyone prefer coffee?'

'Yes, I would,' Laurel said. She looked at Sarah. 'Mrs Grill?'

Sarah Grill slunk to the vacated chair, a pack of cigarettes and a lighter in one hand, a mutinous look on her face. 'Black coffee, one sugar,' she said to no one in particular.

Ethel returned with two more chairs. 'I'll give you a hand, Lily. Mabel, what would you like?'

Mabel didn't take her eyes off Sarah. 'Tea, Ethel. *Thank you*.'

Sarah's look would have frozen an erupting volcano.

Ethel cocked her head at Laurel, and placed a chair between the two protagonists.

'What's this all about, Mabel?' Sarah asked, after lighting up a cigarette and blowing a stream of grey smoke at the ceiling.

Laurel was glad she hadn't aimed for Mabel's eyes. She couldn't see this meeting being very productive and she wished she hadn't come.

'Sarah, I think we're both upset. I shouldn't have lost my head like that. But I didn't like the way you talked to Miss Bowman. She's a dear friend as well as being a colleague. She's been a lot of help to me, and to Stuart. She stayed with me on the beach that night when I was attacked and left for dead,' Mabel said, obviously making a great effort to control herself.

Sarah inhaled deeply; she looked calmer, her face taking on a calculating look. 'Yeh, I'm upset too, after all he was my husband.' The way she said this seemed to imply the loss of a husband was greater than a mother's loss. Laurel thought, in some cases, a wife might be grateful to lose her husband; she wouldn't be surprised if Sarah wasn't one of them. She inwardly chided herself – that was a mean-spirited thought. She looked at Sarah. No, she deserved it.

Ethel and Lily carried steaming mugs to the table, Lily hovering near the door, looking unsure.

'Do you want Lily to stay, Mabel?' asked Laurel.

Mabel turned. 'What do you want to do, Lily?'

Lily twisted her hands. 'Can I go home? See how mum is?'

'You do that, dear. Miss Bowman can talk to you another time.'

Lily smiled at Laurel, but didn't look at Sarah, and made a smart exit.

'Shall I stay?' Ethel asked.

Mabel nodded. 'We've just spoken to your Tom. Heard from him how he found Matt.'

Sarah ground out her cigarette on a saucer. 'Do we have to go through this now? It's really upsetting talking about it. I don't know how you can do it. I'm only just coming to terms with his death.'

Mabel leant across the table towards her. 'You don't believe it was an accident, do you?'

Sarah shrugged. 'The police seem to think so. What else could it be?'

Mabel sat back until she was as straight as a Victorian schoolmistress. 'Matt would never be so slap-dash. What's more, he never wore a scarf. Did you ever see him wear one?' she challenged.

Sarah raised her whip-lash thin eyebrows. 'Not that I remember. I wasted my money buying him a lovely Jaeger scarf one Christmas.' She sniffed. 'He never wore it, even to please me. Anyway, what's a scarf got to do with it? Oh, you mean the one . . .'

Mabel tilted her head as she eyed up her daughter-in-law. 'What did the police say to you about a scarf?'

Sarah took out another cigarette, her fingers trembling as she raised the lighter to it. 'They said his clothing got caught in some machinery.' She took a deep drag, then puffed out a cloud of smoke, immediately sucking on the cigarette again, as if she needed to charge her blood stream with nicotine.

Mabel was staring at her, unblinking, like a ferret trying to hypnotise a rabbit. 'There was a scarf round Matt's neck; that's what choked him. Don't you think that's strange? The first time he wears a scarf since he was a little boy and I'd wrap one round him when those bitter winds from the east blew in winter. Even then he'd pull it off when he thought I wasn't looking. Don't you think that's suspicious?'

Sarah wriggled nervously. 'I suppose so. Perhaps he had a sore throat and wanted to keep warm. We'll never know, will we?'

'Oh, yes, we will. We'll know what happened,' Mabel said, her face as grim as a church warden when he finds a foreign coin in the collection plate. 'Sarah, where's that scarf I gave you last Christmas? I'd like to see it.'

Sarah's cheeks flushed. 'Why? Want it back, now you think you can get rid of me? Don't think I don't know you've never liked me. Not good enough for your precious son, was I? Let me tell you, I've put a lot into this fish and chip shop, worked my socks off, and what for? Don't think you can get rid of me so easily. You owe me for all the effort I've put in.'

Mabel's nostrils flared, and her hands clenched, probably wishing they were round Sarah's neck. Should Laurel try and calm things down? 'Mrs Grill, please, it's all right. Mrs Elderkin is trying to make sure we get the correct verdict—'

Mabel banged her fist on the table. 'You and Matt have had all the profits since I left. I was happy for that, you deserved it, you both worked hard. There was no rent to pay, the only overheads were the rates and gas and electric. I've taken nothing from you since I moved out to work at the school, so don't come that one with me. I wasn't going to ask you to leave, but now you're bringing it up.' She was getting near breaking point, eyes full of tears, her words ragged.

Sarah seemed to sense blood; her expression changed, nostrils narrowing. 'You can keep your greasy old chip shop. I'm sick of it, sick of the stink of fish, sick of my hair smelling of grease. And look at these.' She held up her hands. The skin was reddened and dry, the scarlet nail varnish not improving the picture.

Laurel couldn't stand any more of this. It wasn't her quarrel, but Mabel had asked for her help and the growing animosity between them wouldn't help her investigations. 'Ladies! This is not helping anyone. Mabel, if you want me to continue looking into how Matt died, I need you to calm down.' Once a teacher, always a teacher. 'Mrs Grill, I'm sorry for your loss, but I'm sure you also want the circumstances of your husband's death to be fully understood. Both of you are very upset and perhaps this meeting was too soon. I fully understand it must be difficult for you to talk about this.' She paused, looking from one to the other, knowing her expression was stern, calm and not to be quarrelled with. Her very best Senior Mistress mode.

76

Mabel's shoulders dropped and Sarah's eyes filled with tears.

'What's going to happen to me?' she said, plucking a handkerchief from a pocket and blowing her nose.

Mabel stared at her, and bit her lip. She looked at Laurel, who nodded, and gave her a smile of encouragement. Mabel took a deep breath. 'We're both overwrought, Sarah. Perhaps I've been a bit harsh; put it down to – well. I don't need to explain, do I? Don't worry, I won't turn you out. We'll come to some arrangement, but I don't want to talk about that now.'

'Shall we bring this meeting to an end?' Laurel asked.

Sarah nodded. 'I think that'll be best.'

Mabel shook her head. 'No. If you don't mind, Sarah, I'd like to hear a bit more from you. We can't waste time on this one. I'm not accusing you of anything, but you're his – was – Matt's wife. You may be able to tell us something important.'

Sarah bristled.

Oh God, thought Laurel, here we go again.

'I hope you're not accusing me of anything!' Sarah said.

Laurel shot a warning glance at Mabel. 'Mrs Elderkin isn't accusing you of anything, but it would be helpful, especially to me, if you could talk us through a few things.'

'Such as?'

'Let's start with the last time you saw Matt. How did he seem?' She hoped Mabel would take the hint and shut up. If Mabel started up again, they'd be back to square one, a very unpleasant square one.

Sarah flicked back her hair, then lit another cigarette. 'Oh, all right. Ask your questions.' Mabel leant back against her chair. Thank goodness for that.

'When was the last time you saw Matt?'

'It was last Tuesday evening, Matt had had a bath and I gave him his supper.'

'You ate together?'

'No, I had a sandwich when the shop closed.'

'What did Matt have for his supper?'

Sarah pouted, emphasising her hamster-like cheeks, the one

feature preventing her face from perfection. 'What's that got to do with anything?'

Laurel smiled at her. 'Every little detail helps to build a picture.'

'Cod and chips.'

Mabel let out a sharp breath.

'What time was that, Sarah? Is it all right if I call you Sarah? Please call me Laurel.'

The rebellious look faded. 'About six thirty.'

'What did you talk about?'

Sarah shrugged. 'Nothing really, can't remember.' She paused. 'I said I was sorry I hadn't had time to go to the butchers and get him some steak. I was meeting Mandy, my friend, at seven, so I probably left about quarter to.'

'Did you ask Matt what he'd be doing that evening?'

'Can't remember.'

In other words, she hadn't.

'Where did you meet Mandy? Is she a local woman?'

'There's no need to bring Mandy into this; she wouldn't like it if people came busybodying about.'

'Oh, OK. Did you have a nice evening?'

Those eyes went into ice-chip mode. 'Yeah, we went to the flicks.'

'Good film? I presume you went to the Aldeburgh Cinema?'

Sarah shook her head. 'No, we went to the one in Leiston. Mandy's got a car. There was an arty-farty film on at the Aldeburgh, we didn't fancy that.'

'What time did you get back home?'

Out of the corner of her eye, she saw Mabel lean forward. Please don't interfere, she thought.

'Can't remember, about half-ten, maybe eleven.'

'You didn't realise Matt wasn't in bed?'

Sarah flushed, looking furtive. 'No. I thought he was asleep. I didn't go into our room. I told Matt I'd sleep in the other bedroom; I didn't want to wake him. He has to get up early.'

'You didn't even peep in to see if he was home or not?'

'Why wouldn't he be home at eleven? He always went to bed early, it was a real bore, we couldn't go out anywhere, and if we did, we always had to leave before everyone else.'

'Very understandable,' Laurel said quickly, not giving Mabel a chance to interrupt.

'Just one more question, Sarah. Mrs Elderkin said she gave you a scarf as a Christmas present last year. Would it be possible for us to see this scarf? It would help to clear up one problem if we could see it.'

'Well, I'm afraid you can't,' she said, shrugging.

'Why's that?'

'I lost it, sometime during the winter. Can't remember when exactly. I think I may have left it somewhere – I told the police.' She looked at Mabel. 'I told you I'd lost it when you phoned.'

Mabel, Mabel, please keep quiet.

'Anyway, why do you want to see it?'

'A scarf similar to the one Mrs Elderkin gave you was wrapped round Matt's neck. It strangled him.'

Sarah's eyes widened; her face paled to white then to pale green. She clapped a hand over her mouth and rushed out of the room. There were sounds of heaving and the flushing of a lavatory.

Chapter Eleven

Tuesday, 19 September, 1972

Frank glanced at Stuart; he'd asked to come to Gladham Hall today, desperate to get away from Greyfriars – and Mabel. They were going to pick up the list of staff and hopefully to conduct some interviews. Stuart had hardly spoken during the journey and with every minute his face sagged a little more and increased his resemblance to a bloodhound.

Halfway up the drive leading to Gladham Hall, Frank braked and pulled the Avenger onto a grass verge.

Stuart looked startled. 'Something wrong with the car?'

'No.' Frank tapped his wristwatch. 'We're early, so I thought we could have a stroll. Weather's fine and you can have a pipe before we go in. What do you think?'

Stuart let out a long sigh, one of relief. 'Thanks, Frank, I need to get my mind into detective mode. It certainly isn't there at the moment.'

They walked over turf, kept trim by the cows and sheep they could see in the distance; Stuart plodded behind him. Clouds scudding overhead cast shadows over the grass. 'Horse chestnuts are colouring already,' Frank said.

Stuart nodded, stopping to get out his pipe.

Frank pointed to a nearby tree, one of the many dotting the expanse of the park. 'Look, there's a circular seat built round that oak, why don't we sit there for a bit? You can puff your pipe in peace.'

'I'm not a bloody Red Indian,' Stuart said.

'Not in the mood for pow-wow?'

Stuart gave him a sideways glance. 'Could be.'

It was peaceful under the oak, the breeze rustling the dark green leaves. Already there was a smell of autumn in the air, that whiff of future decay as the supply of water was cut off to the leaves, and they started to crisp and colour. Frank decided he'd have a walk over Dunwich Heath and the nearby woods and search for some edible fungi; they'd make a tasty omelette.

Stuart puffed away beside him as they walked. The grey-blue smoke, caught by the moving air, was whisked under Frank's nostrils, the smell enhancing the scents of the season.

Stuart turned to him. 'I don't know what to do about Mabel.'

'It's understandable, Stuart. She's lost her only child. She's bound to be unstable at the moment. Give her time.'

Stuart shook his head. 'It's not just her grief, I understand that. I'm upset enough and I didn't know Matt all that well, but I know what it's like to lose a wife. I realise it must be worse to lose a child. I can't imagine feeling more devastated than I did when Doreen died. I know *that* grief was different to the grief when my parents died, so I suppose losing a child is a different kind of grief again.'

That was a long speech for Stuart. Frank was lucky, he hadn't lost anyone close to him; he'd been too young to realise what was happening when his grandparents died. He supposed the nearest was when he thought he'd lost Laurel to the North Sea. But it was fleeting, the terrible feeling lasted no longer than a few minutes. 'What do you mean, not just her grief?'

'I've never seen her like this. It's as if she's bottled up her grieving, and is obsessed with trying to prove Matt was murdered. I feel sorry for Laurel, I don't think she really wants to be involved, but you know how kind she is. She'd do anything for any of us.'

Unfortunately, Frank thought, there was one thing she wasn't prepared to do for him. Fall in love with him. He couldn't blame her – if it ever happened, he'd probably put up the barriers, afraid of commitment. Or would he?

'Pity Revie didn't tell Laurel to back off,' said Stuart. 'She'd have been grateful.'

'Don't be too sure of that. Once our Laurel gets a whiff of something dodgy, you won't budge her, and she's excellent at getting facts out of people, even taciturn old buggers,' Frank replied.

'Like yours truly?' Stuart said, giving him his first smile of the day.

'You said it, not me.' He glanced at his wristwatch. 'Right, time to mix with the upper classes.'

Stuart snorted. 'If Lady Trubshaw is an aristocrat, I'm a monkey's uncle.'

'No need to insult monkeys, Stuart. Some of them may have appalling manners but they're our nearest relatives.'

They were greeted at the door by Giddings.

'Sir George has had to attend a meeting in London, but Lady Trubshaw will see you,' he said.

Frank wondered if he was a robot, as his facial muscles didn't seem to move as he talked or was he practising to be a ventriloquist?

'Lady Trubshaw is in the walled garden. Please follow me.' He led them round the side of the house to a terrace at the back, which overlooked a central path flanked by deep borders filled with roses and herbaceous plants.

Giddings started to descend the stone steps.

'Just point us in the right direction,' Frank said. He fancied a slow walk to the walled garden so he could examine the borders at leisure. Whoever looked after them had an eye for excellent colour combinations, and the late-summer flowers formed sumptuous cushions and drifts of mauve, yellow, red and white.

Giddings looked offended, but modelling himself no doubt on Jeeves replied, 'Of course, sir. Follow the path to the end, turn right behind the line of pleached limes and the entrance to the walled garden is to your left.' He turned and glided away.

'Gone back to his crypt?' Stuart asked.

'You've got that wrong, he didn't shrivel up in the daylight.'

Stuart made a sweeping gesture. 'This must cost a fortune to keep up.'

'That's Trubshaw's Toffees for you,' Frank replied. 'I wish Laurel and Dorothy could see these gardens.'

'Well, the garden at Greyfriars has certainly improved since Jim McFall started. Perhaps we could nick a few cuttings on the way out.'

'Stuart, that's what little old ladies do when they visit National Trust gardens. They deserve to have their hands cut off. I believe after a weekend a garden can look as though plagues of caterpillars have been at the plants.'

Stuart snorted.

They came to a wrought-iron gate, wide enough to wheel through two wheelbarrows side by side. The garden walls were old, made of small, pink bricks; they supported espaliered fruit trees and ornamental climbers.

'Those apples look tasty,' Stuart said, pointing to some rosy-cheeked fruit. 'Soon be time for apple pies.'

He'd be lucky to get one before Christmas, Frank thought.

Paths divided the garden into quarters, with deep beds against the walls and four central beds which seemed to house mainly vegetables and soft fruit. At the far end was a greenhouse which took up most of the wall. Voices drifted from it, then raucous laughter.

'Sounds like Lady Hazel. Something, or someone, has tickled her fancy,' Stuart said.

'Don't be crude,' Frank replied, 'you know it upsets me.'

Stuart laughed.

Frank inwardly smiled. Thank goodness Stuart had come today. It was doing him good.

Lady Trubshaw emerged from the greenhouse, or was it an orangery? Greenhouse didn't seem a grand enough name. She looked flushed. She was followed by a man, Frank assumed he was a gardener, as he was dressed in corduroy trousers and gardening boots, with braces over his brown shirt. He was over six feet with broad shoulders and could easily have auditioned for the role of Mellors in *Lady Chatterley's Lover*. Was he the reason for the flushed cheeks?

Hazel Trubshaw waved, and sauntered towards them, carrying a garden trug holding several bunches of grapes.

'Would you like some flowers for the house, Lady Trubshaw?' the gardener asked.

She stooped and turned back. 'Good idea. We've got some guests for dinner. I'll nip back when I've seen off these two.' She flashed him a toothy smile. 'Where will you be?'

'I'll be here. Cook's asked me to bring her some tomatoes and the last of the runner beans.'

'Make sure they're not stringy, can't have the guests cutting their tongues on old beans.'

The gardener didn't reply, but Frank thought he saw a sly wink.

The walk back to the house was filled with inconsequential chatter, mainly from Lady Trubshaw who had no difficulty in filling the time in until they reached the sitting room, via the kitchen, where she deposited the grapes. How many staff did they have? There were two women in the kitchen, then there was Giddings, plus that other man who'd answered the door, when he'd come by himself last Monday. The nation's rotten teeth were supporting the Trubshaws in a lifestyle he thought had gone out of fashion with the Edwardians.

Hazel Trubshaw gestured they should sit down. 'I'll fetch that list. Would you like a cup of coffee, I'm gagging for one? I don't know about you but I need a caffeine fix at regular intervals.'

Frank thanked her and wondered if there were any other fixes she needed at regular intervals.

'Looks like she's a might too friendly with that gardener,' Stuart whispered after she'd left the room.

Frank raised his eyebrows and nodded. He was glad to see Stuart more like his old self, beginning to get interested in the case and losing that bloodhound expression.

Lady Trubshaw came back waving a paper, followed by Giddings carrying a silver tray with three steaming mugs on it. Must be instant, there hadn't been enough time for a percolator to do its business. Stuart's face lit up – it must be the plate of Jammy Dodgers.

She passed the sheet of paper to Frank. There were twelve names on it, topped by Giddings – his title, butler. It was followed by the footman, two cooks, two gardeners, two cleaners, an estate manager and three estate workers. Blimey, it would take a few days to interview this lot.

'You've a considerable number of staff, Lady Trubshaw,' Frank said, waving the paper at her.

She pulled a face. 'Doesn't suit me, but Georgie's been used to this kind of life. I wouldn't mind a smaller place, preferably in London, with help just coming in during the day and then buggering off at night. 'Scuse my language!' She gave a throaty laugh and took a long drink from her mug. 'He wouldn't approve of this,' she said, raising the mug in the air. 'Don't you tell him, will you? He's a great one for keeping up appearances.'

'And you're not, Lady Trubshaw?' Frank asked.

'What do you think?' She turned to Stuart. 'Mr Diamond insists on being formal. How about you, Mr Elderkin, what's your moniker?'

The Jammy Dodger, on its way to Stuart's mouth, froze. 'Moniker? Oh, yes. Stuart, er, Hazel.'

'That's a good name, I had an Uncle Stuart, he was ever so fond of me, used to give me sixpence if I'd sit on his lap.'

Frank nearly choked on his coffee. He was grateful he hadn't had an Auntie Flossy who gave him sixpence for cutting her toenails.

Lady Trubshaw sighed. 'Mr Diamond, I know you won't call me Hazel, but I get cheesed off being called Lady Trubshaw by everyone. It's not friendly, is it?'

There was genuine regret in her voice, as though she longed to be one of the masses and have a knees-up at the Old Bull and Bush. What was the origin of that name – he must find out. 'Perhaps when Sir George isn't here, but you'll have to try and remember to give us our official names when he is.'

She gave him a brilliant smile. 'You're a good sort, and so are you, Stuart. Help yourself to as many biscuits as you like, I can see you've got a sweet tooth. Me too, but,' she patted her belly, 'I need to watch it or Georgie might cash me in for a newer model.' She laughed, as though this was a ridiculous idea. 'After all, he's done it before!' More throaty laughs.

Frank decided Lady Trubshaw was a lonely woman; she must be desperate for company if two detectives were worth socialising with. He put down his mug. 'Hazel, we'd like to start interviewing the staff today. Are there two rooms we could use? I'll start with Giddings and Stuart can take the next one down on the list.' He passed the sheet to Stuart, who took out a notepad from his briefcase and noted down the name.

'We'll return tomorrow and try and interview at least six more members of staff, if that's convenient. Perhaps you could arrange a schedule, and tell the persons concerned. Say, start at ten, and allow half an hour for each person. Is that all right? Or would you like one of us to do that?'

She was looking at him intently. 'No, I can do it.' Her manner had changed; was she worried?

She bit her lip. 'You're serious about this, aren't you?'

'Of course; we always do a thorough investigation of any case we take. We've built up a formidable reputation, we're a good team, there's also a third detective, Miss Laurel Bowman, and we've strong back-up as well.' Not quite as strong at the moment, but he wouldn't mention that. 'Why do you ask, Hazel? Do you think we won't succeed?'

'That's the problem, I think you might,' she muttered.

Frank didn't like the sound of that. Stuart looked up from the list.

'Would you like to explain that?' Frank asked, trying to keep his tone friendly.

'Oh, don't pay any attention to me, I don't know what I'm saying half of the time.' She got up. 'I'll sort out two rooms and send the chaps to you. Be back in a mo.' She hurriedly left the room.

Stuart swept up the last Jammy Dodger. 'What do you think she meant?' he asked before the Dodger disappeared to join four others in his stomach.

'I think it means she knows what happened to those two rings and the bracelet. I wonder if Sir George also knows their where-abouts, or is Hazel hiding something from him, as well as us?'

★

The room Lady Trubshaw gave Frank was Sir George's study, a large airy room, the window overlooking the right-hand side of the house with its formal parterre garden laid out with low box hedges planted in squares and rectangles, the centres filled with standard roses. While admitting the skill of the gardeners in keeping everything in order, he didn't like this style of gardening; it was too rigid, he liked a touch of wildness.

'Giddings will be with you in a sec,' Hazel said. 'He's just finishing a job for Georgie.'

'Lady Trubshaw, er, Hazel, before you go can I ask you if there's anything you'd like to tell me? I thought when we were speaking earlier, you wanted to say something. I'd like to remind you, anything you, or Sir George, or one of your staff, tells any of us, is confidential. We don't report to the police, we have a good relationship with them, but unless you've murdered someone all information stays in-house. You haven't murdered anyone lately, have you?' He smiled at her, hoping she might be tempted to tell all.

She stared at him as though trying to make a decision. 'I can't. I'd like to. I will say this, I wish you'd just tell Georgie you haven't any leads and you think you, or any other detective agency, will be unable to find those dratted jewels.' She turned on her heels and marched out.

What was going on? Why did Hazel want the case dropped? She'd inflamed his interest. He looked round the room. Should he sit in Sir George's hot seat behind the super-sized mahogany desk? He didn't think Giddings would approve. From the notes, he'd learned that Giddings had been with Sir George for over twenty-five years, before he married Hazel and moved to Gladham Hall. A faithful servant? He must have been a young man when Sir George first hired him. He decided the two armchairs on either side of a coffee table would be better. The open grate held a blue and white jug filled with mauve Michaelmas daisies and yellow rudbeckias. Nice touch.

Giddings came in. Shouldn't he have knocked? The standard of staff nowadays! Shocking. He must remember to give his union-mad father a description of how the nobility lived and describe in detail the ground-down staff who worked for a pittance. His father had been born in the wrong century and the wrong country; he should have been a Frenchman at the time of the Revolution.

'Hello, Mr Giddings. I believe you know why we're questioning all the staff?'

Giddings nodded.

'Thank you for sparing the time. Please have a seat.' He indicated one of the armchairs, taking the other himself.

Giddings looked unsure as to whether he should take such a liberty. He pulled at the creases in his trousers and perched on the edge of the chair.

'Please relax, Sir George knows I'm interviewing the staff; he wouldn't want you to stand.'

Giddings slid back. He didn't look at home.

'I see you've been with Sir George for many years. Have you always been his butler?'

Giddings smoothed back his already smooth black hair. 'No, sir. I started with Sir George when he lived in London. He brought me down from the North. I used to work in the factory, on the production side, and Sir George, er, noticed me. He had me trained as a butler and I moved down to London.'

'Trubshaw's Toffees?'

'Yes, that's right.'

'Did you work anywhere else before Trubshaws?'

'I was in the Merchant Navy, before I went to Trubshaws, but I had to leave – I was needed at home.'

'What did you do in the navy?'

'Catering – I was in charge of supplies.'

'That's quite a story – not quite rags to riches, but not far from something you might read in a Dickens novel.'

'Charles Dickens? Yes, I was lucky.' There was a sly smile. 'But you have to make your own luck. Don't you, sir?'

Was he trying to tell him something? 'Please call me Mr Diamond, Mr Giddings. You know why we're questioning the staff?'

'Yes, it's about the missing jewellery, isn't it?'

'That's correct. How did you first hear it was missing?'

'When I came back with Sir George and Lady Trubshaw; they'd been to the races.'

'You were with them?'

'Yes, I also act as chauffeur when needed.'

'Do you stay at the same hotels as your employers?'

'No, it's usually a small hotel or boarding house. Once we get to wherever we're going, I have a lot of free time. Nice little holiday, Sir George gives me some money for expenses, and if they don't need the car, I can use it.'

Could he have driven back to Gladham Hall and stolen the jewellery? 'He's very generous.'

Giddings pulled a face. 'It depends if he's flush. We're all right at the moment, but there have been times when things haven't been so rosy. Then we've had to tighten our belts, staff are dismissed and I have to double up on jobs,' he moaned.

He's loosening up – good. 'But it isn't like that now, is it? Or Sir George wouldn't've asked us to take on this case. Also, there seems to be plenty of staff around.'

Giddings shrugged. 'Yes, at the moment things are going well. Let's hope it keeps that way.'

'When was the last time Sir George had financial difficulties?'

Giddings' eyes looked at the stuccoed ceiling. 'Few years back. Soon after he married *her*.'

So, that was how the land lay. 'Really? Why was that?'

Giddings was relaxing, looking as though he was enjoying a bit of gossiping and a touch of backbiting. 'That last divorce, you know. Took him to the cleaners, did the last wife. Can't say I blame her. She was a cut above *this* one. Had an accent that could cut a slice of beef off the Sunday roast. Then he went potty and spent God knows what on *her*. That's when he bought the jewellery that's been stolen, and a few other things, like a baby-blue sports car and a watch with diamonds instead of numbers. He ignored the business, and I kept telling him he ought to try and keep up with modern trends in confectionery; profits slumped and he was in hot water.'

Giddings must have a close relationship with Sir George. But had Hazel pushed his nose out of joint? He obviously resented her. 'Sir George must set a great store by you, if he listens to your advice.'

'He used to, now I'm just one of the staff. In the past we had really meaningful conversations, I felt I was almost one of the family, having known him for so long. But all that's over.'

Frank tried to look understanding. This was Laurel's territory, pity she wasn't interviewing Giddings, she'd have had him weeping on her shoulder and blurting out even more juicy bits of scandal. 'That's hard.' He hoped he sounded sympathetic, but to his ears the words rang false.

'Thank you, Mr Diamond.'

Perhaps his personal skills were improving? 'Around the time the jewels were stolen, did you see anything suspicious?'

'What do you mean?'

'Was there anyone who came to the house, perhaps delivering a parcel, or asking if there was any work on the estate, or pretending they were lost and asking for directions. Or have you doubts about the honesty of any other staff? You've been in Sir George's employment for a long time, you must have seen staff come and go.' He paused, giving Giddings time to digest the suggestions.

Giddings was frowning. 'I need to look in my Day Book.'

'Day Book?'

'When I started working for Sir George there were a lot of things I had to learn. I found if I kept a log of everything that happened, and also if there was something new I hadn't come across before, I'd make notes and when it happened again, I could check back.'

'Very efficient.' He wished all witnesses kept details of their day's activities. 'Do you still do that now? Surely there isn't any situation you haven't experienced before?'

Giddings gave a smug smile. 'I don't need to, but I got used to writing everything up at the end of the day, if I hadn't managed to jot things down as they happened. I make a note of deliveries, guests, when Sir George and Lady Trubshaw go out, when they come back.'

Frank was impressed. 'How many Day Books have you got?'

'I've quite a little library. Perhaps one day, after I retire, I might get them published in some form. A Mrs Beeton's *What the Butler Saw*, kind of book.' He chortled at his witticism.

'Would you be prepared to loan me the book that covers the period when the jewellery was stolen? I'd keep it safe and return it as soon as possible.'

Giddings looked pleased, his chin disappearing into his neck as he beamed at Frank. 'Goodness, will it be used in evidence? Will I have to read from it in court?' The thought seemed to thrill him.

'Only if we unmask a gang of thieves and we need to use your words to nail them!' he said, hoping Giddings was a fan of crime fiction.

'How exciting. Yes, I'll get it for you, but don't tell Sir George.' He left the room, a man on a mission.

He came back with two black A4 books, each with a year stamped on the front. Giddings had spared no effort.

'I've put a great deal of work into these books. If you find something that might help you solve the case, I think it's only fair I should have some benefit, don't you?'

'What are you suggesting?'

Giddings pursed his lips. 'I think a hundred pounds would be a fair recompense.'

Frank shook his head. 'You'd have to solve the case for that.'

'Eighty?'

Frank took out his wallet and examined the contents. 'Fifty quid. Take it or leave it.'

Giddings' hand shot out. 'That's the one you want.' He thrust one of the books into Frank's hand. 'But the other one might be worth reading,' he said, winking.

'Thank you, I'll keep them safe. When I've read them, I hope I can come back and have another chat with you. There'll probably be questions to answer, or explanations to give. Is that OK?'

Giddings pursed his lips. 'Perhaps it would be better if we didn't meet here. Give me a ring and I'll meet you somewhere else.'

Frank didn't fancy an evening with Giddings. 'We'll see.'

Giddings nodded. 'Can I go now?'

'Yes, and thank you for your cooperation.'

'Do you want me to send anyone else in?'

'No. Mr Elderkin and I are heading back to Dunwich, there are some matters we have to see to there this afternoon.' A meeting with Mabel to help her sort out funeral arrangements. His heart sank. For a few hours he'd managed to forget Matt's death and Mabel's misery; he hoped it had been the same for Stuart.

He was waiting for Frank in the hall.

'Any luck?'

Stuart shook his head. 'No. You?'

Frank patted the two books under his arm. 'I've got some light reading to do.'

Stuart looked interested. 'Lady Hazel's diaries?'

Frank explained.

'So, Giddings is not the loyal servant he seems.'

'I think he's not too keen on Hazel.' Frank paused. 'How about a pint on the way home?'

The grin nearly split Stuart's face in half. 'I thought you'd never ask.'

In the office at Greyfriars, Laurel put down the phone.

Dorothy came in. 'Well?'

She smiled and gave her a thumbs-up. 'Revie said I could say to anyone who objected being questioned by me, I had his full permission, and they could contact him if they wanted to. I felt I had to double-check with him, after clashing with Sarah. I didn't expect her to be so aggressive.'

'Nick's gone up in my estimation, although he was up there anyway, but he's been very thoughtful towards Mabel,' Dorothy said, sitting down at her desk. 'You seem pleased. I thought you weren't keen on doing this.'

'I wasn't at first, but after meeting Matt's wife, Sarah, and also Lily Varley, I'm intrigued. I liked Lily, and Tom Blower and his mother. Even if I don't come up with anything, they're interesting people. I must say I didn't like Sarah; she's an enigma, very attractive, sexy, in a sultry way. There may be something there. Of course, I have no true authority, even though I'm endorsed by Revie. I wouldn't be surprised if Sarah refuses to talk to me.'

Dorothy looked at her over the rim of her blue glasses. 'I think Mabel might have something to say about that.'

'What's Mabel doing at the moment?'

'She's attacking the cupboards in the kitchen and giving them new lining papers.'

'The thought fills me with dread; still, it's better than her moping in her bedroom. She wasn't too pleased when Frank and Stuart didn't turn up for lunch.'

'I don't know why, they said they'd be back for the afternoon meeting.'

The front door opened and slammed shut. Two cheerful male voices heralded Frank and Stuart.

'I bet I know where they've been,' Laurel said, wishing she'd been with them.

'Eel's Foot or Cross Keys?'

'Both probably. Good to hear Stuart laughing.'

'Let's hope Mabel thinks the same way.'

Frank came into the office, grinned at them, sat down and placed two A4 books on his desk. 'Good morning?' He nodded towards the kitchen.

'She's kept herself busy,' Laurel said. 'Revie's played ball, so I can start questioning in earnest. I haven't told Mabel yet.'

Frank moved towards the table. 'Laurel, would you like to tell Mabel and Stuart we'll start the meeting in five minutes?'

'No, I wouldn't, but I will. Coward,' she said as she passed him.

Dorothy sighed. 'I do hope Mabel will manage to get through this without upsetting Stuart. I know she's going through a dark time, but Stuart's feeling left out. If only she'd confided in him about the trouble Matt and Sarah were having, perhaps we could have helped and perhaps the accident might not have happened.'

Frank frowned. 'I can't see your logic, Dorothy. How would that have prevented the accident?'

'It might not have, but perhaps Matt was distracted by worry, and it made him careless.'

'It's a possibility.'

Laurel came back followed by Mabel and Stuart. It looked as though the positive effect of Adnams beer had worn off him already.

When everyone was seated, Frank opened the meeting. 'We haven't a formal agenda, but I thought we could get the Agency business over first, and then Mabel can take over to tell us of the funeral arrangements she wants to make, and we can give her any help she needs. Is that all right with you, Mabel?'

She nodded.

'Great. Laurel, would you go first and tell everyone about your conversation with Revie, then Stuart and I will give a brief resumé of our morning's work at Gladham Hall.'

'And your follow-up at some pub or other, on the way back,' Mabel said, glaring at Stuart.

Oh Lord, Laurel thought, it's going to be one of those meetings.

'You must blame me, Mabel, I needed a drink and Stuart was forced to join me,' Frank said. 'Laurel?'

She quickly told them of her success with Revie.

Mabel almost looked cheerful. 'That's encouraging. Nicholas Revie is a good man, he was really nice to me when I went to see Matt.'

'Yes, he is a good man. I feel easier about questioning people, now I have his back-up; if anyone isn't cooperative I can refer them to him. Perhaps you'll be able to organise a rota for me, Dorothy?'

Dorothy gave a firm nod and made a note.

Frank put them in the picture about what they'd learnt from their visit to Gladham Hall. 'Before we do anything else, I'll go through Giddings' Day Books, then we'll continue questioning the rest of the staff. Right, over to you, Mabel. Remember we'll do anything you want.'

Laurel thought that was a rash statement and hoped he wouldn't regret it.

Mabel pulled the edges of her cardigan together. 'I can't set the date of the funeral yet, as Matt's body hasn't been . . . released. Did Nick Revie say anything about that this morning, Laurel?'

'No, and I didn't ask him. I didn't think I had the right to do that.'

Mabel nodded approvingly. 'I'm going to see the vicar of St James's tomorrow morning; I know what I want for the service.'

'Have you talked to Sarah about it?' Dorothy asked.

'No,' Mabel snapped, 'but I'll show her the hymns and readings I've chosen. I don't think she'll object to any of them. I rang up Tom Blower and asked if he'd give the eulogy. He said yes.'

Stuart's back stiffened.

'You've done well, Mabel,' Laurel said. 'Do you want any of us to do anything special?'

'No. Everything's in hand. We'll have the wake at the Cross Keys, that's where Matt used to meet the other members of the lifeboat crew. They'll carry the coffin.'

During Mabel's monologue, Stuart's face reddened, and he looked hurt and angry.

Laurel shot a glance at Frank. He nodded slightly, hopefully sharing her concern.

'Well, Mabel,' Frank said, 'you seem to have thought of everything. As Laurel said, you only have to ask if you want any one of us to do some particular job. I'll call the meeting —'

'There are a few more things I want to say,' Mabel said.

Frank gestured with his hand for her to continue.

'Matt will be buried with his father, and I've decided that's where I want to go when I die.'

'What about me, Mabel?' Stuart cried. 'Have you forgotten me completely? I've been sitting here listening to you; I'd have liked you to have talked this over with me first. You've never said you didn't want to be buried with me.'

'You're not dead, are you? I always thought you'd want to be buried with Doreen.'

'We've never talked about it, Mabel. If you want to be buried with your first husband and son, I can understand that, but I'd have preferred not to be told about it in a public meeting.'

Mabel sniffed. 'Hardly public, they're all our friends. One last thing, I might as well say it now. I'm going back to Aldeburgh to the chip shop as soon as the funeral's over. Tom's going to carry on fishing and he'll try and get another man to help him. He can't go out alone. I'm not having Sarah working in the shop, or living in the flat.'

'Is this going to be permanent?' Frank asked.

'I don't know,' Mabel said, 'but the shop must re-open, I've got to keep the business going.'

Stuart got up, pushed back his chair and left the room.

This was too much. Laurel wanted to tell Mabel she was acting dreadfully, but how could she add to Mabel's woes, even if she did deserve a dressing-down.

'Well,' Dorothy said tartly, 'we must find someone else to do the catering. Obviously on a temporary basis, but with the understanding it may become permanent.'

Mabel's cardigan expanded. 'I won't be going until after the funeral.'

'So you said, but I'll need to advertise and interview the candidates, that will take time.'

Mabel got up. 'I'm sure you'll have no difficulty in replacing me.' She flounced out.

'Dorothy Piff, you're a brave woman,' Frank said.

'I'm sorry, but she was behaving unreasonably. Poor Stuart is cut to the quick. She's had a terrible loss, but there's no excuse for being unkind, and she was so high-handed about leaving us in the lurch, I'm afraid I couldn't help it.'

'Gosh, this is a mess. If she leaves, what will Stuart do? I can't see him doling out cod and chips to the day trippers, but we might lose him as well,' Laurel said.

'We'll just have to make the best of it until the funeral is over and Mabel has decided what she wants to do,' Dorothy said.

'Do you know of anyone who would fit the catering bill?' Frank asked.

Dorothy frowned. 'I'm not sure what you'd think, but Jim McFall might do. I know he did a catering course when he was in the open prison, that's a bit ago, but the other week he brought me a slice of leek and cheese tart he'd made, and it wasn't bad.'

'He didn't poison his wife, did he?' Frank asked.

'No, we're safe there, he strangled her.'

Chapter Twelve

Wednesday, 20 September, 1972

Frank finished drying his breakfast dishes and decided another pot of coffee was needed before he settled down to the fascinating task of reading Giddings' Day Books. He felt guilty, but it was a relief to have the day to himself, and to be able to cook some food he'd chosen. Mabel was an excellent cook, but sometimes it was good to eat exactly what he felt like, and to be able to sit down and consume it in silence. Not quite silence, as the sound of the waves beating on the shingle shore beneath Minsmere cliffs was always present, together with the mournful calls from passing sea birds. Sounds he never got tired of.

They'd decided Stuart would go back to Gladham Hall to interview as many staff as he could, and Laurel was going to Aldeburgh to talk to Tom and Ethel Blower; she was giving Mabel a lift to the chip shop. Dorothy, apart from looking after Bumper, was going to talk to Jim McFall about the possibility of him helping with the catering. Mabel had prickled when she heard Dorothy's suggestion, and if the situation wasn't so serious, he would have enjoyed Dorothy's quick thinking and Mabel's overreaction.

It looked as though the threat of the Agency folding was solidifying. He hadn't anticipated Mabel wanting to go back to her shop; in the past she'd said how glad she'd been to move away from the town after her husband died, and how she'd enjoyed her time at Blackfriars School – until the murders started. Would her marriage to Stuart be under threat? He didn't want to lose his only male partner; they worked well together, and he was fond of the old bugger. He'd hate him to end up without Mabel. They'd been so good for each other. He blew out a stream of air, and poured himself a cup of coffee. He stood at the window, looking out at the North Sea beyond the heather-covered cliffs. He wasn't in the mood for grinding his way through a list of Giddings' tasks; he wasn't in the mood for work; what he wanted to do was put on his boots and go for a very long walk until the sea air had scoured all negative thoughts from his brain.

He sighed and rinsed out his mug and settled at the kitchen table with the Day Books, an A4 pad and two biros – one black, one red. He decided to find the exact date the Trubshaws went to Newmarket and any other details Giddings had noted. He opened the book. He had to admit Giddings was punctilious in his record-keeping. In a copperplate hand he'd recorded the date and the times of each task or happening. Out of curiosity as to what a butler did, he looked at the first page.

Thursday, June 1, 1972

Served breakfast at 9.30 a.m. Lady Trubshaw came down at 10.00 a.m. Needed to reorder toast as it had become limp. I had to send fresh toast back to the kitchen, as it had obviously been burnt at the edges and scraped. Lady Trubshaw said she didn't mind, but Sir George agreed with me, it was not up to standard.

11.00 a.m. Held brief meeting with kitchen and other staff about tonight's dinner when we are expecting four important guests including the local MP. Made sure all ingredients were present for menu, and reminded everyone there must be no more mistakes. Cook was offended, but I reminded her about the burnt toast.

11.30 a.m. Checked the cutlery, glasses and napkins were all up to scratch.

12.00 p.m. Laid a small table in the conservatory for luncheon. Sir George and lady Trubshaw helped themselves to a light buffet.

God in heaven, he wasn't going to wade through pages of this drivel! The man thought he was living in the Edwardian era. He remembered the last time the pages of a book had revealed so much about a case and about the character of the person who'd written it. That had been riveting. It was the secret diary of Susan Nicholson, the murdered headmaster's wife from Blackfriars School. Giddings' Day Book was the antithesis of that.

He started flicking over the pages. The robbery must have been in August or the beginning of September. He wasn't sure why they hadn't established the date with Sir George. He realised it must have been because of the urgent phone call from Laurel telling him Matt was dead. They'd dropped everything and driven back to Greyfriars as though the devil was on their tail. Ah, here it was.

Thursday, August 31, 1972

8.00 a.m. Set off to drive to Newmarket with Sir George and Lady Trubshaw. Lady Trubshaw did not have breakfast as rising at such an early hour (7.00 a.m.) is too much for her. Sir George made a hearty breakfast and complimented me on the scrambled eggs, which I personally cooked at the side table on a spirit stove.

Frank felt like scribbling all over the page.

11.30 a.m. Made good time, arrived in Newmarket after a smooth journey and dropped Sir George and Lady Trubshaw off at the Lion Hotel, carrying in the suitcases and making sure the correct rooms had been booked.

As I was no longer needed, I made my way to my small hotel on the outskirts of the town. The proprietor, a Mrs Fanshaw, made me welcome. Although the bedroom was small, it was clean and there were no dust balls under the bed.

What did the man expect to find? A potty with a picture of Hitler painted inside?

Dinner at the hotel was adequate. Mrs Fanshaw patrolled the dining room making sure everyone was happy. A good touch. She invited me to have coffee with her in her office. Not my type. Too old and on the plump side. I prefer my ladies much younger and a great deal slimmer. Also, not as voluble.

Worth noting? How much slimmer? He flipped the page until he found details relevant to the case. They'd stayed two nights in New-market and driven back on Saturday, the second of September.

Saturday, 2 September, 1972

9.30 a.m. Collected Sir George and Lady Trubshaw from the Lion Hotel. Lady Trubshaw was wearing dark glasses and soon went to sleep as we drove back. The A12 was busy and progress slow.

Lady Trubshaw woke up and insisted we stop at Yarmouth for coffee. Sir George was not pleased, he thinks little of Yarmouth. I agree with him.

12.45 p.m. We arrived back at Gladham Hall in a shower of rain.

What other kind of shower did he expect? A shower of frogs? A shower of five-pound notes? What a dickhead!

1.35 p.m. Sir George and I were in the study discussing next week's plans and when I would be needed to chauffeur them to two events, one in Ipswich, the second in London. I don't look forward to that, the London traffic is too fast and too dense. Then we heard Lady Trubshaw scream and I followed Sir George up the stairs.

Sir George entered Lady Trubshaw's bedroom and gestured to me to wait outside. Her Ladyship's voice is so loud I can hear her through the door.

With your ear to the keyhole?

'They've gone!' she said.

'What?' Sir George said.

'Those blasted jewels – the two rings and the bracelet – the ones I can't wear in public. Why did you do that?'

'You know why. It was necessary at the time. Why didn't you give them to me to put in the safe?'

'I'm sorry, Georgie, I forgot. It was so nice to wear them again, and we had a lovely dinner, didn't we? Just the two of us.'

I didn't hear any more as they must have moved away from the door.

I was standing several yards from it when Sir George came out.

'Is everything all right, Sir George?'

'No, it isn't. Some jewellery has been stolen while we've been in Newmarket.'

'That's terrible, Sir George. Shall I phone the police for you?'

He looked startled. 'No, I'll deal with it.'

'May I ask which items of Lady Trubshaw's jewellery have been taken?'

He shook his head. 'We're not sure what's been taken at the moment. Please don't inform the other members of staff. This needs to be dealt with discreetly.'

'Is there anything I can do, Sir George?'

'No, thank you, Giddings.'

Why doesn't he want the police involved? If my home had been burgled, that's the first thing I would do – phone the police. I wonder if it's connected to the time some other pieces of jewellery were stolen? Then he was on to the law in a trice.

What followed were the usual details of Giddings checking on the staff, ringing up suppliers to order food for arranged dinners, or driving his employers to social events. Many of his waspish remarks about Lady Trubshaw showed his dislike of her, and also the fact she didn't like him. Frank suspected Giddings might be worried Hazel would give him the heave-ho, if she could. He closed the book. What had he learnt? And was it worth the sum Giddings had extracted from him? He grimaced. Certainly, the words confirmed his own feelings that something wasn't right, the reluctance to inform the police, and the need for details to be kept private. The only intriguing fact was Giddings' suspicions this burglary was connected to another jewellery theft. He picked up the other Day Book, written a few years earlier. God in heaven, was he going to have to sit down to another session of the life of Giddings? Not before he'd had something to eat and possibly – no, definitely – something to drink.

Feeling in a more positive mood after bread and cheese, pickled onions and a bottle of Adnams beer, he settled down to read through the second book. You couldn't overestimate the healing property of good food; he couldn't understand people who had no interest in their meals and looked upon them as just refuelling breaks. Didn't they know you are what you eat? He savoured the last of the hoppy beer before starting to make coffee.

1966. June. He decided to skim until he found the word jewellery. He flipped over pages, tracing down the page with his index finger, trying not to be seduced into reading the exciting goings on at Gladham Hall. It wasn't difficult. His finger stopped. Here it was.

15 June, 1966. It was 8.00 a.m., and I was checking everything was correct in the dining room and that the scrambled eggs were the correct consistency, when Sir George rushed in, his face white and strained.

'Giddings, phone the police and tell them to come over at once. We've been burgled.'

I nearly dropped the silver lid to the chafing dish. 'Good heavens! When did this happen, Sir George?'

'Never mind that now. Get on the phone.'

Frank skipped over the next page, as Giddings set down details of his phone call, the police's response, and then their arrival. Giddings speculated as to what happened between the police and the Trubshaws, but he wasn't present at the meeting. Frank flipped forward to see if he could get more details of the jewellery.

18 June, 1966. Today we had a visit from the assessors from the insurance firm, two men, who were with Sir George in his office for well over an hour. Then they inspected Lady Trubshaw's room, that was where the jewels disappeared from. I had to provide them with refreshments – Sir George had instructed me to make sure they were served with the very best Cook could provide. After they'd gone, he looked relieved, sat down in the sitting room and asked me to fetch him a large brandy.

'I hope the meeting went well, Sir George?'

'Better than I hoped. Thank God it's over. Please ask Lady Trubshaw if she'll join me, I haven't the energy to go upstairs.'

I wondered why he'd been worried about the meeting with the insurance people. It wasn't like him; he was usually so assured. But he hadn't been himself for several months, business was poor, and there was no doubt we'd had to cut our cloth. Two members of staff who left for more pay in other jobs hadn't been replaced. Not to mention other economies, and Lady Trubshaw had cut down visits to the hairdressers to two a month. She's certainly had a face that would curdle milk lately.

Frank wondered if Stuart had remembered to try and find out the name of the insurance firm. Probably not, with everything that had been going on. They needed to discover which pieces of jewellery had been stolen in 1966. Perhaps if the insurance firm were told there might be something fishy going on, they might be willing to tell them details. He wondered how much Sir George got for the stolen jewellery. From what Giddings had written it seemed the Trubshaws were going through a money squeeze. Why? Wasn't Trubshaw's Toffees coining enough money for him to uphold his lifestyle? If there had been an insurance scam it seemed such a dangerous and stupid game to play, when they could have just sold the jewellery. Perhaps Hazel wasn't so keen on that, and if they were presents to her, what right did her husband have to take them away from her? If that's what he'd done, and if it had been found out, the scandal would have ruined his reputation, something he obviously cared a great deal about. Then it hit him. He slapped his hand down on Giddings' Day Book. But was it his job to turn on his client and get him into deep trouble with both the police and his insurers? Now he *was* sure they shouldn't have taken the case.

Chapter Thirteen

Laurel turned the Cortina onto the road leading to Thorpeness; there was a faint smear of water on the wind screen, just a touch of sea mist, and she switched on the wipers. She was on her way to meet Tom Blower in the fisherman's hut near the Moot Hall in Aldeburgh. He was taking the boat out – he'd found someone to go with him – and if he had a good catch, he'd be busy until late morning supplying lobsters, crabs and fish to hotels and restaurants, then selling what was left to the public.

Tom had said to come at about eleven; he'd shut up the hut and they could go for a cup of coffee somewhere, as long as she didn't mind him smelling a bit fishy. She decided to bring a flask of coffee and some ginger cake, and offer her car for them to chat in. She didn't think a local café would be a good place for her to get Tom to reveal his true feelings about Matt's death.

She found a parking space next to the promenade and set out for the hut. As she walked up the concrete steps to the door, two masculine voices drifted out. Tom was putting boxes of fish into the fridge and the other man was wiping down the weighing scales. He dipped a cloth into the sink, wrung it out and started on the counter surfaces.

'Hello, Mr Blower,' she said. The combination of fish and bleach was overpowering; she was glad he hadn't offered to give her coffee in the hut.

'Miss Bowman. We've nearly finished.' He turned to the other man, who was staring at her. He looked to be in his mid-forties, with dark hair set back from a high forehead. He was tall and bulky, starting to go to fat.

'Miss Bowman, meet Alan Varley, he's been out in the boat with me today.'

Lily's father?

'Alan, this is Miss Laurel Bowman, of The Anglian Detective Agency. She's come to ask me some questions about Matt.'

'I'm pleased to meet you, Mr Varley.' She held out her hand and after a moment's hesitation, he gripped it tight, but didn't say anything.

'I believe I met your daughter, Lily, the other day, at the fish and chip shop.'

'Did you?' he said, sounding none too pleased.

'Yes, she's a lovely girl, you must be very proud of her.'

He grunted.

'We'll be a few minutes cleaning up, hope you don't mind waiting,' Tom said, looking embarrassed by Alan Varley's attitude.

'No, that's fine. Did you have a good catch?'

Tom smiled and nodded. 'Wasn't too bad, was it, Alan?'

'No. Not bad at all.' He turned to Laurel. 'Why you asking Tom about Matt? Is something wrong?'

This was difficult, but perhaps she could turn it to her advantage. 'Mrs Elderkin can't understand how Matt could have been so careless, she's asked me to see if I can find out anything more.'

'It certainly wasn't like Matt, he was a stickler for making sure everything was shipshape, always keeping us on our toes with practice drills. We'll miss him.'

The man sounded genuinely upset.

'Mr Varley, would you be willing to talk to me about Matt? Not today – when you can spare the time.'

He stared at her, thinking. His face cleared. 'Yes, I'm willing, but you'll have to come to my house. I've only been able to help Tom, here, because Lily isn't working at the moment. She's looking after my wife, Patricia.'

As he spoke, lines of worry and pain deepened; her heart went out to him. 'Thank you for agreeing. I'd be pleased to visit your home. I do understand, Mr Varley, Lily told me her mother was ill.'

'When do you want to come?'

'Would sometime tomorrow be suitable?'

Varley looked at Tom Blower. 'You did say you'd need me all this week, didn't you?'

His tone suggested he wanted the work. Money must be tight if he wasn't able to keep up a regular job because of his need to care for his wife. 'Please don't worry, Mr Varley, it's more important for Tom to have help.'

'We've mostly finished by one. You could see Miss Bowman in the afternoon, Alan. I can stay on for a bit longer and finish cleaning up, that's no problem.'

'Thanks, Tom. Three o'clock tomorrow, Miss Bowman? That suit you?' Varley asked.

She thanked him and he wrote down his address on a margin of one of the newspapers they used to wrap the fish in.

Tom took his jacket from a peg on the back of the door. 'Right, let's go, Miss Bowman. Alan, can you finish here and lock up and put the key through my letter box as you pass by?'

Varley nodded. 'Same time tomorrow morning?'

'Four a.m., Alan. Let's hope the weather keeps calm.' He turned to Laurel, a grin on his face. 'You can join us if you like,' he said, laughing, no doubt at the expression on her face.

'No fear! I'm an early riser, but not that early.'

'Just as well,' Varley said. 'I wouldn't go out on the boat with you. It's bad luck to take a woman fishing. Bound to give rise to a storm or a sea fog.'

The man sounded serious.

'He's only pulling your leg, Miss Bowman, I think you might be handy pulling up the lobster pots,' Tom said.

She decided not to reply, but was pleased he ribbed her. Perhaps she could offer to be first mate if Tom couldn't get anyone to help him. What would Frank say?

Seated in the Cortina, coffee drunk and ginger cake eaten, Tom

Blower leant back in the passenger seat. 'That was very nice, Miss Bowman. Thank you. Certainly filled a hole. I had a sandwich when we came off the boat, but I was ready for a bite to eat.'

'Good. That was Mabel's ginger cake. I found it in the freezer. She hasn't had much time or inclination to bake at the moment. And please call me Laurel.'

Tom nodded. 'How is Aunt Mabel?'

'I think she'll be able to grieve properly when she's sure Matt's death was an accident.'

'I can't believe it was anything else, although it wasn't like Matt to be careless, but then . . .'

'But then what? You know something that might explain why he lost concentration?'

He was silent for a time. 'Matt was worried about something, he hadn't been himself for quite a time.'

'For how long?'

'Perhaps a few months, but I'd say it was worse these last few weeks.'

'He didn't talk to you about it?'

'No. The night he died he came into the Cross Keys; it was late, about nine. There were quite a few of us lifeboat crew in there, we were at the bar. He came in, ordered a pint, and then went and sat down by himself. Now, that's not like him. Matt was a sociable chap and all the crew liked him, respected him as well, he was a good cox'n.'

'Did anyone speak to him?'

'Yes, I did. I went over and we had a bit of a chat. I asked him if he was all right. I thought he was going to say something, but he didn't. He said goodnight and that was the last I saw of him. Alive. A few hours later I found him dead in the tractor shed. My God, I wished I'd never let him leave the pub until he'd told me his troubles.' Tom's face was riddled with grief and his voice full of guilt.

'It wasn't your fault, Tom. I'm sure we'll confirm it was an accident.' Was that true? She was beginning to feel there was more to his death. 'Have you any thoughts as to what he was worried about?'

He looked down and shuffled his feet.

'Anything you say is confidential; the only people who will hear it are the other members of the Agency.'

'But that'll include Aunt Mabel, won't it?'

'I'll only report anything that I think is relevant.'

'Even so, I'm not sure I should say anything. I haven't anything solid, nothing concrete, you see.'

The car was steaming up, so she wound down her side window. 'Tom, I need some help, something to work with.' She decided to risk it. 'Is this something to do with Sarah, Matt's wife?'

He looked up, his hair a mass of frizzy curls, his eyes wide with shock. 'You know then?'

She smiled. 'No, I don't know anything about Sarah, apart from what Mabel has told me. I think she's prejudiced against her.'

'Why are you asking me about her?'

'I have met her, briefly. I did form an opinion.'

He let out a long breath of air, re-steaming up the patch of windscreen in front of him. 'Yes, I think he was worried about Sarah.'

'Why? Did he ever say anything about her?'

Tom's face twisted; he was obviously uncomfortable talking about Matt. 'He did say a few things, now and then.' He moved in his seat, looking embarrassed. 'Well, you know how men talk when we're by ourselves,' he said.

'No, I don't, but I can imagine!' She laughed and he laughed with her. 'Don't be embarrassed, Tom. I was a schoolteacher, and I assure you, young girls and women can have some frank exchanges, especially when it's about sex.'

He gave her a sidelong glance. 'I didn't think teachers had sex lives.'

'You'd be surprised.'

'Blimey, I better not tell my wife we had this conversation.'

She decided to get down to the nitty-gritty. 'What did Matt say?'

He frowned. 'Several months ago, he complained Sarah had gone off him. Didn't fancy him any more. Said he was living like a monk.'

'Did that change?'

'I don't think so. A few weeks later I asked him if things in the love department were any better, and he said he would soon have to start, er, you-know-what, if it went on any longer.'

'You-know-what?' His face reddened. 'Oh, I see, schoolboy gratification?'

'That's a polite way of putting it. Real teacher talk.'

She decided she liked him, with his expressive clown's face and down-to-earth humour. 'Anything else about Sarah?'

'He worshipped her, you know. She's a good looker, I'll give her that. He said she was spending a lot of money on make-up, going to the hairdressers and buying clothes. He didn't begrudge her, she's a hard worker, but I think he thought she was seeing another man.'

'Certainly, those are all the classic signs: losing interest in your husband, spending money to make yourself more attractive. They do suggest she was playing away. He never said that out straight?'

'No, and I didn't like to ask him. We're best mates – were best mates – but I wouldn't like it if he'd suggested my Betty was shagging another man – sorry, I mean having an affair. If anyone did that, I'd clock them.'

'But you think there was something else, something that had happened recently?'

'Yes, I do. One morning about a couple of weeks ago, when we were on the boat, I saw his face in the light of my torch. He looked awful. Bags under his eyes, his cheeks sunken. I thought something terrible had happened.

'"What's up, Matt," I said. "Is someone ill? It's not your mum, is it?"

'"No," he said, real sharp. "Couldn't sleep, got terrible toothache."

'His cheeks weren't swollen like you have with a bad tooth. He didn't want to talk about it so I didn't ask no more, but from that day to the day he died, he never looked the same. Always with the weight of the world on his shoulders.' His eyes teared up. 'God, I miss him.'

She decided poor Tom had had enough questioning for the time being. 'Thank you for being so open. What you've said has really helped me to form a picture of the state of Matt's mind. I know what you've told me is conjecture and I'll treat it as such. One last question: do you like Sarah? And do you believe she was capable of being unfaithful?'

His face hardened. 'No, I don't like her. She's a flirt and a teaser, she enjoys men chasing after her. She tried me out at a party once, years ago, before they married. I knew she was doing it just to see if she could. Went behind Matt's back – I didn't like that. And yes, I think she's capable, and what's more I think she has.'

Laurel glanced at her watch. She'd driven Tom home and he'd pointed out Alan Varley's house; it was a few doors further down from his own house in Slaughden Road. The ginger cake seemed a long time ago, but she'd arranged to meet Ethel Blower at the chip shop at twelve thirty; she only had half an hour, no time for a proper lunch. She reversed the car and made for Smith's Bakery and hoped there was at least one Cornish pasty left.

She knocked on the shop's side door.

'Come on in,' Ethel said. 'Like a cuppa first? I'm dying for one. Mabel's just left, she wants to see if they've got anything suitable for the funeral at Maddeleys. I said don't come back for a bit, I want to talk to you without her being here, butting in, or arguing with me if I say something she doesn't like.' She switched on an electric kettle.

'You're a braver woman than me, Ethel Blower,' Laurel said, shrugging off her jacket and sitting down at the table.

'Me and Mabel go back a long way, we don't mince our words. Many's the times we've nearly come to blows, but I'd do anything for her. We haven't seen as much of her over the past two years and she lost interest in the shop. I was so pleased when she got together with that Stuart Elderkin, but I never thought she'd marry again. "Good Lord, Mabel," I said, "why do you want to get mixed up with all that at your age?" Well, she blushed like an eighteen-year-old. "I'm as surprised as you," she said.'

Laurel decided she didn't want to hear any more girlish gossip

112

between Ethel and Mabel, she might not be able to keep a straight face. 'I could certainly do with a drink,' she said, eyeing the kettle.

'Sorry, dear. I got carried away.' Ethel warmed a large brown teapot, scooped three spoonfuls of tea from a caddy into it, and poured in the boiling water. 'Like anything to eat?'

'No, I've just eaten a very nice pork pie from Smiths. I was hoping for a pasty, but they'd all gone.'

'You don't mind if I eat while we talk, do you?' Ethel asked, taking out a greaseproof parcel from a shopping bag, opening it and taking a bite from a sandwich it looked like ham.

'Want one?' She pushed them towards her.

Laurel shook her head. Ethel brandished a strainer and poured deep brown liquid through it. 'I hope you like it hot and strong,' she said suggestively, and gave a throaty laugh.

Laurel smiled and decided not to reply.

Ethel sighed after demolishing another sandwich. 'Home-cooked ham and a good dollop of English mustard, you can't beat it. Working with all this fish, you get a real craving for a bit of meat. Mind you, by the time we open, I'll be ready for a crispy cod and a load of chips. Right, ask away, dear.'

Laurel took a sip of tea; plenty of tannin, perhaps a tad too much, but better than dishwater. 'Ethel, did you notice any change in Matt's behaviour over the past, say, six months?'

'Matt was a cheerful bloke. Always a good word or a joke. I think he was putting a face on most of the time, pretending everything was fine and he had no worries, but sometimes you'd catch him unawares, and he looked worried, sad and unsure of himself, which wasn't like Matt.' She started on another sandwich.

'Have you any idea why he was troubled?'

Ethel swallowed and nodded her head. 'That's a good word, describes it exactly, troubled. It can't have been anything to do with the business as the catches have been good and the shop is as popular as ever; we always do a roaring trade in the summer, and in the winter we cover our costs and make a little bit of money.' She poured herself another cup and waved the pot at Laurel.

113

'Yes, please. What do you think was worrying him?'

'It has to be her, doesn't it, his wife, Sarah? But I'm not so sure, I think there might be something else. I think something happened recently. I'm not very good at telling this.'

'Try.'

'Well, in the past, when she'd been nasty to him, or short with Lily, and he's pulled her up, I could see from the expression of his eyes, he was hurt and I'd say, disappointed in her. He did love her, you see. Thought he was so lucky to have her. But lately, I've caught him looking at her in a different way.' She stopped, looking troubled.

'Go on. Was love changing to hate?'

'Oh no, but the look was one of . . . damn, I can't find the word.'

Laurel didn't know whether to try and supply a list of suitable words or remain silent.

'It was as though he was trying to work out a puzzle. You know, when something goes wrong with a machine and you're trying to work out what's happened, and how you can fix it. I don't doubt he was still in love with her, and when she was nice to him, he looked so happy. Pathetic, really. Like a schoolboy who's been given a gold star by his favourite teacher.'

'You've got a way with words, Ethel, even if you sometimes have trouble finding the right one. That's an interesting picture you've painted.'

'Thanks for the compliment.' She swept up crumbs from the kitchen table and put them in the bin.

'Can you tell me a bit more about Sarah? You worked with her. Was she a good worker?'

Ethel nodded. 'When they were first married, she worked in Ipswich, then she decided she'd like to work in the shop. She hadn't any experience of shop or catering work, but she mucked in, and there were no airs and graces. But when Mabel left to go as cook at Blackfriars School, things gradually changed.'

Laurel pushed her empty cup to the side and leant over the table towards Ethel. 'That's quite a few years ago. How did things change?'

'She took over all the bookkeeping and the ordering: potatoes, condiments, paper bags, you know, all the bits and pieces we need, from pickled onions to salt and vinegar. She'd count up the takings at the end of each day and make sure they were safely banked, put up the weekly wages and gradually she eased out of working in the shop.'

'Did you mind?'

'No, not really. When she was in the shop, although she pulled her weight, she wasn't much fun to work with. You need a bit of banter, between the staff and with the customers. Makes the wait in the queue go more quickly, if there's a jolly atmosphere. She didn't know how to do that, or didn't want to.'

'When did things change?'

'I'd say it was in the past year, probably from Christmas. You see, she had this idea of turning the chip shop into some kind of restaurant.'

'Really? I don't think the people of Aldeburgh would have been happy.'

'No, nor the holidaymakers. They look forward to our fish and chips – best in the county, they say. Best in England, I say.'

'I know I always enjoy them, so does Mr Diamond.'

'He looks as though he knows how to enjoy himself.'

Laurel nodded. Unfortunately, that was too true. 'I assume Matt didn't like the idea.'

'He hated it. They had some big arguments over that, I can tell you. She said they should better themselves, that Aldeburgh was going upmarket and nice people, in other words them snobs from London, would pay good money for restaurant food. She thought they could start by converting the chippy and then sell up and find a bigger place with more covers, as she called them.'

'What happened?'

Ethel waved her hand round the kitchen. 'She was in a bad mood for weeks, then suddenly she started to act nice again, but she was going out more, on her own, or with her friend, Mandy.'

The way she said Mandy suggested she didn't think much of Sarah's friend.

'You know Mandy?'

'Wouldn't say I know her, but I know of her, and I used to know her mother who was a flighty piece as well.'

Perhaps she needed to put Mandy on her interview list. 'How did Mabel take all this?'

Ethel blew out her cheeks and rolled her eyes in their sockets. 'When she found out Sarah wanted to turn this place into a restaurant, and had even mentioned selling it, she went ballistic and gave Sarah a right mouthful. I was working in the prep room when the row broke out. They were upstairs but I could hear every word. Mabel made it quite clear that Matt wouldn't inherit until she was dead, and even then, she said, she'd see if she could have a clause put in the will, so it couldn't be sold or changed in any way for a number of years after her death. I don't know if she did that. No need now, is there? Who's she going to leave it to? Sarah? I don't think so.'

'Mabel's thinking of coming back to work in the shop. Did you know?'

'Yes, she told me. But not until after the funeral.'

'How do you feel about that?'

'I'm not sure. I don't mind, it'll be good to see more of her, and sometimes hard work is the best way of dealing with a sad loss.'

'You look worried.'

'I am, but not for me, for Mabel. It doesn't seem right for her to leave you lot without a housekeeper; I'm sure you'll all manage, but if you lose one member of a team, it's always difficult for those left. I've known that myself, when we've lost a good worker in the shop, and my Tom is missing Matt, not only as his best friend, but as the other part of the boat team, and as cox'n of the lifeboat. And what about Mr Elderkin? Will he give up detective work and start shovelling chips? Can't see that myself.'

Laurel inwardly sighed, agreeing with Ethel. Mabel's move could mean the future of the Agency was in doubt. They'd have to find another detective and someone to look after them. She wasn't sure she fancied Jim McFall's cooking.

★

Ethel had gone home and Laurel was waiting for Mabel to return from her shopping trip. She decided she'd prowl around the building, trying to get a feel for the place and imagine life, both in the shop and in the flat above. Although the shop had only recently been closed, it felt deserted, cold and unfriendly. When she'd been to the shop to buy fish and chips it had been warm, winter and summer. The memories made saliva start accumulating in her mouth. She wondered what they'd have for dinner. Obviously, Mabel hadn't prepared anything. She sighed. They'd all been spoilt. Never having to even think about what they'd eat, Mabel always there with a lovely meal. They'd been able to concentrate on their cases. What would happen now?

The sound of the door opening ended her reverie. Thank goodness, Mabel was back. She came in clutching a paper carrier bag, looking exhausted.

'You found something you liked?'

Mabel flopped down on a chair opposite her. 'Yes, you can depend on Maddeleys. I've got a hat, but they didn't have my size in the costume I wanted, but they're going to order it for me. They'll have it by next week. They'll make sure I have it for the funeral. I could have worn what I wore for Rosamund's funeral, but I wanted something special for my Matt. I know that sounds silly, but that's all I can do for him now, give him a good funeral and make sure there's a decent wake.' She eyed Laurel. 'Of course, it isn't the only thing I can do, I can find out who killed him. How did you get on today? Have you found out anything?'

She was tired and wanted to go back to Greyfriars, have a drink, something to eat and possibly take Bumper out to the beach and stop thinking about death for a few hours. The last thing she wanted was an inquisition from Mabel. 'It's early days yet, Mabel. I haven't anything new to report, but I had useful conversations with Tom and Ethel. I also met Alan Varley and I'm seeing him tomorrow.'

Mabel's face registered disappointment. 'You must have heard something interesting? What did they say about Sarah?'

Laurel decided she'd better make her feelings clear now, no use

117

waiting a few days to see if Mabel would stop interfering. 'Mabel, I'm not prepared to talk about this until I've interviewed everyone who was connected to Matt, and reviewed my findings. This isn't an official Agency case, you've not hired me to do this job.'

Mabel bristled. 'Well, if that's what you want, we'd better make it official and I'll pay the usual rates!'

She'd expressed herself badly, she must be in need of some food. 'Mabel, dear, please don't lose your temper. I told you I was happy to do this for you, but I need to keep my findings to myself. If I report every word people have said I'll never have time to think about the case. I want to help you, but I'll only report the truth as I see it. Please be patient and wait until I've completed my work. I know you want *the truth*, whatever it is.'

Mabel crossed her arms over her chest. 'Perhaps I should have asked another detective agency to look into Matt's death.'

This was too much. 'Yes, perhaps you should, and if you want to do that please let me know.' Laurel got up and gathered her things. 'I'm driving home. Do you want to come with me or are you staying here?'

Mabel's shoulders collapsed, her eyes filled with tears and she shook her head. 'Please don't be cross with me, Laurel. I'm sorry, I shouldn't have said that. I'm grateful you're doing this for me. No, I don't want to stay here. I want to go back to Stuart. I'm sorry, please forgive me.' She was sobbing, scrabbling in her handbag for a hankie.

Laurel felt near to tears herself. What was happening? Everything was going wrong. She longed to be back at Greyfriars, for Frank to be there, and for him to fold her in his arms. God in heaven, she was turning into a drippy character in a Victorian novel. She put her arms round Mabel. 'Come on, you old so-and-so. No more squabbling, let's go home. Have we got anything to eat?'

Mabel shook her head. 'No, sorry, I seem to have forgotten about preparing meals.'

'Perhaps Jim McFall has rustled up a tasty meal – haggis and chips, and a few fried Mars bars. That would be nice.'

★

118

Frank looked at Stuart, who was seated at the kitchen table, carefully peeling potatoes, one of Mabel's pinnies protecting his trousers. 'You're a real artist, Stuart. I've never seen such elegant and thin potato peelings.'

Stuart held up a strip of potato skin to the light from the window. 'You can see through it. Army training. Sergeant Major would yell at you if they were thick. "That's a waste of spud, you clumsy oaf," he'd shout, whipping down his swagger stick so it missed your fingers by a millimetre.'

'Those were the days, eh?' Frank said as he placed two enormous T-bone steaks in an oven tray. 'When men were men and women were . . .?' He looked at Stuart.

'Women?'

'Drudges, tied to the oven and the kitchen sink.'

'Now it's us tied to the potato peeler and the oven.'

'For one night only! After this it's Jim McFall.'

Stuart pulled a face. 'I like to see a woman lording it over the kitchen, preferably Mabel. Unless Jim can make a decent apple pie, he's not going to win my vote.'

'Well, it's Jim's cooking, or egg and cress sandwiches from tomorrow. I think it's brave of him to say he'll help out. What does Mabel think of him taking over her kitchen?'

Stuart blew out his cheeks. 'I really thought Dorothy had played a blinder. I was sure when she suggested Jim might do the cooking, Mabel would have a fit, and give up the idea of going back to the chip shop.'

Frank crushed garlic and spread it over the steaks. 'Need a few sprigs of rosemary,' he said, disappearing into the garden. When he came back Stuart was loading the potatoes into a pan. 'Stuart, before you put them on to boil, could you cut them into slices? I'll sauté them later.'

'Wish you'd told me before,' he grumbled. 'Not that I don't prefer sauté to plain old boiled.'

'Who doesn't?'

Frank crushed the rosemary between his palms, and held it to his nose. The cleansing, evergreen smell made him blink. Rosemary, for remembrance. He spread it over the steaks. 'What will you do when Mabel moves to the shop? Will she stay there overnight? Will you go with her?'

Stuart flopped back onto his seat. 'I don't know, I haven't said yet. She says when she's working an evening shift, she'll stay overnight in the flat and come back if it's an early one. I don't like the thought of her being alone at night in the flat, so I think I'll have to stay with her.' He cast a look at Frank. 'I hope it will work out – with the Agency, I mean.'

'We'll have to see,' Frank said, putting a hand on his shoulder. 'Perhaps it might not be for long, Mabel might see it's creating problems.'

Stuart's head dropped. 'Yes, it could be difficult. If I can't pull my weight, and there's no one to run the house and look after us, we may not be able to take on enough work to make the Agency a going concern.' He took off the pinny, and searched in the pockets of his jacket, which was over the back of the chair. 'Mind if I have a smoke?' he said, bringing out his pipe and a pouch of tobacco.

'No, go ahead. Everything's ready for when they come back. Won't take much cooking. I'll check on Dorothy and see if Bumper would like a walk.'

'We all know the answer to that,' Stuart said, lighting up and sucking in air through the bowl of his pipe.

Dorothy's fingers were a blur as she typed up another invoice on her electric typewriter. Frank waited until she pulled out the sheet of paper. 'How's it going? Nearly finished?'

She looked at him over the rim of her blue spectacles. 'Three more to do, two of them reminders. These people, they want immediate action, but when it comes to paying for services rendered, they continue to procrastinate.'

'Where's Bumper?'

She smiled and pointed under her desk. 'Keeping my feet warm.'

'I'll take him out for a run. Did Mabel say what time she'd be back?'

Dorothy sniffed. 'I'm afraid Mabel has lost her consideration mode.'

'She has lost her son, Dorothy.'

'No excuse for poor manners.'

'I thought you were fond of Mabel?'

She looked at him, horrified. 'Of course I am, and Stuart. Good Lord, Frank, I wouldn't have invited them to live with me if I didn't love both of them. Just because you love someone, doesn't mean you have to turn a blind eye to their faults.'

Frank raised his eyebrows.

'Don't look at me like that! I know I've got as many faults as anyone, probably more, but I think Mabel is being inconsiderate; she isn't thinking of how Stuart feels, and how her actions are affecting the Agency.'

So, Dorothy also realised the Agency was under threat. She'd invested a great deal of her own money in changing her house so the Agency could work more efficiently. If it folded, she'd never get her money back, but more importantly she'd lose the structure the work gave to her life. They all needed it. And their friendships.

That decides it, he thought, I'm not going to let it happen. 'The Agency won't fold, Dorothy. I'll make sure of that. We've created something special. I hope Laurel will be able to convince Mabel Matt's death was an accident.'

Dorothy took off her glasses. 'Thank you, Frank.' She blew her nose. 'Bumper!' She prodded him with her foot. There was a yawn from under the table and the dog emerged and blinked at Frank.

He turned towards the door. 'Walk!' Bumper leapt into life, and jogged behind Frank, his tail lashing the air.

When they returned from their walk, Laurel's Cortina was on the drive. He stopped, not wanting to go in. There'd been too many scenes, too much friction and an uneasy atmosphere during the past few weeks. He wasn't like Laurel, she seemed to be able to cope when relationships became strained. She was good at handling people, prepared to put her own feelings on hold as she tried to sort out situations. It was the endless talking, the perpetual analysis he couldn't stand. It was probably why he'd shied away from committing himself to any long-term relationship. Too much touchy-feely stuff. But if he didn't watch it, he'd end up as a miserable old git. Perhaps he was a miserable young git – but not so young.

What would have happened if Laurel had been different that night? Where would they be now? Engaged? Married? Lovers? Ex-lovers? He bent down and rubbed Bumper's ears. 'If there is reincarnation, Bumper, I'm definitely returning as one of your lot. All you need to be happy is lots of food, lots of walks and lots of petting. Not a bad life.' Bumper looked at him, his brown eyes seeming to say, 'I'd like a love life, too.'

'Let's face the music. At least I can get on with the cooking.'

The kitchen was deserted, but he could hear voices coming from the sitting room. He checked Stuart's potatoes. Good. They still had some structure. Cabbage was neatly chopped and soaking in a pan of water. He decided to see if the dining-room table had been laid. It had. He walked into the sitting room.

Stuart was busy at the sideboard pouring out drinks and the atmosphere seemed calm, Dorothy chatting with Mabel, and Laurel reading a book. Bumper rushed up to Laurel and nosed the book aside, his tail thumping her legs.

'Frank! Thanks for taking Bumper out. Could I have a word? There's something I want to ask you.'

'Sure, come into the kitchen, there's a few things I need to do before I start cooking. How are you, Mabel? Found anything in the shops that's suitable?' She looked more like her old self.

'Yes, thank you, Frank. I feel happier now I know what I'll be wearing. That's one thing settled. It's good of you to cook the meal tonight. I'm looking forward to it.'

'I can't promise it'll be up to your standards.'

She smiled at him. 'I'll let you know.'

She turned to Stuart. 'Could you put the telly on, I'd like to see the six o'clock news. Does anyone mind? It'll be over by the time the meal is ready.' She looked at Frank.

'No rush, everyone can relax and have a drink. I'll get a beer from the fridge.' He looked at Laurel. 'Coming?' She followed him out of the room.

'I'll have a beer too,' she said, sitting down at the kitchen table.

He took several swallows of the cool beer before he asked her, 'What's the problem?'

'I talked with Tom Blower and then his mother. Tomorrow I'm seeing Alan Varley, the lifeboat's mechanic. Frank, there are so many members of the crew I need to interview, plus other people, I can't see them all as soon as I'd like.'

He raised his eyebrows.

'Are you going to make me plead?'

'I certainly am! Or better still you could bribe me.'

'And how can I do that?'

He rubbed a hand over his cheek. 'I can think of one way, that would definitely work.'

She picked up a tea towel and flicked it at him. 'Beast!'

'If only.'

'Stop this! Be serious.'

'I am.' She was beginning to lose her cool, he'd better stop. 'I presume you want some help interviewing the "suspects"?'

'If you could give a hand we'd get through this much more quickly. If there's only me it could take weeks.'

'I'll see if I can make room to do a few the day after tomorrow. Make a list. Has Dorothy contacted any of the other members of the lifeboat crew to make your appointments?'

'No. I'll see what I can get out of Alan Varley tomorrow. He was the next person to turn up after Tom Blower on the night Matt died. I met him in Matt's hut when I went to see Tom. I need to sort out who was on duty that night and when they arrived at the tractor shed. I also need to talk with Sarah's friend Mandy, and establish if Sarah was with her.'

'Right.' He got up and took a frying pan from a cupboard. 'Let's talk about it tomorrow night. Over a pint and a bite to eat, if you like? We can chat about who you want me to see.'

Laurel blew out her cheeks. 'Thank you, Frank, you'll have saved me from all this,' she jerked her head towards the sitting room.

There was the sound of a cry from the sitting room.

'Now what's happened?' she said.

They both hurried to join the others.

Mabel was sitting with her hand over her mouth. Stuart was shaking his head.

Dorothy pointed to the television screen. 'It's terrible. Another woman's gone missing.'

Chapter Fourteen

Thursday, 21 September, 1972

There was silence as Frank drove towards Gladham Hall; Stuart was puffing his pipe, blowing grey smoke out of an opened window to join the patches of light fog eddying over the countryside. The smoke blew back into the car.

Frank glared at him.

'Sorry.'

How many years since he'd given up smoking? Well over ten years, probably twelve, but the addictive smell and taste of tobacco smoke hitting the back of his mouth brought on the old craving. The pleasure of a cigarette with a cup of black coffee at the end of a good dinner, or even a mediocre one; helping him concentrate when revising for university exams; the camaraderie of smokers as they passed their packets of fags around and all lit up at the same time. For God's sake, he thought, what about the camaraderie in the cancer wards when the poor buggers couldn't breathe and coughed up black phlegm?

They'd all been shocked last night when the news of another woman's disappearance was on the television. She'd been missing since Tuesday night. Her parents went to bed, not worried when she didn't come in as she was often out late. What were they thinking about! When she wasn't in her bed on Wednesday morning, they thought at first she'd got up before them and gone to work, then realised her bed hadn't been slept in. They didn't call the police until the afternoon, when they contacted the shop she worked in and they said she hadn't turned up. There was an interview with her parents; he was glad her mother spoke of her in the present. Revie would be feeling the strain, he wished he could be there, working alongside him.

Stuart knocked out his pipe, and tried unsuccessfully to empty it out of the window.

'You can get the pan and brush out when we get back and sweep up the mess you've made,' Frank said. He reminded himself of his mother.

'Sorry, my coordination isn't what it used to be.'

Stuart was having a hard enough time, without him adding to his woes.

'Mabel and I enjoyed *War and Peace* the other night. You and Laurel should have watched it. BBC2, you know – the posh channel. Mabel liked the frocks.'

'I'd have enjoyed the peace, we've had enough wars of our own,' he replied.

Stuart snorted. 'Very witty! There's going to be twenty episodes, it'll make *The Forsyte Saga* looked like a skimped story.'

'The licence payers are getting value for money. Got the list of who you're going to interview?'

Stuart patted his jacket pocket. 'Not getting very far with this, are we?'

'No. What's more, I'm losing what little interest I had to begin with.'

'Come, come, Detective Diamond, remember you're a professional, and what's more, we're taking Sir George's money.'

He nodded. 'OK, I'll behave. I'm going to have one more go at Giddings and then see Sir George and find out if he's happy for us to carry on. What's next? I think we need to start going round jewellers and the better antique shops, even pawnbrokers, not that there are many of those in this neck of the woods. See if anything strikes a chord.'

'Won't the jewels have been moved on from this area? It might be better to try the London shops. Why he didn't involve the police, I can't imagine.'

Frank glowered. 'I can.'

'Really? Going to tell me?'

'No. I want someone to keep an open mind, mine is closing down rapidly.'

'You need a pint, or several, I should say,' Stuart said hopefully.

Frank grinned. 'Get thou behind me, Satan.'

It was Giddings who opened the front door to them. 'Do you wish to see Sir George, or will you be starting to interview the rest of the staff immediately?'

'First of all, I'd like to have another word with you, Mr Giddings, then I'd like to see Sir George. Perhaps you could take Mr Elderkin to his interview room and bring the first of the staff on the list I gave you. As each interview finishes, the interviewee can fetch the next one.'

Giddings opened his mouth, no doubt to protest, but Frank cut him short. 'I'll wait for you in my interview room.' He glanced at his watch. 'Ten minutes?' He walked briskly away, wishing he could see Giddings' face. Treat them rough and they'll love you, it was one of his father's favourite sayings. Frank had never believed him.

When Giddings arrived, Frank indicated to him which chair to sit in. He opened his briefcase and took out Giddings' Day Books, and passed them to him. 'Thank you, there were some interesting details. I'd like to ask you some questions about some of the remarks you wrote.'

A smile briefly played on Giddings' lips. 'I'm glad you thought your money was well spent.'

'I didn't say that.' Frank had a good idea what was coming. He'd been to the Midland and drawn out more money than he hoped he'd need.

'Oh dear, that's a pity. I'm afraid my memory may need the resuscitation of hard cash.'

'You made a fair sum for a small amount of information.'

'There may be someone else who'd be willing to be more generous.'

'Really? Who?'

Giddings rubbed his forefinger against his nose. 'That's my business.'

'The police?'

Giddings paled.

'You may well look a tad upset. The police don't pay for information, and they might regard you as an accessory.'

'An accessory to what? Burglary? I don't think so.' His nostrils flared.

'How about fraud? Who's to say you weren't involved?'

Giddings swallowed hard.

'Look, I know you're worried about your position here, I don't blame you for trying to make a bit on the side, but the Agency is going through a lean period. Another fifty quid if you answer my questions. And I want honest answers.'

Giddings looked relieved, then he frowned. 'How do I know you won't tell Sir George about this?'

'You should have thought of that before you offered to accept money for a peek at your Day Books. I'm not going to tell Trubshaw I've been bribing his butler, am I?'

'Give me the money.' He leant forward, his face glistening. A smell of grease, like duck fat, pervaded Frank's nostrils. Body odour? Or was it what he used to produce that smooth hair? 'Not until you've answered the questions. Shall we get on with it?'

'Yes, I suppose so.' He sounded like a sulky schoolboy who'd agreed to eat up his greens in return for a Walnut Whip.

Frank opened his notebook and glanced at a short list of the questions he wanted answers to. 'First, when you came back from Newmarket, what did you think Lady Trubshaw meant when she said she couldn't wear this jewellery in public?'

Giddings pinched his nose with thumb and forefinger. 'You've guessed, haven't you? I don't need to tell you.'

'I want to hear what you think.'

'Sir George and Lady Trubshaw had decided to dine at home. I served them at dinner, there was just the two of them. I think Sir George had had good news about the profits from the sweet factories and the three new shops he'd opened in Lancashire. It seems Lancastrians have a taste for cheap sweets,' he said scathingly.

'Watch it, Mr Giddings, I come from Liverpool.'

Giddings' nostrils widened.

'Go on.'

'Lady Trubshaw was loaded down with jewellery. I didn't know which jewellery had been stolen in 1966, but I hadn't seen those rings or that bracelet for several years. She was flashing them around; half-cut she was.'

'You started wondering if they could be the same pieces of jewellery stolen in 1966?'

Giddings nodded.

'Good. Now, when Sir George said "it was necessary at the time", what do you think he meant?'

Giddings patted one of the Day Books. 'I think you know. It's all there.'

'Indulge me.'

'In 1966 Sir George had a bit of a financial crisis, I wrote about it in the book. Staff weren't replaced, the sweet business for some reason took a nose dive –'

'I expect all those Northerners started eating healthily: raw carrots and sticks of celery.'

Giddings tittered behind his hand. Frank decided Giddings might grow on him. Anyone who laughed at his jokes couldn't be all bad. But, perhaps not. 'Sorry, go on.'

'He'd recently married Lady Giddings.' He sniffed and looked as though he'd smelt something nasty on the sole of his shoe. 'He'd been spending money hand over foot: furs, new car – a Bentley – bought a villa in France, well, a chateau, which he re-furnished. Her Ladyship chose the furniture and fittings.'

'As good as Versailles?'

'It looked more like a house of ill repute, if you ask me: red velvet everywhere, gold-plated taps, sunken bath and a huge bar in the long gallery. Then suddenly money is in short supply. Economies had to be made, and of course it was us, the staff, who suffered, each of us doing the work of two or three people, and for no extra money. I even had to turn my hand to some cooking!'

'What do you think was meant by "necessary at the time"?'

'I think they needed the insurance money. I don't think those pieces of jewellery were stolen. I don't know how much they got from the insurers, but it was enough to see them through a lean time. He got back to concentrating on the business and turned it around.'

'So, when Sir George said "Thank God, that's over", when the insurance claim was settled, what did you think?'

'I think he'd got away with fraud.'

'Why didn't you report it to the police, or the insurance firm?'

Giddings looked horrified. 'I liked Sir George, I still do. Sir George was good to me, I wouldn't be where I am today if it wasn't for him. But things have changed.'

'How?'

'Sir George doesn't treat me like he used to do. *She* hates me; the first opportunity she gets, she'll get him to fire me. I expect he'll do it nicely, give me a parting present and a good reference, but not many families can afford to pay for a butler. I could end up in a hotel with a top hat and a flashy tailcoat, greeting customers at the door, taking their car keys and accepting tips.'

Frank thought he'd do very well in that role, though he'd have to be a touch friendlier.

'Thank you, Mr Giddings. I'll see Sir George now.'

'Haven't you forgotten something?'

'Forget my head, next.' Frank took out his wallet and passed him five ten-pound notes.

Giddings counted the notes and carefully slid them inside a pig-skin wallet he took from an inside jacket pocket, his movements precise and careful. There were no thank yous.

What a fuss-pot, Frank thought. He wondered if . . . he was aware of the danger of stereotyping, and from the remarks about women in one of his Day Books, but . . . 'Mr Giddings, is there a Mrs Giddings?'

Giddings' eyebrows arched, he looked deeply offended. 'There certainly isn't. Women are good for one thing only, if you know what I mean.'

Frank had a shrewd idea what that was, but he wasn't going to agree. 'I presume you mean their place is in the kitchen?'

The butler snorted. 'Only if they're peeling potatoes or washing the dishes. The best chefs are men, no doubt about that. There's only one thing women have that men haven't, and who'd want to make use of it after they are twenty-five? Most of them are either dried-up old spinsters or fat old frumps with varicose veins.'

Frank had met some misogynists in his time, but Giddings took the biscuit. He must tell Laurel when he got back. Perhaps arrange for her to meet Giddings, he'd enjoy that confrontation.

'I'll take you to Sir George.' Giddings walked to the door and held it open.

A young woman, dressed in a dark dress and white apron, carrying a tray, was passing as they entered the corridor.

'Olive!'

She stopped, her colour rising. Frank glanced at Giddings; the tip of his tongue was touching his upper lip.

'Yes, Mr Giddings?'

'There's something on the carpet in front of you. Pick it up.'

She glanced around, probably looking for a place to put the tray. Normally, he'd have offered to hold it for her, or picked up the offending article, a leaf, himself, but he was curious about Giddings' motives. Was he demonstrating his power and standing in the household? Did he get a kick from humiliating the other staff?

The girl turned so she was facing Giddings and bent down, put the tray on the floor and picked up the leaf, whilst keeping her back as erect as possible. She put the leaf on the tray and with her face becoming redder by the second, she rose, her hands gripping the tray's brass handles, her rate of breathing increasing, her face hardening into a scowl.

Giddings' nostrils were pinched. He didn't look too pleased either. Frank suspected this wasn't the first confrontation between the pair. Was he hoping she'd bend down with her back to him?

'May I get on with my work, Mr Giddings?' Olive asked.

'Yes, get along. Make sure if you see anything else out of place, you rectify it at once, don't wait to be told what to do.'

If looks could kill, Giddings would be hitting the floor faster than his granny's hand moved as she played snap.

Giddings watched Olive as she walked down the corridor. 'Slut. She'll be pregnant before too long. Flaunting herself to everyone who comes within spitting distance.'

But not to you, Frank thought, if it was true, which he didn't believe. He admired Olive's reactions to Giddings' bullying. She wasn't a pushover. A quiet word with her might be profitable. Giddings may have laughed at his joke, but the way he'd treated Olive made up Frank's mind. He didn't like Giddings.

Giddings opened the sitting-room door. 'Mr Diamond, Sir George.'

'Thank you.' Sir George rose from his chair. 'Well, Mr Diamond, I hope you've something concrete to tell me. Have you finished questioning the staff? This is causing a lot of gossip and unease. They're offended I've let you question them. I'm not too popular at the moment.'

Frank took the proffered seat. 'No, I haven't anything to report yet. Mr Elderkin should have finished interviewing the rest of the staff. We'll exchange information and decide which leads to follow.'

'This is not progressing as well as I hoped, Mr Diamond. I'm used to getting fast results. Perhaps if you haven't solved this case, say by the end of next week, we'll call it a day. I don't enjoy spending money and seeing nothing for it.'

Frank decided he'd ask Dorothy to bump up Trubshaw's bill; the sooner he could finish having to come to Gladham Hall the happier he'd be. What a motley crew! 'Certainly. However, there is one line of enquiry I'd like to explore.'

'Yes?'

'Could you give me the colour photographs of the missing pieces of jewellery?'

Sir George drew back in his chair. 'Why?' He looked offended.

'We'll make copies of the photos and take them around jewellers, especially those specialising in antique jewellery, also, antique shops and possibly pawnbrokers. They may have been offered for sale, or even bought.'

'There aren't many shops like that round here.'

'Correct. There are a few in Aldeburgh, and some of the other small towns, like Southwold and Saxmundham, but we'll try the Ipswich shops as well, and some in London if needed. I think I know which ones to target.'

Sir George sniffed. 'Contacts from when you were in the police force, I presume?'

He nodded.

'You haven't mentioned this to any of your police friends?'

'You asked me not to.'

'Yes, sorry, but sometimes things slip out. I'll go to my study and bring them back to you. Is there anything else you want to discuss?'

'No, I'll get back to you by the end of next week, and then you can make a decision whether you want us to continue with the case.'

Sir George half-rose. 'Perhaps I've been a bit hasty. I know you're doing all you can, and I realise the death of Mr Elderkin's stepson must be upsetting and distracting. Do your best.' He marched from the room.

Frank sighed. They could be on this case for weeks. It wasn't straightforward. It looked as though Trubshaw had made a false claim years ago, the insurance money getting him out of a financial hole. Then the *stolen* jewellery had really been stolen. Did the thieves

133

know about the scam? Knew Trubshaw couldn't go to the police? But who had told them? How many other people were in the know? The Trubshaws and Giddings? Had Giddings told anyone else of his suspicions? Had Hazel Trubshaw blabbed to anyone else, apart from Anne? How about that gardener she obviously fancied? Pillow talk? What a fucking mess.

Chapter Fifteen

Laurel found a parking space close to Alan Varley's house on Slaughden Road; the car directly in front of the house was a Vauxhall, which she presumed was his. She glanced at her watch, two minutes to three. Good timing. She'd managed to fit in a quick walk after lunch with Dorothy and Bumper; Frank and Stuart had gone to Gladham Hall, and when Stuart came back, he was driving Mabel to Southwold to visit antique shops and see if any owners had been offered the stolen jewellery.

Revie had phoned and said Matt's body would be released for burial, although the inquest wouldn't be for two more weeks. He'd sounded bone tired; probably been up all night. He didn't ask how her questioning was going, and she didn't mention it.

The brass knocker on Varley's front door was in the shape of a ship, a three-funnelled liner, and it looked in need of a clean. She knocked and the door swung open silently – at least the hinges were well oiled.

'Miss Bowman, come in,' Alan Varley whispered. He wore an England rugby shirt and grey cord trousers.

'Thank you.' She stepped directly into a front room furnished with a brown three-piece suite grouped round a small television; there was a sideboard against the wall opposite to the front door, and a few other pieces of nondescript furniture. He pointed to one of the chairs. She took out a pad and biro from her briefcase.

'Formal meeting, is it?'

'We all take notes, but if you don't want me to . . .?'

'No, it doesn't bother me.'

'Thank you for seeing me. I take it we need to talk quietly. Is your wife in bed?'

He nodded. 'Yes, I need to keep the door open.' He pointed to a door leading, probably, into the kitchen and staircase. 'Pat's got a bell she rings if she needs me.'

'I see. I hope our talking won't disturb her.'

'I looked in just before you came, she's asleep. So, how can I help you?'

It seemed awful to bother him when all he was thinking of was his poor wife. However, he'd said he was prepared to talk about Matt.

'Could we start with the night Matt died? I understand you got to the tractor shed just after Tom found Matt. Could you tell me what happened after you heard the maroons?'

'When the maroons went off, I got up as quietly as I could –'

'Pardon me for asking, but do you sleep in the same room as your wife?'

His face reddened. 'Yes, I've a camp bed I put up every night.'

'Did your wife wake up?'

'No, she'd had her morphine. She'd been in a lot of pain that evening. She was still asleep.'

'Then what did you do?'

'I got dressed and left the house.'

'What about Lily? Did she wake up?'

'No, it takes a lot to wake her in the middle of the night. I looked in, she sleeps in the other bedroom.'

'Did you wake her?'

'No. I decided as Patricia was asleep, I'd let Lily sleep too.'

Only two bedrooms. A two up and two down house. Not an ideal situation if you were looking after a seriously ill woman. She wondered about the washing facilities. Was there a bathroom? 'As you went towards the lifeboat house, did you notice anyone else? Or did you hear anything?'

He frowned, as though trying to remember. 'No. I was running as fast as I could.' He patted his stomach. 'I'm not in the best shape at the moment. Lily brings back too many fish and chip suppers, but as they usually don't cost us anything, I'm grateful.'

So, money was tight. What could you expect if he hadn't a regular job, and she didn't think Lily's wages would add up to much?

'Did you hear the noise of the tractor engine before you got to the shed?'

'Yes, I ran down the High Street and I could hear it. In God's name, I thought, what's Matt playing at?'

'Why did you think it was Matt?'

'Because he always gets there first, I suppose it could have been Tom, as he's usually there second. It's a real rivalry.' He smiled and then the smile faded. 'Not any more though, eh?'

Laurel nodded and waited.

'I think I'd got as far as the Midland Bank when the engine stopped. I have to admit I was angry. Matt does do that sometimes, to make sure it'll be working when we get back. But I always tell him there's no need. I keep that engine sweet. Then I went into the shed and saw them.'

'Take your time, Mr Varley, and describe everything you can remember.'

'I couldn't make out what was happening. I was expecting to see both of them geared up, with their life jackets on, ready for the launch, hopping up and down with impatience, waiting for the rest of the crew to put in an appearance. Matt couldn't stand waiting about for anyone, he used to give them the rough edge of his tongue if anyone was tardy.'

'What did you see?'

'Tom was kneeling on the floor by the tractor engine, I could hear him sobbing. There was a shape on the floor, he was crouched over it, trying to get something off it, tugging at it, like a madman. Then I saw it was a body. "My God, what's happened, Tom?" I said. He turned his face to me. "It's Matt," he said. "He's dead. Get to a phone, call the coastguard, say we can't make a launch. They'll have to get another crew out. Then phone the police and the ambulance."

He bowed his head over Matt's body and howled. It was terrible, I've never heard a man make that noise, it was like a wolf caught in a steel trap. I ran out and did as he asked.'

Telling the story had taken its toll, his face was white, his eyes enormous, and he clasped his hands together so tightly the knuckles shone through the skin. He sighed deeply, closing his eyes, looking like a praying monk.

'Thank you for telling me this, Mr Varley. I'm sorry, I can see it's upset you. I'm not surprised.'

He opened his eyes and slowly nodded.

'Can I ask you a few more questions? Or would you like a break?'

He didn't reply. She hoped he'd agree to continue; she didn't want to have to come back and bother him again. Also, she had so many other people she needed to talk to. 'I'd be grateful for a glass of water, if that's not too much trouble.'

He blinked at her. 'I'm truly sorry Matt's dead,' he said. 'He was a good man.' He bit his lip. 'I can make some tea, would you like a cup?'

'Yes, thank you.'

He went to the kitchen. A tap turned on and there was a pop as a gas ring was lit. A door opened and shut and he muttered something. He came back, looking cross. 'We've hardly got any milk left, I told our Lily to buy some this morning. Pat might need a cup at any moment.'

'Please, a glass of water will be fine. Save the milk for your wife's tea.'

'Would you do me a favour, Miss Bowman?'

'Of course, if I can.'

'I can go to the Co-op and get some milk, it'll only take me a few minutes in the car. If you could stay here, just in case she wakes up. She gets panicky if she rings the bell and no one comes.'

'What shall I do if she does ring?'

'Could you go up? She'll know who you are, I told her you were coming.'

'That's fine.'

'Right.' He took a jacket down from a hook behind the door, felt

138

in a pocket, nodded, snatched car keys from the sideboard and opened the front door. 'Won't be long.'

As soon as the door closed, she was on her feet, looking round the room. What was she looking for? She didn't know, it was an automatic action, the urge to look and learn about the Varleys, to find clues to their characters, examine the detritus of their lives. It was the detective in her, she wasn't sure it was a good trait, but now it was second nature.

She looked closely at the room: there was a mirror over the small fireplace and only one picture on the wall over the sideboard, it looked religious, a print of a bound sheep; she was sure she'd seen it before in a newspaper or magazine. Were they Catholics? She opened the sideboard. A bell rang from upstairs. She started. She'd better go up. She was torn, she wanted to see what Alan Varley's wife was like, but she'd been nosing in the front room of a terminally ill woman. She felt a heel.

The kitchen was clean and tidy, with a gas stove, fridge and work tops. The staircase to the left of the door was carpeted with a striped runner held down with brass rods. A question answered – at the back of the kitchen was a lean-to, the door was ajar and the room contained a white enamelled bath, standing on curved feet. She presumed there was also a lavatory. Was there one upstairs or did poor Mrs Varley have to come downstairs, or even worse have a commode in the bedroom?

The steep stairs led to a small landing; there were two doors, one was open. 'Mrs Varley,' she said gently. 'I'm Laurel Bowman, I've been talking to your husband. He's just gone out for some milk. Can I come in?'

'Yes.' The voice was clear, but faint.

The room smelt of disinfectant, stale air and the underlying taint of death. Patricia Varley was lying in bed, propped up by two pillows. Once she must have been very beautiful, her translucent skin drawn tightly over fine bones, her brown eyes enormous in her wasted face; an exceptionally beautiful woman, but her body hardly raised the bedclothes. Lily looked like a healthy and bonnier version of her.

'Hello, Miss Bowman. It's good of you to stay while Alan goes out.'

'How can I help you?'

'I woke up and my magazine has fallen onto the floor.' She waved a hand to the right of the bed.

There was little room to manoeuvre, as there was the folded camp bed Alan Varley slept in. No wonder he looked shattered if he had to try and get some sleep on that. And, yes, there was a commode. A chest of drawers, with a silver-backed mirror, brush and comb on it, a spindly chair, and a single wardrobe took up the remaining space in the room. She edged round, conscious of her height and build; Patricia Varley made her feel like a giant. She stooped and picked up the magazine, *People's Friend*. Not one she knew.

'Thank you.'

She nodded and made to leave the room.

'Please don't go. Can you stay until Alan comes back? I don't see many people. Only Alan, Lily and the doctor, sometimes a nurse. Lily told me about meeting you. She's so upset about Matt Grill. Wasn't that a terrible thing to happen?' Her eyes were glistening, her breathing rapid.

'Would you like some water? Are you all right?'

There was a little throaty laugh. 'I'm afraid I'll never be all right again. You know, don't you? Didn't someone tell you?'

Laurel swallowed. 'Yes. I'm sorry.'

A small hand, with delicate bones, closed over hers. 'Don't be sorry. If it wasn't for my Lily, I'd be glad to go. I've had enough of this life.'

Was the pain so bad she wanted to die? Laurel couldn't imagine feeling like that. The thought of leaving everyone she loved, never to see them again, was too horrible to contemplate. Never to see her parents, or Dorothy, Mabel and Stuart. Most of all, Frank.

'Could you help me to sit up, please?'

Laurel slipped an arm behind Patricia's back to ease her upright, using the other hand to pull up the pillows. There was nothing of her. How she managed to give birth to bonny Lily didn't bear thinking about.

'Thank you. That's better, I was slipping down the bed.'

'Is there anything else I can do for you? Can I get you a drink?'

'Just sit with me until Alan gets back.' She sighed. 'I'm sorry it's so cramped in here. Sit on the edge of the bed. There's plenty of room.'

That was true.

'We had a lovely house in Lee Road, but when Alan left the Merchant Navy to look after me, we had to sell it. This place was cheap compared to the old house; the profit Alan made from the sale saw us through the first two years, but now . . .'

'When did your husband leave his job?'

'1969. He was a ship's engineer, very good pay. He used to be away for long stretches of time. Now he's here all the time.'

The last sentence was said in a voice which suggested Patricia preferred the former arrangement.

'You must have been lonely – sorry, of course you had Lily. I presume your husband was away for long periods, if he was travelling all round the world?'

'Yes.' She shivered. 'Could you pass me my bed jacket, please? It's on top of the chest of drawers.'

It was very feminine, pink angora wool. She placed it carefully round Patricia's shoulders.

'Thank you. Yes, Alan mostly went to the Far East, but also Australia and Japan. After every trip he'd bring me back a lovely present, usually something to wear.' She pointed to the wardrobe. 'I've got a pure silk kimono in there, saris and I don't know what else.'

'You must have caused a stir in Aldeburgh if you went out in those.'

Her cheeks flushed momentarily, giving her a fleeting resemblance of health. 'I only wore them at home.'

A car drew up outside. 'It's Alan,' she said.

'You know the sound of the engine?'

She nodded. 'Alan bought the car new, when he left the Navy. Said at least he'd have a decent car. I hope he doesn't have to sell it.' Her eyes filled with tears. 'I wish it would all end soon. I've got used to the thought of dying. I'll be glad to go, except I don't want to leave Lily. I'm afraid what might happen to her.'

141

Laurel took her hand again. 'I've only met Lily briefly, but she seems a sensible girl. She's lovely, inherited your looks and she's quick on the uptake. I'm sure she'll be all right, eventually.' How long would it take for Lily to get over her mother's death? And why was she working in a fish and chip shop? Surely she could have aimed higher? 'How old was Lily when she left school?'

Patricia's head dropped. 'Sixteen. She wanted to stay on to the sixth from.'

'Why didn't she?'

'Her father put his foot down. Said it was a waste of time and money any girl staying on at school. Said Lily would soon be married and having babies. What good was a load of certificates then? I'd have liked her to continue. Especially with her music. She's got a lovely voice. Sings in the church choir.'

There were footsteps on the staircase. Patricia pulled her hand away from Laurel's and she made shooing motions with it. Laurel stood up and moved away from the bed.

Alan Varley came into the room. 'What's the matter? Has the pain come back?' he asked.

She shook her head. 'I rang the bell. I didn't know you'd gone out. I dropped my magazine, Miss Bowman picked it up for me, and she straightened my pillows. She's been so kind.'

Varley stared at Laurel. 'Thank you for that, Miss Bowman. Patricia, I'll take Miss Bowman downstairs and when she's gone, I'll get your next dose ready. Would you like anything to eat?'

'No, dear, just a cup of tea and a biscuit. A tea biscuit would be nice, if you've got one.'

He nodded and waved Laurel out of the room. Back in the front room he didn't ask her to take a seat but moved to the front door. 'No more questions, I hope?'

'Just one, Mr Varley, and then I'll let you get on. I, or my partner, Mr Diamond, will be interviewing all members of the lifeboat crew and other people who knew Matt. I know this is a difficult question, as I'm sure the crew are, if not close friends, then people you know and respect, but is there anyone who you think we should interview

142

first? Someone who might have a reason for wanting to harm Matthew Grill?'

He rubbed the first finger of his right hand over his upper lip, his eyes hard and calculating. 'If I were you, I'd start with Calum Tyner.'

'Calum Tyner? I'm afraid I don't know who he is. Is he a member of the lifeboat crew?'

'Yes, but he's not a fisherman, he runs a yacht, he's an experienced sailor, goes on long runs to the Med and Aegean. Owns an antique shop in the High Street.'

'The one opposite the cinema?'

'That's it. Tyner's Antiques.'

'I've never been in, seems expensive.'

Varley sneered. 'Over-priced load of tat.'

'Why do you think we should talk to him first?'

'You're the detective, not me.' He moved to the front door and held it open.

'Thank you for your help, Mr Varley. Can I come back and ask you more questions, if I need to?'

'It may not be necessary,' he said enigmatically.

'It was lovely to meet your wife. She's a beautiful woman. If I can be of any help, please let me know. It was nice to talk to her. If she'd like me to come back and spend some time with her, it would be a pleasure.'

'We don't need or want any help. Goodbye.' He shut the door in her face.

Chapter Sixteen

It was after six when Frank parked his Avenger next to Dorothy's Morris Traveller; he frowned, it really was time she jacked that rust-bucket in and bought herself a new car – if you wanted to dim the headlights you had to take your foot off the accelerator and stamp on a button on the floor. It was 1972, not the 1950s. No sign of Laurel's car, and he knew Stuart and Mabel wouldn't be there. Stuart was going to Southwold to take the photos of the stolen jewellery round the jewellers and antique shops; he was taking Mabel with him and they'd have their evening meal out. Stuart had confided that Mabel couldn't stand the thought of sitting at the dining-room table and eating Jim McFall's first meal. Frank had made sure he had a tasty piece of cheese and some crusty bread back in the cottage, just in case.

He decided he'd better enter through the front door; it would look too nosy to go directly into the kitchen. In the hall his nose twitched as the smell of leeks assailed him; not one of his favourite vegetables. He made for the dining room/main office to find Dorothy laying the table.

'Need any help?'

'Hello. No, but you can pour me a drink.'

'Usual?'

'Yes, please, make it a generous one.'

'Where's Laurel?'

'She's taken Bumper out in the car, said they'd have a walk on

Minsmere beach, she should be back soon. I told her dinner at six thirty.'

'Shall I ask Jim if he'd like one?'

'Good idea. He's eating with us, I wasn't going to have him sitting in the kitchen by himself.'

'Excellent. Smells . . . tasty?'

'He's made a real effort, a thoughtful and interesting menu.'

'So, what's he cooking?'

'Go to the kitchen and find out, but could you give me my drink first? I know you, you'll start talking about football, or that wretched Blackfriars School.'

Frank had first met Jim McFall when he was a detective inspector in the Suffolk Police Force, working on the case of the murdered headmaster's wife, Susan Nicholson. Jim was the school groundsman, and at one time a suspect. During the investigation it came out he'd served ten years in prison for strangling his wife: a crime of passion – he found her in bed with another man. The previous headmaster had known this and had offered him a job as groundsman. When the school closed, Jim had stayed in the area and Dorothy helped him to find work, which included being her gardener. Now, he'd been promoted to temporary cook.

Having watered Dorothy, Frank opened the kitchen door. Jim had his back to him; he was stirring something in a pan with a wooden spoon. The smell of leeks was even stronger. 'Hello, Jim. Everything all right? Want a hand?'

Jim turned. 'Och, hello there, Mr Diamond. No, I'm OK. Thank you.'

Frank liked his soft Glaswegian accent. 'Like a drink? We usually have one before dinner – I'm having a beer. Want one?' He made his way to the fridge, trying to get a peek at the contents of the pan.

'Ay, that would be very welcome. This cooking lark is thirsty work. I'm not used to fuddling for so many.'

Jim was a couple of inches taller than Frank's five eleven, with a scrawny, wiry body. His pale red hair was greyer than two years ago, otherwise he hadn't changed. Frank got two bottles of Adnams from the fridge. 'Handle or straight?'

Jim cocked his head. 'Straight, please. My. I wasn't expecting this, being waited on by the polis.'

Frank handed him the glass. 'Not any more, and please call me Frank – I guess you might have called me a few other names in the past.'

Jim took a long pull, sighed with pleasure and then returned to his stirring of the pan.

'What's on the menu?'

'Miss Piff said I was not to tell you, to let it be a surprise. I dustn't disobey Miss Piff.'

'She's not the school secretary now, Jim.'

'No, but she's my boss and I won't go against her.'

The kitchen door was flung open and a rush of cool air preceded Laurel and Bumper. Bumper skidded to a halt and looked at Jim suspiciously.

'Hello, Jim, this is Bumper,' Laurel said.

'Ay, we've met before when I've chased him off the vegetable patch.'

'I hope you're going to be friends,' she said.

Bumper sat back on his haunches, not taking his eyes off Jim.

'Ay, I expect we'll learn to rub along together, won't we, boy?' He conjured a biscuit and tossed it to the dog, who leapt and neatly mouthed it, flopped on the floor and took two seconds to send it down the bone shoot.

Laurel smiled. 'You planned that, didn't you?'

Jim grinned at her. 'I hope all my customers are as easily satisfied.'

'Come on, Frank, let's get out of Jim's way – also I'm behind on the drinks front.'

Jim was looking at Laurel with affection, but who wouldn't, Frank thought.

Twenty minutes later, Jim put his head around the sitting-room door. 'I'm ready to serve the first course.'

Thank God for that, Frank thought, his stomach was rumbling.

They went to the dining room and Jim came in with a large tureen and placed it in front of Dorothy, nipping back to the kitchen and returning with soup plates. 'They're hot, be careful.' He handed Dorothy a cloth. She lifted the lid.

'I thought as this was the first dinner, and who knows, it might be the last I cook for you, I'd do a Scottish menu.'

Oh, no, thought Frank, not haggis!

Jim removed the lid of the tureen. 'This is leek and tattie soup.'

It smelt good, and was laced with cream and chopped parsley; the texture was smooth on his tongue – delicious.

'This is lovely, Jim. Congratulations,' Dorothy praised.

Jim's pale face flushed. 'Och, it's nothing, but thank you.'

After seconds all round, Jim retired to the kitchen and shortly reappeared. 'I've plated this up, but there's more veg if you want it.' He'd cooked grilled salmon and beside it was a heap of what? Frank wasn't sure. 'What's this, Jim?'

'It's clapshot. Neeps and tatties, with lots of butter and chives.'

It was tasty. So far so good. This was much better than expected and the clapshot was a dish he'd cook for himself.

Pudding was cranachan.

'I saw some autumn raspberries in Aldeburgh so I thought I'd make this, nice and easy, a few oats, some cream and a drop of whisky, that's all you need.'

Lots of delicious flavours and textures. Excellent.

It had been a pleasant meal, good food, and a more relaxed atmosphere than late. There was a tad too much cream for him, but better too much than none at all. 'I enjoyed that meal, Jim, thank you.'

'It was excellent,' Dorothy said. 'When you said you liked cooking, I wasn't sure what we'd get, but you're a good cook. Beside the work you did when you . . . where did you learn to cook? Your mother?'

Jim gave her a wry grin. 'I'm afraid my ma only had to look at a piece of bread and it burnt. I learnt a lot in that open prison in Norfolk, where I served my last two years. It was helping in the kitchen or the laundry. My custard was well received.'

147

'Do you still follow Glasgow Rangers?' Frank asked.

'Ay, me and Ayla we went to Barcelona in May, I wouldn't have gone, but Ayla she's doing languages at Glasgow University, she persuaded me.'

'Blimey,' Frank said, 'you must have been pleased she did.'

'Ay, 3-2 we beat Dynamo Moscow, won the European Cup. Up with your team now,' he said, nodding to Frank.

'You need to win it a few more times before you can say that.'

'How is Ayla?' Laurel asked.

Ayla was Jim's daughter, brought up by his parents-in-law while Jim was in prison, but now reunited with her father. Frank remembered the photo he'd proudly shown them during the Nicholson case: a small, pretty, red-haired girl, a few years older than the Blackfriars schoolgirl, Felicity, who reminded Jim of his daughter. He'd helped Felicity, and was devastated when she disappeared, and later was found to have been murdered.

'She's doing fine.' He looked at Dorothy. 'She's coming down to stay with me for a few weeks before she goes back to do her final year.'

Dorothy looked at him over the blue rim of her spectacles. 'You must bring her round, if that fits in with your plans. I'd like to meet her.'

'Ay, she'd like that. I've told her about you lot, and all the things you've got up to over the past two years. She's really interested, said she wouldn't mind going into the police, but she's a bit too small.'

Frank rubbed his upper lip. 'You'll be pleased about that. You've never been keen on the boys in blue.'

'You're right there,' Jim snorted.

'Well, I better wash up and get home. I'll be back at five tomorrow to cook the next meal. Will Mr and Mrs Elderkin be here tomorrow night?'

Who knows? thought Frank.

Laurel nudged him. 'We can do the dishes, Jim. You've worked hard and it was a really lovely meal.'

'Very kind of you, Miss Bowman, but the arrangement was I was to cook and wash up, that's what I'm being paid for. That's right, isn't it, Miss Piff?'

'Correct,' Dorothy replied. 'I agree with Laurel, it was a very good meal. I look forward to tomorrow night's supper.'

'I'll get on with the pots, I've enjoyed cooking for you and thank you for letting me eat with you. It's a nice change to eating on my own. In case I don't see you all before I go, sleep well, and I hope none of you have indigestion.' With a smile and a nod, he disappeared, closing the door firmly behind him.

'Goodness, that was a long speech for Jim,' Dorothy said.

'He's a far better cook than I thought he would be,' Frank said. 'I enjoyed that meal.'

'Why didn't you say something before he left?' Laurel challenged.

'I said I enjoyed it earlier, he's received enough fulsome praise already. I'll wait until we get three good meals in a row before I start laying it on.'

'Do you think he's a better cook than you?' she asked.

'That's not for me to say. You can't judge, you've not had many meals at the cottage.'

'Whose fault is that?'

Dorothy tapped the table with a fork. 'Children! Children! No bickering.' She glanced at the clock on the sideboard. 'Shall we wait for Mabel and Stuart to come back before we have coffee?'

Frank pulled a face. 'Who knows when they'll be back? We need to sort out a few things tonight. I hope Stuart has had some luck with the photos of the stolen jewellery.'

'Frank?'

'Yes, Laurel?'

'You might be able to kill two birds with one stone tomorrow.'

He raised his eyebrows. 'Really? And how can I do that?'

'One of the lifeboat crew who needs to be interviewed about Matt is a man called Calum Tyner, he's the owner of an antique shop in Aldeburgh. If you went to see him, and asked him about Matt, it would be another tick on my list, and you can ask him about the jewellery at the same time. Is that OK?'

He shrugged. 'Don't see why not. Do we know anything about him?'

'He's an experienced sailor and has a yacht. Also, Alan Varley doesn't like him. When I asked him if he knew anyone who might want to harm Matt Grill, he suggested I start with him. He wouldn't tell me why.'

'Interesting. If I don't find anything incriminating from Tyner about Matt's death, perhaps you can see Mr Varley again and see if he'll tell you of his suspicions. What was Varley like?'

'Perhaps I'd better wait on that one until the terrible twins are back, or I'll only have to repeat myself.'

'True.'

The front door opened and Stuart's voice carried into the dining room. Frank stiffened. He hoped there wouldn't be another scene, it was too late in the day for arguments.

'I think you should come in with me, Mabel. We need to have a meeting, and you're one of the partners. You need to know what's going on.'

There were mutterings.

'Don't you want to hear what Laurel's found out?'

Laurel gasped. 'Not very much,' she whispered.

More mutterings.

The door swung open and Stuart ushered Mabel into the room. 'Finished dinner? We had a nice meal at the White Lion, didn't we, dear?'

'Very nice, made a change to not put a pinny on and slave over a stove,' Mabel said.

The augers were not good.

They sat down.

'Shall I make some coffee?' Laurel offered.

'I don't want any. We had some lovely coffee after our dinner, didn't we, Stuart?'

'Yes, but I wouldn't mind another one,' he replied.

Laurel got up and left the room.

'Anyone like something to go with it?'

Dorothy shook her head. 'No, if I'm taking notes, I'd better keep a clear head.'

'Stuart?'

He shook his head.

Frank decided he'd have a Scotch when he got back to the peace of his cottage. He wanted the meeting over as quickly as possible.

'I'd like a Tia Maria,' Mabel said. 'Thank you for asking!'

'Certainly. Well, you both missed a grand meal, Jim is a talented cook.'

Dorothy shot him a startled look. Yes, he shouldn't have said that, but Mabel was getting on his wick. She was going through a bad time, but why take it out on her friends?

'Really?' she replied, her back stiffening. 'High praise indeed from someone who fancies himself as the best cook in Suffolk!'

'I'll see if Laurel needs a hand,' Stuart said.

Frank put the liqueur glass with its dark liquid in front of her. 'There you are, Mabel, I *hope* you enjoy it.'

'What's that supposed to mean?'

'What I said – I hope you enjoy it. *And* I hope it puts you in a better mood.'

'I'll go and get my notebook and biro,' Dorothy said, scuttling from the room.

Mabel looked up at him, her eyes welling with tears. He should have kept quiet. He sat next to her and put his arm round her shoulder. 'Sorry, Mabel. You didn't deserve that. Forgive me?'

'Oh, Frank, what's happening to all of us? Is it my fault? I don't want to make everyone unhappy, but all I can think of is Matt, lying in that tractor shed, strangled to death. I know you all think I'm mad, but I'm certain it wasn't an accident. I want justice for my boy. Please forgive me if I've been horrible, I don't want to lose your friendship, or Dorothy's or Laurel's. You've all helped me so much after I was attacked and nearly died. I was so happy when Stuart asked me to marry him, and I felt I was part of something important being a partner in the Agency, doing something worthwhile, helping people, bringing criminals to justice . . .' He passed her his handkerchief and she loudly blew her nose.

He squeezed her shoulder. 'Mabel, I understand how you feel.'

'Do you? How can you? You haven't got children – never mind losing one.'

'No. But I know what it feels like to nearly lose someone I was . . . fond of. I think how you feel must be a hundred times worse.'

'Are you talking about Laurel?'

He gave her an old-fashioned look.

She smiled through her tears. 'I'm sure she feels the same way about you.'

He didn't reply.

She blew her nose again and made to give him back his handkerchief.

'Please keep it, Mabel.'

'I'll wash it for you.'

'Thanks. Laurel has asked me to help her interview some of the people who knew Matt.'

Mabel's eyes widened. 'Has she? Will you?'

'I will on one condition.'

'What's that?'

'I don't want you having another tantrum.'

'You make me sound like the three-year-old I saw on the Aldeburgh promenade, lying on his back, screaming and shouting because he'd dropped his ice-cream cone.'

The thought of Mabel performing such antics made him laugh. 'I'll only help if you agree not to be present at the meetings when we discuss our findings.'

'Why? Why shouldn't I be there? I was his mother, I've a right to know what's happening.'

'And what would you do, if and when we have a suspect for Matt's murder, and you know who it is?'

'Why I'd . . . I see what you mean. I'd mess up the investigation, wouldn't I? I wouldn't be able to help myself. I'd be after them.'

'Correct. Do we have an agreement?'

'I suppose so. Does that mean you think Matt was murdered?'

'I've got an open mind, Mabel. You'll have to trust us.'

'I do.'

'Also, you'll have to agree you won't give Stuart the third degree when you've got him under the bedclothes, using your feminine charms to wheedle information from him.'

'Do I look like Mata Hari?'

'Only when you wear that new pinny with the roses on it.'

She giggled.

Emboldened, he decided to risk it. 'If you don't think you can do that, then we must cut Stuart out of any investigation and meetings.'

'He wouldn't like that.'

'He certainly wouldn't.'

'Oh, Frank, I'm not sure I can stick to all this.'

'You have a choice. What is more important to you? Finding out the truth about Matt's death, or never knowing? You must face up to this like the woman I know you are. We'll find the truth, but I can't promise it will be what you want to hear. If you don't accept my terms, Mabel, and live with the results of our findings, you, and Stuart, will never know a moment's peace and I'm afraid the Agency could be finished.'

Her face whitened, her shoulders sank, and lines of worry etched her face. 'I have been behaving like that toddler on the prom, haven't I? This is serious, isn't it?'

He nodded. He'd taken a risk, spoken from his heart, told her the truth.

'I shall never get over losing my son. I know when Bill drowned, I thought I wouldn't be able to cope, but I had Matt to help me. I haven't got Matt, but I've got all of you, haven't I? And Ethel and Tom, and lots of other good people. I'll do as you say. I'll get the shop up and running when the funeral is over. Then we'll see what happens. I agree to your terms, Mr Diamond. If I look as though I might step over the line, you can read me the riot act. Again.'

'Mabel, you're an angel. Jim's cooking was good, but we all want you back in the kitchen. Also, what are we going to do if we have to call on Nick Revie's help? I can't see him wanting to scoff Jim's bacon butties. Or Jim wanting to make them for the polis!'

She blushed. 'Silver-tongued devil!'

'Like another Tia Maria?'

She passed him her glass. 'Won't you join me?'

'I will. I think Laurel and Stuart are cowering in the kitchen and Dorothy must have driven off to buy a new notebook. I think everyone deserves a drink. They'll want one when they hear what you've got to say.'

'Me? You can tell them.'

'No, Mabel. You say what you've decided. Once those words pass your lips, you're more likely to keep them.'

She took a deep breath. 'You're the devil, a right fiend.' He passed her the filled glass. She took a sip. 'Right, round them up.'

Chapter Seventeen

Friday, 22 September, 1972

Despite the day being warm, Frank had dressed in his one and only suit; he'd decided to do a bit of role playing. He was on his way to Tyner's Antiques, in Aldeburgh, and was going to pose as a prospective buyer, before reverting to his real role. When he told Laurel his plan, she'd said, 'Whatever do you want to do that for?'

'I want to see him in his role as an antique dealer, see how good he is, how much knowledge he has.'

'But what will happen when you tell him you're a detective? I don't think I'd be pleased if someone pulled that trick on me. He might refuse to help you.'

'True, but it'll be interesting to see if the mask slips, if he's worried about Matt's death; after all, I'm the next best thing to a policeman.'

She shook her head. 'I hope you're not expecting me to pick up the pieces and smooth him down if he refuses to cooperate.'

He pursed his lips. 'What are your smoothing-down techniques? Softly stroking? Tickling under the chin? Buying him lunch?'

'Oh, you're exasperating!'

'You're just jealous you hadn't thought of having some fun by pretending to be a channel swimmer when you interviewed Mr Varley.'

'What good would that have done? You're in a very silly mood, Frank Diamond, I'm not sure it's safe to let you out interviewing people. I don't think Mabel would approve.'

'I think it was trying to counsel Mabel last night that's addled my brain. He's got quite a reputation, this Mr Tyner. He might be able to help us on the other case.'

'The stolen jewellery?'

'I'm hoping he can point us in the direction of some dodgy jewellers and antique dealers if he's got as much knowledge as I've heard.'

'How did you discover all this?'

'I rang a few contacts early this morning, including Nick Revie. He's in a right state after the latest disappearance. I asked him if he'd like to unload over a few pints, talk it over with us again.'

'What did he say?'

'Seems keen, or I thought I could invite him over for a meal, here, or at The Ship.'

'What about Jim? You know his feelings about the police.'

Frank grinned. 'Might be fun, he might hit Nick with a haggis or throw a pan of scullen kink over him.'

Laurel looked at the ceiling. 'For goodness' sake, get out of this house.'

'Your command is my pleasure, ma'am.'

'By the way, you look lovely in your suit. I almost fancy you.' She was biting her lip, trying not to laugh.

'Almost? So near and yet so far. Would it help if I wore a cape, tight trousers and riding boots?'

She picked up a ruler and threw it at him.

The shop opposite the cinema was double-fronted. He'd seen it many times before, with cursory looks in the window at the few choice items displayed there; usually a bronze statue of a naked lady balancing on one foot, holding aloft a globe, a clock or a tennis racket. Today, again on one foot, she was attached by leads to two running wolf-hounds, and wore a short-skirted number, revealing her smooth and perfect legs. A gold-edged card said: *Art Deco Bronze Circa 1923.* There was no price on the card.

He pushed open the heavy door. The inside of the shop – surely it merited a more salubrious name – art salon? – was spacious, with several cabinets each housing different collections: silver, pottery, glass, small clocks, watches, more bronzes. They looked to be all of the same periods, Art Nouveau or Art Deco, Deco winning. There were a few pieces of quality furniture dotted about, but the emphasis seemed to be on small antiques.

A dark-haired man, about five nine, came out of a back room and stood behind a glass-topped counter. 'Can I help you, sir? Or are you browsing? Please take your time and I'll help you if needed.'

There was no Scottish lilt in his voice, which his name suggested, rather English public school, definitely not your secondary modern. He had a touch of the Sean Connery's: thick dark hair, straight eyebrows to match, narrow-eyed and seemingly incisive, but the picture was spoilt by tight lips, and too much space between a rather snub nose and mouth. Frank was glad he was wearing his suit as he didn't think this well-tailored man would have been impressed by his leather jacket.

'I hope you can help me. I'm looking for a piece of jewellery as a present.'

The man walked towards him. 'I'm Calum Tyner, I'm pleased to meet you.' He thrust out a strong, well-manicured hand.

'Frank Diamond.'

Tyner blinked and frowned, as though the name meant something to him, but he couldn't remember what. 'Pleased to meet you, Mr Diamond. Over here, in this cabinet, we have a very good selection of Art Nouveau and Art Deco jewellery. These are the periods we specialise in. I'm afraid if you're looking for Victorian or anything after the 1950s, I won't be able to help you.'

'No. I find the objects of those periods, especially Art Deco, very attractive.'

Tyner smiled at him. 'You have excellent taste, and I agree with you, it's my favourite period.'

'Really? I sometimes get the two periods confused.'

Tyner tilted his head, as though weighing him up. 'Art Nouveau was a reaction to fussy Victoriana, but Deco was a reflection of the dynamic times.' He then went into a lengthy discourse on the two

157

movements, pointing out various pieces of furniture and small objects to illustrate his comments.

Frank's patience was wearing thin. 'This cabinet is handsome,' he said.

'It's also of the period, mahogany, maple and chrome, it is for sale, but not what you're looking for today?'

'Quite.'

Tyner took a key from his trouser pocket and opened the cabinet. 'Are you interested in nature?'

Was the man a mind reader? 'Yes, I am.'

'In that case we have a beautiful selection of animal-inspired jewellery.' He took out several pieces and placed them on a black velvet cushion on top of the cabinet. 'This one, in the form of a butterfly, made of sterling silver and plique-à-jour enamel can be worn either as a pendant or a brooch.'

'Price?'

'Three hundred and eighty pounds.'

'And that one?'

'Again, a piece with two uses, as a pendant and also a locket.' It was in the shape of a moth, triangular, in silver with gold details.

'Lovely. How much?'

'Four hundred and thirty pounds.'

'Really? What about the one in the form of a toucan?' He really fancied giving that to Laurel, it was lovely and fun, made of white and yellow gold with diamonds in its tail.

'Ah, I see you like quality, Mr Diamond. Yes, charming. Its beak is inset with onyx and coral. Eight hundred and thirty-nine pounds.'

'Goodness, that's a lot for a small bird.'

Tyner's thin mouth got thinner. 'Here's an amusing brooch, 1950s, ruby and diamond, set in gold . . . in the form of Daffy Duck.'

Did he look like a cartoon aficionado?

'It's only two hundred and fifty pounds. Has your friend got a sense of humour?' The tone was snotty, he'd put him down as a time waster.

'She has indeed and so have I. I hope you've also got a sense of humour, Mr Tyner?'

'It's not functioning at the moment, but I have been known to enjoy a cutting witticism.'

'Could we talk in private?'

'Why? You obviously aren't interested in buying anything.'

'You're correct, I'm afraid, but I'm impressed by the quality of your stock and your deep knowledge of the periods, I believe you could give me some valuable assistance.'

'Mr . . . er . . . sorry, I've forgotten your name?'

'It's Frank Diamond, one of the partners in The Anglian Detective Agency. As I said before, could we talk privately?'

'What's your game, Mr Diamond? You've been wasting my time.'

Although his words were harsh, the tone was not uninterested. He waited.

'Very well, follow me.' He turned and led him into the back room which was laid out as an office. A young woman was seated at a desk, looking at something.

'Iris, could you take over the front, I need to talk to this gentleman.' She closed the ledger, smoothed down her tight black skirt, and eyed Frank in a calculating manner. She was tall, blonde and pencil thin, except for breasts attractively swelling her striped silk blouse. Unsmiling, she stalked out on impossibly high heels.

Frank looked at Tyner enquiringly. He gave a tight smile. 'Iris hasn't got the sense of humour you say your friend possesses, but she's a wizard at adding up and taking away.'

He was beginning to take to Mr Tyner, he liked *his* sense of humour.

Tyner pointed to an upright chair, shades of Rennie Mackintosh; Frank lowered himself carefully into it, thinking he might be charged if he broke its slender legs, or leant back too heavily and shattered its pierced slats.

Tyner moved behind the desk.

Here we go, Frank thought, power play.

'What was that all about? Why did you pretend to be a customer?'

'I hope you'll take it in good part, as one businessman to another.'

159

Slight exaggeration; he was several rungs down the executive ladder compared to Tyner. 'I wanted to get a feel for the place and to assess if you would have enough knowledge to be able to help me.'

'Your conclusion?'

'I suspect I'd be hard put to find another dealer with more knowledge of the Art Nouveau and Art Deco periods, and especially jewellery.'

'So, I come up to scratch?' Although there was a smile on Tyner's lips, his eyes were hard and calculating.

'I need some advice about some jewellery that was recently stolen.' Was it his imagination, or had Tyner's lips imperceptibly moved? His eyes were unblinking.

'Stolen goods? I assure you I wouldn't buy anything unless I knew its provenance, or I was buying from a reputable auction house or jewellers. I have my reputation to think of.'

Frank laughed. 'Oh, no, Mr Tyner. Please don't think I'm accusing you of buying hot goods. I wondered if you could point me in the direction of antique shops or jewellers who might be tempted to buy such items if the price was right.'

Tyner's shoulders dropped a millimetre. 'I see. Can you give me details of the stolen items?'

Frank reached for his briefcase and took out photos of the missing pieces. He passed them to Tyner. He studied his face as he looked at them. Not a trace of recognition or concern.

'Can you give me any more details?'

Frank told him what he knew.

'You say they were recently stolen? Locally, I presume?'

'Yes. They're worth a great deal of money.'

Tyner nodded. 'Indeed, but the bracelet will be difficult to shift, it's unique, and if it was broken up, its worth would be considerably diminished. I hope none of these pieces get taken apart, they're all beautiful. I'd be pleased to have them – legally, of course.' He laughed, showing small white teeth behind those tight lips. 'Yes, I can give you a list of jewellers that might be worth a visit from you, but I think these items will be well away from this area already; on their way to the States, I wouldn't wonder, they're big on Art Deco there.'

'Thank you, that's very helpful. Can you do that now?'

'Give me half an hour. Are you going anywhere else?'

'Possibly, but before I go, can I ask you a few questions on another matter?'

'Really, Mr Diamond, you're pushing your luck.'

'I'm sure you'll be only too willing to help me when I tell you this is about Matthew Grill, the former lifeboat cox'n.'

The reaction was strong – his eyes widened, and for a moment he looked shocked. Then he smoothed his features back into urbanity. 'Matt? Yes, it was a terrible shock to everyone in Aldeburgh and especially to us, the lifeboat crew. I found it hard to believe.'

'The Agency has been asked by Matt's mother, Mrs Mabel Elderkin, to investigate the circumstances of his death. Naturally, we're talking to all his relatives, friends and colleagues to help form a picture of the man, and to see if we can either confirm the findings of the police, that this was a tragic accident, or if there are any facts that point in a different direction.' As he talked, he could see Tyner was shaken, worried, and was trying hard not to let this show. Interesting. He hadn't expected this reaction, but then Varley had said to Laurel that Tyner should be one of the first to be asked about Matt's death. It looked as though he was right.

'Of course, I'll help in any way I can, though I'm not sure how.'

We'll find a way, Mr Tyner, Frank thought. 'How long have you been a member of the lifeboat crew?'

'I applied soon after I moved to Aldeburgh, it must be seven years ago.'

Frank decided they must check his past history. 'Where did you move from?'

Tyner frowned. 'Is that relevant?'

'No, just curious. Have you a problem telling me?'

'Of course not,' he snapped. 'London.'

'Really? What attracted you to this area?'

Tyner looked at his watch. 'If you want that list of names, you'd better get down to questions about Matt and not my personal history.'

He was getting tetchy – excellent. 'Of course, sorry. Just interested. What was your relationship with Matt like?'

'What do you mean? We didn't have a relationship. I saw him in the lifeboat when we were having drills or doing rescues, I didn't see him socially.'

Frank took a risk. 'What about his wife, Sarah, did you see her socially?'

Colour briefly flared in Tyner's cheeks. 'No, of course not.'

'You've never met her?'

'Yes, of course I've met her. At the various lifeboat dos, you know, annual fundraising events, Christmas parties, things like that.'

'What's your opinion of her?'

'What do you mean?'

'She's an attractive woman, don't you think?'

'I really haven't an opinion.'

'Come, Mr Tyner, you don't strike me as a monk, most men notice a beautiful woman. I know I do.'

'Well, yes, I suppose you can call her attractive.'

'Did you ever hear that the relationship between Matt and Sarah was unhappy?'

Tyner bit the inside of his lip, seemingly unsure what to say. 'Er, yes, I believe some of the other members of the crew did say Matt was not himself, but that could have been about something else, not his wife.'

'That's true. How did you get on with Matt?'

'Me? He was a good cox'n and I respected him as a sailor and fisherman, he was top quality as far as knowledge and understanding of the sea went, especially round here; the shifting sandbanks and reading the weather. We'll be hard put to find another cox'n like him.'

His voice held genuine respect, but did he respect Matt in other areas? 'Did he ever buy anything from you?'

Tyner's eyes flickered. 'Yes, he did come in once, a few years ago. He'd mentioned to me, when we were on one of the lifeboat drills,

162

he wanted to buy his wife something special for her birthday. I told him to come to the shop and I'd see if I could do something for him, but I wasn't sure he could afford my prices.'

'Can you remember what he bought?'

'Goodness, it was years ago.'

'Don't worry, I expect Mrs Grill will be able to remember when we talk to her.'

'I really can't see the relevance of these questions.'

Frank shrugged. 'Neither can I at the moment, but I often find one thing leads to another.'

Tyner frowned. 'Oh, yes, I remember now, he bought a piece of Clarice Cliff pottery. I was able to give him a good price as there was a small fault in the glaze, nothing anyone would notice.'

'Did he tell you if Sarah Grill was pleased with her present?'

'Yes, he obviously wasn't au fait with her tastes. The next week when we met at the next drill, he said the present wasn't a success. I told him to bring it back and I'd see if I could find something she'd like, for about the same price.'

'Did he do that?'

Tyner frowned again. 'I seem to remember Mrs Grill came into the shop herself. I was surprised, she showed remarkably good taste. I think she went away with an antique ring.'

'So, you did meet her?'

'Only in the way of business, I'd forgotten all about it until you asked.'

Frank didn't think so.

'Right, I'll disappear for half an hour. Thank you for talking to me and for helping me with a list of shops to visit. I shall certainly recommend you if I meet anyone who wants to buy Art Deco antiques.'

They both got up and Tyner opened the door to the shop.

Iris whirled round, and put the emerald and diamond bracelet back into the display cabinet. Tyner shook his head at her. 'Not on your wages, Iris.' She shot him a look of dislike.

Frank thought a chat with Iris might be productive.

★

Laurel decided she'd copy Frank and dress up a bit for her meeting with Sarah Grill. From what she'd picked up about her she thought a smart appearance would cut the mustard. Her decision to do this reminded her of when she went 'undercover' at the holiday camp, posing as a swimming coach; she'd enjoyed dolling up with more eye make-up than usual, and platform sandals that gave her another two inches — as if she needed them.

Sarah had moved back to live with her parents, and as the chip shop was closed until her husband's funeral, she wasn't working. She'd agreed to meet Laurel in a snack bar situated towards the Thorpeness end of the High Street, away from the busy centre. Laurel parked near the fishermen's huts and cut through a side street by the Mill Inn.

Laurel peered through the steamed-up window of the snack bar; it was empty. She glanced at her watch, five to eleven, she was five minutes early. She pushed open the door and a bell announced her arrival. The room was small with half a dozen Formica-topped tables; the rest of the furnishings were basic: a red-topped counter on which was a cane basket filled with wrapped biscuits and chocolate bars, plus a plastic dome covering small cakes; lino covered the floor, and wall light-fittings, shaped like vertical water lilies, completed the decor. No one appeared through the open door behind the bar.

She decided to sit where Sarah could see her, at a table facing the window. She hoped she'd turn up; on the phone she hadn't seemed too keen.

'I can't see what all the fuss is about. I've got enough to cope with at the moment without raking up Matt's death. Why should Mabel want to make me go through it all again? I just want to be left alone to grieve.' Her voice didn't convey someone who was heartbroken; rather someone who was fed up with the situation.

'Hello, dear. Sorry I've kept you waiting.' The voice came from a large, blonde woman, who appeared behind the counter. 'What can I get you?'

Laurel got up and moved towards her. 'Would you mind waiting

164

for a few minutes before I order. I'm hoping to be joined by . . . a friend.'

'No, of course not, dear. Give me a shout when you're ready. We're only serving tea, coffee and cakes. Lunch is served from twelve o'clock.'

'That's fine. Thank you.' She wasn't too keen on anything, as there was a lingering smell of stale fat, the place could do with fresh air being blown through it. She settled back in her seat and went over the questions she wanted to put to Matt's widow.

The bell rang as the door opened. Sarah Grill closed the door behind her, and leant back on it, staring at Laurel. She was wearing a black skirt and jumper, a single row of pearls round her neck. She looked beautiful, sexy and perfectly in control.

'Hello, Mrs Grill, thank you for coming.' Laurel got up, holding out her hand.

Sarah moved towards her, her high heels clicking on the floor. She shook hands, but didn't say anything.

Laurel indicated a chair. 'What can I get you?'

'A coffee – white.'

'Anything to eat?'

Sarah sniffed and cast a disparaging glance over the embalmed cakes. She shook her head, shuddered, sat down and placed a crocodile-skin handbag on the table. She frowned, put the handbag on her lap and snatched a paper serviette from the holder on the table, wiped the top down, and threw the soiled paper on the floor.

'Hello,' Laurel called. The blonde woman reappeared. 'Just two white coffees, please.'

'Is that all? Can't I tempt you to a cake?' She sounded desperate.

'I'll have a KitKat. Would you like one, Mrs Grill?'

At the sound of that name the woman behind the bar leant over to get a closer look, her mouth turning down at the corners. Sarah stared back at her, and flicked back her blonde hair. 'No, thanks.' She spat out the words.

'That'll be four and six,' the woman said.

Laurel paid and sat down opposite Sarah; there were noises of a kettle boiling, a jar being opened and the clash of crockery.

'Daylight robbery,' Sarah said. 'She'll probably spit in mine, yours as well if she thinks you're friendly with me.'

'Do you know her?'

'Not really, but she knows who I am, and like the rest of the town, she's turned against me. It's my mother-in-law's fault. Getting you lot to start asking questions about Matt's death. Makes everyone think there's something suspicious about it.'

'You don't think that?'

'The police are satisfied. I don't know what Matt was playing at, stupid man, he's got me into a right mess. Mabel's taking over the shop, and I'm certainly not working for *her*.'

'Have you thought about what you will do, later on, when you can cope with life without your husband?'

'I'll be all right.' Her face showed doubt. 'I'm moving out, I'm not living in that dump.'

'What about your parents? They'll want you to stay with them until things get sorted out, won't they?'

She shrugged. 'I can't say they've made me welcome, they see it as their duty, not their pleasure.'

Laurel was beginning to reassess her opinion of Sarah Grill; she wasn't exactly the grieving widow, but she didn't look happy and she was obviously worried about something, presumably the attitude of the town folk.

'I'm sorry to have to ask you questions about your husband, but Mrs Elderkin genuinely believes his death wasn't an accident.'

'Your drinks and KitKat are on the counter,' the blonde woman shouted, closing the door behind her.

'Miserable cow,' Sarah said. Laurel got up and brought the drinks back; she pulled off the paper wrapping and tore open the silver foil of the chocolate biscuits. 'Like a piece?'

'Oh, go on then, it'll help to take away the taste of this coffee.'

The coffee was instant, hot and milky, not too bad though she didn't think Frank would have approved. 'Sarah, is it OK if I call you Sarah?' Somehow, she had to get her onside.

166

There was a little smile. 'That's OK.'

'Please call me Laurel.'

'That's a classy name, pity it's not Lauren, like Lauren Bacall, she's so elegant.'

'Gosh, that's who you remind me of – I hadn't realised until you mentioned her name.'

Sarah glowed. It wasn't strictly true, as Sarah was more voluptuous than the feline film star, but it seemed to have worked.

'Do you really think so?'

Laurel nodded and passed her another piece of KitKat.

'Sarah, I know the police have probably asked you all these questions I'm going to ask you, but I'd be grateful if you'd answer them again.'

'That's OK, I'd rather talk to you than that inspector, I didn't like him, didn't like the way he looked at me.'

'Really? What, do you mean, he fancied you?' She'd decided flattery would be productive.

'You must be joking, he looked down his nose as if I was something nasty he'd trodden in.'

'Was that Inspector Revie? Probably wore a Gannex raincoat and trilby?'

'Shortish, built like a brick shit-house?'

Charming. There seemed to be a faecal theme running here. She must remember to tell Revie what he reminded Sarah of. No, that wouldn't be fair, to either of them, but Frank would have a laugh. 'Yes, he's got wide shoulders.'

Sarah sniffed.

'Could you tell me about the night Matt died? I believe you were with a friend.'

'Yes, I was with Mandy.'

'Where did you and Mandy go?'

'Went to the flicks at Leiston, then we had a drink in a pub.'

'When you got home, you thought Matt had gone to bed?'

Sarah confirmed all the details she'd learnt from Revie and Frank;

she told her story confidently, looking Laurel straight in the eye. She was either telling the truth or was a most accomplished and practised liar. 'You know the scarf found round Matt's neck?'

Sarah shivered. 'That was weird.'

'It was yours?'

'Oh, yes, it was. One of the few presents Mabel bought me that I liked, it was classy.'

'Do you think Matt picked it up in the house and kept it?'

'Why would he do that? I know some men get worked up by different items of women's clothing, but not Matt. No, I'm pretty sure I lost it a few months ago. I remember looking for it a couple of times.'

'Have you any idea where you might have left it? Perhaps when you were with Mandy at the cinema? Or in a pub?'

Two lines were drawn between Sarah's eyebrows, she was obviously remembering something; either the word cinema or pub had struck a chord. 'Yes, I remember wearing it to go to a pub, I chose it because it went with my new coat.'

'Can you remember which pub you left it in?'

She leant back, withdrawing slightly. 'No.'

Laurel didn't believe her. She'd obviously thought carefully about what she was wearing that night – did she always dress to impress Mandy? Or was it someone else? 'If you did leave it there, someone must have picked it up, someone who knew you. This is really important, Sarah, did you see anyone in that pub, someone you recognised?'

Sarah's eyes darted from side to side, her face paled. 'No . . . I don't think so.'

'Could the person you were with have taken it?'

She looked horrified. 'God, no!'

'Who were you with that night?'

She didn't reply.

'Was it Mandy?'

She glanced at Laurel. 'Yeh, it was Mandy. She wouldn't have taken it. I must have left it on the seat, or it might have slipped off my lap, it was silky and it's done that before.'

She was sure Sarah was lying. If someone had seen her drop the scarf and they'd picked it up, why hadn't they returned it, or left it at the bar?

'Sarah, you must try and think which pub you visited. I think you ought to go back and see if it was handed in. They may not remember after so much time passing, but it's really important to try and find out.'

'Why? Why should I go to all that bother? It's only a scarf.'

'Because if someone picked it up, knowing it belonged to you and they didn't give it back, they must have kept it for a purpose.'

'What do you mean?'

'It means Mabel may be right, and Matt's death was not an accident. By placing the scarf on Matt's body, they were trying to implicate you, and whoever you were in the pub with, in his death.'

Sarah laughed. 'You must be joking! What a silly idea. Why would I want to murder Matt?'

'I didn't say you murdered him, I said someone was trying to fix you up.'

Sarah abruptly pushed her cup and saucer away, and picked up her handbag. 'I've had enough of your silly questions. I've got better things to do.'

Laurel placed a hand on her arm. 'Sarah, if you know anything, even if it's only tentative, I really do think you should tell me. Everything you say is confidential; only if it's vital to the case will you have to tell the police.'

She pulled her arm away. 'What do you mean? I haven't done anything wrong.'

'I'm sure you haven't, but if this *is* a murder case, the person who killed Matt is still at large. We don't know what the motive was, but you could be putting yourself in danger if whoever took your scarf thinks you recognised them that night.'

'How many times do I have to tell you – I didn't see anyone. I'm off.' She flounced out of the café, the door and bell vibrating as she slammed it shut.

The blonde woman poked her head round the door. 'Oh, it was

her trying to break my door. Don't think much of your choice of friends, if you don't mind me saying.'

Laurel agreed with her. 'Sorry about that. I'm afraid she left in a huff.'

The woman sniffed. 'Little tart.' She gave Laurel a sly look. 'What was all that about? I couldn't help overhearing some of it.'

She must have had her ear to the door, probably pressed a glass to the wood. Laurel decided to find out if the woman knew anything, or was just full of hot air and scandalous gossip. 'My name is Laurel Bowman, I work for The Anglian Detective Agency.'

The woman bristled with interest. 'Oh, I thought I knew you from somewhere. Why are you talking to her? Has something happened?'

Something you don't know about? You can't bear it, can you? 'I'm afraid, much as I'd like to tell you, I can't, but perhaps you can help me.'

The woman's cheeks plumped up with pleasure. 'Anything I can do to help. Shall we sit down? Would you like another coffee? On the house.'

Laurel refused, but went back to her seat and the woman plonked herself down where Sarah had been sitting a few minutes ago.

'Call me Evie, dear. Now, how can I help you?'

'You obviously don't like Mrs Grill. Would you tell me why?'

'Oh, I'm not sure if I should do that, her being recently widowed, it doesn't seem fair, does it?' she said coyly.

'I understand your feelings, but it would help me to get an understanding of the case. I'd be grateful if you'd help.'

'If you put it like that, and you think I'm being of help.'

'Thank you.' She'd add more than a pinch of salt to her words.

'I've known about that Sarah since she was a girl, Sarah Yarde, she was then. She comes from a good Aldeburgh fishing family, got two boats, church-going, very respectable. She was always a handful, she was,' she said, pulling a face. 'Mind you, she was clever, went to college in Ipswich, did well for herself, but she was always one for the boys; dressing up in clothes no respectable girl would want to wear. I was real upset when I heard she'd got her claws into Matt Grill. A nicer man you couldn't wish to meet.'

Evie maliciously droned on; Laurel decided she'd been a fool to encourage her. 'Is there anything more recent you feel I should know? Anything specific.'

Evie pursed her lips. 'If I were you, I'd see if she was meeting another man, I wouldn't put it past her.'

'Anyone in mind?'

'There's a few men in this town who'd be only too quick to get their leg over, if you'll pardon the saying, I could give you a long list, but my money would be on one not too far from here.' She winked suggestively at Laurel.

'And who's that?'

She leant closer, her breath hot and meaty. 'When you leave here to walk towards the town, you'll come to an antique shop. He's the one.'

Laurel nearly cried: Calum Tyner? 'Who's that?'

'You'll see his name over the door. I've seen her coming out of his shop.'

'She might just be a customer.'

Evie shook her head. 'Coming out like she was the cat who'd got the cream? I don't think so.'

It was the second time Tyner's name had been brought up, first by Alan Varley and now by Evie. 'You've been really helpful, Evie. Thank you.' She looked at her wristwatch. 'I must go.'

'I'm glad to have been of help. If I see anything going on, I'll give you a ring, shall I?'

Laurel gave her a business card. 'Thank you, if I'm not there leave a message, probably with Miss Piff.'

'I knows her too, everyone does. Nice lady, it was terrible her sister being murdered.'

Laurel nodded her agreement. She wasn't sure she'd describe Dorothy as a nice lady, but she wasn't going to argue the toss.

She decided, as she was passing Tyner's shop, she'd give it the once-over. Frank was meeting Tyner earlier that morning, so he'd probably have left by now. She'd noticed the shop on several occasions and thought how attractive the window display was; she'd never been inside as it looked expensive and she wasn't keen on antiques.

A dark-haired man in a well-cut suit came out of the shop, and went to a Jaguar car, unlocked it, took out a small box and returned to the shop. Calum Tyner? Was he the kind of man Evie had described? A ladies' man? She smiled to herself, pleased she'd taken more care than usual with her appearance, and also pleased she was wearing navy pumps rather than high heels as it looked as though he was her height, or even a bit shorter. This wasn't in her plans for the day, and she wasn't sure Frank or the other members of the Agency would think it was a good move, but it was a challenge. Would she come up to Tyner's standards?

She looked in the window, tilted her head as she looked at the statue of the girl with the two dogs. Not a patch on Labradors. She surreptitiously glanced into the shop and saw he was behind the counter staring at her. As Frank would say – excellent. She lingered, giving the girl and dogs a thorough examination.

The door opened. 'Good morning. I see you're admiring my statue.'

His voice was pleasant, his smile charming, but she didn't like the look in his eyes. 'Hello. Yes, it's full of life, but somehow I wonder if the girl and the dogs were sculpted by two different artists?'

'Really? Why do you say that?'

'The dogs are very realistic, there's a lot of movement there, but the girl is very smooth, and a little bit static compared to them.'

'But girls and dogs are different, aren't they?'

'True. Do you think I'm right? What's your opinion? Not that it makes any difference to the charm of the statue, it's lovely.'

He held out his hand. 'Calum Tyner. It's a pleasure to meet such a discerning woman.'

She mustn't give her real name, he might recognise it; especially if he'd just met Frank, he might make the connection. 'I'm Lauren McCall.' She blamed Sarah Grill for that name.

172

'Would you like to come in and have a look at some other antiques?'

She hadn't been prepared for the bait to be taken so quickly, in fact she wasn't prepared at all. However, she might find something out and at least she'd get a clearer idea of Tyner's character.

'Thank you, that would be very interesting. However, I must tell you, I'm not in the market for buying anything, so please don't waste your time if you think I'm a potential customer.' Now what would he say?

'I'm not interested in selling you anything,' he said, opening the door.

What was he interested in? She could almost smell the waves of testosterone coming from him.

'Would you like a coffee?'

'Yes, please.' She was sure it would be superior to Evie's brew.

He went to a door behind a counter and said to someone on the other side, 'Iris, two coffees, please.' He turned back to her. 'Black?'

'Just a touch of milk, no sugar.'

'Did you get that, Iris?'

'Yes,' Iris snapped.

Tyner showed her several items of jewellery, insisting on putting a necklace round her throat and giving her a mirror to judge the effect. 'That suits you. Elegant, and beautiful.'

Was he referring to the jewellery? She hoped not.

A woman came out of the back room carrying a tray with two posh cups and saucers. She placed it on the counter.

'Iris, you can take your lunch break now,' he said. She glared at him, went back to the room and returned with a coat and handbag.

'Be back promptly at one, please.'

'Yes, Mr Tyner.'

Goodness, she was thin, thin and peeved. He was certainly a quick and smooth operator. Was he going to try and seduce her in the back room? He must think she was easy if a cup of coffee would do the trick.

173

'Shall we drink it here, or would you prefer some privacy?' he asked.

She wondered if there was a director's couch in the back room? But she might see something interesting. She imagined the riposte Frank would make to that. 'I think it would be more relaxing to drink coffee out of the public's gaze. Also, you might have a customer and then you can deal with them while I finish my coffee.'

He looked pleased, picked up the tray and nodded to the back room. 'Follow me.'

He placed the tray on a large desk and rearranged two chairs so they were close together.

'These chairs are very elegant. I'm surprised they aren't for sale,' she said.

'Well spotted. They will be. I bought them recently; I like to have the use of some of the pieces for a few weeks before they're sold. I've already got a customer for them.'

'Really? What a quick turnover, that must be good for business. Are they expensive? Sorry, do you mind me asking?'

'Not at all. They're two of a set of five Gustav Stickley dining chairs, they'll fetch about one thousand, five hundred pounds.'

'Gustav Stickley? Sorry, that's a name I don't know, I'm afraid my Art Deco furniture education stopped at Heals and Liberty.' She was pleased she'd remembered those names. Tyner seemed knowledgeable and from the sound of it, well-heeled.

'You know more than most people who come into this establishment.' He passed her a coffee. She hoped Iris hadn't spat into it.

'The chairs are American; Gustav Stickley was one of the greatest exponents of the Arts and Crafts movements in the USA. The chairs are more Art Nouveau than Art Deco.'

She nodded and sipped her coffee; it was better than Evie's, just.

'Are you working at the moment, Lauren? Is it all right if I call you Lauren? A lovely name, it suits you.'

She was enjoying the flattery and the admiring looks he was giving her. It seemed a long time since any man had devoted himself to trying to seduce her. She presumed that was what he was after. At least he was one step up from the stripy coat at the holiday camp who'd been keen to form an intimate relationship, or as Dorothy would put it, remove your French knickers quicker than a magician plucking a sixpence from behind your ear.

'Thank you.'

'Are you working at the moment? Day off?' he repeated the question.

'A day off, well, a week off actually.'

'What do you do?'

'I'm a swimming instructor, at a holiday camp near Orford.' When she got back to Greyfriars, she would phone John Coltman, the owner of the holiday camp, and ask him to tell the staff that if anyone phoned asking for Lauren McCall, they'd say she was on holiday. She knew John would do anything for her, or any of the Agency, as last summer they'd saved his life and returned him to his father.

'Salters? The one where there was all that scandal last year?'

'The same, but now renamed Coltmans. It's a good place to work, adults only, so no naughty children to deal with.'

'Just naughty adults?' He gave her a sleazy smile.

'I have no problems with the campers.'

'And the staff?'

'Ditto.'

'Have you always been in that line of work?'

'I was a PE teacher, but I thought I'd have a change. I'm not really sure what I'd like to do with my life – professionally speaking.'

'I thought you must have some academic background. Thought of going into the antique trade?'

She smiled and shrugged. 'I don't think so, I haven't got any experience, although I envy you working with such interesting things – like these chairs. How can you be sure they were made by Gustav Stickley?'

'Like everything else, it's to do with experience, you get your eye in, but all his furniture is beautifully made, usually of oak, with simple construction showing obvious signs of handiwork – like exposed mortice and tenon joints. These chairs are going back to the States. We do a lot of business over there – I send out a full container nearly every month.'

She wondered if Frank or Stuart had done woodwork at school and could explain what a mortice joint was? Tyner's business was much bigger than she'd thought, he wasn't some small Suffolk dealer, he had tentacles reaching over the world. Things could get shipped out in containers and who knew what was in them? Stolen goods? She was sure she was doing the right thing by trying to get closer to Tyner. But, not too close!

The phone on the desk rang. 'Sorry, I'd better take it.'

'Do you want me to go out?' She nodded towards the front sale room.

'No, just a client, I expect. I'll make it brief.'

He picked up the receiver and held it to his ear. His face changed from relaxed urbanity to irritation. 'You know I can't talk to you during office hours.'

Laurel pretended to be examining the joints on her chair – mortice or otherwise.

'What?' He sounded shocked. 'What did she want?'

If only she could hear the speaker on the other end of the line.

'Her male counterpart was here this morning,' he said, lowering his voice and turning away from Laurel.

Was he talking about Frank? Was this Sarah Grill talking to him? There was a long pause as the speaker went on about something at length. 'Yes, tonight, about eight. Usual place?'

Another pause.

'Very well. I'll pick you up outside the Moot Hall, don't be late, I won't wait.' He put the phone down.

'A problem?'

'No. No. Well, just a small one. A client being difficult, nothing that can't be fixed.'

'You seemed worried.' She hoped she sounded concerned.

He smiled at her. 'Don't worry that elegant head of yours about me – I can sort out any problems.'

Possibly not this one, she thought. 'I must be going, thank you for the coffee and the interesting lesson on antique furniture.'

'I hope I can see you again. Would you have dinner with me?'

'Thank you. I'd be delighted.' As long as it's not in an Aldeburgh restaurant, or any nearby.

'Tomorrow night?' He was keen. 'Where do you live? I'll pick you up.'

'As I'll be visiting someone in Aldeburgh tomorrow, would you mind meeting me here?'

'No, of course not. Any preferences where to eat?'

'The White Lion in Southwold is a good place. Is that too far?'

He shook his head and reached for her hand. 'I'd go a long way to have dinner with *you*.' He raised her hand to his lips and flickered a kiss over the back; it was like being licked by a lizard's tongue. Quite erotic – she must tell Frank, see if he looked jealous. What was she thinking? Did she want to rekindle his interest? She wasn't sure.

'Where shall we meet?' he asked.

'I could come to the shop?'

'Good. Seven o'clock?'

'Yes. That's fine.'

'Until then.' He ushered her to the front door, opened it and half-bowed as she left. It was all very Italian.

She strolled away, but as soon as she was out of his sight, she wiped the back of her hand with a handkerchief and speeded up. She must get back to Greyfriars.

'You've done what?' Frank said, his voice full of disbelief.

They were all sitting down to an early dinner, cooked again by Jim. Even Mabel had decided to grace the table.

Dorothy gave her an old-fashioned look over her blue spectacles. 'I hope he's dishy, there should be some perks in this game.'

'When you hear what I've learnt you won't be so sniffy about it,' she said to Frank, and told them about her meeting with Sarah, Evie's gossip and her mention of Tyner as a likely candidate for

Sarah's lover. 'I had little difficulty in attracting his attention, he came out of the shop and before you could say Jack Robinson, I was in the back office having coffee.'

Frank glared at her. 'Tart!'

She told them about the telephone call and the strong possibility the caller was Sarah. 'Someone, and it'll have to be Stuart, or you, Dorothy, could follow them from the Moot Hall, even if you lose them, at least we'll know whether the caller *was* Sarah.'

'It can't be me,' Stuart said. 'If it is Sarah, she knows me.'

'Yes, of course, stupid of me. Dorothy, what about you? Does Sarah know you? Also have you ever been in Tyner's shop?' Laurel asked.

Dorothy grimaced. 'I'm sure Tyner wouldn't recognise me. I'm not too sure about Sarah, we've never formally met, but . . . What do you think, Mabel?'

Mabel's face was full of anger, her lips tight as though choking back the words she wanted to spit out.

'Mabel, I'm sorry, I should have told you first. It may not be Sarah,' Laurel said.

Mabel got up and walked out of the room. Stuart started to get up. Frank took hold of his sleeve. 'Give her a few minutes, she may come back.'

Jim came in from the kitchen carrying a casserole dish. 'What's the matter? Did you not like the soup?'

Dorothy was scraping the last from her dish. 'No, delicious, Jim, but I'm afraid I have to go out soon. Could you plate up some of the main dish for me? I'll warm it up when I get back.'

Laurel looked at Frank and tilted her head towards Jim. He raised his eyebrows and grinned.

'Dorothy, if you had a man with you, and it appeared you were a couple enjoying an evening out, you wouldn't be so conspicuous, if they went, say, to a pub. You'd be able to follow them in and possibly hear what they were talking about.'

'True, but where am I going to acquire a man from? You two,' she nodded to Frank and Stuart, 'are *verboten*!'

'Jim isn't,' Frank said.

178

Jim, who'd been listening to the conversation as he doled out the casserole, nearly deposited a ladle-full into Stuart's lap. 'Are ye going to turn me into a flat-foot?'

'No, Jim, not a policeman, but would you be willing to help us, just this once? All you'd have to do is cosy up to Dorothy and look as though you're enjoying her company,' Frank said. 'That shouldn't be difficult, she's an interesting lady.'

Dorothy had taken up her fork and was waving it at him in a threatening manner, however on hearing the last comment, she nodded graciously. 'Well, Jim, are you willing to do a bit of sleuthing? I have to tell you I need support. My undercover role as aunt to Sam Salter, the owner of the holiday camp last year, was not one of my best moments. I need all the help I can get.'

Last year, Dorothy, as well as Laurel and Frank, went undercover at Salter's Holiday Camp in Orford to try and discover the whereabouts of two missing members of staff. Dorothy found it difficult to subdue her normal characteristics: organising people's lives and not being pleased when they didn't obey her instructions.

Jim put the ladle back in the casserole. Stuart sighed, presumably with relief. 'I learnt a few tricks about acting against my inclinations when I was in prison, so I'd be proud to help you, Dorothy. What time do we need to leave?'

Laurel looked at the clock on the sideboard. 'You've plenty of time, stay and eat your dinner.'

'No, parking spaces near the Moot Hall get filled up in the evening, especially as there's something good on at the Aldeburgh Cinema tonight. We don't want to miss Tyner and whoever he's with.'

Mabel marched back into the room and passed a photo to Dorothy. 'This is one of Matt and *her* taken not long after they married. She's not changed much, you know her, Dorothy, but Jim doesn't.'

Jim took it and held it at a distance. 'Good-looking girl.' He made to hand it back.

'Keep it for tonight,' Mabel said.

Dorothy nodded and got up. 'OK, Jim, let's go. We'll be a happy couple out on a date. What are sleuths wearing nowadays?'

'What about the rest of the dinner?' Jim asked.

Laurel got up. 'We'll cope, don't worry.'

Mabel bounced up. 'I'll see to it, Jim. Thank you for doing this, it means a lot to me. At last we seem to be getting somewhere.' She marched into the kitchen.

'Get your coat, Jim. If we end up in a nice pub, we can have something to eat there. If not, I hope you lot will save us something for when we get back,' Dorothy said.

'We'll all be up, waiting to hear what's happened,' Frank said.

'What does Tyner look like?' Dorothy asked.

Laurel gave a brief description. She noticed Frank was relaxed, and smiling at her.

'He drives a black Jaguar, at least I saw him take something out of one parked outside his shop, I presumed it was his.'

Jim came back. 'I'm ready, Dorothy.'

'I'll meet you by my car, I'll just get a coat.'

After they'd left, the three round the table looked at each other and laughed.

Mabel came in with vegetables, smiling at them. 'You never know, this might be the beginning of a beautiful romance.'

Chapter Eighteen

Dorothy backed into the nearest parking spot to the Moot Hall she could find. 'I think Tyner will probably pull up and whoever he's meeting will get in straight away, so I'll have to be ready for a quick getaway.'

Jim nodded. 'Ay, I've heard of those before.'

Dorothy chuckled. 'This is an adventure, isn't it? I'm glad you're with me, if I lose them, I can blame you.'

'I beg your pardon, I'm not the one driving.'

'I'll say you were nervous when I speeded up, so I had to slow down.'

'And you think they'll believe you?'

'No, but it'll amuse them.'

'I thought this detective business was serious?'

'It is, most of the time, and it can be dangerous as well. Laurel and Frank could both have lost their lives in the past two years. Goodness, Frank could have been burnt to death last year when that unexploded bomb went off on Orford Ness.'

'Ay, they're brave people, especially Laurel, her being a woman.'

'I'm not sure I follow your logic, Jim. Just because we're classified as the weaker sex, doesn't make us less brave.'

'Shouldn't we be keeping our eyes peeled?' he said, probably wanting to change the subject.

She glanced at her wristwatch. 'Ten to eight. But you're right, I'll stop chattering.'

'Och, I didn't mean you should stop talking. I can listen as well as watch.' He nudged her. 'Look, that woman who's just walked up to the Moot Hall, is that her?'

The woman was smartly dressed in a black suit, the pencil skirt so tight it restricted her movement. She stood near the hall, impatiently tapping the toe of a high-heeled shoe against the pavement. She turned and started to walk towards them; as she got nearer, Dorothy saw her face was heavily made up, lashings of black mascara, blue eye shadow and bright red lips.

'Turn and face me, Jim, don't look at her. Say something!'

Jim's brow was furrowed. 'What do you think about the electricity union asking for a thirty-eight per cent pay rise? The industry lost fifty-eight million last year!'

'I'd say they were living in cloud cuckoo land,' she replied.

'And what do you think about that Space Conference in Nice – saying sex is necessary on a long space mission! Typical of the French, it's all they think about.'

She put a hand over her mouth to stifle her sniggers. Wait until she told the others about Jim's conversational gambits.

Sarah walked past them, she didn't give the car, or them, a glance but kept looking back towards the town. Her hips swayed from side to side and the slit in her skirt revealed slim legs encased in black tights. Dorothy presumed they were tights, not stockings, as who bothered with a suspender belt nowadays, except certain ladies, either like herself, who thought tights were unhygienic, or ladies of the night, who no doubt indulged in red satin jobs.

'Is that Sarah Grill?' Jim asked.

'Yes, it's her.'

'It's a good job Mabel's not here, she'd leap out of the car and attack her.'

'She's certainly not dressed for church,' Dorothy added.

'She looks a right floozie,' Jim said, shaking his head. 'Her husband dead less than two weeks and here she is all dressed up to go out with another man.'

'She's certainly flaunting her wares. I'm beginning to realise why

182

Mabel thinks Matt's death might be more than a tragic accident. This has obviously been going on for some time.'

'Ay, another unfaithful wife. Ye can't trust women.'

'Really, Jim, all women aren't like that. In fact, I think most are faithful to their husbands.' She paused. 'Can't say the same about the men!'

He glared at her.

'It was a joke. Look out, she's coming back.' She took out a map from the side compartment, unfolded it and they both pretended to be studying it.

'I'd start the engine, Dorothy. It's nearly eight,' he whispered.

'Good idea.' She turned the ignition key.

Sarah Grill halted by the Moot Hall; her body looked tense.

A black car approached from the right and stopped by her.

'It's a Jag,' Jim said. 'Pull out slowly.'

'All right, all right.' She hated being told what to do when it was bloody obvious.

A figure inside leant across and opened the passenger door. Sarah bent forward and said something, then got in. Before her door closed, the Jag accelerated away. Dorothy ground the clutch into first gear and followed.

The Jag drove smartly through Market Cross Place and turned right at the Mill Inn, stopping at the junction at the High Street. Dorothy pulled up behind. It crossed the junction and went up Church Hill.

'They're heading inland, out of Aldeburgh,' Dorothy said. 'I thought they'd go north, along the coast.'

'I hope you've got plenty of petrol in the tank, they may be on their way to Ipswich,' Jim said.

'Job's comforter. I think we'll be OK fuel-wise. Or were you hoping I'd run out of petrol and then you could claim I was trying to proposition you?'

Jim laughed. 'Miss Dorothy Piff, and you a stalwart of the village.'

'I think they must be heading for the A12. Then they could go either way, north or south.'

The distance between the Jag and her Morris Minor Traveller was increasing; she floored the accelerator trying to keep up. 'If they get on the A12 and he puts his foot down I'll lose them.'

'No, he's signalling a left turn, they're taking the B1069 to Tunstall.'

'Nothing much there.' She grimaced. 'Lord, I'm going to lose them, I can't keep up with him.'

'Och, don't worry, we've found out it was Mrs Grill he was meeting, that's the main thing.'

Dorothy mentally willed her old banger on, but the tail lights of the Jaguar became fainter until they completely disappeared.

'Damn and blast, if I'm going to be involved in car chases, I need to get a new car.'

'Why didn't you borrow Mr Diamond's or Miss Laurel's? You could have kept up then.'

'I didn't think, also I'm not sure they would have been keen on my driving their cars. We may as well go back home.' She was disappointed with herself, it seemed so feeble to say she couldn't drive fast enough. She was fond of her old car, with moss growing in the wooden sills. She didn't want to part with it and it did her very well getting her around the locality.

'I think we should drive on,' Jim said. 'If they took this road they may have been heading for Woodbridge, if they were going to Felixstowe, he'd have kept on for the A12. Why don't we drive on to Woodbridge and look in the car parks of some of the classier pubs? I don't think Mr Tyner is the type who'd go to a spit and sawdust place.'

'Good thinking, Jim, and even if we don't find them, we can treat ourselves to a drink and a bite to eat.' His suggestion cheered her; if she could go back to Greyfriars and tell them they searched the Woodbridge pubs, even if they didn't find them, somehow, she wouldn't feel such a failure. She remembered how disappointed she'd been with herself the last and only time she'd acted as a detective, she'd found keeping up a false persona difficult and her naturally bossy nature couldn't seem to help asserting itself and spoiling the rapport she was supposed to build up with a suspect.

'Ay, I'll go along with that, I wouldn't mind a pint of Adnams.'

'My treat.' She was conscious of his body stiffening.

'If I take a lady into a pub, or restaurant, I pay. I don't agree with all this new-fangled women's liberation.'

'I shouldn't let Laurel hear you say that, or Frank for that matter. However, I haven't burnt any of my bras, so thank you, I accept your kind offer of a drink.' She glanced at him; his face looked darker, or was it the fading light? Perhaps mentioning sex had been too much for him. That was the trouble, she was so used to saying whatever came into her head with the rest of the team, and being amused by Frank's sometimes cheeky wit, she was forgetting Jim wasn't one of them. Yet, he'd fitted in so well, and he was obviously liked by the rest of the team.

'Do you know any pubs in Woodbridge, Jim?'

'Noo, I don't. I'm not much of a pub man, although I like going into The Ship and talking football with some of the men. I dare say you don't know many pubs in Woodbridge either.'

'You're wrong there; my sister and I used to have at least one day out a week, visiting different towns and villages, on market day if possible. We often had lunch in a pub.'

Jim sighed. 'I did feel for you when you lost her – it was hard to tell you apart.'

'We looked alike, but we were quite different. Emily was a gentle, kind soul, not bossy and wanting to organise everyone, like me. Much the nicer of the two of us.'

'Don't you put yourself down, Miss Piff, you've helped a lot of people, including me, we think the world of you.' He coughed. 'I hope that wasn't too personal.'

Dorothy swallowed and gripped the steering wheel. 'No, thank you. I'm glad you think so.' She decided to move away from analysis of her character, her eyes were misting up and she couldn't see clearly. She blinked several times. That was better.

'There's The Butley Oysterage,' she said.

'I've never been in there.'

'We're near the Butley river, it flows into the sea. Do you like oysters, Jim?'

He pulled a face.

She laughed. 'I take that as being no.'

'Ugh, who would want to eat something that looks like a load of phlegm!'

'Well, until your description, I did – now I'm not so sure.'

'Sorry.'

They passed through Rendlesham Forest and at a junction joined the B1438. 'This road goes through Woodbridge by the riverside, where the oldest pubs are. I presume we'll drive around looking for the Jag.'

'Ay, unless you've a better idea.'

'I'm a one-idea woman, and that's all you'll get. Have you a better solution?'

'I do have an idea.'

'Let's hear it.'

'It's eight thirty, I propose we give it until nine, and then if we don't have any luck, we go to a pub you like and have a drink and a bite to eat.'

'Excellent, as Frank would say. In that case we'll leave the Old Bell and Steelyard until the last and have a drink there. It's a lovely old pub, Tudor, fifteenth century, all wattle and daub and black timbers. Delightful.'

'Ay, sounds very pretty, but is the beer decent?'

'Philistine!'

They slowly made their way through the streets of Woodbridge checking out pubs, their car parks and nearby streets. They didn't sight a black Jag near The Duke of York, The Anchor, The Old Mariner, or several others.

'It's nine, Miss Piff, shall we make for this Old Bell?'

She puffed out a deep breath. 'I think we'd better. They must have driven through the town.' She glanced around, getting her bearings. 'It's in New Street, near Market Hill, nice little museum nearby.'

'That's a queer museum we've got at Dunwich.'

Dorothy bridled. 'It's a jolly good museum. Have you ever been in?'

Jim rubbed his top lip. 'Er. No, I haven't.'

'In that case, you've no right to criticise. There's an excellent model of Dunwich when it was a great city, before the sea gobbled it up. We've a rich heritage.'

'I'm sorry, Miss Piff. I promise I'll pay it a visit, then I'll have the authority to tell you it's a queer little place.'

'You did say you were paying, didn't you? I think I'll have a double malt.'

'And you a respectable churchgoer and sober driver! I'm having a bad influence on you, Miss Piff.'

Dorothy braked. 'Look!' Parked in front of The Old Bell and Steelyard was a black Jag.

'Bingo!'

She found a spot nearby and smoothly backed into the space. She turned off the engine, took a deep breath and squared her shoulders. 'Right, Jim, let's get our story straight before we go in. Are we a married couple? I haven't got a ring.'

'In that case, we're just good friends.'

'Agreed, I won't need to nag you or straighten your tie.'

'Thank God for that.'

'You go to the bar, and I can look around for somewhere to sit, and hopefully it will be near them. We might be able to hear what they say.'

'What do you want to drink?'

'A malt whisky, a small one, with a splash of water.'

'What about eating? I'll ask at the bar, but at this hour I doubt there'll be anything.'

'If that's the case, crisps and peanuts will do.'

'What'll we talk about? If we stay silent it'll look suspicious.'

'Take your lead from me, I think a discussion on vegetables and

187

all things horticultural would be suitably innocuous, but don't talk too loud, or we won't be able to hear them.'

Jim straightened his tie. 'Do I look like a detective? Or have I still got that jailbird air about me?'

Dorothy looked at him. 'You look like a distinguished intellectual with that sombre face and serious mien.'

'I don't understand a word you've said, but I'll take it as a compliment. Right, let's get in there.'

He sounded nervous; she realised this must be an ordeal for him, as he kept himself to himself, and since she had known him had little respect for authority and none for the police. Now he was one of 'the good guys' trying to help catch the murderer of Matt Grill, if there was one to catch.

The pub was just as she'd remembered it: picture-postcard pretty, typically Tudor, with white wattle and daub between black beams, and red window frames with bull's eye windows. Inside it was warm and smoky. Jim went to the canopied bar, sat on a red-velvet-topped stool and leant against the mahogany top. She felt proud of him, he looked calm and perfectly in control. He ordered drinks from a plump, motherly woman behind the bar.

There were two couples in this room, but no sign of Sarah and Tyner. She wandered to an open door, catching Jim's eye and nodding towards the next room. He smiled at her, then turned back chatting to the landlady as she poured the drinks.

This room was cooler and less smoky, set out with dark wooden tables and chairs; there was a corner cupboard and a Welsh dresser, blue and white plates covering its shelves. Sarah and Tyner were seated at a table at the far end of the room, and the next table was empty. There were three other people playing cribbage. She made her way to the table next to Sarah and Tyner and sat down with her back to them. They'd been talking before she sat down, but now they were silent. Had either of them recognised her?

Jim came into the room carrying a pint in one hand and a small glass in the other. 'Here you are, dear,' he said. 'I'm sorry, but they don't serve food in the evening. Would you like plain crisps or cheese and onion?'

'Plain, please, and some peanuts if they've got them.' Good thinking calling her dear, her name might have prompted Sarah's memory.

'I'm having some pork scratchings. Would you like some?'

Dorothy shuddered. 'No, crisps will be fine.' Jim went back to pick up the snacks.

Their mundane conversation must have allayed Sarah and Tyner's worries as they started talking in whispers. Dorothy pretended to be rummaging in her handbag; she was concentrating hard, trying to pick up the gist of their conversation and hopefully be able to make sense of it.

'They think I had something to do with it. What am I going to do? Supposing they find out about us? That'll give them a reason, won't it?' Sarah said.

'Sit tight, say as little as possible. It'll blow over.'

'It's all right for you. That Miss Bowman, I could see she didn't like me, and my horrible mother-in-law is paying her to fix me up. *She* won't be happy until I'm behind bars!' Sarah's voice became hysterical as she reached the final sentence.

'For God's sake, turn it down.'

Jim came back and as he approached, they stopped speaking.

Jim opened a packet of crisps and placed it between them on the table.

'Only one pack?' Dorothy said. 'I've heard Scotsmen are tight, but this is ridiculous.'

'Tut, tut, dear,' he replied, 'they're all yours.' He opened his packet of pork scratchings. 'What's more, here are your peanuts.'

'Sorry, I take it all back. I've been meaning to tell you I was disappointed in my potato harvest this year, the Foremost skins were scabby.' She dug out the twist of blue paper containing salt and sprinkled it on her crisps. She realised she was hungry.

'Were they? It was probably too dry for them, it's the dryness that encourages the fungus, you ken.'

They continued in this vein for a few minutes more. She found it hard to concentrate on the next table's conversation. Jim leant across and whispered, 'You listen, I'll talk.' She nodded and Jim proceeded to drone on, all she had to do was say an occasional 'Really? Fancy that!' or 'Well, I never'.

'I think we'd better not meet until after the inquest, and probably not for several weeks,' Tyner said.

There was silence but Dorothy could almost taste the rising tension.

'Are you trying to get rid of me?' Sarah hissed. 'You promised we'd be together. If they try and fix it on me, you'll also be involved. You do realise that?'

'Only if you blab about us. I've told you, sit tight and say as little as possible. You'll have to be patient. We can't be together for several months.'

Would it be years soon?

'That's no good to me. What am I going to do? Live with my parents for ever? Mabel doesn't want me in the shop and I don't want to be with the miserable cow. I put a lot into that shop and what have I got to show for it? Nothing!'

'Didn't Matt take out life insurance? Won't you get that? And she'll have to compensate you for the years of work you put in. Although you and Matt took the profits, didn't you? And you took more than your fair share, so you told me. You must have a bit stashed away.'

She hissed something back that Dorothy couldn't hear.

'I was pleased with the raspberries this year,' Jim said. 'I was proud when you won first prize with your raspberry jam at the annual show.'

'Thank you,' she muttered, pulling a face as the voices from the next table became even more difficult to decipher. Raspberry jam! It wasn't her thing at all; Emily was the one who took prizes at the local shows.

'Calum,' Sarah said, 'do you remember the night I lost my scarf? I left it in that pub we went to in Framlingham. You went back for it, but it wasn't there. Someone must have taken it.'

'So?'

He sounded bored, in fact from everything she was hearing, he didn't seem fond of the woman, there was no warmth in his voice. Was the affair fizzling out? Sarah was sounding increasingly desperate.

'That scarf was found round Matt's neck; it had caught in the machinery and choked him to death.'

'What, your scarf? Do the police know it's yours?' Now, he did seem interested.

'Yes, Mabel identified it, she'd given it to me as a Christmas present, only decent thing she ever gave me.'

'Do you think someone picked it up and gave it to Matt? Someone who'd recognised us?'

Tyner was a quick thinker.

'I don't know, although I thought I saw . . .'

'Thought you saw what?'

'Never mind. If the worst happens, you'll back me up, won't you?'

'What do you mean: "the worst"?'

'Mabel is determined to change the verdict on Matt's death to one of murder. At the moment it looks as if the coroner will say death by misadventure. But if she can dig up enough dirt on me, they could use the scarf as evidence. I'll need you to say I lost it that night.'

There was a deep exhalation of air. 'What? And who do you think would be in the frame then? If the police find out about us, they have a motive, don't they? Keep me out of this. Well out of it. Understand?' He sounded angry.

'But, Calum, I need your help.'

'Keep your voice down.'

'Would you like another drink, dear,' Jim said, waving his empty glass. 'It's thirsty work, all this chatting.'

She realised she'd swigged her whisky and would have relished another, but she was driving back. 'I'll have half a pint of shandy, thank you.'

Jim smiled, got up and retreated to the next room.

'Calum, you promised we'd go away together, after you'd . . . I have saved a bit. When can we leave? I can't stand it in Aldeburgh any more, everyone's against me, even my parents are looking at me as though I've done something wrong.'

There was the scraping movement of a chair. 'You have done something wrong. You're an unfaithful wife. This'll have to be the last time we meet until all this blows over. It's too risky. Just keep your nerve, sit tight. Don't admit anything. Dress in deepest mourning and try and look as though you miss him. You've often fancied yourself as a film star, haven't you? Now's the time to do a bit of acting.'

What a horrible man! Dorothy almost felt sorry for Sarah – almost.

'You can't do this to me,' she hissed. 'I know what you're like. You're not going to deprive yourself of female company for months on end. Or have you got someone already lined up to replace me? If they accuse me of murder, I'll t . . .' She mumbled the end of her sentence.

What a disgusting pair. She was glad to see Jim returning. He looked at her, his face concerned. She'd never been able to hide her feelings.

'Would you like anything else to eat?' Jim asked.

She shook her head. What she'd heard had made her sick to the pit of her stomach. Poor Matt, working hard, risking his life at sea to support his cheating wife. 'No, thanks,' she whispered. From what Tyner had said, Sarah had managed to squirrel away money for herself. Dorothy wished she could turn round, denounce them and tell them exactly what she thought. She smiled as she pictured Frank and Laurel's faces if she did that as she announced in triumph what she had done when she got back to Greyfriars.

'What did you say?' Tyner snarled.

'You heard me. If I'm arrested for murder, I'll tell them about us.'

A chair was pushed back, its feet scraping the floor.

'Don't you threaten me.' His voice was closer, louder, as though he was leaning over towards Sarah. Dorothy glanced at Jim. He was staring at them, looking ready to intervene. She pinched her face and slightly shook her head. He took a long pull at his fresh pint.

'What's more, I know more about you than you think. I've kept my ears and eyes open,' Sarah hissed.

There was a brief pause. 'Let go, you're hurting me.'

'We'll finish this conversation outside.'

Dorothy buried her nose in the half pint of shandy. She looked up to see Tyner leading Sarah from the room, a hand gripping her arm.

Jim started to get up.

'No, Jim, sit down. Let them go.'

'He might do her harm.'

She wanted to say she deserved it, but didn't want to go down in Jim's estimation. 'Drink up, we'll see if we can follow them back to Aldeburgh, I presume that's where they're going.' She doubted if her Morris Traveller would be able to keep up. The mood Tyner was in she could imagine he'd have his foot down.

Jim thumped the half-full glass onto the table. 'Let's get out of here. I can't say I enjoyed that, I don't think I'm cut out to be on the right side of the law.'

'You did well, blathering on about fruit and veg,' she said, as they made their way to her car. No sign of the Jag.

'What did you learn?' Jim asked as she pulled away and headed the car towards Aldeburgh.

'Quite a lot, and I'll tell you as I drive, so you can try to remember all the details and butt in if I forget something when we tell the others. Let's hope they can make some sense of it.'

'Will you tell Mabel?'

'No, she'll have to leave the room. It was a condition of the case continuing that she wouldn't be involved.'

There was a sigh of relief. 'I'm mightily glad about that. I don't think I could have borne to watch her face when you told her Matt's wife is a whore.'

'Steady on, Jim. That's a bit strong! I don't think he's paying her for her favours.'

'Well, what would *you* call her?'

This was a sensitive subject as far as Jim was concerned; he'd served time for strangling his own unfaithful wife. 'Slut?' she offered.

He sniffed. 'And a few other things.'

Frank's nerve endings were sizzling after hearing what Dorothy and Jim said. Laurel came back from the kitchen with another percolator of coffee, which was passed round to refill their empty mugs.

'You've both done fantastic work tonight. A special thanks, Jim. You came to help us out with the meals; this was well above anything you might have expected to do,' Frank said.

'Jim was brilliant,' Dorothy said. 'You'd have thought he'd been snooping all his life.'

Jim scowled at her. 'I'm not sure I like that description.'

'Sorry, but the way you managed to witter on about fruit and vegetables for so long was remarkable. I was able to concentrate on trying to hear their conversation.'

'I'll summarise what we've learnt and suggest further lines of investigation. Everyone chip in. Dorothy, I know it's asking a lot, you must be bone tired, but could you make notes? Just the relevant points,' Frank asked.

'Of course, I don't feel at all sleepy, I'm so fired up at doing some detective work and not messing up.' She picked up a notebook from a nearby table.

Frank raised two thumbs. 'Firstly, you've established Sarah Grill and Tyner are having an affair, but from what you heard it seems as though he's cooling off and might want to end it. Correct?'

'Ay,' Jim said. 'I nearly lost my temper with him, the way he spoke to her. He's a nasty piece of work.'

'And so's Sarah,' Laurel said, looking disapproving.

'Let's try and be professional, folks. Well done, Jim, for not clocking him, and remember, Laurel, if you talk to her again, try not to have that look on your face,' Frank said.

'What look?'

'As though you've swallowed a slug.'

Laurel glared at him.

'Shall I put those remarks in the notes?' Dorothy asked, smiling at Laurel over her glasses.

Frank sighed. 'We'll be here until the small hours unless you all behave.'

Jim was looking from one to the other. 'You started it, Mr Diamond, I'm sure Miss Bowman knows how to act professionally.'

Laurel gave him a satisfied smile. 'Thank you, Mr McFall.'

Frank groaned. 'Next, Sarah seems to be panicking and isn't responding to Tyner's pleas to sit tight and say nothing.'

'She's sure Mabel is using Laurel to fix her up for Matt's death,' Dorothy said, waving her biro in the air. Frank looked at her and she went back to her notepad.

'You think Tyner is definitely wanting to end the affair?' he asked Dorothy.

Before she could reply, Jim butted in. 'Och, if I've heard a brush-off that was it. I didna hear much, but I heard that.'

'She was threatening him if he deserted her?' Frank asked both of them.

'He didna like it. He's used to being the boss,' Jim said.

'You say he mentioned life insurance. That's an area we haven't covered. Stuart, do you think Mabel will know about that?'

Stuart removed the stem of his pipe from his mouth and blew a stream of bluish smoke ceilingwards. 'I'll check.'

Frank's nostrils twitched at the scent of tobacco. It was times like this when you were concentrating, trying to connect tenuous threads to weave them into a complete garment, that he longed for a drag from a cigarette.

'Dorothy, you say it sounded as though Sarah was creaming off money from the shop for herself?'

'That's what Tyner implied. You'd think Matt would have noticed if that was happening,' Dorothy said.

Stuart shook his head. 'Sarah did all the bookkeeping and banking. Mabel will go ballistic if it's true.'

'For God's sake don't tell her yet,' Frank said.

Stuart grinned. 'She's probably got her ear to the keyhole.'

The rest looked towards the door. Frank was tempted to rush over and pull it open. The thought of Mabel, stooped with a hand cupping her ear, was too much. He started laughing and they all joined in.

Stuart put up a hand, palm out, like a bobby holding up the traffic. The laughter died as he left the room. They sat in silence. He returned. 'She's reading in bed,' he said. Sighs of relief.

'Phew, you had me going there, Stuart,' Frank said. 'Next, the bit about the scarf is interesting. Sarah said she left it in a pub in Framlingham. Stuart, could you do the rounds and see if any of the staff in any of the pubs remember finding a missing scarf, or Tyner going back to look for it? If we find evidence she did lose the scarf, this means someone else found it, and didn't hand it in to the bar, but kept it.'

'I'll do the pubs on Monday, if that's all right,' Stuart said. 'I'll try and get Mabel out in the car this weekend, take her out for a meal.'

'Excellent, they shouldn't be too busy then,' Frank said.

'It was a lovely scarf,' Dorothy said. 'Mabel showed it to me before she gave it to Sarah. You could be tempted to keep it.'

'How did it find its way back to Matt?' Frank asked.

'If someone in the pub recognised Sarah, perhaps they gave it to Matt and told him about Sarah and Tyner,' Laurel suggested.

Frank nodded. 'Excellent. Good theory, or perhaps someone planted the scarf on Matt's body to implicate Sarah.'

Laurel raised a finger. 'Good, we've got two theories.'

'Dorothy, what was your gut feeling about how Tyner felt about Sarah? I know you couldn't see their faces –'

'But I could, even though I didna hear much,' Jim said.

'What a combination,' Laurel said.

'Go on then, do a duet,' Frank said.

'From what I heard he didn't sound like a man who was in love, or infatuated, or even lusting after her. He sounded annoyed and bored. Then when she threatened him, he was furious.' Dorothy turned to Jim.

'It looked to me like this relationship was coming to an end. I didna think either of them had deep feelings for the other. He, as Dorothy said, looked as though he'd rather be somewhere else. Och, I think he'd had what he wanted, and didna want it any more. Now the lassie, she was keen for it to go on, but not because she was fond of him, but for what he offered; I'm thinking money and protection from the polis.'

The rest looked at him in silence.

'What's the matter? Why are ye all looking at me like I'm a bletherskate!'

'A what?' Laurel asked.

Jim blushed. 'I take the word back, I shouldna have used it in polite society.'

'What does it mean?' she persisted.

'Idiot,' he replied.

Dorothy looked at him over her glasses and slowly shook her head.

'We were astonished, Jim, by your detailed observations. You've obviously made a study of human nature,' Frank said.

'You've plenty of time in prison to look at people and wonder how they got there, what they did, and why,' he replied, looking pleased.

Frank continued. 'There are two more comments, both from Sarah, which are worth thinking about. Firstly, you said she threatened Tyner, implying she knew more about him than he realised. Any ideas what she meant? Give me your thoughts, don't worry if they seem ridiculous. One can spark off another.'

'It suggests that Tyner must be doing something that isn't legal,' Laurel said.

'Could it be connected to the lifeboat?' Stuart asked.

'It must be something he wouldn't want people to know about,' Dorothy said.

'Has he had another affair with someone whose husband might be violent if he found out?' Laurel asked.

'Or, he might be worried he'd be cited in a divorce case and lose his reputation,' Dorothy said.

'What reputation?' Laurel replied.

'Can I suggest something?' Jim asked.

'Go ahead,' Frank replied.

'It seems to me, the man could be up to something criminal. What, I've no idea.'

Frank looked at Stuart. 'Are you thinking what I'm thinking?' Stuart nodded and puffed out more smoke.

'Oh, for goodness' sake, stop being mysterious. Tell us!' Laurel said.

'Tut, tut,' Frank said. 'Little Miss Impatient.'

Dorothy tapped her wristwatch. 'It's well beyond my bedtime.'

'Sorry. The case Stuart and I have been investigating concerns the theft of Art Deco jewellery. Tyner specialises in that area, and in the conversation I had with him he displayed a deep and wide knowledge of the period.'

'You're right,' Laurel enthused. 'He had some gorgeous items for sale, but the prices were well beyond my means.'

'You think he's a fence?' Jim asked.

'It's a possibility, but I don't think he'd be selling stolen goods in his shop, far too risky,' Frank said.

'I wonder if he knows Lady Trubshaw,' Stuart mused.

Frank nodded. 'Shrewd remark. She seems to have a penchant for younger men, there was certainly something going on between her and the virile gardener we saw. It's a possible connection.' He bit his lip. 'I wonder if Sir George, say before the first burglary, asked Tyner to look at the jewels, possibly for a valuation.'

'Jim,' Laurel asked, 'with your experience, would you say Tyner was a criminal type? Does he remind you of any one you met in . . .?'

'No need to beat about the bush, Miss Bowman – in prison, ye mean. Let me think.' He frowned. 'Ay, I met that type in the open prison in Norfolk; there was a better class of criminal there: forgers, conmen, white-collar types fiddling the books, serial bigamists, not like the thugs, bank robbers, murderers and hit men I met in Her Majesty's Prison Barlinnie. I suppose the nearest I can think to him, was a man doing time for making fake bronzes. He was proud of his skill, told me how much he used to make from selling them to antique dealers, like Tyner, and also putting them into auctions. Ay, now I think of it, Tyner does remind me of him. Full of himself, proud about how he'd sold so many fakes to the suckers. He had an eye for the ladies as well, boasted about his conquests.'

'What happened to him? Do you know?' Laurel asked.

'He got out before me. One of the guards told me a probation officer got him a job helping in a museum, he didna say which one.'

'One of us,' Frank said, pointing to Stuart, 'and I suppose it'd better be me, seeing as you're looking into Matt's life insurance and trekking round Framlingham's pubs, had better pay a visit to Sir George and find out if there is any connection between him, or Lady Trubshaw, and Tyner. I'll try and get a word with her ladyship alone, she won't admit to anything if Sir George is about.'

'Is that it?' Dorothy said. 'My wrist's aching.'

'One last thing. Dorothy, you said when Sarah was talking about losing her scarf, she said something like "although I thought I saw". What do you think she meant?'

Dorothy frowned. 'It was after she talked about Mabel giving her the scarf . . . Tyner thought someone in the pub, who knew Sarah, or him, or both, took it and gave it to Matt.'

'Yes, we've got that. What was her voice like when she said that? Any clues there?'

'It was as if she'd suddenly realised something.'

'Could it have been she remembered seeing someone she knew in the pub?'

'Possibly.'

'Then that someone could be the murderer.' He turned to Laurel. 'Can you talk to her again tomorrow? If it was the murderer, and he realises she saw him, she could be in danger.'

'Surely that can't be right, otherwise he'd have made a move before now,' Laurel said. 'But I'll certainly get in touch, make her realise how important it is for her to come clean.'

'That's it. The meeting is closed. Thanks, everyone, it's been very productive and all made possible by our two sleuths.' He smiled at Dorothy and Jim.

Dorothy, rubbing her wrists, graciously nodded.

'Back to the day job,' Jim said. 'Any ideas what ye'd like to eat tomorrow?'

Chapter Nineteen

Monday, 25 September, 1972

Frank was once more seated opposite Sir George Trubshaw in the sitting room of Gladham Hall. Trubshaw – he refused to think of him as Sir George, despite having to give him that moniker to his face – Trubshaw was looking peaky, and he'd the impression he was wishing he'd never started the search for the missing jewellery.

'How are you, Mr Diamond?'

'Well. And you, Sir George?'

'Feeling considerably better having heard about the discovery of the oil field off Shetland. They say it's bigger than either the Fortes or Brent Fields. We won't need to be so reliant on those Arab chappies. It'll meet half of our needs by 1980. Yes, very good for business, shares are going up.'

Didn't he want to know how the case was going? 'There's a new line of enquiry I'd like to follow, Sir George, but before I can start, I'll need some information from you.'

'Really? I was actually wondering if . . . you know, if . . . Perhaps it would be better to forget the whole thing, you know.'

Frank inwardly smiled. Getting a bit dodgy, is it? 'I do think I may be able to find out who burgled your house and stole your property. Give me another week?'

Trubshaw shrugged his shoulders. 'Oh, very well. What do you want to know?'

'I take it you have the receipts for when you bought the stolen jewellery?'

'Er, yes. I do.'

'Excellent. Could I see them?'

'Why?'

'I like to have all the facts at my fingertips.' And all criminals by the throats.

'I'll get Giddings to fetch the file. He's acting as my secretary as well as butler at the moment; my secretary is on holiday.'

'A man for all seasons?'

Trubshaw sniggered. 'Not quite Thomas More, but he'd suit the hat!' He picked up the telephone on a nearby table and dialled. 'Giddings?' A pause. 'Please find the file with the receipts of the purchases of all Lady Trubshaw's jewellery and bring it to the sitting room.'

'Apart from the receipts, did you ever have those pieces valued? Depending on when you bought them, their value could have increased or decreased by the time they were stolen.'

Trubshaw sagaciously nodded. 'Of course, it's extremely important to have up-to-date valuations on any possession of worth.'

Bumptious prick. 'Were these the valuations used by the insurance firm when assessing your loss?'

'Er, yes. Is this important?'

He doesn't like this line of enquiry. 'I need to know who did the valuations. I presume those details might be in the same file?'

'Yes, yes, I think so. But I can tell you that without having to look in the file. It was a local antique expert, he specialises in the Art Nouveau and Art Deco periods. A very interesting man, in fact we saw quite a bit of him socially after he came to the house to do the valuations. Lady Trubshaw was quite taken with him, said she learnt so much about those two periods from him.'

And a few other things, Frank thought. 'Who is he?'

'Tyner, Calum Tyner; he's a . . . it's too special to call it a shop, more an antique centre, in Aldeburgh. You may have seen it.'

Implying a hoick like me wouldn't frequent such place. 'Yes, I believe I have. Not my kind of place.' Might as well corroborate his prejudices.

Trubshaw smiled pityingly. 'I understand.'

The door silently opened and Giddings glided in holding a box file before him, looking like a priest carrying a sacred object to be placed on an altar; a coffee table acted as a substitute. 'Is there anything else, Sir George?'

Trubshaw turned to Frank. 'Can Giddings fetch you some refreshment?' The question lacked enthusiasm.

'No, thank you, but perhaps I could have a word with Giddings when I leave you?'

There was a slight movement of Giddings' head and a half-lowering of his eyelids.

'May I ask why?' Trubshaw was increasingly tetchy.

'I want to check a few dates with him. Attention to detail, Sir George, attention to detail.' He might as well add to the boring repartee.

'Very well. Where will you be, Giddings? Mr Diamond will be finished here very soon.'

'I will be in the library, Sir George, dusting the first editions.'

Frank raised his eyebrows.

Giddings inclined his body and glided away.

'Good man, Giddings,' Trubshaw said, rummaging in the file; he handed Frank several sheets of paper.

Frank swiftly glanced through them. All the valuations, made by Tyner, were greater than the original purchase prices. He made no comment. It wouldn't do to point that out just yet.

'Thank you, Sir George. Most helpful. I'll see Giddings now. I won't take up too much of his valuable time, just a date I need to check.' He tried to do the Giddings glide, but his feet wouldn't obey.

Giddings was in the library, which smelt pleasantly of old paper and polish. He was wielding a feather duster, holding a hardback book with a lurid cover at arm's length, as though afraid of contamination.

'That doesn't look like an expensive first edition,' Frank said.

Giddings' mouth turned down and he shook his head despairingly. 'Sir George collects first editions of the James Bond thrillers. He believes their value will increase. It has already.'

'You prefer something more esoteric?'

'If you want to read a book, the cheapest way is to go to the local library. I prefer to spend my money on other things.'

'Very true,' Frank said.

Giddings shoved *Dr No* into a gap in the shelf between two other Ian Fleming books.

'You told me, Mr Giddings, you were in the Merchant Navy before you left and went to work in one of Trubshaw's factories. How did that come about?'

A brief smile played over Giddings' lips, possibly appreciating being given a title, and someone asking with interest about his former life. He gestured to a captain's chair and sat down on its twin on the other side of the table.

'My mother was a widow, but her brother, my Uncle Joseph, was in the Merchant Navy, and he persuaded me, when I was old enough, to apply to join. I never regretted it, as it gave me a range of skills.'

'Do you still have any connections with the Navy? Do you sail?'

Giddings pushed himself back against his chair and eyed him suspiciously. 'Your questions, are they pertinent to this inquiry?'

Frank laughed. 'No, just interested. I've met so many men with connections to the sea on this case. I was talking to another ex-Merchant man the other day.' Not strictly true, but Laurel had. 'What was his name? Barley? Darley? Marley?'

'You don't mean Varley? Alan Varley? Lives in Aldeburgh?'

Frank lifted a finger in triumph. 'That's it, Varley. Well done, Mr Giddings. You obviously know him.'

'Yes, we were on the same ship for a few years, obviously a time ago. I sometimes bump into him.'

'Friends?'

Giddings' lips twisted lasciviously. 'We shared a common interest.'

'Oh? What was that?'

'That's for me to know, and you to guess,' he said, wriggling in his chair, and spreading his legs.

My God, the man's got an erection. Whatever he got up to, the memories were strong. Frank was tempted to call an end to this conversation. Steel yourself, boy, he thought. 'I'd guess you both liked the ladies,' he said, miming the international sign for shagging, with a bent arm and a pumping action.

Giddings sniggered, indulging in a spot more wriggling. 'In the Far East they supply very young ladies indeed.'

Frank decided he would give Giddings' name to Revie as a person of interest. 'The younger the better, I say.' Thank God Laurel couldn't hear him.

'They may be young, but they've been taught how to please a man,' Giddings said. 'More than you can say for what you can get round here.'

Frank felt like grabbing him by the throat and stuffing a first edition down his gullet. 'Did you share any other interests?'

'Such as what?'

'Oh, I don't know? What do sailors do? Tie knots? Do they still teach young tars such things?'

Giddings looked offended. 'They do indeed. It's surprising how often I use that skill in my job, especially when it's Christmas; Lady Trubshaw relies on me to tie up all her Christmas presents.'

'Really?' He had to get away from this disgusting specimen of a human being before he tore him apart. 'I need to speak to Lady Trubshaw, any idea where I'll find her?'

Giddings consulted his wristwatch, and smirked. 'I'd try the kitchen garden.'

Frank made his way through light rain. He pushed open the wrought-iron gate; the garden seemed deserted. It smelt of decaying compost heaps mixed with floral notes from the rows of cutting flowers. He walked up the brick path towards the greenhouse, but apart from the plants and grapevine, it was empty. At the end of the right-hand wall was a low building, with small windows set high in the red brick walls, their panes of glass dulled by spiders' webs on the inside. A superior potting shed?

He grasped the handle of the green-painted door and turned it.

A woman screamed.

The interior was dim, but not that dim he couldn't see Lady Trubshaw pulling up her knickers and the lookalike Mellors zipping up his corduroy pants.

'Sorry.' Frank retreated. Why hadn't they locked the door? Had they become blasé?

He decided to wait. Faint feminine hysterics and low masculine rumbles penetrated the door. Several minutes passed, then the door opened and a red-faced, tearful Lady Trubshaw emerged.

She gasped. 'Oh, it was you! What were you doing snooping round here?' she said accusingly.

'I was looking for you, Lady Trubshaw.'

She stared at him, her eyes moving from side to side, no doubt trying to work out what line to take. Mellors was staying safe in his potting shed.

She gulped, then took a deep breath. 'What are you going to do?'

'Do you mean am I going to inform Sir George I caught his wife in flagrante with the gardener?'

'Don't use those posh words with me. Are you going to tell him? I'll deny it, say you made it up.'

'Will he believe you?'

She looked uncertain, and once more her eyes filled with tears. She walked towards the greenhouse and gestured for him to follow. It was pleasantly warm, with bunches of grapes hanging from a vine trained over the roof on wires. Whiffs of a heavy perfume pulsed from Hazel's cleavage.

Inside she sat on a stool and pointed to another. 'Please don't tell him, he'd be so upset. I do love him, but . . .'

'But what?'

'Do I have to spell it out?'

'I'm afraid you do.'

She twisted her hands together. 'Sir George is not the man he used to be . . . you know?'

'You mean he's not well?' This was cruel, but she was cheating on her husband. Hypocrite, he thought, he'd been a whisker away, or should it be a pubic hair away, from committing adultery with a client's wife not so long ago. Who was he to judge?

'He's very fit, apart from . . . oh, damn it, he can't get it up.' She looked at him, put a hand over her mouth and tittered. 'Sorry, I shouldn't laugh. I don't know why I did.'

'Embarrassment?'

She pursed her lips and blew out a stream of air. 'I know I shouldn't do it, but I'm . . .'

'A passionate woman?'

She nodded. 'Are you going to tell him?'

He wanted to reassure her that he wasn't a do-good busybody, but this was an opportunity to get some answers to some questions. 'I'll keep your secret.'

'Thank God. Thank you, thank you.'

'But there's a proviso.'

'A what?'

'A condition.'

'I'll pay whatever you ask.'

Anger rose from his stomach. 'I'm not a blackmailer.'

'If you don't want money, what do you want?' She sounded desperate.

'Some honest answers.'

Her body shrank back. 'What about?'

'To begin with, the jewellery that was recently stolen.'

Her face tightened. 'We've told you everything we can about that.'

'I don't think you have. First of all, when was the last time you wore those particular pieces of jewellery?'

Her face flamed. 'I can't remember.'

'I think you can, because you didn't wear them very often, if at all, and certainly not when you were in company, perhaps only at home when you and Sir George were alone.'

'If you know so much, why are you asking?' she spat.

This was going to be a leap of faith. 'Changing the subject, I believe you are having, or have had, a close relationship with Mr Calum Tyner. That's true, isn't it?'

Hazel Trubshaw looked deeply shocked. 'How did you find out? Did the bastard tell you?'

'I don't have to answer your questions, you have to answer mine.' No good being soft on her.

Her shoulders drooped, and she hung her head.

'I suggest you tell me about it.'

She looked up, her face a picture of misery and fear. 'If George finds out about that, he'll divorce me. He's a proud man, and even though I know he loves me, this would be too much. I've made a fool of him and myself.'

'Start from when Tyner came to value the jewellery.'

'Oh, you know about that as well?'

'Sir George just confirmed it.'

'You didn't say anything?'

'No, and I promise I won't if you're honest with me.'

She shook her head. 'I can't help it. All my life I've had a weak spot for confident, good-looking young men.'

'Men who make it clear they find you attractive?'

'It's always the same, as soon as I see that look in their eyes, I just can't resist playing up to them.' She sighed. 'Sometimes George is away, visiting the factory, having meetings with supermarket giants, building up the business. They ring, I'm lonely, I fancy them and they fancy me.'

'So, Tyner?'

'He's a charmer, at least I thought he was.'

'When did the affair start?'

'It was after he'd been here to value the jewellery. I went to his shop and bought some jewellery. That's when it started. We'd meet

208

in the shop after it closed for the day, I couldn't afford to be seen with him in public. It didn't last long.' She sighed.

Frank's nerve endings twitched. 'I take it the affair has resumed recently?'

In the short time they'd been talking, her face had aged ten years; all the liveliness disappeared, and lines and grooves of age cut deep into her face as it sagged with misery. 'I'm such a bloody fool. I've risked everything I love for a few hours of being flattered and not such good sex.'

'You're risking a lot with the gardener. How do you know he won't talk?'

'He knows he'll lose his job if he does,' she said, tartly.

His sympathy took a dive. 'Let's get back to your recent meetings with Tyner.'

She was starting to look grumpy. 'I was in Aldeburgh and I saw the sweetest little silver ring in his window. I went in, he was there, and . . .'

'You started meeting in the shop again?'

She nodded.

'You wore the jewellery to one of these meetings?'

'What jewellery?'

'The jewellery you couldn't wear except when you and Sir George were alone.'

'I don't know what you mean.'

'Remember that word – proviso?'

She glared at him. 'George was going away for the weekend and Calum persuaded me that if we went somewhere where we weren't known, we could have a few days together.'

And nights.

'Where did you go?'

'He drove to a posh hotel in Derbyshire, near some big house belonging to a duke or someone. Calum told me to pack a couple of nice dresses for dinner. I took along some jewellery as well. It was a lovely couple of days, apart from being dragged round this stately home. Room after room, full of old furniture and pictures of miserable people.'

'Chatsworth?'

Her eyes widened in surprise. 'That's the name – you're a clever bugger.'

'So I've been told. The jewellery. Were they the ones recently stolen, the ones I'm trying to recover?'

She snorted. 'You'll soon be telling me what I had for breakfast and the last time I had a pee.'

Not if he could help it. This was taking too long. 'Answer my question.'

She drew back, as though shocked by the tone of his voice. 'Yes, they were. It was lovely wearing them, I could see other women looking at me and Calum. Envying me. I know you shouldn't feel like that, but it was good to know I could still be fancied, it made me feel young again.'

'Did Tyner make any remarks about the jewellery?'

'He said how beautiful I looked, not many women could carry off wearing such lovely pieces without being outshone by them. I was thrilled when he said that, it's stuck in my head, even after I knew he'd probably stolen the fucking pieces, or told someone else where I kept them.'

'You told him where you kept them?' What an idiot.

'Don't rub it in. He said he hoped I kept them safe, and I told him I was always forgetting to put them in the safe and I usually kept them in my bedroom, so I could look at them.'

'Does Sir George think Tyner may have had a hand in the burglary?'

She looked horrified. 'How could I tell him? I wanted him to just forget about them, after all we'd had the . . .'

'The insurance money?'

'I told him it was a stupid idea. Why couldn't he have borrowed some from his pals? Look at the trouble it's got us into.'

'Tyner obviously realised these were the same pieces he'd valued and sussed out they were supposed to have been stolen?'

210

'Yeh, he knew all right. He didn't come out with it straight, but one night when we were in Derbyshire, he took my jewellery off and said something like, "I was a clever little girl, having my cake and eating it."'

'Do you think, if he stole them, he knew you wouldn't be able to go to the police as you'd claimed the jewels had been stolen before?'

'I do. He's a clever bugger – I'm sure he had a hand in stealing them.'

'Why did your husband ask us to find the missing jewels? Wouldn't it have been better to swallow the loss? After all, he'd had the insurance money.'

'He's never liked losing, and he thought you had a good chance of recovering them; he was impressed by your reputation and discretion.'

'Well, Lady Trubshaw, I think you've answered all my questions.'

She stared at him, her face strained. 'What are you going to do?'

'I'm going home. I need to think this over.'

'My God, you promised not to tell him about Calum . . . and the other chap.'

'I did, but I don't think the Agency should be involved in helping you and your husband to continue to fraudulently claim for jewels that weren't stolen, even if now, they have been.' It wouldn't do her any harm to stew for a few days. 'Goodbye, I may be back with a few more questions. Hold your nerve, Lady Trubshaw, but if I were you, I'd stick to cutting flowers for the house when you go into the walled garden.'

As Frank drove away from Gladham Hall, or Glad Eye Hall, thinking of Lady Trubshaw's weakness, he glanced at the dashboard clock. If he got a move on, he might catch Iris as she left the antique shop.

He parked the Avenger at the seafront, near the Moot Hall; the temperature was falling, but he was glad of the fresh sea air after being in Gladham Hall. He stepped out briskly until he reached the

211

High Street near Tyner's shop. Tyner's car was parked outside. Frank pretended to be interested in the display in the window of a nearby bookshop, looking sideways to make sure he didn't miss her.

Just after five thirty, Iris, the acid-faced one, came out and turned left, walking towards the centre of the town, moving at a good pace despite the high heels. He followed, keeping a distance until they were well away from the antique shop. He speeded up.

'Iris,' he said as he came alongside her.

She stopped and stared at him.

'Don't you remember me? I came to see Mr Tyner last Friday. Frank Diamond.'

Her expression changed from one of puzzlement to recognition. 'Oh, yes. I remember, you put Mr Tyner into a very bad mood, that is until a blonde came in and gave him the glad eye.' His feelings vaulted from being pleased at the effect he'd had on Tyner, to peeved at the thought of Laurel flirting with the antique dealer. Then he smiled – here was another one using the glad eye. Laurel would love having her morals equated with those of Lady Trubshaw.

'I wonder, would you do me a favour and have a drink with me? I think you may be able to help me.'

She tilted her head. 'You're a detective, aren't you? He didn't like that.' She sounded pleased. She must have sharp ears unless she had them pinned to the door when he was talking with Tyner. 'Do you want to ask me about him?'

'Would you object?'

She sniffed. 'No, I wouldn't.'

Perhaps she'd hoped for a different kind of relationship with Tyner, not one of employer and employee, then she'd found he wasn't interested. 'Thank you. Would it be convenient to talk now? Or we can arrange another time, if you'd rather.'

'No, I'm only going home to a night of telly with my parents. Where were you thinking of going?'

He hadn't expected it to be so easy and he hadn't thought of anywhere. 'Would you prefer to go out of town?'

212

'Might as well, wouldn't do for him to see us. Not that I care, I'm looking for another job, I'm not staying there. Have you got a car?'

This looked as though it might be a productive session. 'Yes. Why don't we drive to a pub? Can I offer you a bite to eat, as well as a drink?'

She smiled, her thin face lighting up, as though she didn't get many offers like this. 'Thanks, Mr Diamond. And if I help you, perhaps you can help me.'

'Of course, if I can.' He imagined Laurel's face when he told her this. 'Be careful, Frank,' she'd whisper.

He decided not to go too far and they arrived at The Dolphin, in Thorpeness, just as it was opening at six. At the bar he ordered a pint for himself and a gin and orange for Iris. 'I've ordered fish and chips,' he said as he placed her drink before her. 'I hope that's all right, there wasn't much choice.'

She raised her glass and saluted him. 'Cheers. No, that's fine. I'm really glad you bumped into me, I've been wondering what to do for ages.'

He raised his glass to her. 'Really? I'm interested. Want to talk now, or wait until we've eaten?'

'You're nice, most people would just want to get what they want. *He's* like that. Not a bit interested in what I think. He promised he'd teach me about the trade and pay for a course on antiques, but I've just been a dogsbody. I really thought I'd clicked lucky when I got the job, but all he wanted was someone who didn't look like a dog's dinner to front the shop and deal with the punters who came in for a nose round. As soon as a customer showed interest, I had to get him and so I never made any good sales. He pays me a pittance, you know. I thought I'd make a good wage, because I was on commission, but he saw to it I never made an expensive sale.'

'Here comes the fish and chips, Iris. I'll get you another drink. Same again?'

'Yes, please.'

He wondered what culinary delight Jim had rustled up and

wished he was sitting with Laurel and the others. But the smell of the fried fish and chips made his mouth fill with saliva. What was it about fish and chips? Was there anyone who didn't love them? The cod was fresh, the batter crunchy, and the chips crisp on the outside and fluffy inside. Iris was tucking in with gusto, how she managed to keep her wraith-like figure was a mystery. Perhaps everything settled on her chest? Keep your mind on the case, he thought.

Iris eagerly accepted a pudding and after a quick look at the menu decided on three scoops of ice cream: vanilla, chocolate and strawberry. He settled for a coffee and sipped it as Iris made quick work of the ice cream and wafers. She settled back against her chair, looking relaxed and pleased. With herself? With him? Or with a full belly? He hoped the latter.

'Right, Iris. Do you feel up to telling me your concerns about Mr Tyner? I don't mean as an employer, I've already formed the opinion he isn't a man who looks after his staff. You said you were wondering what to do. What was that about?'

She leant towards him, a conspiratorial look in her eyes. 'People always think blondes are thick,' she began.

'Not me,' Frank said. 'One of my partners is a blonde, she's as sharp as a newly honed knife.'

She squinted at him. 'She wouldn't be a tall, blonde woman, good-looking, with long hair?'

This girl was sharp, that was an accurate description of Laurel. Iris had put two and two together and matched the woman who came into the shop and fascinated Tyner, with his partner.

'Could be.' He tried to look enigmatic.

'You're going to fillet him, aren't you?' She looked delighted at the thought.

'Yes, with your help, Iris. Tell me what you know.'

'I have to be truthful, I haven't got any firm evidence, just suspicions.'

'They'll do for a start.'

'I think the shop's a front for stolen goods.'

'He sells hot antiques? He didn't strike me as reckless.'

214

'You're right. He's very careful, all the articles for sale in the shop have good provenances. He's got a lot of contacts and some of them seem a bit ropey to me. About six weeks ago a man came into the shop just as we were about to close. He certainly wasn't the usual type we get, either as a customer, or as a person who wants to sell to him. He was well dressed, but very flashy, bit like a spiv you see in a movie. I was in the shop, making sure all the cabinets were locked and this man barges in, left the door swinging. He startled me. I thought he was going to rob us and I picked up the baseball bat we keep behind the counter.'

He was beginning to reassess Iris.

' "Where's Tyner?" he shouted.

' "Take a seat and I'll fetch Mr Tyner," I said. I hadn't time to do that as Mr Tyner rushed in from the back room.

' "What are you doing here?" he asked. "I've explicitly told you never to come to the shop." He turned to me. "Iris, you may leave now." He waved at the cabinets. "I'll lock the cabinets."

"It won't take me long –"

"*Now*, Iris." I got my coat and handbag from the back room. He gestured to the man and they went into the office and closed the door.'

'And?'

'I crept up to it and put my ear to the keyhole.'

'Keyhole Kate?'

She tilted her head. 'Surely you don't think I look like *her*.'

'Much more glamorous.'

She smiled. 'I couldn't hear what Mr Tyner said, but the other man was shouting and I caught a few phrases. I didn't stay at the door very long, especially when the man seemed to have calmed down and I couldn't hear anything, just the odd word.'

'Tell me what you can remember.'

She frowned. 'I should have written it down when I got home. I'll remember next time.'

Was she going to make a habit of snooping? 'You must be careful, Iris. I'm not sure how ruthless Mr Tyner is. You mustn't put yourself in danger.'

She looked at him for a few seconds. 'That's nice of you, but I'll be careful. The first words I heard were "If you don't cough up within twenty-four hours, it'll be the worse for you." He was really shouting at the top of his voice at that point. Then a few seconds later, "I've got my boys to pay . . ." and then, "How would you like your shop windows smashed in and the rest of the shop wrecked . . .?" After that it was just the odd phrase or word. "You can kiss my arse" and "the filth" and "recce" and lastly "knock-off". I'm not sure what those last two mean. I know the filth is a term for the police.' She sounded cross at this.

'Correct. Recce is short for reconnaissance, and knock-off is stealing, or it can mean stolen goods. You've done well, Iris, and possibly your evidence could be used in court.' He hesitated. 'That's if you would be willing to do that.'

She pulled back her shoulders. 'It would be a pleasure.'

'You mentioned you wanted my help, what can I do for you?'

She played with her ice-cream spoon, suddenly looking unsure of herself. 'You may think I'm silly to even think of this, but after I became suspicious of Mr Tyner, and I started to notice how he behaved, I thought I'd like to join the police.'

Frank wasn't often taken by surprise, but he hadn't expected this. 'You're tall enough, you've got a sharp mind and from what you've said, you wouldn't mind a bit of danger –'

'I wouldn't mind at all! It would be exciting.'

'It isn't all chasing criminals in cars; like any job there are boring bits, and the training is tough. Also, it can be hard on a woman if you get a misogynist bastard sergeant shouting at you.'

Her face was serious. 'I'd like to try.'

'Then apply and good luck. I can't pull any strings for you, but I'll make sure an inspector friend of mine knows you've given us help, and I'm sure that would count in your favour. Contact me if I can be of any help – filling in forms, helping with interviews.' He smiled. 'You won't be able to wear your high heels and the uniform is no great shakes.'

'I may not look like a fashion plate, and I must say I don't fancy the hats they wear, but I think I can cope with that.'

'Excellent. Are you prepared to keep your eyes and ears open when you're in the shop and let me know if you hear or see anything suspicious?'

'I certainly will. Give me your phone number.'

'Thank you, Iris. Ready to go home?'

Chapter Twenty

Laurel had arranged to meet Lily Varley outside the Cragg Sisters' Tea Room. Alan Varley was crewing for Tom Blower and would be away until late morning; as the fish and chip shop was still closed, Lily wasn't needed and she'd managed to get a neighbour to look after her mother for a few hours, on the understanding she wouldn't tell her dad.

Laurel wasn't sure if Lily could tell her anything new about Matt, but she'd taken a shine to the girl and wanted to see if she could help her in any way. Lily was standing to the right of the shop window, close to the wall, looking as though she was trying to make herself inconspicuous; not an easy task for a tall girl. When she saw Laurel, she looked relieved, and gave a tentative wave.

'Thanks for coming, Lily. Shall we go straight in? I'm dying for a coffee.'

Lily didn't reply, just smiled. She was a most attractive girl, and Laurel had to admit she was biased towards her as Lily was no porcelain doll, but a well-built girl, who didn't make her feel like an elephant.

Most of the tables were occupied, but Laurel pointed to a table away from the window. The air was full of the smells of baked cakes and pastries, and the aroma of freshly brewed coffee; bird-like chattering filled the room from the mostly female customers. A pot of coffee, a jug of cream and a plate of fancies were soon on their table.

'This is lovely,' Lily said, helping herself to an almond slice. 'Thank you.'

'I see you have a good appetite, like me.'

Lily blushed. 'My dad says I'm fat.'

'Nonsense. I wonder what he says about me?'

Lily's face reddened.

Laurel imagined the remarks he'd made. 'Beauty comes in many forms: delicate and petite, like your mother, and Junoesque like you and me.'

'You mean the goddess Juno?'

'Yes, you'd make an excellent goddess.'

Lily grinned. 'I wouldn't mind having a few of her powers.'

'Ditto,' Laurel said, and they both laughed. Laurel let her eat two more cakes and refilled her cup before starting to ask questions.

'Lily, have you had any more thoughts about Matt Grill? Has anything occurred to you since we last met? Any detail you can remember might be important; nothing is too trivial, even a tiny fragment of knowledge can fit with another piece and be an important part of the jigsaw.'

Lily wiped her mouth with a paper napkin. 'I've tried to think of anything else I can tell you. I've told you how kind Mr Grill was, he'd listen to my worries and took them seriously. Sometimes he'd just say I was fretting too much and he was sure things would get better, but the last time we talked he said he'd have a think about what I'd said.'

'Can you tell me what that was?'

Lily bit her lip. 'It doesn't seem right for me to talk about it. After I told him, I regretted it.'

'But you did tell Mr Grill?'

'He found me crying in the kitchen, he thought his Ethel had been harsh with me, but it wasn't that.'

Laurel leant towards her and placed a hand over Lily's. 'Did he talk to you again about your worry?'

'No. A few days later he was dead.'

Could this have any relevance to his death? A young girl's worry? She couldn't see the connection. 'Lily, if you can summon up the courage to tell me, I might be able to help.'

'I don't see how anyone can help, it's a family matter.'

'Is it to do with your mother?'

'In a way.'

Laurel remained silent, her hand still holding Lily's.

Lily frowned. 'It's my dad, since he gave up his job to look after Mum, you can't predict what kind of mood he's going to be in. He thinks the world of her, but sometimes he flares up and blames her for how his life has changed. Because he has to look after her, he can't get a permanent job.'

'I think that's understandable, he made a big sacrifice giving up his job in the Merchant Navy. He must have been used to travelling the world. Was he an engineer?'

'Yes. We were well off then. None of us liked having to move to a smaller house and do without all the things we were used to, but I don't mind, Mum comes first.'

'Is that what you're worried about?'

Lily's face reddened. 'This sounds awful, but I'm not sure what I'll do when Mum . . .'

Laurel squeezed her hand. 'Don't think about that now. I'm sure everyone will rally round and help you and your dad.'

'No, no, you don't understand. It's what I told Mr Grill, I don't want to stay with my father after Mum goes.'

Laurel was shocked; she hadn't particularly liked Alan Varley, but he was Lily's dad. 'He'll need you when it happens, and you'll need him. You'll be a support for each other.'

Lily looked at her and slid her hand away. 'I'd better go now, I need to get back to Mum.'

'I've really enjoyed talking with you, Lily. Would you like to meet again tomorrow? Perhaps you can think a bit more about Matt? It's really important for us to try and find out if his death was really an accident.'

Lily didn't reply, looking unsure.

'Or we could just have a chat and more buns!'

'I want to help. I do miss Mr Grill, and I miss being in the shop, Mrs Blower is always kind to me, even if she does shout at me sometimes.'

'Good, what time?'

'In the afternoon, Dad'll be looking after Mum. I can say I'm going shopping.'

What wasn't she telling her?

'What do you make of that?' Laurel asked Mabel as they walked away from Greyfriars. She'd persuaded Mabel to take an early evening walk with her and Bumper. 'It'll give you an appetite and I'll have someone to talk to, he's never been a good conversationalist,' she'd said, pulling Bumper's ear. She told Mabel what Lily had said.

'She didn't give any inkling why she didn't want to stay with her father?'

'No, she didn't want to tell me.'

'Mm,' Mabel said. 'Did she look embarrassed?'

'I'm not sure, perhaps frightened.' They stopped at a path running up between trees. 'Shall we walk to the Abbey and then go through Greyfriars Wood?'

Mabel blew out her cheeks. 'I'm not sure if I'm up to it.'

'Come on, Bumper's dying to get off his lead. You're not cooking dinner tonight and the exercise will help you to sleep.'

'All right, up we go.'

'I can always put Bumper back on the lead and he can pull you up.'

Mabel laughed. 'I don't think he'd be too pleased.'

They climbed in silence up the stony pathway, trees forming a tunnel, cutting off views of the nearby sea. At the top, the path levelled out and now there were glimpses of the cliff edge and the blue-brown water beyond.

'You used to be able to see loads of old gravestones here,' Mabel said, 'but I think there's only one left, the rest have been washed onto the beach.'

Laurel shuddered as she thought of the skulls and bones tumbling down with the gravestones and remains of coffins.

They turned through a gate onto a path bordering a field, its grass cropped by rabbits, the ruins of the Abbey in the distance. She was glad to get away from the cliff edge, afraid Bumper might take a fancy to chasing a rabbit, and end up falling over the cliff edge, although she knew he had more sense than his appearance suggested. They stopped to look back at the Abbey ruins, then walked into another wooded area.

'Why did you ask if Lily looked embarrassed?'

'I was wondering if she was beginning to feel uncomfortable around her father?'

'Really? You mean in a sexual way?'

Mabel nodded. 'I was quite friendly with Patricia Varley, not bosom pals, but when Alan was away, and he was often on long hauls, she sometimes used to give a hand in the shop when we busy – bank holidays, the Aldeburgh Festival. She'd bring Lily with her and she'd play in the yard. When we closed the shop, we'd have a cup of tea and a chat with the rest of the girls. Well, you know what women are like, we always seem to get on to the subject of our men, their good points, their bad points. This one's romantic and gives her chocolates and flowers, another hasn't a romantic bone in his body and she's likely to get a hairdryer for a Christmas present.' She paused for breath.

Laurel thought if she had a husband, she wouldn't want to discuss him with a load of women. She wondered if the husbands talked about their wives, and what did they talk about? Their culinary skills? If she could darn a sock? Or perhaps more intimate matters? She shuddered at the thought.

They turned into Greyfriars Wood; Bumper charged after a squirrel.

'One of the women,' Mabel resumed, 'said she wished her husband was keener on sex, she said it was once a week if she was lucky, and it was so quick it was over before she'd . . . you know what.'

Laurel was surprised at Mabel's frankness, perhaps it was only her own sex life she didn't like talking about. Where was this leading? 'What's this got to do with Lily?'

'I'm coming to that,' Mabel said impatiently. 'Patricia said, "You're lucky, when Alan comes home it's sex, sex, sex, and then more sex." We all laughed, but she wasn't laughing, you could see she didn't like it.'

'Why do you think that's a reason for Lily . . . oh, I see. You think she knows about that, and it upset her?'

'You can't tell me if it was happening that often Lily wouldn't have known and also have seen the effect it had on her mother.'

'He can't be having sex with Patricia when she's so ill. Can he?'

'I hope not, poor woman,' Mabel said.

They walked in silence, dried sycamore leaves crunching underfoot, releasing smells of autumn as they passed isolated houses, none of them showing signs of life.

'I wouldn't like to live round here,' Mabel said. 'It's too dark, and too quiet.'

'You wouldn't think we were quite close to the cliffs, would you?' Laurel said. She pointed left down a rough road, a single house on the left. 'If you go down to the end of the road you come to the cliffs and the sea.'

Mabel sniffed. 'I'm still not tempted.'

'I remember when I walked in these woods for the first time on my way to see Dorothy, Emily was still alive then, I was seriously spooked and wished I'd gone by the road.'

'Was that when we didn't know who'd killed Susan Nicholson?'

'Yes. But after I'd been with them, when I walked back, I didn't feel like that – their company had blown my fears away.'

'A lot has happened since then,' Mabel said.

Laurel linked her arm through hers. 'Some good, in fact most of it good, but some bad.' She glanced at Mabel, who was slowly nodding in agreement, a stoic look on her face.

'I nearly died, then I found a man to love, something I wasn't expecting to happen, and now this.'

Laurel squeezed her arm.

'I'll get over it. I'll have to.' She looked at Laurel. 'But I'll not rest until we get to the truth about how Matt died.'

'I know. We're doing everything we can, Mabel.'

'I know you are.'

Where was Bumper? Where was that damned dog? 'Bumper! Bumper!'

They both stopped, listening. 'He'll come back, don't worry,' Mabel said, 'when he's finished eating the squirrel he was chasing.'

'Remember Muffin being ill after wolfing down a rabbit?'

Mabel laughed. 'I do. He wasn't the most obedient dog, poor lamb.'

'Bumper! Bumper!' Laurel turned, and shouted in the direction they'd come from. 'I think I'd better walk back. Do you want to wait here?'

'No, I'll – listen, over there, I think I can hear him whining.'

Laurel's heart leapt. 'God, I hope he's not hurt.' She turned from the path, making her way between trees, brambles and ferns over uneven ground. Mabel was crashing through the undergrowth behind her.

The whines were loader. 'Bumper. Good boy. Stay. We're coming.'

The whines became more frantic.

'I'll kill him if he's rolled in something disgusting,' she said.

'He's upset,' Mabel panted.

Bumper jumped over a clump of male fern, still whining, but perfectly fit, his black coat shining as beams of sunlight caught his fur, his pink tongue lolling from his mouth. He rushed up to Laurel, who was ready with the lead, but as she bent down, he turned and ran away from her.

'Whatever is the matter with him?' Mabel said.

Laurel's temper was rising. He'd never been so disobedient. He was whimpering again. She rounded a clump of brambles and froze. Bumper was lying on the earth, head between paws, tail straight, softly moaning; guarding the body lying next to him.

Laurel stretched out her right arm. 'Stay where you are, Mabel. Don't come any further.'

'Why? What's the matter? Oh dear, is Bumper hurt?'

'No, he's all right. Just stay there.'

Mabel didn't reply and the sounds of panting breath and crunching leaves told Laurel she wasn't heeding her warning. She turned and tried to shield Mabel from the dreadful sight.

'Laurel, don't be silly, I'm not a baby.'

It was useless. 'Steel yourself, Mabel. Bumper's found a dead body.' She grabbed hold of Mabel in case she fainted.

'Oh, no! An animal? Is it a deer?'

Mabel's body went rigid and she uttered a gasp of horror, burying her head into Laurel's shoulder.

The half-naked woman lay on her back, her arms outstretched as though in supplication, the lower half of her body exposed, black threads of dried blood encrusting the white skin of her thighs, her purple tongue poking obscenely at them as she looked up into the trees with sightless eyes. Her long blonde hair was partly covered with fallen leaves.

'Christ in heaven,' gasped Mabel. 'It's Sarah, my Matt's wife.'

Chapter Twenty-one

Laurel held Mabel tight. 'Yes, it's her. We need to get help, Mabel. Are you OK? Can I let go of you? We must decide what to do.' She was always amazed her voice sounded so normal when she was in a tight or distressing situation. People must think she hadn't any feelings.

'I won't faint. When you said it was a dead body, that was bad enough . . . but when I saw her . . .'

'I know. It was Friday when I talked to her in the café. It's hard to realise she's dead.' She slowly released Mabel from her grip. She tried to turn her round so she didn't have to look at Sarah, but Mabel pushed her away.

'I'm all right.' Mabel put a hand to her throat and looked down on Sarah's body. 'Do you think it's *him*?'

Laurel pointed to Sarah's neck. 'She's been strangled, you can see the rope or whatever he's used, it's cut deep into her flesh. I can't imagine there are two murderers in this area.'

'What shall we do?'

'Are you happy to go back to Greyfriars by yourself? You can take Bumper with you. I'm sure you'll be safe, she wasn't murdered in the last few hours. I'll stay here and guard the body.'

'How do you know that? He might still be around. I think we both ought to go back.'

Laurel didn't want to say she'd seen a few lazy bluebottles crawling over Sarah's face and a smell of decay was drifting from the corpse; also, one of her eyes was damaged, probably pecked by a corvid. 'There are signs she didn't die recently. I think it's important

I stay here and make sure she's not disturbed. Make for Greyfriars and phone Revie, tell him where we are. We're not far from the road, in fact you can see where he must have dragged her in.' She pointed to flattened ferns and brambles. 'Don't argue, Mabel. Keep to the road, no short cuts.'

'Supposing I see a car, should I flag it down? I'll get home quicker.'

Laurel shook her head. 'No. Unless the driver is someone you know and trust.'

Mabel blew out her cheeks. 'I feel awful. I didn't like her, and I blamed her for Matt's death. Now she's *dead*. I feel as though I've killed her. I've wished she was dead and Matt was alive.'

Laurel wanted to tell Mabel what Dorothy and Jim had found out about Sarah and her affair with Tyner, and then she might not feel so guilty. 'Sarah's murder has nothing to do with you, Mabel. It looks as though she's another victim of the mass murderer, although she doesn't seem to fit in with his usual victims in one way.'

'What do you mean?'

'She's taller than all his previous victims, although she fits in the age range and she is . . . was, attractive.'

Mabel sighed. 'I'll get off, but I'll leave Bumper with you.'

Laurel bent down and hugged him. 'No, it's better he goes with you. You be a good boy and go with Auntie Mabel.' She attached the lead to his collar and handed it to Mabel. 'Get him home, he needs a drink and a meal.'

Mabel pulled him towards her and Bumper reluctantly followed, turning to look at Laurel.

Laurel gulped, she wanted to keep him with her, he was so solid and comforting whatever the situation. 'As soon as you've phoned Revie get someone to come back and keep me company until the police arrive.'

'I hope Stuart's back; he said he was going to some antique shops in Wycombe Market.'

'Don't go through the track the killer made,' Laurel ordered. 'They may be able to get some footprints.'

Mabel veered to the right and the sounds of her and Bumper

crashing through the undergrowth faded, to be replaced by the cooing of wood pigeons and a far-off yaffle of a green woodpecker. Laurel moved away from the body and stationed herself beside a sycamore tree, its leaves already coating the woodland floor, the bright autumn colours spoilt by black patches; Frank told her they were caused by a fungus. The air was tainted with decay: rotting leaves and fungal spores, mixed with dead flesh.

She shivered as she remembered the last time she had guarded a body; Mabel, barely alive, smashed on the head, lying on Minsmere beach. It had been night-time, and Frank had left her to get back to Blackfriars School and phone the emergency services. She'd been alone, talking to the unconscious Mabel, trying to keep her warm with her own body heat, and filled with rage at the unknown person who'd tried to kill her and had succeeded in killing Muffin, Mabel's little dog. Then, she was afraid the murderer might return to finish the job. But she didn't believe this murderer was nearby. He'd completed his work.

Who was he? Someone she'd met? Someone unknown? She thought of the men she'd met recently: Tom Blower, Alan Varley, Calum Tyner, and the other members of the lifeboat crew. Could she imagine any of them doing this? Calum Tyner had threatened Sarah. That was Friday night. Today it was Monday and she was dead.

A police car was parked in Greyfriars' drive, near the round pool. Frank's stomach tightened. Was someone hurt? Not Laurel? He turned off the engine and leapt out of the Avenger, slamming the door behind him. He looked in the kitchen. No one there. Voices came from the dining room, one of them was Laurel's. He stopped, took a deep breath and sauntered in.

Seated round the table were Laurel, Stuart, Mabel, Dorothy, Jim, Nicholas Revie and Johnny Cottam, Revie's sidekick, who was making notes. Looking at their grim faces, the quip on his lips died. 'What's happened?'

Revie pointed to a chair. 'I'm glad you're back. The rest of your team have been waiting for you to join them, before they'll give me some information which they think may be relevant.'

Frank frowned. 'Relevant to what?' Everyone looked upset, even Jim, but Mabel's face was white and drawn.

'There's been another murder, another woman strangled and raped,' Revie said.

Frank's cheeks hardened, and his breathing seemed to stop. It must be someone they knew. 'Who was it?'

Revie looked at Mabel and nodded.

'Laurel and me, we found her. Sarah, Matt's Sarah. She's dead, Frank.'

Sarah Grill, the possibly unfaithful wife. Tyner? He'd threatened her. Frank realised why they'd waited for him. They hadn't told Revie. They'd waited until he'd returned. His cheeks softened. 'You haven't told him about Tyner?'

'We felt we should wait until you came back,' Laurel said.

'Tyner? Who's he?' Revie snapped.

Frank explained how Dorothy and Jim had tailed Tyner and Sarah on Friday night. 'I think you ought to hear what they overheard.'

Dorothy unfolded the story, with Jim chipping in. As the tale progressed, Mabel's face whitened, her nose pinched – she was having difficulty controlling her anger.

'You'd swear to that in court?' Revie asked.

'Certainly,' Dorothy said.

Revie looked at Jim McFall. 'What about you?' he said, eyeing him suspiciously.

'I dinna like helping the polis, but I'll make an exception in this case. And I didna like the lassie, she said some nasty things, but no woman deserves what she got. It's a pity you've done away with hanging, that bastard deserves to swing.'

'I think you ought to be grateful capital punishment had been abolished when you strangled your wife, or you might have dangled on the end of a rope,' Revie snapped.

Laurel gasped. 'Inspector Revie, that was uncalled for.'

Jim had half-risen from his chair, looking as though he was about to attack Revie. Stuart grabbed his arm and pulled him back.

Revie's face turned red.

'What are you going to do?' Frank asked Revie.

'We'll go back to the murder site, see if Ansell can give us any more information, then I'll bring Tyner in for questioning, see if he has an alibi for the time of death, which I hope Ansell will provide.' He started to get up.

'Before you go, I've got information about Tyner.' Frank told them of his meeting with Iris and what she'd told him. 'I think it would be worth getting a search warrant for his shop, his yacht and wherever he lives. Hopefully you might find some stolen property. By the way, Iris wants to join the police, I'd say she'd make a good copper, perhaps when things quieten down you might invite her to the station so she can see the force in action.'

'Is she a looker?'

A sharp intake of breath from Laurel.

'Yes, tall, attractive. Great figure.' He might as well embroider it a bit, just to see the look on Laurel's face.

Revie's face lit up. 'Good news all round. If Tyner hasn't got an alibi, and we can find evidence of Sarah being in his car, or yacht, or his house, we may kill two birds with one stone.'

'Inspector Revie, I do admire your way with a cliché,' Frank said.

'Cheeky bugger,' Revie replied, looking his old cocky self. 'Right, Cottam, let's get going.' At the door he turned. 'Sorry about that remark, Mr McFall, Laurel was quite right, I spoke out of turn.'

Jim's eyebrows met his hairline. 'I accept your apology, Inspector Revie. You're the first polisman that's apologised to me. I'll go to court and swear as to what we heard Tyner say.'

'Thanks. I'm sorry, Mabel, you've had enough to bear without this. Hopefully we can clear it up soon.'

They sat in silence until the sound of the police car's engine faded and all was quiet.

'Supposing Tyner hasn't got an alibi?' Laurel asked.

'Does that mean he killed those other girls?' Dorothy asked.

'This isn't helping find out what happened to Matt,' Mabel said.

Stuart blew out his cheeks. 'I need a smoke.'

'And I need a drink,' Frank said.

There was a chorus of 'yes, please's.

'We havnae eaten yet,' Jim said. 'Do you want me to fix up something?'

'I had some excellent fish and chips with Iris.'

Mabel put her hands on the table and pushed herself up. 'Come on, Jim, I'll give you a hand, we'll make some sandwiches and cheese and biscuits. I think I'd like a long drink tonight. Have we any wine?'

'There's a few bottles of Merlot in the cupboard and I think there's some white wine in the fridge. However, Frank, I'd like a large Scotch,' Dorothy said.

With a plate of beef sandwiches and one of cheese and biscuits in the centre of the table and everyone with drinks, Frank looked round at them.

'Hands up if you think Tyner is the killer,' he said.

No one raised their hand.

'Supposing he did kill Sarah and tried to make it look like the work of the mass murderer?' Laurel asked.

'A copy-cat killing?' Stuart mused.

'But he'd need an alibi,' Frank said. Again, he wished he was there with Revie and Cottam to hear Ansell give the approximate time of death and then go with them to bring in Tyner. He was sure he was at the centre of the jewellery thefts, but was he also a mass murderer?

Chapter Twenty-two

Tuesday, 26 September, 1972

When Laurel came down to breakfast, Frank was already in the kitchen drinking coffee: 'Where's everyone?'

'Hello, slug-a-bed. Dorothy's in the garden giving Jim instructions, Mabel and Stuart have gone to Aldeburgh; Stuart's going to finish going round the pubs tomorrow. He wants to go to Aldeburgh with Mabel, she got a phone call from Ethel. It seems the locals are starting to complain, they want their fish and chips, so Ethel wants Mabel's permission to open the shop.'

'What's Mabel's attitude?'

'I'm not sure, I know she feels it wouldn't be proper to open before Matt's funeral, but the inquest isn't until next week and she wants to wait until after that before burying him.'

'I don't see why the shop can't open, she won't be working there. If she doesn't look out people will start going somewhere else.'

'Where? The nearest chippy is probably in Leiston. Long way to go for cod and chips.'

Laurel put two slices of bread in the toaster.

'Want some coffee?' Frank asked.

'Yes, please. Where's Bumper?'

'He's with Dorothy – speak of the devil.'

The kitchen door opened and Bumper ran in followed by Dorothy. He tried to climb onto Laurel's lap. 'Bumper, down. I'll get your breakfast when I've had mine.'

Frank poured coffee for all of them, and Laurel started buttering her toast.

A phone rang out in the office. 'I'll get it,' Frank said.

'You had a good sleep,' Dorothy said. 'It's not like you to be so late.'

'It's finding dead bodies, it makes me sleepy.'

Dorothy cocked her ear towards the office. 'Frank's not saying much, that's a change.'

'Swallowed a lemon, have we?'

Dorothy looked at her over her spectacles. 'Your long sleep hasn't improved your manners.'

'I didn't know they needed improving.'

'Oh, very sharp.'

'Stop squabbling, my children,' Frank said as he came back into the kitchen. 'That was Revie, keeping us up to date.' He sat down and took a swallow of coffee.

Although he'd got up early, he looked fresh and alert. His hair was freshly washed, curls caressing the collar of his leather jacket, and no sign of stubble. Perhaps he was sprucing himself up for the lovely Iris. 'Aren't you going to tell us the news?' Laurel asked impatiently.

'If you've finished spatting.'

Dorothy rapped her mug with a teaspoon. 'If you don't tell us at once, I'll have to chastise you.'

'You sound like Burt Lancaster in *Sweet Smell of Success* – "I'll have to chastise you, Sidney," he said to Tony Curtis. Great film.'

Laurel inwardly groaned; he was in one of his perky moods. 'You look a bit like Tony Curtis, all that curly hair.'

'Very good, Laurel. Your cinematic knowledge is improving.'

'For goodness' sake, you two, stop word-fencing. Frank, tell us what Revie said.'

He laughed.

It was good to hear. It seemed an age since the last time there'd been light-hearted banter at Greyfriars. She'd missed it.

Frank drained his mug. 'Revie said Tyner hasn't got an alibi for the time Ansell has given for Sarah's death, and it seems he also can't produce alibis for the times of deaths of the other women.'

'Gosh. Do you think he's the killer?' Laurel asked.

'Also, they found rope on his boat which matches that used to strangle the girls. I don't think that will carry much weight, as it's commonly used, you'd probably find it on ninety per cent of boats.'

'But it is another piece of evidence,' Dorothy said.

'If they don't get him for murder, Revie has definitely got him for possession of stolen property, and possibly theft as well.'

'Jolly good,' she said. 'I'm pleased about that.'

'So, no more intimate dinners with Mr Tyner,' Frank said.

'Perhaps I'll visit him in prison and take him some lovely food,' she retorted.

'Don't take the cake and file mix, it's so old hat,' Dorothy said, smiling at her own joke.

'The police will also be visiting Sir George and Lady Trubshaw,' Frank said.

Dorothy looked surprised. 'Why? What have they done?'

'Some of the jewellery found on the yacht was the pieces we've been trying to recover. They were reported as stolen by Sir George a few years ago. Tyner's denying he's the murderer, but he's accepted he's been caught red-handed with the stolen jewellery, and he's landed the Trubshaws in the mire. The insurance wallahs will be after them for false claims; they'll get done for fraud.'

'That's a terrible example for the nobility to set,' Dorothy said.

'There's nothing noble about those two. I feel a bit sorry for Hazel, but not too much, she's a real tart, keen on anything in trousers. As long as they're young and good looking,' Frank said.

'Like you?' Laurel asked, pulling a face.

'Correct. I think she's an insatiable sexual appetite – that young gardener looked shagged out.'

'Frank! Language,' Dorothy remonstrated.

'So, that case is wound up,' Laurel said.

'I don't suppose we'll get any more money from them,' Dorothy said, looking sad.

'What? You got some already?' Frank asked.

'Of course, and he paid up. I hope the cheque doesn't bounce.'

Laurel sighed. 'We still haven't made much headway finding out how Matt died.'

'I think you should tell Mabel you can't find any evidence it wasn't an accident,' Dorothy said. 'The sooner you do that, the sooner she'll accept the verdict.'

'I'm not so sure it was an accident, Dorothy. The night you followed Tyner and Sarah to Woodbridge, and she told Tyner her scarf was found round Matt's neck?'

'Yes.'

'I think you said Tyner thought someone in the pub must have picked it up, and recognised them. We need to check again what Sarah said. Could you get your notebook, please?'

'Of course. I'll go and get it, I wrote everything down when we came back. Hold on, I won't be a minute.' She rushed from the room.

'What do you think, Frank? Could he have been murdered?'

Frank's green eyes bored into hers. 'If he was, what was the motive? Could he be another of Tyner's victims? Removed, so he could safely carry on his affair with Sarah?'

'But Dorothy and Jim thought he wanted to finish with her, there was no warmth or passion shown between them. Why would he risk killing Matt?'

'True. Perhaps Matt found out about his other criminal activities, and threatened to expose him if he didn't give up Sarah.'

'That's a good theory.'

'Thank you, but only a theory. You've spent time with Tyner, do you see him as a rapist and murderer of young women?'

Laurel wrinkled her nose. 'I didn't like him, he fancied himself rotten and couldn't understand why I didn't want to melt into his arms. He was certainly shirty by the end of our evening out, when he realised all I had done was consume an expensive meal, a few glasses of ditto wine, and asked him numerous questions.'

'But he wasn't violent, or menacing?'

'Quite the opposite, couldn't wait to dump me back in Aldeburgh once it was obvious I wasn't going to play ball.'

'He didn't appeal to you one little bit, not a tiny smidgen?'

'Not my type.'

'What is your type, Laurel?'

'Black, furry, with a cold nose.'

He rubbed his chin. 'I've got dark hair, I could grow a beard and if I stuck my head in the fridge for half an hour, I'm sure my nose would come up to scratch. Will that do?'

She looked into his eyes, a half-smile on her lips. 'I prefer the stubble, it's sexy, so don't bother with the beard, in fact don't change a thing.'

He started to move towards her.

'Here it is,' Dorothy said, waving her notebook as she came back into the kitchen. 'Frank, why are you glaring at me? I know I've been a time, but I couldn't find the right book.' She sat down next to Laurel and flicked through the pages. 'Yes, here it is. Tyner said something like "Someone gave it to Matt. Someone who'd seen us?" and Sarah replied, "I don't know, although I thought I saw . . ." She didn't finish the sentence, it was as though she'd just realised what she'd seen in the pub. Then she fobbed Tyner off when he questioned her about that remark.'

'We come back to the two theories we came up with before: Sarah realises she'd seen someone she knew and they gave the scarf to Matt, or she made another connection and wondered if he, I'm presuming it was a he, had murdered Matt with the scarf and was trying to implicate her,' Frank surmised.

'In that case, why didn't she go to the police?' Laurel asked.

'Because she'd reveal who she was with, and even though Matt was dead, she wouldn't want all Aldeburgh knowing she was a tart,' Dorothy said, waving her biro in the air.

'Of course,' Laurel said. 'I don't think I'll have another lie-in, it's affected my brain.'

'Really?' Frank said. 'I haven't noticed any difference.'

'Perhaps you ought to grow a beard.'

'Frank! No! You're not going to turn into a hippy, are you?' Dorothy said.

'If Laurel wants me to, what alternative have I?'

Dorothy looked from one to the other. 'You're both in peculiar moods. What do we do next?'

'There'll be no more trips to Gladham Hall. Stuart and I may need to make some statements for Revie, or for the insurance firm. It might be worthwhile, Dorothy, to contact them, and claim any reward going for the recovery of the stolen jewellery. What do you think? Worth a try?' Frank asked.

'Well, it can't hurt, our coffers need replenishing,' she said. 'I really think, Laurel, you should give up on trying to find the cause of Matt's death. We had an enquiry this morning about a case in Ipswich, it sounds like a few weeks' work, and it will need at least two of you to tackle it. Your skills are needed elsewhere. We are running a business, you know.'

Laurel sucked on the inside of her cheek. 'I want to keep going for a little longer, and I certainly won't stop asking questions until I've talked it over with Mabel, and she agrees there is nothing more we can do.'

'Do you expect the Agency to run on thin air?' Dorothy snapped.

'No, I don't, but surely Mabel is more important than money? She's lost her only child, Dorothy. I can't imagine what that feels like. I lost my sister, so did you. We both know the pain of losing someone before their time. But to lose a child . . .'

Dorothy didn't reply.

Frank moved between them and put an arm round each of them. 'Come on, you two. This isn't the time for quarrelling. I think you're exaggerating, Dorothy, I don't think our finances are that bad. We've had some very lucrative cases over the past few years.'

'We've also had a lot of building work done, which wasn't cheap. The modifications to the house so Mabel and Stuart could live here were costly.'

Laurel looked at her, shaking her head.

'Yes, I know they paid most of the cost, but now it's likely Mabel will leave the Agency to run her fish and chip shop. That means Stuart will also move out, and who knows, perhaps he'll leave the Agency too. Then where will we be?'

Laurel realised Dorothy wasn't really worried by the lack of incoming money, she was frantic with worry the Agency would dissolve before her eyes, and her reason for getting out of bed in the morning and busying herself being the administrator would disappear. She may seem like a woman of steel, but the Agency helped her to cope with the death of her twin sister, Emily. She knew Dorothy was especially fond of Mabel; she'd known her for years, they were the same generation, they belonged to this stretch of coast, both Suffolk born and bred. Come to think of it, so was she, but this stretch of coast was special, with its shifting sandbanks and crumbling cliffs, a wild low sweep of land meeting an ever-changing sea. She turned to Dorothy and put an arm round her, it met Frank's and he clasped it.

'The Agency won't crumble. I'm sure of that. I'm not sure what Mabel will do, but Stuart won't want to leave, I can't see him in a white coat, shovelling chips for Mabel to put salt and vinegar on and wrap in newspaper. *I'm* not going anywhere,' Laurel said.

'And where Laurel is, that's where I want to be,' Frank said, squeezing her hand.

Oh Lordy, she thought, we're getting into deep waters.

Dorothy sniffed. 'This is getting maudlin. You're right, I'm overreacting. Well, if you're going to carry on looking into Matt's death, Laurel, what are you going to do next?' She got up.

Laurel pulled her hand from Frank's; he raised a quizzical eyebrow. 'I'm not sure. What do you think, Frank?'

He sat down and rubbed a finger over his top lip. 'Shall we go into Aldeburgh tomorrow? I think I'll talk to Tom Blower again. Surely, now he's had time to get over the shock of Matt's death, there might be something he's remembered, some remark Matt made, that might give us a clue.' He looked at her.

'Good idea. I'm meeting Lily Varley and possibly Ethel Blower. She was meeting with Mabel this morning.'

'I wonder what she wanted to see Mabel about? The fish and chip shop is opening soon, so it can't be that?' Dorothy pondered.

'We'll find out at supper,' Frank replied.

'Is Jim cooking tonight?' Laurel asked.

'Yes. Boiled ham, and veg from the garden: baked potatoes and cabbage. All good hearty stuff.'

'Pass the sick bag,' Frank said, pulling a face. 'I'll give that meal a miss, I'll see to myself.'

'No, you won't,' Laurel said. 'I need you here, we've got to stick together until this is sorted out. What's more, you could do with some greens, I think you've got a spot coming on your nose.'

He looked aghast. 'What? I'm turning back into a pimply adolescent? I need to check on this.' He rushed from the room.

'I can't see a spot,' Dorothy said.

'Neither can I, but I know how to get under his skin.' Laurel put her hand over her mouth and silently laughed.

Dorothy lowered her spectacles and gave her an old-fashioned look. 'Laurel Bowman, you're going to have to make up your mind, one way or the other, about Frank.'

She stopped laughing. Dorothy was right.

Chapter Twenty-three

Mabel pointed to a parking space in Aldeburgh High Street. 'That's as near to the shop as you'll get,' she said to Stuart.

He turned the steering wheel of the Humber Hawk and it groaned as he eased into the spot.

'Is that you, or your old banger?' Mabel asked.

He stared at her. 'They don't make cars as good as this any more.'

'I think it's time we got a new one. And I've never liked the colour. Sea-green – I'd call it cabbage green, and boiled cabbage, at that.'

He pulled on the handbrake. 'You don't want me to come in with you, do you?'

Mabel let out a long, sad breath. 'That's the worst of being married to a detective; I can't get away with anything.'

Stuart reached out and took her hand. 'I won't interfere, but I'm your husband, I've a right to know what's going on. The decisions you make will not only affect you and me, but there's the others to consider. We're like a family, us, Dorothy and Laurel and Frank. I need to know what you're thinking, Mabel.'

She looked up at him. Good, solid Stuart. He'd been a rock these past years. What would have happened to her if two years ago they hadn't all met at Blackfriars School? The murder of Susan Nicholson had brought them all together. She'd known Stuart for years, and realised he liked her, but if they hadn't been thrown together would their friendship have blossomed into romance? She never thought she'd marry again. Now Matt was dead, did she want to leave the security of her friends at the Agency to go back to running the chip shop?

'Come on, love,' he said. 'Ethel will be waiting for you.'

The wind almost took the car door away from her as she got out. It was strengthening, blowing in from the North Sea, and flecks of rain clipped her face. She pulled up the collar of her coat, and they ran towards the shop. They'd agreed to meet in the flat above the shop at ten, it was just past that now; she didn't like being late, she didn't want Ethel to think she didn't care what happened to the business. She'd been proud of the reputation she'd built up with her husband, Bill. The freshest fish, the best potatoes, everything prepared before opening and the fish and chips hot and tasty, the service efficient and friendly. Everyone said you can't go to Aldeburgh without having Aldeburgh Fish and Chips. When Bill drowned, she'd been too proud to let her friends and customers see her miserable face behind the counter. Would she be any better now? Wouldn't she be worse?

Mabel opened the door with her Yale key and led the way up the flight of stairs to the flat. She frowned: the stair runner was worn on the edges and looked in need of a good clean, and the brass stair rods were dull, the stained woodwork scuffed. Why hadn't she noticed that before? She thought of the staircase at Greyfriars, with its fitted blue carpet and oak balustrade, gleaming with polish and worn smooth by centuries of hands.

There was the sound of the scraping of a chair against the floor. Ethel must be here already. She tried to quell a surge of anger. She'd given Ethel a set of keys to all parts of the shop, including the living quarters. It didn't seem right though, she felt like a visitor, not the owner. How many years since she worked here? Matt, Sarah and Ethel had run the business. She'd left it to them. Calm down, she thought, remember Ethel is your friend, treat her like one.

'Hello, Mabel – Stuart – I wasn't sure if you were coming.' There was a clean tablecloth and crockery laid out on it. 'I came a bit early, thought we could have a coffee. Do you want to make it, Mabel, or shall I?'

She sounded nervous. That wasn't like her. 'You make it, dear. Thank you for thinking ahead.' Stuart softly exhaled. He'd been expecting Mabel to make a fuss. Not surprisingly, she hadn't been too clever lately. Stuart pulled out a chair for her and she sat down.

'It's instant, hope that's all right.'

'Fine by me,' Stuart said. 'It's not Frank Diamond you've got here.'

Ethel laughed. 'He likes his food rich, doesn't he? Tom saves him a Dover or a lobster, if he knows he's coming into town.' She brought a plate of scones from the kitchen. 'They're from Smiths, I'm not up to your cooking standards, Mabel.'

'You can fry a nice bit of cod, when called upon to,' Mabel replied, taking a scone, biting into it and nodding with approval.

'Frying's a man's job. I've done it, but it's hard work.' She hesitated. 'I've asked Tom to join us. He'll be here in a minute. Hope you don't mind.' She nervously glanced at Mabel.

'Be nice to see him. How's he managing?'

'He's been out a few times by himself, I don't like him doing that. If anything should happen . . .'

Mabel put down her cup. 'We can't have that. I'll tell him it's not worth it. I don't want you going through that.' She shuddered. 'No one should lose a son.'

Ethel reached over the table and took her hand. They sat in an uneasy silence.

'I see the Norwegians have voted not to join the EEC,' Stuart said.

'Sensible people, they're not going to let foreigners ravage their fish stocks,' Ethel replied. 'Here he is.'

Quick and heavy footsteps raced up the stairs. 'Sorry I'm late.'

His mop of hair was wilder than ever, blown about by the strengthening wind. He took out a handkerchief and wiped the rain from his clown's face.

Mabel gave him an indulgent smile. He never failed to cheer her up. 'Good to see you, Tom. Have a seat.' She slapped Stuart's hand as he reached out towards the plate. 'There's only one left, Tom, but you'd better be quick.'

Tom laughed and even Stuart raised a smile.

When the coffee was finished, she decided this was the right time to talk, as Ethel didn't seem to want to begin the meeting.

'Well, Ethel, what did you want to talk about?'

Ethel gulped and shot a sidelong look at her son. His face was serious; he nodded encouragingly at his mother. Ethel took a deep breath.

Mabel's stomach clenched. What were they going to say?

'I know you don't want to open the shop until Matt's buried, I can understand that, but I'd like you to reconsider.'

She thought that was going to be it. 'Why would I want to do that?'

'Because the people who work here, myself included, want to get back to work. If there's no work, they can't have their full pay. I've been giving them a token payment, but even if we opened up, I haven't got enough money to pay the wages until we start selling.'

'But there's a kitty, it's kept in a strong box under the bed. I told you about it, I gave you the key,' Mabel said. 'Why haven't you been using that? I don't want anyone to go short.'

Ethel breathed in, her shoulders rising to her chin. 'There's no money in the box, Mabel. I didn't like to worry you. I thought you'd made a mistake, not surprising with everything that's happened.'

Mabel felt the blood rush to her cheeks. 'My God, she must have taken it. The thieving bitch. God forgive me for swearing at the dead.'

Ethel nodded. 'She didn't like it when you put me in charge, even if it was only keeping an eye on things as we weren't open.'

Mabel whipped round and faced Stuart. 'I still say she was mixed up in Matt's death, I don't care what you and Frank say.'

'Calm down, Mabel. I think Ethel has more to say,' Stuart said.

She glared at Ethel. 'Well?'

'Don't start on at me, Mabel. It's not my fault if Sarah was siphoning off money.'

'You knew?'

'She was always buying things for herself, expensive things.

243

Either someone was giving her money, or she was getting it from somewhere else. I didn't know it was from the shop's takings.'

Stuart tapped firmly on the table. 'I don't think this is a subject which is going to get us far, this morning. Is this why you wanted the meeting, Ethel?'

She shook her head. 'Only partly. I'm sorry it's gone that way, but you had to know sometime. Mabel, me and Tom, we've a proposition to put to you. Tom, do you want to say something first?'

Tom looked at Mabel squarely, his face unusually serious. 'Auntie Mabel, I can't operate the boat if I can't sell the majority of the catch. If the shop isn't open, I'm left scrabbling round trying to sell it. I haven't time to be in the hut selling a bit of fish here and there, if I'm going round the hotels and cafés trying to flog them cod and haddock. It's the fag end of the hotel and restaurant season, the freezer's full – I'm throwing fish away, the gulls are loving it.'

'Why didn't you say?'

'I'm saying it now.'

This was awful, she hadn't thought about him, or the people who worked in the shop. In her grief it hadn't seemed important. She'd let them down. 'What's you proposition?' she said, looking at Ethel.

'We don't expect an answer straight away, take as long as you like, but Tom and I would like to buy the business.'

It was as though a hand had grasped her heart. Lose her fish and chip shop? She'd no longer be Mrs Grill, owner of the famous Aldeburgh Fish and Chips. But she wasn't Mrs Grill, she was Mabel Elderkin and she hadn't worked behind that counter for years. She hadn't even taken any of the profits, happy to think Matt was keeping the business going and upholding its reputation. 'You don't know what the business is worth, or how much I might want for it,' she said.

'I know, but if you said yes and we could agree a price, Tom's prepared to sell his house and live over the shop, Betty is happy with that. She'd work in the shop with me.'

Mabel's nostrils flared. 'You've certainly thought it through. How long have you been plotting this?'

Ethel's face flushed. Tom put a restraining hand over hers. 'Matt and Sarah's deaths have changed everything. You haven't worked in the shop for years, you left Matt and Sarah to run the business, which is as it should have been. It's only in the last few days we've come up with this idea. Someone's got to run the shop.'

'And how do you know I won't want to do that? Stuart and me, we can move back. Stuart wouldn't mind that, would you?'

All she saw was panic in his face. He was glancing round the room, looking at the out-of-date furniture and the worn carpet. She thought of Greyfriars and of their bungalow in Leiston, Stuart's home which he'd rented out when they moved in with Dorothy. There was the new kitchen, the well-kept garden, the comfy lounge. 'Don't answer that, Stuart, I shouldn't have asked you until we've talked it over.'

'I'd need to buy the rest of the shares in the boat as well, I realise that,' Tom said. 'Did Matt tell you I bought forty per cent of it?'

'Yes, I was happy with that, Tom. It was only fair. You were a good team.'

'I'd try and find someone I could work with and offer them a share in the boat and catch.'

'I suppose you're thinking of Alan Varley?'

Tom frowned. 'No.'

'He'll need something when his wife passes on.'

'I don't think it'll be long now,' Ethel chipped in.

'I know it seems heartless, but I wouldn't be happy working with him permanently.'

'For what reason?' Stuart asked.

'I'd rather not say at the moment.'

'You really think you'd be able to afford my business?' Mabel asked.

'With what Tom gets for his house, and I've got some savings, it might be enough. But if not, I hope you might be willing to let us make payments over a number of years, with interest, of course.'

She could almost hear Stuart shouting, 'Take it! Take it!' He didn't want to move into a flat with no garden and the perpetual

245

smell of fish. She couldn't see him in a white overall, sweating over a pan of bubbling beef dripping. 'I'll think about it and I'll let you know after Matt's funeral.'

'Can we open the shop?' Ethel asked. 'I really need to, the people of Aldeburgh are missing their fish and chips.'

Mabel got up. 'Yes. Open up. You,' she pointed to Tom, 'get back to fishing, but make sure you have someone with you.' She hesitated, looking out of the window at the rain lashing down. 'Don't go out until this one blows over, or they'll be sending up the maroons for you.' She gave Ethel a hug, then Tom. 'Whatever happens, I won't forget you're my friends, and you, Tom, I know you'll never stop grieving for my Matt.' She put a hand on Stuart's shoulder. 'Let's go home, love.' Dorothy, Laurel and Frank: she'd miss them.

Chapter Twenty-four

Wednesday, 27 September, 1972

The easterly wind buffeted the Avenger; Frank pulled the steering wheel to the left to stop it veering to the wrong side of the road. He and Laurel were approaching Aldeburgh from Thorpeness, and there was no shelter from the roaring wind. His mind was seething with conflicting thoughts. When Mabel and Stuart had returned to Greyfriars, Mabel went to their rooms, saying she had a headache, and Stuart told them about Ethel's offer. He also mentioned Tom's reluctance to take on Alan Varley as a partner.

'Might be worthwhile you asking Tom about him, being as you're going to talk with him this afternoon,' Stuart said.

He would need to gain Tom's trust as the town folk usually stuck together, and wouldn't talk about grievances to a stranger. As a Liverpudlian, he was regarded as some exotic creature from the North, who pronounced any word with a double o in a most peculiar manner.

The other matter dogging him was Laurel. He didn't think of her as a cock-teaser, but she'd make some flirty remark, with a definite sparkle in her eye, and if he made a move it was regarded with horror – no, perhaps that's too strong a word, but certainly a degree of panic set in. They needed to resolve their relationship once and for all. He'd have to decide what he wanted; but it would probably depend on her. Hopefully she might want their relationship to become physical; but would she want more than that? Apart from her near miss with the doctor, she hadn't been involved with any other man since they formed the Agency. As far as he knew. Did she like sex? She certainly wasn't a prude, and had a ribald sense of humour, and a general love of people. His instinct said . . . he shivered.

'Are you cold, Frank? I hope you're not coming down with something nasty.'

He glanced at her, hoping she wasn't a mind reader. A fresh, flowery perfume hit his nostrils; her blonde hair was tied back in a ponytail, and she was geared up for the wild weather in a blue anorak. Sexy. 'Must have been the devil having his daily walk down my backbone.'

'I wonder if his hooves have left marks? Perhaps I'd better examine you when we get back to Greyfriars.'

There she goes again, getting me all worked up! 'I'll go for that, Laurel, unless, as usual, you welch out of your commitment.'

She sat up straight. 'Frank! What do you mean?'

'I'm only human, Laurel, and what's more I'm male, in case you haven't noticed. Or did your human biology tutor at college forget to mention males are easily aroused?'

'Frank Diamond, what's got into you? We're in the middle of an investigation, and you seem to have lost the plot. You should be thinking about how you're going to question Tom Blower, not fantasising about me and my lack of empathy with your sexual urges.'

She laughed, obviously pleased with her witticisms. She wasn't taking him seriously. Now was not the time.

There was a parking space opposite Tom's shed. It wasn't really Tom's, it was Mabel's, but he was sure he wasn't the only one who had started to think that way. He turned off the ignition, the engine's revs faded and the wind shook the car. Almost horizontal rods of rain exploded against the windscreen.

'I'm thinking of going to see Nancy before I see Lily,' Laurel said.

'Nancy Wintle? Why?'

'She knows everyone in Aldeburgh and because her husband was a local doctor, she's trusted, and people do tell her their problems.'

Nancy was a friend of Dorothy's and over a year ago she'd asked the Agency for help. Laurel and Nancy had become friends too, and

248

when Nancy wasn't on one of her cruises, Laurel would visit her, sometimes with Dorothy.

'Can't do any harm.'

'I might get a drop of malt whisky if I'm lucky.'

'At this time of the day?'

'Whenever Nancy has a visitor it's a good excuse for her to get the decanter out. The time of day is unimportant.'

'Good job I'm driving.'

'What time shall I get back?'

He looked at his watch. 'It's quarter to two. Four?'

'Fine. Will it take you that long to talk to Tom?'

'I doubt it, but I can have a prowl round the shops. See if I can find anything interesting. Perhaps something to eat when I get home tonight.'

'What? After Jim's repast?'

He smiled at her. 'Sure thing. See you later.'

'Frank, were you being serious before?'

'What about?'

She shrugged. 'You know . . . me not following through.'

His smile faded. 'Yes, I was.'

She bit her lip. 'Do we need to have a talk?'

'We do.'

She looked like a worried teenager wondering if she should let her boyfriend get to first base. 'Hey, Laurel. We're mates, we always will be. We like each other.'

'That's putting it mildly.'

'How about putting it hotter?'

She punched his arm. 'I never know whether you're being serious or silly.'

'That's part of my irresistible charm.'

'It hasn't worked so far.'

'Bugger off and talk to Nancy. See you here at four. Don't be late.'

She had to push hard to open the passenger door. 'That's what I adore about you. You're so masterful.' She hopped out and the wind slammed the door shut.

★

Nancy Wintle lived in a terraced cottage on the right of the High Street as you walked towards the car park. Laurel was surprised she hadn't moved to a larger house, possibly one on Crag Path, after she inherited money when her brother Sam was murdered. 'This place suits me,' she'd said, 'I'd be lost in a big house.' As Nancy reminded Laurel of an exotic sparrow, she could understand her thinking.

The window box and pots surrounding the blue front door were overflowing with geraniums, bedraggled in the rain, and petunias; they didn't like this weather. Laurel raised the dolphin-shaped door-knocker and gave it several raps. Scuttering footsteps.

'Who's there?'

'It's Laurel, Laurel Bowman, Nancy.'

'Hold on.' A latch clicked. 'Wait a second while I step back, then barge in, dear.'

Laurel sighed. It was time Nancy had this dratted door fixed, there was the same palaver every time she visited. She put her shoulder to it and pushed. The door groaned and the swollen wood parted company with the frame.

Nancy, brown eyes gleaming and violet hair shimmering, beamed at Laurel. 'Dear girl, lovely to see you. Come in and tell me all.' She hopped towards her chair near the electric fire which, as usual, was sending out too much hot, dry air.

'You've changed your hair colour, Nancy.'

Nancy flicked her fingers through it, revealing a shiny pink scalp. 'Do you like it? I thought it was time for a change.'

It had been pink the last time Laurel saw her. 'I'm not sure. I'll reserve judgement, I need to get used to it.'

'That's what I said to the hairdresser. I wanted to try green, but she persuaded me to go for this.'

Thank goodness for that, Laurel thought.

'Sit yourself down. Tea? Coffee? Or a wee dram?' Nancy cocked her head, and nodded to the decanter on the sideboard.

'The usual, please. Don't forget the water. Thank you.' She took off her anorak and put it on a hook on the back of the door.

Nancy's red-trousered legs nimbly slalomed between the crowded furniture; she disappeared into the kitchen, returning with a small jug of water.

Laurel settled in the chair opposite Nancy, wishing she'd worn fewer clothes.

'Here you are, dear.' She passed Laurel a cut-glass tumbler, half full. A peaty, heathery smell filled her nose – heavenly. Nancy's glass contained the same amount of liquid, but a darker colour. No water. She didn't believe in diluting malt whisky.

'Well, Nancy, what was the latest cruise like?' Since inheriting money, Nancy had been on several cruises, taking a friend for company.

'Marvellous, dear.' She spent half an hour detailing the ports visited, the standard of food and drinks, and her position on the captain's table. It wasn't a chore listening to Nancy, she was a lively and funny raconteur. She stopped, blew out her lips and took a good mouthful of whisky. 'I think next year I'll fly to Australia; time I visited the other half of the world.' She settled back in her chair. 'What about you? Have you and Frank done it yet?'

'Nancy! And no, we haven't.'

'It's time you did. You're not getting any younger, Laurel. I'd put you down as a passionate woman, and I don't think I'm wrong.'

Laurel gave her a stern look.

'Don't give me your teacher's glare. I care about you and Frank. I'll never forget how you found out who murdered my dear brother, Sam, not to mention you both nearly getting killed.'

'Nancy, can we talk about that another time? I need to pick your brains.'

She cocked her head again. 'Really? That's interesting. Anything to do with poor Matthew Grill's death?'

Laurel took a sip, and hoped the alcohol didn't addle her brain. 'In a way. I wanted to hear your opinion of a few people. You have such a good knowledge of the town and everyone who lives in it.'

Nancy looked pleased. 'That's a bit strong, but I'll help if I can.'

Laurel leant forward, then retreated, waving a hand.

251

'Shall I turn a bar off?'

'Yes, please.' That was a relief. 'Could you tell me anything about the Varleys?'

'Which one: Patricia, Lily or Alan?'

'All of them, and your opinion of their relationships.'

'With whom?'

'Each other, or anyone else you can think of.'

Nancy pressed her lips together. 'Hmm, let's see. I'll start with Patricia, poor woman. You know she's dying?'

'Yes. Lily's told me.'

'I've known Patricia since she was a child. Such a pretty girl, a tiny doll of a thing. She was everyone's pet. But she wasn't like some spoilt children, she *was* spoilt but that didn't spoil her. You see what I mean?'

Laurel nodded. 'Go on.'

'She grew up into a most beautiful woman, as lovely if not lovelier than some film stars. I'm sure if she'd wanted to she could have been a movie queen, although she is petite. But some male stars are short, they'd have been grateful to have a co-star shorter than them. Alan Ladd wasn't more than five foot six, I believe—'

'She didn't become an actress, so what did she do when she left school?' If she let her, Nancy would have rambled on for ages about stars of the silver screen and who was her latest male pin-up.

'She'd always been a quiet, retiring girl, didn't seem that interested in boys, although, as you can imagine, most of the local lads worshipped her. She passed her School Certificate with good grades and got a job in the library. It suited her, the quiet, orderly way of working. I can tell you, library applications went up leaps and bounds, the town's youths mooned in and out of the library.'

'Did she stay long as a librarian?'

'She went to night-school in Ipswich and passed her Higher School Certificate in English and History with good grades.' Nancy paused, frowning. 'I wouldn't say she was an intellectual, but she loved books, especially the classics: Dickens, Austen, George Eliot, and she certainly improved the children's section. The kiddies liked her, she was calm and patient with them.' She sighed. 'Then she married Alan Varley.' She pulled down the corners of her lips.

'You didn't approve?'

'It wasn't my responsibility who she married, but I was shocked. Such a big man for such a little woman.' She shivered. 'I didn't like to think of them . . . it didn't seem right. She should have married someone who looked like Prince Charming, a young, handsome man, who would treat her with kid gloves.'

Laurel stared at her, and raised an eyebrow.

'I'm sorry, Laurel. I suppose I can relate to Patricia, being small myself. I can't imagine what it's like to be so tall. You're lucky Frank is about the same height.'

'He's half an inch taller.'

'That much?'

'Can we get back to Patricia? What has their marriage been like?'

'I'm not sure I know. She may have been attracted to the security he gave her, and perhaps I'm mistaken about her love of the library, as she gave it up when they married. He'd a very well-paid job, you know. A mechanical engineer in the Merchant Navy. That could have been another attraction, and he was away for months on end. Patricia was well provided for, he didn't keep her short. Once she'd had Lily, she blossomed, she doted on that child.'

'Lily looks like her mother in some respects.'

'She does, and she's a bonny girl, attractive, but not beautiful. It's a great pity Varley wouldn't let her go on to the sixth form, I think she's got more brains than her mother, and a beautiful singing voice. She's wasted serving in a fish and chip shop.'

'She seems happy there and Ethel Blower looks after her. Did she have a crush on Matt, do you think?'

'I don't know, but I wouldn't be surprised.' She shook her head. 'His death was terrible. He was a lovely man. Another one who married the wrong person.'

'We'll talk about Sarah later, if you've time. Tell me what you know about Lily, apart from being an intelligent girl.'

'I'm not sure I can tell you much more, except she adores her mother. I think that's one of the reasons she's stuck with her job; she knows the people working at the fish and chip shop will support her and give her time off if she needs it; they do already. Alan Varley does most of the care, except when he's short of money and has to do a session on the boats.'

'He made a big sacrifice giving up his job to look after his wife. You can't fault him on that, Nancy.'

She tossed back the last of the whisky. 'I suppose most people would think that, but he's made it difficult for people to see Patricia. I'm not the only one who's wanted to pay her a visit, and has been thwarted by Varley saying she's too tired, or the doctor has said she must rest more. I checked with the doctor, he wouldn't say anything but I could tell by his face he hadn't said any such thing. The poor woman must think we don't care about her.'

'I should think Lily will let her know a lot of people want to see her.'

'Possibly, but Alan Varley is a bit of a control freak. He bought all her clothes well before she became ill. What woman would want a man choosing her jumpers, never mind her underwear?'

'If they were made by Yves St Laurent it might be all right,' Laurel said.

'A Frenchman? No fear!'

'Any more thoughts on Alan Varley?'

'He's aged since he left his job. He doesn't pass the time of day, no small talk.'

'The strong, silent type?'

'He's no Gregory Peck. There's something about him I don't like.' She squeezed her eyes shut. 'I think he doesn't like women. I'm not sure if he likes anyone, I always feel as though he thinks I'm beneath his notice. A useless old woman, no good to anyone.'

'I hope you don't think of yourself in that way, Nancy?'

Nancy scrunched up her face and laughed. 'Only when I look in the mirror at the hairdressers when they've shampooed my hair and I look like a drowned old rat.' She glanced at Laurel. 'Don't look like that. I soon recover after a colour rinse and a blow dry. I've had my

254

day; a lovely marriage to a wonderful man. I hope you might be able to say the same soon.'

'Nancy Wintle, you're good at changing tack. I heard something secondhand about Alan Varley, but I'm not sure if it's true. Someone said Patricia once told her, when Alan came back on leave, he made considerable demands on her.'

Nancy's eyes widened. 'Those kinds of demands?'

'Yes, he'd been away at sea for months, I expect he was . . . you know. From what was said it seemed it was excessive. Do you think it could be true?'

Nancy was silent, looking down into her lap. 'Perhaps it could be. I remember, it must have been several years ago, I met her in the chemist. She looked awful and as soon as she'd got whatever she came for, a prescription, I believe, she rushed off, almost doubled up, clutching her stomach. I was worried, and the pharmacist was concerned. I said I'd go and see her straight away. The pharmacist said, "Tell her to drink plenty of water." He looked angry.'

'Did you go?'

'I did. Varley had just gone back to sea. Lily was still a schoolgirl. I had to wait for several minutes before she let me in. Her legs were stained, she hadn't quite managed to wipe all the blood off. She said she had cystitis, but if it was that, it was the worse cystitis I've seen.' Nancy looked distressed as she relived the scene.

'Your husband wasn't alive then?'

'No, dear, my James was dead. A pity, he'd have made sure she had the right treatment.'

'What happened then?'

'She didn't want me to come in, she tried to shut the door on me, but she was still in pain, and she was still bleeding, clutching her stomach. I took hold of her and helped her to the bathroom.'

Laurel put her hands on either side of her face. 'What had he done to her?'

Nancy's mouth turned down at the corners. 'She wouldn't talk about it. I sat her on the lavatory, then when it looked as though that wave of pain had lessened and the bleeding stopped, I got her to bed,

255

elevated her feet with a pillow and found a hot water bottle. She took the antibiotics from the chemists and some painkillers.'

'She said nothing?'

'Not about her husband. She was very grateful and I stayed with her until Lily came back from school.'

'It must have been difficult for you.'

'Not really; you can't be a doctor's wife and not learn something. James would sometimes discuss cases with me, he never said who the patient was, but sometimes I guessed. Also, I'm naturally curious, and I'd ask him about various illnesses and their treatments.'

'Did you see Patricia again, after that?'

'I did, I called round several times to make sure she was getting better, but I also spoke to Lily when she came back from school that day. I explained about cystitis, drew her a little sketch of where the bladder is, told her how she could help her mother by getting her to drink as much fluid as possible, and I persuaded her to ring their doctor and get him to pay a visit. I felt I couldn't do that.'

'Did she ask any awkward questions?'

'She wanted to know how her mother had caught cystitis. I fobbed her off with details of bacterial infection. I think she had some idea of the cause, as she kept clenching her hands together. I thought she was angry.'

'Can you think of anything else about the Varleys? Anything that's worried you, or you couldn't understand?'

'All I can say is it's an unhappy household. I don't think there's much shared laughter. Lily and Patricia are close, but I don't think Patricia has confided in her daughter, and that probably means Lily doesn't feel she can talk to her mother about any problems she has. They love each other, but is there mutual trust? I don't think so.'

'Thank you, Nancy. Those are shrewd words. I need to get Lily's trust and hopefully she'll open up to me. If what she has to say will have any relevance to Matt's death, I'm not sure.'

'Good luck. Be careful.'

Laurel stood up and looked down on Nancy. 'Be careful? Who should I be careful of?'

Nancy looked up, her brown-button eyes wary. 'I meant be careful when talking to any of the family: Patricia is dying and both Alan and Lily will be in a fragile state. Tread warily.'

Laurel smiled at her. 'I will.'

'Give Mr Diamond my regards.'

'Certainly.'

'He's a good man. Very attractive. Sharp mind.'

'Are you trying to say something, Nancy?'

'No, just musing. Give Dorothy my love and I hope Mabel can come to terms with her son's death. Don't say that to her.'

'I wouldn't dare.'

Chapter Twenty-five

Alan Varley rapped on Lily's bedroom door. 'What are you doing in there? I told you, we need some bread. Hurry up.'

Lily opened the door, a book in her hand.

'Wasting your time reading again. Get down to the Co-op.'

'I'll go now.'

'And don't dawdle, chattering to people. I need to catch Tom Blower in the hut. I need some more work.'

She retreated into the bedroom. She spent too much time there. What was she up to? Thinking about boys? Thinking of that boy he'd found out about? He wasn't having his daughter labelled as a tart by the rest of the town. Women – all the same. Except for his lovely Patricia.

Lily came out; their bodies were close on the small landing.

'When are they opening the chip shop?'

She sidled past him, body close to the wall. 'Ethel said it might be tomorrow, if Mrs Elderkin agrees.'

'We need the money.'

'I gave you what I got the other day. Ethel is still paying us, but she can't afford to give us our normal wages.'

'It's not enough. We need you to be doing overtime.'

'I'll see if Ethel knows when the shop is opening; she might give me some work to do if I explain to her we need the money. I might be gone a few hours. Is that all right?'

'I suppose so.' What a lump of a girl. Her size offended him. 'What are you waiting for?'

She shot him a look of hate, and ran down the stairs. The front door banged shut.

He went into the front bedroom and looked at his dying wife. She was disappearing, shrinking, flesh evanescing. Soon she'd be gone. What would he have left? Nothing. Before, he'd had everything.

Life had been perfect. He thought back to – was it only a few years ago? It seemed like someone else's life. He'd served on the same ship for twenty-one years, working his way up to first engineer on the SS *Shanghai*. A top-class ship for the post-war people of Britain, taking them on cruises to the Orient and the Far East. He'd been someone, in charge of a spacious engine room, constantly checking the control station, making sure she kept up to 23 knots. Such a beautiful ship, with all the latest marine technology; the first ocean-going passenger ship to be fitted with anti-roll stabilisers. The best.

Sitting at the captain's table, when off shift, dazzling the passengers with his knowledge and stories about former voyages. The purser said it was the white uniforms that got them. The lady passengers – easy-peasy if you wanted one, whether married or not. They didn't attract him – most of them big-boned, with mannish shoulders, or plump little hens, twittering away.

Not like his beautiful Patricia, her features refined, delicate, her almond-shaped eyes a deep brown, her body perfect, childlike, with small, perfect breasts; they were shaped like exotic fruits, his to lick, nibble and suck. He shivered at past memories of her. Now her body was a travesty of its former glory. She opened her eyes, but didn't seem to see him, the pupils black pin-pricks, the whites a muddy yellow. The doctor had warned it wouldn't be long, today, tomorrow, next week. Would he like a nurse to help him? No. Never. He didn't want anyone else. He'd be there when it happened. Lily could give him a break, but he didn't want anyone else in the bedroom. He'd be there when she died. He even didn't want Lily in the room, but he had to try and get some money. Patricia might say something. The morphine was loosening her tongue. What did she know? Yesterday, she'd said, 'Alan, did you do it? Tell me you didn't?' Lily had been in the bedroom, putting clean nightdresses she'd ironed into a drawer.

'Dad, what does she mean?' She'd moved towards the bed.

'Nothing, she's rambling. Make some tea. I need a drink.'

She paid him no attention, coming nearer. 'Mum, what's the matter? What's Dad done? Has he hurt you?'

He got up and blocked her way. 'Do as you're told. You're upsetting her.'

'It's you who's upset her, not me,' she said, her voice full of contempt.

'Get out of this room. I'm not telling you again.'

'Lily, do as your father asks . . . please.' Her voice was weak, the words came with difficulty.

'Look what you've done, you've upset her. Get out.' He'd raised his fist. The look she gave him was one of loathing. He hated her. She'd always been difficult, rebellious. Too tall. Like the women in his family. Too big and too bossy. Why couldn't she have taken after her mother, dainty and quiet, always compliant? How he liked them.

Where was Lily? She should have been back by now. What was she doing? Who was she talking to? That Miss Bowman? God, she should be ashamed to call herself a woman, as tall if not taller than most men, with shoulders like a navvy. He curled his lip. Who'd want her?

His mind drifted back to his time on the SS *Shanghai*. Five hundred first-class and three hundred tourist-class passengers, looked after by a crew of five hundred. And the food – superb. The ship had its own bakery, a butcher's shop with a huge cold larder, but it was the engines – geared steam turbine engines, built by Vickers-Armstrong – that were his pride and joy. They were his. Until. He shouldn't have given up his job. But what choice did he have? He'd quit it on an impulse. He hadn't thought it through. He'd presumed he'd be able to return in a few months, but the months turned into years. Would they take him back? Someone else was in charge of the main engine room, someone else checked the boiler room, making sure everything was functioning correctly. What was he now? Nothing. What had he to look forward to? A funeral to arrange, a grave to purchase; a bed he never wanted to sleep in again. Bitterness rose from his stomach, crept up his gullet and seeped into his mouth. He spat into his handkerchief and wiped his lips. He should have stayed at sea. He was safe there.

Patricia's cheeks moved slightly as she breathed in and out; a sour smell hit his nostrils; he knew that smell: a harbinger of death. He'd smelt it when he'd sat by his mother's deathbed, outwardly solemn, but inside rejoicing. His father sat opposite, a picture of misery and despair. My God, how could he have loved her? She'd bossed him for as long as Alan could remember, along with the rest of the family. But by then she was silent beneath the sheet tucked tight around her, as if to stop her escaping. He'd wished she would open her eyes and see him sitting looking at her, the winner at last. She'd know what he was thinking, she always did. If only she'd wake up and say something, then he could press his mouth close to her ear. What would he say? 'I hate you, I'm glad you're dying. You're a fucking tyrant.' He never had the chance. His two sisters had been there as well. They were just like her: big, dominant women, wanting their own way, with timid husbands. They were crying; surely, they couldn't love her? Perhaps they admired her – she'd set them an example.

Patricia moaned, her forehead wrinkling. Was she in pain? Was the morphine wearing off? He leant over her wasted body and kissed her dry lips. From a bedside table he took a pad of cotton wool and dipped it into a basin of water, then smoothed it over her mouth. The tip of her tongue protruded and moved backwards and forwards over her upper lip, like a snake testing the air for prey. 'Patricia, Patricia, why did this have to happen? You've driven me to this. If you hadn't got cancer, I'd never have done it. Never.'

Her eyes opened, brown pools, close to his. 'Alan, what have you done?'

He jerked back.

261

Her hand crept over the edge of the eiderdown, fingers plucking at the material. 'Alan. What have you done?'

He took her hand and put it under the sheet and pulled the bedclothes higher. 'I've not done anything, except give up my job to look after you. Not many men would have done that, so think yourself lucky. What are you? Lucky. Say it. I'm lucky. Say it.'

Her nostrils widened and she tried to edge down under the bedclothes.

He leant over her. 'Say it, Patricia. Say it and I'll give you your next dose. Then you can sleep. Say it.'

Her lips quivered, followed by her cheeks, then all her body shivered like a trapped rabbit cornered in its burrow by a sharp-toothed ferret.

He took hold of her shoulders and shook her. 'Say it.'

'I'm lucky,' she gasped.

He opened his hands and she slumped back against the pillows.

She wasn't his Patricia any more. She was an ugly bag of bones. Her breathing was starting to rasp. It wouldn't be long now.

After Laurel had left, Frank didn't move for several minutes; he didn't like his brain being jumbled. Why had he brought the subject up? Laurel was right, it wasn't the time to try and sort out their relationship, but he was tired of shifting emotions, tired of longing to kiss her, to feel her body close to his, of waiting for her passion to match his. What was the matter with him? Was he just a frustrated male who needed a woman? Hardly.

In past relationships with women they'd always had something special, something he'd found attractive, beside physical attraction: kindness, intellectual ability, idiosyncrasy, a crazy sense of humour. He'd liked them as people; they'd inflamed his interest. But there'd never been one he'd wanted to spend the rest of his life with. Or even a few decades. He thought of some of his friends' marriages, when, after a few years, they lapsed into boredom, or one was unfaithful or, even worse, it ended in violence. Perhaps he should choose his friends more carefully.

He decided to stop picking at the problem, leave it until they'd dealt with the cases. Was Matt killed? If so, would they be able to find the murderer? Was Tyner the mass murderer? From his brief acquaintance with him, he wasn't convinced. But he'd been fooled before. He needed to spend time looking at the evidence, analysing characters and possible motives.

The trouble was he couldn't stop thinking about Laurel. Lying in bed at night she floated like a ghost into his mind: her smiles, her flowing hair, the vision of her running half-naked down the beach to dive into the sea to try and stop a murderer escaping. The agony of nearly losing her to the black foaming water, and her frozen body in his arms when he pulled her from the North Sea. Was he in love? For the first time in his life? Why hadn't it happened before? He shrugged. This was getting him nowhere. Time to see Tom Blower. He hoped he was a better detective than a potential lover. God damn you, Laurel Bowman.

There was a lull in the rain as he stepped out of the car, but by the time he'd reached the hut another sheet of water had lashed his face. The door of the hut was shut; he knocked and opened it. 'Hello, Tom, can I come in?' He didn't wait for a reply.

Tom and another man – Alan Varley? – were sitting on stools, mugs in their hands. Tom looked relieved to see him; Varley nodded, his face sour. Tom made the introductions.

'We were waiting for the rain to slacken before we locked up, but I think we'll give that up as a bad job,' Tom said. 'Like a cup of tea?'

'Wouldn't mind a coffee, if you have one,' he replied.

Tom glanced at Varley. 'I think you'd better get off, Alan. I expect you'll want to get back to Patricia.'

'I'm sorry to hear about your wife, Mr Varley. It must be very difficult for you and Lily,' Frank said.

Varley's cheeks stained red. 'What's Lily been saying?'

'I don't know Lily, I've never talked to her, but I think Mabel, Mrs Elderkin, may have mentioned your family. I apologise if I made a hurtful remark.'

Varley got up and threw the dregs of his mug into the stone sink. 'I'm off, Tom. Sure you don't need me tomorrow?'

Tom got up and opened the door, holding it tight against the buffeting wind. 'The boat won't be going out in this weather. Forecast says this will keep up for a bit.'

Varley sniffed. 'I might go out in my boat, see what I can catch. A bit of wind doesn't bother me.'

Tom's face stiffened. 'Then you're a bloody fool, risking your life in that boat. I wouldn't risk mine, and my boat's built for rough weather. Your boat would soon be swamped by this sea.'

Varley's chin jutted. 'It's not the boat that's important, it's the skill of the man sailing it.'

Tom jerked his head. 'I'll give you a call if I need you again.'

Varley stumped off, leaving a trail of misery behind him.

Tom slammed the door shut. 'That's the last time he sails with me. I'm down enough already, what with Matt, and now Sarah. A day with Varley makes me feel ten times worse. He's a good sailor and a hard worker, but I can't stand the man.'

Frank decided to stay silent and see what else emerged.

Tom filled up the kettle, switched it on and got a jar of Nescafé from a cupboard.

Frank inwardly flinched, but decided to brave it. At least it would be hot and wet.

Tom spooned coffee into two mugs. 'Like it strong?'

'One spoon's enough, no milk, thank you.'

'Sorry about that. You must think me a right heel, going on about a man whose wife is dying. If Betty could have heard me, she'd go berserk.' He hesitated. 'Although she doesn't like him, either.'

Frank took the mug and blew on the surface of the black liquid. 'Really? Why is that?'

Tom sat down and sipped his coffee.

Christ, he must have a throat lined with asbestos.

'She doesn't like the way he looks at her, says he gives her the creeps. He hardly speaks and when she asks if Patricia would like to see her, he fobs her off.'

Frank wasn't sure how to put this, he didn't want to upset Tom, he needed to keep him onside. 'Did Betty – is it all right if I call her Betty?'

Tom laughed. 'She doesn't like being called Mrs Blower, says it makes her sound like a whale letting off steam.'

'Big girl, is she?'

Tom laughed again. 'My little Betty! She says she's five feet, but I tell her she's only four feet and eleven inches. Drives her wild.'

The hairs on the back of Frank's neck stiffened. 'Has he made a pass at her? I presume not, or you'd have had his guts for garters.'

Tom shook his head. 'Not heard that phrase in a long time. I certainly would. No, she said she didn't like the look in his eyes, he kept looking at her as though she was a piece of meat he was thinking of buying.'

'Is that the reason you don't want to work with him again?'

Tom took another gulp of coffee. 'I suppose it doesn't help, but no, that isn't the main reason.'

'Can you tell me what it is?'

Tom squirmed uncomfortably. 'Why do you want to know? I thought you were coming to see if I'd any more thoughts about Matt.'

Frank winced. Laurel was so much better at getting people to open up. Sometimes brisk, police-like questioning didn't cut the mustard. 'I'm not being nosy, Tom. It may appear like that, and sometimes the questions we ask seem to have no relevance to the case, but every bit of information helps to build up a picture of the different people who knew Matt. It's strange, but sometimes the smallest remark can suddenly connect to another piece of information and lead to solving the case.' And, he thought, that's just happened.

Tom nodded. 'I think I understand, but everything's a bit complicated at the moment. What did you want to know? I've forgotten what you asked.'

Frank inwardly sighed with relief. Talked himself out of that one. 'About why you didn't want to work with Varley.'

265

'Oh, yes.' He gnawed at his bottom lip. 'I'd never worked with him regularly until the past few weeks. He did occasional shifts when Matt was alive, when Matt or I were sick, or had to go somewhere special. But these past days he's opened up about . . . he's started talking about . . . women . . . sex.'

'That's not unusual when you get men by themselves. The subjects are either sex, cars or football; although I have known some men whose favourite topics are spanners, and nuts and bolts. We all like to fantasise.'

Tom nodded and grinned. 'I don't mind chatting about film stars you fancy, like Brigitte Bardot, or Marilyn Monroe, dream women who if they winked at you, you'd run a mile.'

Frank burst into laughter. 'Away or towards?'

'You know what I mean. Lovely from a distance, but they're not real.'

'Varley wasn't talking about film stars?'

Tom wrinkled his nose in disgust. 'He certainly wasn't. He talked about all the women he'd had when he served on the SS *Shanghai*. Prostitutes he'd paid for when the ship docked in Hong Kong and places like that. Fairly slavered as he talked about them. Started to tell me details about what they'd do for a man, and how he loved them because they were so dainty and wanted to please him. He's disgusting. I told him to shut up. But the next day he started again. You could see he got a real kick out of going over what he'd done.'

Like Giddings. It was coming together. 'I know you don't want to talk about it, but did he talk about prostitutes from other countries, like Italian or Spanish women?'

'No, he said he can't stand buxom women, said they reminded him of his mother and sisters. The ones he went on about were always Chinese or other Oriental women. Dainty little women.' Tom frowned. 'God, do you think that's why he fancied Betty?' Tom's face whitened. 'That's it. He's never coming on this boat again.'

Frank drank the last of his coffee, got up and rinsed out his mug. 'Before I go, Tom, have you thought of anything new that might relate to Matt's death?'

Tom frowned. 'We've spent all the time talking about Varley. Why do you want to know so much about him? Do you think he'd anything to do with Matt's death?'

No, he couldn't make that connection, but he could make a connection with the murders of the young women. But it was tenuous. 'No, I can't think of a reason why Varley would want to murder Matt. Can you?'

Tom slowly shook his head. 'No. He had a great respect for Matt, as we all did. That man knew the sea like the back of his hand, and he was as brave as a lion. I do miss him.' His voice was breaking.

'I wish I'd known him.'

'He certainly wasn't himself before he died. I told you we talked in the Cross Keys that night, and I said I was always there for him. God, I wish I'd said more, got him to tell me what was worrying him.'

'Have you any idea what that was?'

'I thought it was Sarah, up to some hare-brained scheme, wanting to posh up the shop and turn it into a fancy restaurant again.'

'Anything else?'

Tom blew out his cheeks. 'No, nothing I can think of.'

'Varley's got a boat? Isn't it seaworthy?'

Tom screwed up his face. 'Perhaps I was a bit rude about his boat – it's a nice little motorboat. He bought it when he was in the Merchant Navy, he said he may have to sell it soon.'

'Would it be dangerous to take it out in this weather?'

'Very dangerous, but I think he was being awkward because I didn't offer him any more work.'

'Mabel tells me you and your mother made her an offer for the shop. I hope she takes it. We don't want to lose her from the Agency.'

Tom's eyebrows shot up, animating his clown's face. 'You won't mention it to anyone, will you? If she doesn't agree, it would be better if it's kept quiet.'

'Of course. Best of luck on that. I'll go now; thank you for being so open. You've been a great help.'

'Have I? Don't see how. Mind how you drive back to Dunwich, that wind's so strong it could take you right off the road.'

'I came over with Laurel, she's talking to someone else, so we'll go back together, she's strong enough to grab hold of the wheel if the worst happens.'

'She's a bonny lass.' He laughed. 'Not Varley's type. She's safe from him.'

The wind was stronger as he walked to the car. The thought of Varley fancying Laurel made him want to get hold of him and shake him until his teeth rattled. But Varley liked them small. Like his wife, Patricia, like Betty, like the Oriental prostitutes. Like the murdered girls? And what about Tom? With Matt gone, he and his mother could benefit by taking over the shop and boat. It wasn't a certainty, but if Mabel agreed, no doubt they'd get a good bargain. Was that reason enough to kill a man?

Chapter Twenty-six

Laurel ran through the rain from the Cragg Sisters' Tea Room towards the sea, Lily by her side. She was laughing as the wind caught her hair, sending it streaming behind in drenched snake-locks. Laurel felt like a teenager herself, the hood of her anorak blown back and her hair free and madly dancing. It reminded her of when she and Angela were young, moments of madness, silliness, uncontrollable laughter. Precious times. She hoped everyone had such memories to look back on.

It was joyous to see Lily running like a young pony, full of zest, her worries momentarily forgotten. They'd had tea together and she decided to let Lily enjoy the treat and not bother her with questions. But that had to change. She'd suggested they brave the weather and make for the public shelter on the promenade.

The four-sided shelter, with its hipped roof, provided refuge whatever way the wind blew. They darted into the side facing the town and collapsed laughing on the wooden bench. Laurel took a handkerchief from a pocket and wiped her face, shaking her head, sending a spray of water over Lily.

'Do you mind? I'm wet enough already.'

'Sorry. Here, use this.' She offered her handkerchief.

Lily giggled and tossed it back. 'That's no use, it's sopping wet.' She scrabbled in a pocket and wiped her face with a grey piece of cloth. She looked at it and bit her lip.

'Goodness, Lily, you've made me feel ten years younger. Oh, to be a teenager again.'

The colour in Lily's face, whipped by the wind and rain, was starting to fade, the gleam in her eyes dimming and the worried look returning. 'I wish I was as old as you, Miss Bowman. Old and independent.'

Laurel's feeling of youthfulness was dwindling. 'How old do you think I am?' Always a silly question to ask.

Lily frowned. 'Twenty-five?'

'That's another cream tea I owe you.'

'Really? You're more than that?'

'Just a tad, but I'll settle for twenty-five.'

'You're like my mum, she didn't like the thought of getting old.' Her face hardened. 'Not that her age matters now.'

'How is she?'

Lily took a deep breath. 'Not long now.'

'Did the doctor say that?'

'He came yesterday evening. Dad won't let me in the room when they talk, but I creep to the door and listen. I'm getting good at that. It's not a skill I'm proud of, but if I didn't do it, I wouldn't know what's going on. And I need to know.'

Laurel's heart went out to her. She must feel so alone. How could she get back to the conversation of the previous day, when Lily said she didn't want to live with her dad after her mother died? She was torn. She needed to investigate the family dynamics, but all she wanted to do was take Lily in her arms and try to give her some comfort and reassurance. She wished she could help her. But, how could she? It would be cruel to build up her hopes with hollow promises, if she couldn't turn them into reality. 'I'll try and help, Lily, but unless you trust me, I won't know how.' Sometimes she hated herself.

Lily reached out and squeezed her hand. 'Thank you, Miss Bowman. You used to be a schoolteacher, didn't you? I expect you know a lot about young girls. I loved being at school, I wish I could have stayed on into the sixth form.'

Laurel's spirit rose. That was one way she could possibly help. 'It's not too late, Lily. You could still go back to school when . . . it's all over.'

'I'm too old and it's too late. I suppose I could go to college, but I'm not sure they do the subjects I loved.'

'What were they?'

'I wanted to take A level music. I did really well in my O level. I used to dream of going to music college and studying singing. I'd imagine going on stage and bowing to the audience and they would applaud, and after I'd sung, they'd stand up and shout "Encore, encore".' She turned and looked at Laurel. 'That's a silly dream, isn't it?'

'No, Lily, it isn't. We all need our dreams. I used to imagine I'd represent Great Britain in the Olympics and win a gold medal throwing the javelin.' She laughed. 'Too late for me, but not for you. I've got a few connections, and when it's all over, we'll talk and if you want, I'll explore the possibilities.'

Lily's eyes glowed. 'Do you mean that?' She sounded as though she couldn't believe it was possible.

'Yes, I will. It'll give me great pleasure to help you. How good is your voice?'

'My music teacher at school said, with the correct training, she thought I would be good enough to sing professionally. She said opera might be too much, but concert performances would be possible. I didn't tell her I'd really love to sing in musicals, like *Oklahoma!* or *Carousel*. She didn't approve of them. I always took a main part in the annual Gilbert and Sullivan opera, from when I was in Form Three. I'm not sure she was happy doing those, but the headmaster was a G and S fan, so she had to toe the line.'

'Have you seen any of the big West End shows?'

'No. I'd love to go, but I saw *Carousel* in Ipswich; it was an amateur production. Mum and I went when Dad was at sea. She loves musicals as well.'

'I saw the film, but that's a bit ago. Mr Diamond, my partner, is very fond of "You'll Never Walk Alone".'

'Really?'

Laurel grinned at her. 'Only because Liverpool fans sing it. He's a Scouser.'

'Does he sound like one? Like the Beatles?'

'You get the occasional twang.'

'I've seen him round the town. He's very good looking. Ethel fancies him, says he looks like Action Man. Has he got a girlfriend?'

There was a twinge under Laurel's rib cage. 'Not that I know of. We're dedicated to our work.' She needed to change the direction of this conversation. 'What about you? Have you got a boyfriend?'

Lily blew out her cheeks. 'No, and I never will have while my dad's around.'

'Why's that?'

'He won't let me have one.'

'Couldn't you go out with a boy without his knowing? It's what I used to do when I was younger than you. I don't think any teenager tells their parents what they're up to.'

Lily's eyes rounded. 'I wish I was as brave as you. The trouble is in this town everyone knows everyone else. There was a boy I went out with for a few weeks. We were in the same form. He was lovely. I did like him. But Dad found out and went round to his house and shouted at his parents. They didn't know anything about us. The way he went on they thought he'd been fresh with me and they punished him – kept him in for a fortnight. He was furious with me and wouldn't speak to me for ages. After that it didn't seem worth having a boyfriend. I felt humiliated.'

'Why is your dad like that? Do you know? He must realise he can't stop you seeing boys when you get older.'

'He called me a slut. He thought because I was going out with a boy, we'd . . . you know. He couldn't believe we just wanted to be together. We did kiss. I admit that, but when Gary tried it on, he didn't dump me when I said no. I think he was relieved. You know what boys are like, they all say they've done it, but most of them are lying.'

Oh, to be young and innocent, Laurel thought. 'Lily, yesterday, you said you didn't want to stay with your dad after your mother . . . is that the reason? He won't let you live your own life?'

Lily's head dropped. 'Partly.'

'There's something else? Something more serious than that?'

'Yes.'

'Have you talked about this to anyone?'

'Yes.'

'To Matt Grill?' She held her breath, waiting for a reply. Lily sat unmoving, as though a spell had been cast over her. Laurel bit back the chivvying words dancing on her lips and waited.

'I wish I hadn't told him. It seems terrible to even think my dad could do such a thing. I don't like him, but he's still my dad. I used to love him; he'd come back from being months away, and it was exciting. He'd bring us presents from foreign countries, lovely things, toys for me and wonderful clothes for Mum. Beautiful silk kimonos and tiny silk shoes. Saris of different colours and jewellery, usually gold. He liked her to wear them in the house – not when they went out. He had to sell the jewellery.' Her head drooped.

'They sound like good times, Lily. Or wasn't it always good?'

'I don't like to talk about it.'

'Do you know why you find it difficult to tell me? Are you embarrassed?'

Lily raised her head, faint colour in her cheeks. 'It's hard to talk about your parents having sex. A girl at school told us how she could hear her parents through the bedroom wall . . . she'd laugh about it, as though it didn't matter, as though it was normal. She said they were as regular as clockwork, Wednesday night and Sunday morning. She said she and her brother always waited until they'd done it, then they'd ask their dad for more pocket money, or persuade him to take them to the pictures. He was always in a good mood after . . . usually said yes.'

Laurel laughed. 'Little tykes. But it is normal, Lily. Sex isn't the exclusive right of teenagers and twenty-year-olds. A couple can be married for ages and still want to express their love for each other, they can still turn each other on.'

Lily looked doubtful.

'One day, I'm hoping I'll meet someone, fall in love, and want to spend the rest of my life with him.' Laurel sighed. 'I haven't given up hope. If your mum and dad love each other there's no reason to be embarrassed.'

'You don't understand.'

'Then tell me, so I will.'

Lily looked up into the roof of the shelter, a few tears leaking from her eyes. She sniffed and impatiently wiped them away with her hand. 'It's not like love. It's not like those other parents. Whenever he came back on leave, it was every night, two, three times. I'd hear her asking him to stop. He hurt her. By the time he went back she was a wreck. Sometimes she could hardly walk. I didn't realise what was happening when I was little; she'd say she'd caught a nasty bug and needed to rest. She'd get better, then he'd come back and it would start all over again. She'd hide it from me, but when I got older and started secondary school, I learnt a few things about life and suddenly realised what was happening. I was about thirteen when I started my periods and Mum was so good. She gave me everything I needed and told me about how babies were made, and the dangers of having unprotected sex. I knew most of this from biology lessons and the other girls, but I didn't tell her that. I felt so close to her when she was talking to me, she wasn't embarrassed, she was lovely. She hoped if I met a boy and we loved each other, I'd want to talk to her about it.'

'That was good of her, Lily. If her own experiences of sex were bad, she wasn't laying it on you.'

'What do you mean?'

'Sometimes, if women have bad sexual experiences, or even difficult pregnancies, they go on about these things to their daughters. It can have a big influence on their lives, and put them off sex or having babies. Your mother is generous.'

More tears needed to be wiped away. 'I love her, what am I going to do when she dies?'

'Was this what you told Matt?'

Lily looked horrified. 'No. I didn't go into such detail.'

'What did you tell him?'

'Something I'd noticed.'

'About your dad?'

'Yes.'

This was difficult. One wrong word and Lily would dry up. 'When did you first notice this . . . change?'

'It was when he left the Merchant Navy, gave up his job and was with us all the time.'

'What happened?'

'At first it was fine. He concentrated on helping Mum. He busied himself round the house, doing everything. He does love her . . . he did . . . But now I'm not sure.'

'When did it start to change?'

'He started to get moody, snap at both of us. I think . . . no, I'm sure, he still wanted to have sex with Mum, even though she was ill. To begin with she made an effort – having a bath, putting on a nice dress. I know she was doing it for him; he liked to see her dressed up. Wearing high heels, jewellery, but some days she was too tired. It took her hours to get ready.'

Laurel's mind reeled at the thought of the costs Varley's demands had made on Patricia. 'What happened next?'

'It was a pattern. His moods would get worse, he'd say vile things to Mum and me. He'd say she was a useless wife and the sooner she died the better, then he could go back to work. He'd call me a fat cow. No man would ever want me. I was too big, clumsy, ugly and he was ashamed to be my father.'

Laurel felt like going to see Varley and telling him what she thought of him. 'That was vile.'

'Then all of a sudden he'd change. He'd buy Mum flowers, tell her she meant everything to him. He'd even be nice to me, and if he managed to get some work on a boat, he'd give me a few shillings and tell me to go to the pictures. I didn't like doing that, it meant he was alone with Mum.'

'What do you think brought about these sudden changes?'

275

Lily let out a deep breath. 'It was the last time it happened. He'd been horrible, cursing us. He hurt Mum, started shaking her, saying she was driving him mad. I came back from work and heard him shouting at her, and she was crying. I rushed upstairs and punched his back until he let go. He turned and tried to hit me, but I dodged. I shouted if he didn't stop being horrible to Mum, I'd tell the doctor.'

'What time of day was this?'

'Evening. I'd finished a shift at the shop, we closed about half-eight. He stormed off and drove away.'

'What time did he get back?'

'I don't know. Late. I'd stayed up with Mum in case he came back. I think I went to bed after midnight. I'd dozed off sitting beside her. When I woke up, she was asleep. I was cold so I went to bed.'

'Your father wasn't back?'

'No. I looked out of the window. The car wasn't there.'

'Was he in a better mood the next day?'

'He was with Mum.'

'But not with you?'

'No, he threatened me. Said if I ever attacked him again, he'd kill me, and if I ever said anything, he'd kill both of us.'

Was what she was thinking possible? She needed to go carefully. 'You told Matt this?'

'Yes.' She stopped and looked at Laurel, her face worried. 'I also told him the terrible thoughts I had.'

'What were they?'

'It was the day after he threatened me. I was still fuming, mad with him. I was on an early shift at the shop, doing prep for the lunchtime opening. I was so angry with Dad, the way he was treating Mum and how he couldn't possibly love me. When I was leaving the shop, it must have been about quarter to twelve, I bumped into Mr Grill. He'd finished early at the hut, sold all his fish. He was in a good mood.'

'"Hello, Lily." He stopped and caught hold of my arm. "Hey? What's the matter?"'

'His voice was kind and concerned as if he was upset to see me unhappy. I started to cry. "I'm sorry, Mr Grill, I'm all right really."

' "I don't think so. Come on. Let's have a cup of tea together and see if we can sort it out."

'He opened the door to the flat above the shop. I'd never been there before. We went up a flight of stairs to the lounge. He sat me down and went into the kitchen and made tea for us. It didn't seem right, me being there; I was afraid Sarah might come back. I knew she didn't like me. Mind, I don't think she liked anyone who worked in the shop.

' "Here we are." He brought in a tray of tea, teapot, cups, everything. "Like a Penguin?"

'I nodded. "They're my favourite biscuits."

' "Mine too, I've got a secret store. Sarah doesn't like them. We can be Penguin buddies."

'That made me laugh. He let me drink the tea and eat two biscuits before he asked me why I was upset. It was lovely sitting there, he was so good looking, so nice. I wished I was older and prettier and I thought how lucky Sarah was to be married to him. So, I told him why I was upset.'

'Everything you told me?' Laurel asked.

'Everything.' She bit her lip. 'Also, the terrible thoughts I'd had.'

'What were they?'

Lily stared at her, her eyes widening. 'Another girl went missing that night. The night my dad went out in a foul temper. I began to think about the other nights, when he'd gone out angry and the next day came back and was nice to us. I tried to remember the dates, but I couldn't. I shouldn't have had such thoughts and I should never have told him.'

'What did Matt . . . Mr Grill say?'

'He looked horrified and shook his head. "No, Lily, you mustn't think such things," he said.

'I felt awful. You're supposed to love your parents, aren't you?'

' "Your dad's been through some really tough times, Lily," he said. "You all have. It's hard on a man when he's not working. I know how I'd feel if I lost the boat, or we had to give up the shop. A man wants to be able to look after his family. Your father is doing the best he can, but I'm sure he wishes he could do more for you and your mother."

'He was so reasonable, so calm. I began to think I'd been silly thinking my dad could do such a thing. But then I thought of how he'd been with my mother – wanting to have sex all the time. Making love to her until she bled. There, I've said it.

'He could see I was still unsure. "I'll think about what you've told me. I've taken it seriously. I'm not dismissing it. I'll see if I can sort it out."

'"Please don't talk to him! You won't say I told you, will you?" I was afraid my father would attack me if Mr Grill told him I talked to him.

'"No. I'll go carefully." He raised a finger. "I know what I'll do. I'll check on the dates those girls were murdered and then I'll check on the lifeboat rotas. If your dad was out on the lifeboat on any of those nights, then we'll know it couldn't have been him. I wouldn't need to talk to him." He smiled. "I'm sure you're mistaken."

'I was so relieved Mr Grill had found a way to check up on him without bringing me into it.

'"I know your dad is grumpy at times, but I can't believe he'd do anyone any harm," Mr Grill said.

'He escorted me down the stairs and I walked away feeling ten times better than when I walked in.'

'Did you talk to him again about it?'

'No.'

'You don't know if he was able to check the lifeboat rotas?'

'No. A few days later he was dead.'

In that time, he might have been able to match up Varley's presence on the lifeboat with the dates the women were murdered. Suppose he found Varley wasn't present on the nights when a disappearance coincided with a call-out, or a practice run of the lifeboat? Suppose he tackled Varley, not wanting to involve Lily? Was Varley not only the mass murderer but Matt's killer as well?

278

'I need to get back to Mum,' Lily said.

'Will your father be there?'

'Yes. When I get back, he's going to Southwold to see if he can find some part-time work on a fishing boat while I look after Mum. We can't leave her alone, not for a minute, now. Someone needs to be by her all the time. Even through the night.'

'Lily, when you get back, make sure you don't upset your father. Promise me you'll not answer back, or inflame his temper in any way.'

Lily looked puzzled. 'I can't stand by if he turns on Mum again. I won't do that.'

'Please, you must try.' She needed to get in touch with Frank, wherever he was, and if she couldn't find him in the town, she needed to phone Revie. Would he think there was enough evidence to arrest Varley? She doubted it. It was all circumstantial.

'I think you must be very careful, Lily. Your father is obviously disturbed in some way. The strain of looking after your mother, not having a proper job, wondering how he'll cope, has upset him. He obviously loves your mother very much, to give up everything to look after her, but he is acting strangely. If you upset him, he might blow a fuse. You must be careful. Promise me.'

Lily frowned. 'Do you think he'd really hurt me?'

'It only takes a split second for someone to lose control. Your father's a big, strong man. Please don't provoke him. Not at this time. Do it for your mother. She needs a peaceful end.' Laurel felt sick – she was worried. If Varley was the murderer then he'd killed several times. With that behind him, how much easier to do it again?

'I promise. What are you going to do? I can see you're thinking of something.'

'You'll have to trust me, Lily. I can't tell you what I have in mind, but I'll be acting in good faith, and I'll be thinking of the safety of you and your mother.'

'Do you think he could have killed those girls?'

'I need to look into things. I'm not leaping to any conclusions.

279

I'm sure Matt Grill was right, it doesn't seem possible, but I'll have to check and make sure. Try and make your mother peaceful. That's the main thing at the moment.'

Lily nodded. 'Yes, it is. I must go.' She clasped Laurel's hand. 'Thank you. I don't feel as though I'm on my own any more.' She ran out of the shelter, the wind blowing her homewards.

Chapter Twenty-seven

Alan Varley poured himself a half-tumbler of gin and added a slug of Noilly Prat. He wasn't a great drinker, but he needed one today. A good one. He'd always enjoyed a drink when the captain of the SS *Shanghai* held cocktail parties for the first-class passengers. This had been his drink – Gin and It, a good gin with clear French Vermouth, not that sweet red stuff from Italy. He'd enjoyed the look in the passengers' eyes when the captain had introduced the crew to them. 'Ladies and gentlemen, may I introduce the most important man on board, our chief engineer, Mr Varley. Without him, we wouldn't be going anywhere.' Polite laughter. Then, glass in hand, he'd circulate. The men were always interested in what he did, the ladies in other things. Sometimes he'd invite them to visit the engine room. There was rarely any woman amongst the passengers who turned him on. Very rarely – but if there was some small and delicate female she was often too young, a twelve-year-old beauty, who in a few years would be ruined when she matured into a gross teenager, with big breasts and wide hips.

He sipped his drink and thought of Lily. She'd been a lovely child, he'd thought she'd mature into a replica of Patricia, but when puberty hit her, she put on a growth spurt, and the next time he came home he couldn't believe how she'd changed. Tall, with breasts and curving hips. And more confident, challenging him, arguing, wanting to know things. He'd started to hate her – she was turning into his mother. She was better looking, but with the same dominant character. She was quiet most of the time, but every now and then she'd rebel, want to go out with boys. His breathing was quickening. That's how she made him feel. He knew what she'd got up to with that boy. He'd put a stop to that. He wondered if she was seeing boys behind his back? Sneaking off to do it in some field, rutting like a bitch. He gulped down another mouthful, the spirit searing his gullet, making his empty stomach contract. Where was the bitch? She should be back here, cooking him some food, relieving him from sitting with Patricia. He'd better go upstairs and she how she was. My God, why did this have to happen? He thought of the past when the ship docked in Hong Kong, or Hanoi. By then he was usually desperate, having trouble keeping his temper with the men working in the engine room. Turning in his bunk at night, fantasising about the next time he'd have a woman. Not any woman. He had his favourites. He thought of Anna, pictured her naked body. 'What you want this time, Alan? Same as before? Or I try something new?' He gulped another mouthful, looked at his glass and refilled it. Body aroused, he climbed the stairs to the bedroom.

She lay beneath the bedclothes. Was she breathing? He put the glass on a side table and bent over her, putting an ear to her mouth. A weak spurt of breath touched his ear, followed by the rancid smell of a dying body, her skin glistened like old, worn silk. His lovely Patricia – ruined.

The women in the ports were skilled – but when he came home, she was the best. She was more beautiful than any of the prostitutes who served him, and the contrast between their expertise and her innocence and vulnerability was incredible. He couldn't get enough of her. She didn't like sex. She didn't say that, and she never refused him. He knew she got no pleasure from it. Neither did the bitches in the ports, they did it for money. With them he was never in charge. They pretended, but it was a business proposition. They were good at their job, but to take Patricia and see the look in her eyes as he penetrated her, to see the pain as he had her again and again, there was no substitute for that. Then he thought of the others. Yes, there was a substitute.

Her eyes opened. 'Alan?' Her voice was hoarse and faint.

'I'm here, Patricia.'

'Water. My throat.'

He poured water from a jug into a glass. He wanted her to die. He wanted to get away from this charnel house. To get in his car. To start driving. Looking. He placed the glass against her cracked lips. Lips he'd never kiss again. He wanted to pour the whole glass down her throat and make an end of it.

His nostrils flared as he steadied his hand and let a small amount of water enter her mouth. Her tongue was cracked too. He hated her. She was disgusting.

'Thank you.'

He raised his own glass to his lips and emptied it.

'What are you drinking?'

'Water.'

'You never drink water.'

'Perhaps I've changed.'

Her eyes, dark as treacle, were huge in her shrunken face. She was looking at him intently, studying his face, as though waiting for an answer to a question.

Lily took out the front door key from a pocket, but as she inserted it into the Yale lock, the door swung open. She stiffened and drew back. Why hadn't he closed the door properly? Was he home? Perhaps he'd left in a hurry and forgotten to lock it. She edged into the hall and listened. No. His voice filtered from the bedroom. Her heart sank. For a moment she'd hoped she would be alone with her mother. They'd be able to talk if she was awake. Every moment was precious, but if he was in the room, he probably wouldn't even let her stay and be near Mum. She'd have to go to her bedroom, or be ordered to the kitchen to make tea, or whatever he wanted.

She sidled to the bottom of the stairs. What was he saying? His voice was different, louder than usual. On tiptoe she climbed the stairs, placing her feet carefully so she didn't make a sound. Slowly, cautiously, she inched over the landing carpet until she stood outside the bedroom door.

★

'Why are you looking at me like that? What's wrong?'

Her eyes were unblinking, the skin of her face wrapped tight over cheekbones, dark hair matted to her skull. This travesty of a woman wasn't his beautiful Patricia; she was an evil crone who'd stolen her place. A witch staring at him.

'You're drunk. Go away. I want to die in peace. Where's Lily? What have you done with her?' The lines etched from mouth to chin deepened.

'What do you mean? What do I want with your daughter? She's a clumsy clod of a girl. Don't think I'll look after her when you've gone. I'll be off to sea. She can fend for herself.'

Her eyes widened. 'Thank God for that.'

He got up and leant over her. She didn't flinch. 'What does that mean? Think I might be interested in her? Not with those big hands and feet; she's got legs like an elephant. Now look at you – a fucking collection of skin and bone. You're revolting.'

'I'm glad you find me revolting. Anything to get rid of you. Why don't you leave now?'

'I want to see you dead and buried. I'll sell the house and then I'll leave.' He lowered his head until he was staring into those huge eyes. 'You never liked it, did you? Never liked sex?'

'I might have done, with someone who was kind and tender.'

Had she been with other men when he was away? The thought seared his mind. He grabbed her wrist. 'Did you do it with other men?' He shook her. 'Answer me.'

'No. Never.'

He dropped her arm and sat down.

'But you went with other women, didn't you? It's driving you crazy, isn't it? Now you can't, now you don't want me.' Her voice rose in triumph.

He leant towards her. 'I've had plenty of women, women who knew how to please me. They didn't whimper and lie like a corpse. They used every part of their bodies to please me, they didn't moan and say, "Alan, please stop, Alan, you're hurting me." Lovely little Chinese women, dainty Japanese girls. Every port a different

284

experience. Soon I'll be seeing them again and you'll be a rotting corpse six feet under. Or perhaps I'll have you burned up and chuck your ashes into a dustbin.'

Her mouth opened in horror.

He laughed – that had hit home.

Laurel went into the bookshop; she looked around. No sign of Frank. 'Has a man in a black leather jacket been in here?' she asked a young woman behind the counter.

'Oh, you mean Mr Diamond,' the assistant said, her face turning a shade pinker.

Laurel nodded.

'He was in here about half an hour ago. One of our regular customers, he always chooses such interesting books.'

Laurel suspected she was not only enamoured by his choice of literature. 'Really?'

'Yes, today he bought a book about the Sutton Hoo ship burial; we had to order it for him. It's published by the British Museum, you know.' She was obviously impressed not only with Frank's charms, but his intellectual abilities.

'I must ask him if I can borrow it when he's finished reading it.'

The girl's face dropped.

'I need to find him urgently. Did you happen to notice which way he went when he left here?'

'Yes, he turned left towards the main shops.'

'Did he say where he was going?'

'No.'

She probably wouldn't tell me if she knew, Laurel thought. 'Thank you. If he does come back could you tell him Miss Bowman needs to see him at once. It's very important.'

The girl nodded, turned, and started stacking books on a shelf behind her.

Laurel stepped out into the High Street and strode towards the town centre. Frank! He'd probably been flirting with the girl, enjoying her simpers and fluttering eyelashes. She stopped outside Calum

285

Tyner's antique shop, its windows boarded up. She was jealous. Jealous of a silly girl. Jealous for no good reason. Or had she reasons? How many other females did he flirt with? Did he date any of them? Come to your senses, she thought. Look for the bastard.

Where would he go? Adnams' wine shop? She checked. No Frank. She wasn't going to go in and ask the old man who ran it; Frank might have been flirting with him. The butcher's? The fish shop? She darted down the left-hand side of the road, peering into shop windows, putting her head round doorways. Where was he? Should she have checked Matt Grill's hut? Was he still with Tom Blower?

She was filled with indecision. Supposing Lily went home, annoyed her father and he lost control? She might reveal her suspicions. She needed to make sure Lily was safe. She'd go to Varley's house. What excuse could she make for going there? Think of one on the way. She started to run.

Lily bit into her clenched fist as she listened to her father goading Mum. She wanted to rush in and pull him away from her. She was strong, but not as strong or as big as him. She hated that he was her father. A man who'd been with prostitutes, a man who'd . . . raped . . . yes, raped her mother. It was rape if you said no. Some men didn't think that way, but it was.

'You can't hurt me any more, Alan.'

Lily moved closer. Mum's voice was faint, but she sounded . . . firm, determined.

'You're brave now you haven't got long, aren't you?'

'Yes. You won't be able to torture me any more. I'll be at peace.'

The sound of a chair being pushed. 'Perhaps I am interested in your lovely daughter. What's more, I'm beginning to think she's not my daughter. Who knows what you were up to when I wasn't here? I'm getting desperate. I need a woman. If Lily's not mine, it wouldn't be incest, would it? Think of that – Lily on her back, screaming.'

Silence.

'At peace now?'

286

Lily clasped a hand over her mouth, forcing back the bile rising in her throat. She gasped for breath as she imagined her father raping her. She started to retreat. She had to get out of this house. No. No, she must stay. Listen. Find out everything she could. Protect her mother.

'You are evil.' Mum's faint voice was filled with terror.

'You don't know how evil. Don't think I wouldn't do it. In fact, the more I think of it the more it appeals. That girl hates me.'

'Leave Lily alone.'

Lily's fear started to turn to anger. She moved back towards the door, arms stiff by her sides.

'What's more, I can get away with it. I'll rape and strangle her, dump her body far away from here. Won't everyone feel sorry for me? My wife's died of cancer and my only child has been killed by the serial rapist. I was here all the time, caring for my dying wife.'

His voice was louder, slurry. He'd been drinking. Was that why he was talking so freely?

'It was you! You murdered those girls.' Mum's voice was shrill.

'I wondered when you'd figure it out. Your body may be a wreck, but that sharp little mind of yours, when it's not full of morphine, is as clever as ever.'

Lily's body went rigid. It was true – her father was the murderer. When he'd said he'd kill her, she hadn't believed him, she'd despised him for trying to frighten her mother, but now she realised he'd meant it. He would rape and kill her as he'd raped and strangled the others. Sarah Grill – he'd murdered her. What should she do? She was static, like a steel girder, she couldn't move – transfixed with horror by the enormity of what she'd heard.

'It was *your* fault I did those things. I gave up everything to look after you. You became useless.'

'My fault? You're a murderer. Those poor girls.'

He laughed.

Lily felt the floor start to move. She was swaying.

'Poor girls? Sluts, every one of them. Out at night – looking for sex. They got what they deserved.'

'Sarah Grill? Her as well?'

Lily reached out and pressed a hand against the wall, steadying herself.

'She deserved it most of all. She was playing Matt Grill false. I saw her with Tyner, that antique dealer. Sex with her wasn't the best, but I enjoyed killing her. I think she put Matt on to me. It must have been her.'

Acid filled Lily's mouth. Matt. Mr Grill? What was he talking about?

'What do you mean? What has Matt got to do with it?' Mum's voice was full of dread.

An icy chill crept over Lily's body as though she were turning into a block of ice.

The bed springs groaned. He was sitting down. 'I didn't want to do that. I had to. I knew as soon as he asked to talk to me. I knew he suspected. I couldn't make out how he'd put two and two together.'

His voice was full of regret. What did this mean?

'You're making this up to upset me. How can you be so cruel? Matt died in an accident. Why are you saying this?'

The bed springs groaned again. 'I'm telling *you* because I can never tell anyone else. You can't bear witness. You'll be dead. Your cracked lips will soon close for the last time. I killed him. I strangled him with his wife's scarf. I'd been driving around, hoping to see a woman walking by herself, but no luck that night. I went for a drink in a pub in Framlingham, and I saw her and Tyner in a pub and she left it behind. I took it, I don't know why, I think I was going to show it to Matt and tell him his slut of a wife was fucking someone else.'

Shallow gasps.

What should she do? What could she do?

'Then I thought better of it, the bearer of bad news often gets shafted by the person they're trying to help. I needed the work on his boat. I kept the scarf, but I didn't do anything with it.'

Her mother moaned again. It seared her heart and stiffened her resolve.

288

'I made a plan. I hoped I wouldn't have to put it into action. I liked Matt as much as I liked anyone. He'd always been fair with me. Always pleasant. I knew he wouldn't let that cow Lily get up to anything while she worked for him. I trusted that man.'

There was a long silence. Lily strained her ears; the only sound was her father's heavy breathing.

'If you'd been a proper wife, I'd never have killed those girls. You don't understand – a man has to have his needs met. You don't know how it feels when you've not had a woman for ages. It takes over your life, all you can think about from when you wake up until you go to sleep is about doing it, being released. To have a dainty little body, as small as a frightened bird, in your power. Then you feel like a god. All-powerful. Supreme. You gave me that, Patricia. You were better than the whores. They could handle it – they'd do anything for money. If I went too far, hurt them too much, their screams would bring men to drag me off, ban me from their whorehouse. But you couldn't do that, could you? Why didn't you scream? Why didn't you go for help? I sometimes thought you might, when I'd run you ragged. Why didn't you?'

Silence.

'Answer me, bitch.'

Silence, then a whispering voice. Lily leant closer.

'I was too proud . . . I didn't want everyone to know what kind of man I'd married . . . I didn't want Lily to grow up ashamed of her father, being teased by the other children . . . I kept hoping you'd change. When you went back to sea it was another life, peaceful with my lovely Lily.' The words were gasped out between shallow breaths.

Tears spurted from Lily's eyes. My lovely Lily.

'Time you had another dose of morphine. Your last one, Patricia. A good, big dose. I don't think the doctor will want a post-mortem. He's expecting you to die any day soon.'

Sounds of movement. The bottle of morphine was on the dressing table. He was going to kill her.

★

Frank knocked back the whisky in the cut-glass tumbler. 'Thanks, Nancy, that was a good drop of Scotch.'

'I think you enjoyed it more than Laurel; she only had one to keep me company.'

'How many tots have you had this morning?'

'A good few, and I feel all the better for it.'

'You old soak!'

'Frank!'

'Sorry, Nancy, only kidding. Where's your sense of humour?'

'I expect young gentlemen to be polite to old ladies.'

'I can't see a lady in this room and I'm no gentleman.'

Nancy's laughter was like a tweeting robin. 'You should come and be rude to me more often, Frank Diamond, I like a bit of banter.'

'I'll add you to my list of women who need cheering up.'

'Who's at the top of the list?'

'Need you ask?'

'You really ought to do something about Laurel.'

'Any tips?'

'I'm so old, my memory has faded. I'm sure you don't need any help.'

'Well. If you won't help me, I'd better go. Thank you for telling me what you told Laurel about Varley. I think I need to find her, make sure she doesn't do anything silly.'

Nancy pursed her lips. 'Find her and look after Lily as well. Poor girl.'

Frank got up and made for the door. 'I will.'

He stepped out into the High Street and turned left, walking back towards the centre of town. Laurel was meeting Lily. Knowing her skills, he was sure she'd be able to gain Lily's confidence. Supposing she started to have the same suspicions he had? What would she do? He hoped she'd try and find him, so they could discuss tactics. But would she think of looking for him at Nancy's?

He stopped and looked in the window of the art gallery, under new management after the owner was murdered. He hadn't felt any sympathy for him. He gazed at the paintings sitting on gilded easels. Supposing she went back with Lily, and Varley was there? He *would* be there – he'd left the hut to go home. Where did he live? Slaughden Road, somewhere near Tom Blower. He should have paid more attention, asked more questions when Laurel was reporting back on her visit to Varley's house. He turned back. He'd ask when he got there. Everyone knew everyone in Aldeburgh.

Lily looked round the landing for something to hit her father with. Nothing. No time to go downstairs. Quivering with a mixture of anger and fear she burst into the bedroom. Her father was bending over the bed, a bottle of morphine in his right hand, his left hand clasped round her mother's jaw, forcing her mouth open. He jerked round, face white, eyes staring in disbelief.

She sprang to the right of the bed and bashed his hand with her forearm. The bottle shot out of his grasp, sailed through the air and exploded against a wall.

He let go of Mum. Her head flopped to the pillow with a thud.

Lily shot back before he could grab her. Get help, her brain said. Don't leave Mum, don't leave her. He'll kill her, her heart cried. She backed to the wall. Make a noise – lots of noise, her brain said. She found she couldn't shout – her chest was caving in.

He stood there glaring at her. 'You interfering, fucking bitch.' He moved towards her, arms outstretched, hands curled ready to encircle her throat.

He lunged. She screamed as loud as she could. 'HELP. MURDER –'

His grip was strong. Fingers dug into the flesh of her neck. She clawed at his hands, kicked his legs. She raised a knee and with one supreme effort stabbed between his legs.

He screeched with pain and for a second the pressure of his fingers relaxed. She tried to get hold of his hair and force him off her, but her fingers couldn't get a grip on his short hair.

'Bitch!' he roared and tightened his grip on her throat. He pushed her hard against the wall, his body tight on hers; she couldn't move

291

her legs. She tried to struggle free. She couldn't breathe. His eyes were close to hers, staring into her soul.

'Now I've got you,' he said.

She was dying. Her eyes were exploding out of their sockets. Her tongue filled her mouth. Darkness was falling.

Laurel ran up Slaughden Road. Perhaps she was panicking for nothing. Lily wouldn't be pleased if she disturbed her mother, or annoyed her father. She didn't care. She'd learnt it was better to look a fool than to have regrets for not acting on instinct.

'Help. Murder—'

She froze. A cry for help.

Arriving at Varley's front door she was prepared to break it down, but the door was ajar. Thank God. She pushed it open. Sounds of fighting, a struggle from above. She leapt up the stairs two at a time and exploded into the bedroom.

Varley had Lily pinned against the wall. Hands round her throat. Squeezing the life from her. Lily's body was sagging. He was so intent on his task he hadn't heard Laurel, hadn't seen her. She picked up a chair, raised it high, and smashed it down onto the back of his head.

Stunned, he collapsed onto Lily. They both slumped to the floor, Lily beneath him. Laurel threw away the remains of the chair and hauled his body off Lily, pulling her to the other side of the bed, moving her body into the recovery position. Her mind was seething with conflicting emotions, her breathing rapid, but her hands were steady as she tried to find a pulse. Was she breathing? She pressed an ear to Lily's mouth. She couldn't feel the slightest breath. She needed to start artificial resuscitation. She put an arm round Lily's shoulder to turn her on her back.

Varley pounced down on her. His hands gripped her throat.

'You interfering bitch,' he hissed in her ear. 'I'll see to you and then finish her off.'

No way. She grasped his hands, inflated her lungs and with a scream of anger and fury tore them from her neck and dug her right elbow sharp into his ribcage.

Woof! Air shot from his lungs past her ear.

She had to get them off Lily. She rolled him over and dragged him away from the side of the bed. It took all of her strength; he was bulky, heavy. Her muscles strained with the effort of moving him in such a confined space. He was gasping – bent double. She needed help. She grabbed a silver-backed mirror from a chest and shielding her face with her other arm she smashed it into the window. The glass shattered. She hit it again. And again. Regardless of the shards sticking out of the frame she put her head out and shouted.

'HELP. I NEED HELP. VARLEY'S MURDERING HIS FAMILY.'

Doors were opening. Someone was running towards her. 'Frank!'

Chapter Twenty-eight

Frank slowed down as a man approached him. 'Where's Slaughden Road?' he shouted.

'Keep going straight on, it's a continuation off the High Street.' The voice was much posher than the worn tweed suit the man was wearing. Frank speeded up. As he ran past the fish and chip shop, the road narrowed, with rows of smaller terraced houses on the right-hand side.

He changed to a jog, searching for clues as to which was Varley's house. The sound of breaking glass brought him to a halt. Silver shards spun through the air from a house farther up the street on the right, the wind catching the shining splinters, arcing them across the street. Doors opened. People came out. He ran towards the house. Crack. More glass shooting out. A blonde head poked out between glass daggers. Laurel.

'Help. I need help. Varley's murdering his family.'

A surge of adrenalin hit his already tense body. He surged forwards.

'Frank!'

She'd seen him. The hope and relief in her voice made his heart swell. Then a cry of pain and her head disappeared. Panic and anger seared through him. Varley was attacking Laurel.

He pounded to the house, shouting to the people in the street. 'Phone for the police and an ambulance.' He glared at their frightened, puzzled faces. 'NOW. Get the local doctor.'

The front door was open. He leapt up the stairs. Sounds of a struggle. Grunts and a sharp intake of breath. A cry of pain – Laurel! He saw red. Varley had his back to him. He'd pinned Laurel to the far wall, his hands round her throat. Laurel was trying to prise his hands away, kicking at Varley, but he'd pressed his body tight against hers. Lily was lying on the other side of the bed. Patricia was motionless beneath the bedclothes.

He tightened his jaw, drew back his right leg and rammed his knee into Varley's kidneys. Varley doubled up, releasing Laurel. Frank grabbed hold of Varley's clothes and pulled him round, clenched his fist and hit Varley's chin with a vicious right upper-cut. There was a satisfying crunch as Varley's lower jaw rammed into his upper. His knees buckled and he slumped to the floor. Frank dragged him away from Laurel, kicking him in the stomach. He'd never wanted to murder anyone before, but he did now.

Laurel staggered away from the wall, her eyes narrowed, gasping for breath, hands at her throat. Frank took her in his arms, holding her tight. Squeezing her to his body. Never wanting to let her go.

She wriggled, choking. He slackened his grip. 'Laurel. Laurel.'

'Lily,' she rasped. Blood was running in scarlet threads from her scalp, there were red fingermarks on her neck. Rage replaced passion.

Holding her by the shoulder he turned to look at Varley.

'Lily. I must go to Lily,' Laurel wheezed.

He nodded. 'Hold on to the bed,' he said. She grasped the bottom rail. He released her. 'OK?'

She nodded.

Varley was crawling towards the door; he tried to get to his feet, staggered, then lost control. Frank rushed at him. They shot out of the room onto the landing. Varley hit the bannisters. Wood cracked. Frank hauled him up and punched his belly. Well below the belt. Varley's breath stank of fear. He swung an arm and hit Frank's right cheek. Coppery blood filled his mouth. Enraged, he let fly a left-hook to Varley's jaw, causing him to stagger back and half fall, half scramble, down the stairs.

Frank started after him.

'Frank! I need you.'

He stopped. His desire to kill Varley was immense. His love for Laurel stronger. She was crouching over Lily, who was on her back. 'Is she dead?'

Her bruised face turned. 'No. I can feel a breath. I couldn't before.'

He knelt down beside her, took hold of Lily's left wrist and pushed two fingers deep into the flesh. There it was – the pulse of life. 'It's weak. Can you manage?'

'Yes. Go after him, Frank. Kill the bastard.'

His warrior woman. He started to get up. Lily suddenly jerked and coughed, blood running from her mouth. Her eyes opened. She tried to speak.

Laurel held her tenderly. 'You're safe, Lily. He's gone.'

Lily shook her head, her eyes frantic. She tried to mouth words. She looked at them, her face creased with frustration.

'Try to catch her words, Laurel. She's desperate to tell us something.'

Laurel bent close, her ear touching Lily's lips.

Frank moved as close as he dared, not wanting to harm either of them. Laurel's hair smelt of coconut. Her eyes widened at Lily's whispered words, horror, shock and anger playing over her features. She carefully withdrew her body from Lily's. 'Varley killed those women,' she said. 'Lily heard him confess to her mother.' She paused and closed her eyes. 'He also killed Matt Grill.'

His rage exploded again. 'Can you manage? There should be an ambulance soon – and the police.'

'Bring him to justice, Frank. I can manage.'

He was torn in two, leaving her with two injured women. Was Patricia Varley alive? Laurel's face was streaked with blood, her voice broken. But her words sobered him. It wasn't his job to administer judgement. He knew she didn't want him to turn into a killer.

He bent down and kissed her broken lips. She winced. He wanted to say he loved her. He got up and made for the door. Why hadn't he told her? He raced down the stairs.

A woman came into the hall. 'What's happened?'

'Has someone called an ambulance?'

'I did as soon as you said.'

'Good. Which way did Varley go?'

'I'm not sure, I was phoning.'

'Go up, see if you can help. What about the doctor?'

'He's coming.'

He pushed past her. 'Anyone see which way Varley went?' he asked the small crowd gathered near the door.

'He tried to get into his car, but it was locked and he didn't have the key. He swore something dreadful and then ran off,' a woman said.

'Which way?'

'Down Hertford Place.' She pointed. 'The road to the left of the Brudenell Hotel.'

Making for the sea.

'Anyone got first-aid experience?'

They shook their heads.

'Don't go up. Keep things clear for the ambulance,' he shouted as he raced off.

Chapter Twenty-nine

Footsteps coming up the stairs. My God, was it Varley coming back to finish them off, now Frank had gone? Laurel desperately looked round for a weapon. She scrambled up, blinking and grimacing as pain shot through her body. Where was the mirror?

'Hello? Can I come in?' A tentative female voice.

Laurel's body sagged. 'Yes.' She turned back to Lily. She'd collapsed. God, had she stopped breathing?

'Oh, my Lord. What's happened?'

'See to Mrs Varley. I haven't had a chance to look at her.' A body squeezed past her. 'Lily! Lily! Can you hear me?'

No response. Her face was tinged blue. She put an arm beneath Lily's body and raised her so she could press an ear to her mouth. Nothing. She should have kept Frank with her. No time for that. She tipped back Lily's head, pinched her nose and tried to push down the rising panic. She hoped she'd enough puff to keep *her* breathing going before help came. She inflated her lungs and closed her mouth over Lily's and breathed out. Lily's chest rose.

She withdrew and breathed in again.

'Is she dead?' the woman said.

Laurel shook her head before she breathed out into Lily again.

'Pat's alive, she's breathing, but she's unconscious.'

'Keep her warm.' Another breath.

'Can I do anything else?'

'Hold Pat's hand. Talk to her. Tell her Lily's safe,' she snapped, between breaths.

A drone of comforting words, said in a quiet, calm voice.

She paused and put a hand over Lily's chest. No movement. Another inhalation. Another breath out into Lily's lungs. Again, she placed a hand over her chest, against the sternum, and briefly waited. Nothing. Had she lost her? Grief seared her brain. No, he wouldn't take another life. She tried not to panic and resumed her efforts, keeping to the rhythm. Five more breaths. Her hand against Lily's ribs. Yes. A feeble movement. Another. Another. Getting stronger. Puffs of air coming from between Lily's lips. Tears of joy erupted and sobs of relief tore from Laurel.

'Oh, my God!' the woman said. 'Has she gone?'

Laurel raised her head to see a middle-aged woman with frizzy dark hair staring at her from the other side of the bed. 'She's breathing.'

The woman pressed her palms together and bent her head. 'Dear Lord, thank you.'

Laurel pressed a hand over her mouth to block the hysterical laughter welling from her.

The screech of brakes. A car door slamming. Urgent footsteps. 'Laurel! What's happened?'

It was Doctor Oliver Neave. Things were complicated enough without this.

Chapter Thirty

Frank wished he was as fit as Laurel. Was this the right thing to do? Varley could have gone anywhere. More people were coming out of their homes as he ran up Slaughden Road.

'Frank! What's the matter?' It was Tom Blower, a small woman by his side. He swerved towards him.

'It's Varley. He's attacked Lily – and Laurel. He's escaped. I think he might be making for his boat. He was seen running towards the sea. Do you think he'd manage to launch it by himself?'

Tom looked shocked, rain plastering his curly hair to his scalp; the woman put a hand to her mouth, her pinny slapping like a wet sheet. 'Why did he do that? Has he gone mad?' Tom asked.

Frank hesitated. 'Lily heard him telling her mother he'd killed those girls and . . . he murdered Matt.'

Tom's eyes widened, his nostrils flared and his mouth took on a mean look. 'By God, I'll murder the fucking bastard.'

'I need to find him. He must be brought to justice. His boat – could he get away in it?'

'Yes, he could. He keeps the key hidden on the boat.' Tom turned to the woman. 'Betty – we'll go and check his boat. If it's gone, we'll launch the lifeboat.' He turned to Frank. 'What's the situation?' He nodded towards Varley's house.

'Ambulance and police are on their way. Local doctor, too. Laurel's battered but in charge.'

'Betty, you see if she needs help. Right, let's get going.'

It was good to have someone else to help him. Ready to take responsibility for a sea search, if it was needed. He started running.

Tom grasped his shoulder, pulling him back, nearly sending him flying. 'Phil,' he shouted to a man walking towards them. 'Go to the shed. Send up the maroons. Get the boat and crew ready. We won't have the first engineer, so make sure you get Ivo. Wait until we get back. We may not need to launch.'

'There'll be trouble if we launch without asking,' Phil said.

'Bugger that. They can have an inquiry later.'

'Why are we doing this?'

'It's Varley. If you see him, you and the others grab him. Be prepared for a fight.'

The man stood there, his face a picture of bewilderment.

'Get shifting, you bugger. The man's a killer.' He started to run and Frank followed him.

'Who's that?' he shouted, as they reached Crag Path.

'He's the bowman, in charge of getting the boat ready and sending up signals.'

The wind and rain battered them, slowing their progress. Frank knew Varley's boat was beached near the Grill's boat and shed. This stretch of Crag Path seemed to have lengthened since this morning. He was buffeted landwards, having to push to keep himself upright, his sodden clothes heavy, the legs of his jeans wet and cold against his legs; it was like running through a bowl of congealed porridge. The wind sucked away his breath, and as they got near to the Moot Hall, he was gasping like a long-time smoker climbing a flight of stairs.

A great explosion rent the air. Even the storm couldn't dim the sound of the maroons and the explosive light high up in the heavy clouds.

'Good man, Phil,' Tom shouted, the wind tearing his words into shreds.

They stopped opposite where Varley's boat should have been. It had gone.

'Tom!' Another fisherman was running towards them. 'The maroons? What's happened?'

'Get to the boat, Col. I'll brief everyone. Tell Phil we'll be launching.'

'Who's that?' Frank asked.

'Another crew member. Good man. They all are.' He breathed deeply and let out a stream of air. If he'd been a dragon, it would definitely have scorched Frank's eyebrows.

'Right, I need to get to the boat.' He stared at Frank. 'Want to come with us? It's against the rules, and you must promise to keep out of our way. You deserve to be there.'

His heart leapt. 'Got a spare life jacket?'

'We'll find you one. Let's go.'

Chapter Thirty-one

They were inside the lifeboat shed. Frank looked at the tense faces of the crew as they focused on Tom. All, himself included, were ready in orange life jackets, fixed securely over oilskins. The men looked uncertain; some whispered. 'What's happened?' 'We've never done a launch ourselves.' 'Who's that man?' 'Is he going with us?' They seemed unhappy to see a stranger in their midst.

'Good work, Phil, getting the maroons up, and well done everyone for getting here so quickly,' Tom said.

'Scorched my fingers. Glad we don't have to do it too often. Striking that bloody stuff to light the delay fuse wasn't funny,' Phil replied.

'Don't worry, the salt water'll soon cure it,' Tom quipped.

The crew laughed as Phil shook his reddened hand at them.

'Right, let's make this briefing short. The mission is to find Alan Varley who's gone out in his boat. I'm not sure which direction he's taken. He can't have got far in this swell. We'll head out, decide on a Datum position, and start the search from there. We'll use the expanding square search.'

Grunts and nods of approval. 'Bloody fool. Why's he done that? We'll be risking our lives for an idiot,' growled a bearded man.

'I think you'll want to find him when you've heard what Mr Diamond has to say,' Tom said, pointing at Frank. 'He'll be coming with us.'

Low mutterings and shakes of heads. Was this a good idea if most of the crew were against it? Perhaps he should stand down.

Tom looked at him, frowned and shook his head. He gestured with his hand. 'Frank Diamond.'

He took a deep breath. He was going on what Laurel told him. He had no proof. He thought of Laurel. Lily and Patricia in that bedroom; Varley with his hands round Laurel's throat and Lily lying on the floor, life nearly choked out of her. 'I'm Frank Diamond, a detective from The Anglian Detective Agency. We've been asked by Mabel Elderkin to investigate the death of her son, Matt, your former cox'n.' Briefly, clearly and succinctly he told them what had happened.

As the story unfolded the men's expressions changed from suspicion and uncertainty to horror, disbelief and then anger. The atmosphere was charged with a thousand emotions, jumping from body to body, until the collective groans of pain and anger seemed to make the walls vibrate. The air turned blue with curses.

'The fucking cunt killed Matt?' 'He'll fucking pay for this.' 'Killed his wife as well?' 'Raped those poor girls? God have mercy on his soul, cos I won't!'

The room seemed to boil with anger, disgust and revenge.

'That's enough,' Tom shouted. 'We'll launch when I think you're in control. There'll be no thought but a good search and rescue. It's going to be difficult conditions. I need everyone to do what you always do. You are going out there to save a life. To bring a man to justice. The justice of our land.'

The swiftness of the reaction of the men to his words was astonishing. They seemed to soak back their anger and grief and the engine room was deadly quiet. 'Good,' Tom said. 'I share all of your feelings, but we know our jobs. Are you ready?'

'Ay. We're with you.'

'Prepare to launch,' Tom shouted.

Some of the men, those who worked on shore to aid the launch, darted outside. The rest followed them, but turned to the lifeboat, the RNLB *James Cable*. Frank was always astonished at the sheer size of lifeboats, and how majestic they looked. He'd never been aboard one, and now he would be on one about to be launched into

304

a rough sea. She was about forty-two foot long, her hull painted blue, her upper work orange, everything trim and neat. They climbed aboard. Tom shouted to him. 'Get in the shelter,' he said. 'I'm the only one allowed in there. If you want to come out, hold on to the rail.'

Frank was grateful and decided he'd stick with the shelter; it was where the ship's wheel was housed; he was curious to see how skilful Tom was at steering. He hoped he didn't make landlubber mistakes, calling things by their wrong names.

He'd sometimes watched the lifeboat being launched, usually for an exercise. Once he'd talked to an older man, who had helped with the launch. As the lifeboat entered the water, he'd turned to Frank. 'Nice, smooth launch,' he'd said. They'd got talking and he'd explained what he and the other men on land did.

'You got any sea experience?' he asked.

He'd looked disappointed as Frank shook his head. He didn't think a brief trip with Benjie Whittle off Minsmere beach, as they tried to save Laurel from her reckless swim in the North Sea, would count.

He'd envied the crew as the boat was tipped forward on its cradle and at a signal from the cox'n the Senhouse Slip on the securing chain was knocked off, and the boat started down the slipway. Now he was on board and his heart was racing. *Boys' Own* stuff!

'Everything ready, Ivo?' Tom shouted.

'Ay. Everything's working.'

'Start the engine.'

A powerful thrum shuddered through the boat, as though a great heart had been brought to life by a thunderbolt.

Tom leant over the side, hand raised. 'Launch!' The boat seemed to hang in the air, then it tipped, pointing down to the raging sea. Slowly, then faster, faster, it gathered speed. Frank steadied himself. Down the slipway, noise building in unison with the screaming wind. Like a fairground ride, she bumped over the skids. She hit the high waves with a tremendous thud and a quivering of metal and wood. The sea sheering up her sides, drenching the men. His throat was tight with a mixture of excitement and fear. Tom, at the wheel, eyes narrowed, was a different man. Hands firm, body taut, face grim, totally in command. Frank kept well back, out of his way. The rain had joined with the water below to form one mass, drenching sheets of solid water hitting the boat, as heavy and dense as though a giant was throwing enormous buckets of water at them.

He leant towards Tom, marvelling that he appeared so calm, his grip on the wheel firm, not knuckle-clenching. 'How does this rate?'

'This is bad, but I've seen worse.'

'That's encouraging.'

'But not much worse, and once we get out there, it won't get better.'

Frank wished he hadn't asked. He tried to think of something else, afraid fear would overtake excitement. He needed to turn his mind away from the angry sea as it landed heavy blows, like a giant boxer pummelling at his opponent's ribs.

He'd mixed feelings about the sea. Laurel had lived by it all her life and seemed unafraid of its deviousness. Despite living in Liverpool, a port on the Mersey, with the Atlantic Ocean not far away, he'd never felt a close bond to those waters. Especially the Mersey; although it looked majestic it was an open sewer. You only had to go over on one of the river ferries to New Brighton and you'd find the beach littered with turds. Certainly, if you could find a living fish in those waters, he wouldn't want to eat it.

An enormous wave, spume dancing high on its crest, dropped onto them. The lifeboat shuddered, was pushed down, waves rolling over the sides. She heaved up, hung in the air, then thudded down, into the sea. Tom's stance hadn't changed.

Frank let out a long breath; he hadn't realised he'd been holding it. Think of something else, he told himself. Liverpool University had a field station on the Isle of Man and he'd enjoyed the trips there, usually in the Easter break. The field work was good, sorties to the beach below the Port Erin cliffs, scavenging the rock pools, collecting animals, identifying the different seaweeds; at low tides, searching the giant Laminaria fronds for the elusive blue-rayed limpet. Equally satisfying were the rowdy evenings: eighty-odd students, and some were certainly odd, billeted in one hotel – the owners must have been desperate, but it was March, and there were few holidaymakers around. They'd organised their own bar, and fuelled by cheap alcohol they'd danced the nights away. Who says youth is wasted on the young?

Tom turned to him. 'OK, Frank?' he shouted.

He nodded and tried to look in control. 'Are we near the point you'll start a search?'

'Yes. I reckon we'll start soon. I'll note the Datum position and the first leg will be directly into the wind, then we'll turn ninety degrees and the second leg will be the same length as the first. We keep doing that, the next two legs will be longer than the first two until we've done six pairs of legs, unless we sight his boat before then.'

It was difficult to catch all the words. 'Sounds efficient,' he shouted.

'Here comes, Ivo, he's the second engineer,' Tom said.

Ivo worked his way towards them, hand over hand on the rail. 'No sign of the bugger.'

'I'm starting the first leg of the search. Tell the others. Everyone all right?'

'We're OK. This is a good one. We've got our eyes peeled, if the wind hasn't peeled them already.' Laughing he turned and crabbed his way to the bows.

God in heaven, Frank thought, these men are made from a different stuff to the rest of us.

He loved the beauty and restlessness of the sea; perpetually moving, reflecting the colour of the sky and the position of the sun, most beautiful of all, he remembered a still bay, surrounded by cliffs, a full moon arrowing a path to the shore, its light silvering the sides of the waves. A naked woman lying on the ravaged bed.

'Hold tight,' shouted Tom.

A wall of water towered over the boat, smashing down on them; the boat seemed to dive beneath the sea, shuddering as it fought its way back above the giant wave.

'That were a good one,' Tom shouted, his words almost inaudible in the shattering noise of breaking water and howling wind.

Frank hoped it wasn't going to be bettered.

Did Tom know where they were? It all looked the same to him. The sea was like a many-headed giant serpent, striking the boat in different directions at the same time. It thudded against the sides, swamping the deck, making the lifeboat shudder and creak as though it was fighting the beast.

Ivo worked his way to the cabin again. 'No sign of anything yet, Tom. I think the rain is easing a bit.'

Frank hadn't noticed.

'What leg are we on now?' he asked.

'First of the fourth leg.' Tom screwed up his face, leant forward and looked up at the sky. 'You're right, I can make out some clouds. He couldn't have got very far out to sea in that boat of his. Let's hope we find him soon. This leg will take us nearer the shore. I think if we don't see anything on the fifth leg, we won't find him, or his boat.'

Ivo nodded. 'Bastard.'

'Anyone seen anything at all?'

Ivo shook his head, sending a spray of water over Frank. 'Sorry, mate. Nothing but sodding water, salty and cold.' He poked his head outside. 'Definitely easing. I'll get back and tell the others. Hope this hasn't moved any sandbanks.'

The sheets of rain had separated into individual rods of horizontal water, needling his face; but it was possible to make out the sky. Thick clouds were hanging low, threatening to envelop and smother them in their cloying wetness. Briefly the clouds parted and a shaft of sunlight touched the lifeboat, like a benediction from above.

Tom let out a great sigh and turned to him. 'That's better.'

Frank admired the understatement. 'Thanks for letting me come with you.'

'Got a taste for it?'

'I haven't quite acquired it yet. I'll let you know. At the moment I'll be glad to get back to shore.'

Tom pulled at the helm, now the sea was bashing the side of the lifeboat. God knows what all the fish were doing underneath the waves. What did they do in such a storm? How many fathoms down before there was relative calm? He wished he'd paid more attention when he'd been forced to take an Oceanography unit at university. But the lecturers had been as dry as old rope.

It was slow progress, and still no sight of Varley's boat. What was happening on land? Were Laurel, Lily and her mother safely ensconced in an Ipswich hospital? He longed to be there, to hold Laurel, to tell her how proud he was of her, how much he loved her. He should have resisted the temptation to board the lifeboat. The initial thrill of the launch and the excitement of the storm were fading as hours of being buffeted, cold penetrating even the protective clothes, and stinging rain and sea water scouring the skin from his face were taking their toll. All this didn't seem to get to Tom or the rest of the crew; he began to realise that not only did the men risk their lives, but they coped with the sheer drudgery of covering miles of sea, and being permanently on the lookout. The crew took it in turns to report back to Tom, but they didn't linger, eager to return to searching the restless waves for any sign of life.

'Tom, afraid still no sign of the fucking bastard,' Ivo said.

'We'll be going into the second fourth leg any minute. Four more sweeps after that, and if we don't sight his boat, we'll head back to base. I don't think we can do more than that today. We'll resume the search tomorrow.'

Frank was relieved. He desperately wanted to know how Laurel and the other two women were. Was Patricia Varley still alive? He hoped, for Lily's sake, she hadn't died during the fighting. Lily needed to say goodbye to her mother and Patricia deserved a peaceful end.

As Tom turned the boat towards the land, the force of the sea and wind pushed her forward and for a moment she seemed to surf the waves. His admiration for Tom, the crew and all fishermen, grew as the voyage went on. He thought how Matt and Tom went out every day, regularly risking their lives to bring fish, crabs and lobsters to the hotel tables and people's dining rooms. He'd never moan about the price of a Dover sole again.

The rain was easing, wind dropping, clouds lightening, and streaks of sunshine hitting the sides of the waves and candy-flossing the clouds of spume. A lone seagull wheeled round the boat. God, he was thirsty; his mouth parched, lips cracked. He rubbed a hand over his face, it felt like sandpaper. Definitely a pint of Adnams tonight.

'A BOAT,' roared from the bows.

Ivo rushed up. 'Starboard, Tom.'

'Could be a wreck brought up by the storm,' Tom said.

'Don't think so. Looks like it could be his.'

'Any name?'

'None I can make out at this distance. Binoculars a bit salted up.'

'Right, let's get closer.'

Frank moved out of the shelter and grasped a rail. An empty boat, low in the water, was tossing in the waves.

'Looks like a Slaughden Quay boat,' one of the crew shouted.

Now they were close enough to make out the name painted on the stern. THE PATRICIA.

'Is he in her?' Tom asked.

They moved closer.

'Only thing in her is water,' Ivo said.

'We'll make a search,' Tom said. 'Back to your positions.'

'Could he have survived?' Frank asked Tom.

'It would be a miracle if we found him alive.'

'I don't think he deserves a miracle.'

'I'm with you there, but it's always a failure if we don't save a life.'

They quartered the sea for another hour.

Ivo came up. 'No sign. I think he's gone.'

'He has,' Tom said. 'He'll not face justice in this world. But he'll face it in the next.' His expression was grim. 'I'm sorry, Frank. We won't see him in the dock.'

'There will be no trial, no confirmation of his guilt, no explanation of his motives, no chance for him to show remorse and understand the terrible pain he's inflicted on those girls' and Matt's families. It's not what I, or you, and the rest of the crew wanted.'

'Ay, The Great Shroud has got him, along with thousands of other men, women and children. He's unfit to share their grave,' Tom said.

'You've read *Moby Dick*?' Frank asked.

Tom looked puzzled. 'What? Never heard of it.'

'Then why do you call the sea The Great Shroud?'

'Don't know; my dad did, and my granddad. Good name for the sea. Makes you remember to respect it.'

Frank couldn't argue with that.

'We'll put a tow on *The Patricia* and then head for Aldeburgh,' Tom said.

'Ay, can't have her drifting and being a danger to shipping,' Ivo said.

Tom manoeuvred the lifeboat close to the side of *The Patricia*; soon a tow line was attached.

'Right, let's get back to shore. Can you tell me any details about what happened, Frank? What did Varley do to the women? We haven't had a chance to talk until now.'

It was the least he could do.

'You sure Lily will be all right?'

'I hope so.'

'My God, it's going to be difficult for that girl. How will she feel knowing her father was a rapist and murderer?'

'I'm not sure. I know Laurel will support her, so will I.'

'What about Mabel? Will she be able to cope with Lily being the daughter of the man who murdered her son?'

Frank thought of Mabel and her past erratic and emotional behaviour. 'I'm not sure. What about you? He was your best friend.'

Tom sighed deeply. 'He was, but this is none of Lily's doing. It would be awful if she felt she had to move away. She needs support, her mother's dying, she may be dead already. She must feel alone in the world.'

Frank hoped the rest of Aldeburgh would feel the same as Tom.

Chapter Thirty-two

Wednesday, 13 December, 1972

Laurel stepped out of Frank's Avenger into the school car park. It was the first time she'd returned to her old grammar school in Ipswich since she'd left over two years ago. The car park was busy with parties of parents, their daughters and other family members disgorging from cars, shouting greetings to each other as they made their way towards the school buildings.

'What a racket,' Frank said.

'It's the end of term, it'll soon be Christmas. You always get an atmosphere like this at the end of the autumn term.'

'Do you miss it?'

She looked at the school buildings, golden light shining from the windows, the Christmas tree at the front entrance glowing with coloured fairy lights. High girlish laughter echoed into the night, like a flock of nocturnal parakeets who'd spotted a tree full of berries. 'Until tonight I hadn't, but I must admit this scene is nostalgic. There are times in the school calendar when everything seems magical. The last few days of term before Christmas is always special; the teachers are relaxed, they might even allow their classes to play games instead of lessons. The pupils are excited, looking forward to school finishing and lots of Christmas presents. It is a time of goodwill and we forget all the hard times, the traumas, the disappointments.'

'Want to go back?' He was close to her, his arm round her shoulder.

'I'll let you know at the end of the evening.'

Dorothy parked her Morris Traveller next to the Avenger. Jim McFall nipped out, shot to the other side, and helped Dorothy from the car.

'Thank you, Jim. I'd given up waiting for *you* to open the door for me, Frank.'

He turned. 'Sorry, Dorothy. Laurel was giving a speech on the wonders of Christmas in a grammar school.'

'Don't be sarky,' Laurel said.

Dorothy sighed. 'No squabbling tonight, please.'

Stuart's Humber Hawk drew up beside them; he and Mabel got out, as well as Ethel, and Tom and Betty Blower.

'Good. Everybody's here. Follow me. They've reserved seats for us.' Laurel strode out, making sweeping motions with her hand as though marshalling a group of first years onto the hockey field.

'She's in her element now,' Mabel said. 'Will she give me a gold star if I behave nicely?'

Laurel smiled. It was true. You never lost it. She couldn't remember how many times she'd reverted to 'bossy teacher' when she'd met a difficult situation during the past two years.

The main school building was an Edwardian pile, originally the lavish mansion of a railway magnate. Modern buildings were clustered round it, and the extensive grounds stretched to several acres. Inside the imposing entrance Miss Banks, the headmistress, was greeting the girls and guests; her tall, lean figure, gowned and gracious, black and silver hair swept up into an untidy bun. Laurel knew she'd be dying for a fag. Whenever she'd been summoned to her office, there was always one dangling from a lower lip.

'Miss Bowman, how very nice to see you again,' she said. 'I see you've brought your party.' Her gaze moved to the Blowers. 'Mrs Blower senior, and Mr and Mrs Blower, welcome. Good to see you again. As you know, Lily has settled in well. She's had a few difficult moments, but that's only to be expected.'

Ethel smiled. 'She loves the school. I often tell her to stop doing her homework and relax a bit.'

313

'She's a conscientious girl, working hard to catch up on all she's missed,' Miss Banks said. She looked enquiringly at Laurel, who introduced the rest of the party.

'I'm so pleased Lily is well supported this evening. Phillipa!' She summoned a tall girl dressed in a short blue dress. 'Please show Miss Bowman's party to their seats, front row, right-hand side.'

It seemed the sixth form had been allowed to wear mufti, they'd made the most of it, and there was plenty of mascara and eyeshadow on display. They looked grown up, not like the schoolgirls she'd left behind two years ago. 'Hello, Phillipa. How's the tennis going?'

'I lost in the singles in the semi-final to Judith Collingwood,' she said, pulling a face. 'I wish you'd come back, Miss Bowman, we still miss you.'

Laurel smiled at her.

Frank watched Laurel as the girl led them to the front of the hall. Was Laurel a trifle more erect? Her shoulders just a little bit squarer? She was looking round the hall, but he couldn't see her expression. Was she realising she'd missed being a teacher? Missed the camaraderie of the other staff and the atmosphere of the school community? He couldn't imagine anything worse, trying to enthuse teenagers with what? He'd have been a science teacher – didn't they wear tweed jackets with leather elbow patches?

Several girls waved to her, calling out her name, turning round, chattering to friends, pointing at her. A popular teacher? He was certain she'd been a good one. From the girls' expressions it looked as though she was well liked. Would he have expected anything else?

Phillipa pointed to their seats. He sat next to Laurel. She was radiating happiness and excitement, turning round, smiling, waving to people. A woman, obviously a teacher, moved from the side of the hall where she'd been supervising the girls stewarding people to their seats. She grasped Laurel's hands. 'So glad to see you. We've all been thrilled reading about your exploits.' She glanced sideways at Frank.

314

'Good to see you, Sylvia. This is one of my partners, Mr Frank Diamond, Sylvia Neal.'

He shook her hand; it was like grasping hold of a brush loaded with glue. She gave him a searing look from come-to-bed eyes. Laurel's face was a picture. He was tempted to play up, but decided instead to play safe, and peeled away his hand. After a few more effusions Sylvia went back to her duties.

'Who on earth is that?'

'She is commonly known as Sex-mad Sylvia. No man is safe within half a mile of her,' she said.

'If only I'd known.'

She gave him a snide kick in the shin.

He winced. 'She's bringing out the beast in you.'

'Quiet. The concert's going to start.'

The hall lights dimmed, and the stage's brown velvet curtains parted. Laurel was pleased her friends had wanted to come to the concert; she was proud of her old school. If she still had the love and support of the man she was engaged to when her sister was murdered, she wouldn't have left. By now they would have been married, possibly with a baby. Something twisted inside her. She'd loved the school, but when Simon and his family reacted in such a horrible way to Angela's death, there was no way back. She'd had to get away from the school, from her parents, from Felixstowe.

Don't think about it. Tonight wasn't her night, it was Lily's, but she was nervous for the girl. How would she feel when she stepped onto the stage and faced hundreds of people, including her fellow pupils? The last few months had been filled with terrible moments. Her father's bloated body found floating ten days after the storm, revealed to the world as a rapist and murderer, her mother dying the day after she was admitted to hospital, her mother's burial, her father cremated and his ashes broadcast God knows where. Lily wouldn't have them scattered at sea. She said she didn't want the sea and all the people it contained contaminated. The town folk, especially the lifeboat crew and fishermen, were glad of that.

But good things had happened: Lily had made a swift recovery from her physical injuries, her voice undamaged, and Ethel had offered her a home. The house her father had owned was in the process of being sold and the money would be turned into a trust fund for Lily. Ethel had persuaded her to work in the fish and chip shop at weekends, it had helped her to realise no one held her father's actions against her. But the school made the biggest difference. Laurel had seen how she'd changed as the weeks went by, growing in confidence, loving the lessons, and the music lessons most of all.

The atmosphere at the Agency had also changed. Mabel had sold the shop and boat to the Blowers, much to Stuart's delight. She glanced at Mabel. She'd lost weight, but the old Mabel was starting to return. Laurel had asked the team if they'd like to support Lily at the Christmas concert, and been overjoyed when Mabel said she'd come. 'I always liked Patricia, and I'd like to show Lily I have no ill feelings towards her,' she'd said. The rest of them didn't need persuading. Stuart had hugged Mabel. Was the blanket of grief lifting from Mabel's shoulders?

The school orchestra filled the stage. Frank sighed. She gave him a nudge with her elbow.

'Bear up. It'll soon be over.'

The first half of the concert was devoted to seasonal music interspersed with carols and appropriate biblical readings, mostly read by members of the lower forms. The curtains closed and the audience rose from their uncomfortable plastic chairs and made for the dining room, mince pies, tea and coffee.

'I think I'll stay here,' Frank said.

She wasn't going to persuade or cajole him. 'Make sure you're still here when I get back. Don't go off with you-know-who. Shall I bring you a mince pie?'

'Do they serve Adnams?'

She tweaked his ear as she swept past him. The dining hall was jammed, the noise ferocious; the school cook and staff were busy at the hatches, and Miss Banks in command as she swept round the dining room, doling out praise or admonishments as appropriate. She waved Laurel over.

'You did well bringing Lily to us. She's enormously talented. University material, no doubt about that.'

'I'm very grateful you took her.'

'I was concerned for her to begin with, I thought it would be too much for her. It's difficult to come into a school after the start of term, and to have *that* albatross round her neck.'

'Thank you for getting the Education Department on her side.'

Miss Banks smiled. 'I know which strings to pull.'

Laurel didn't doubt that.

'Time you went back to your seat, Miss Bowman. Where's your handsome partner?'

'He's contemplating his navel.'

Miss Banks snorted. 'Was it safe to leave him unprotected? I saw Miss Neal making a bee-line for him.'

Laurel wondered if Miss Banks had a Frank hidden away somewhere.

The audience settled down, the chatter died and the hall lights dimmed. The muffled sounds of scraping of bows and tinkling of piano keys drifted from behind the curtains into the auditorium.

Laurel's heart was fluttering with nervousness. Dorothy, on her other side, looked at her, grimaced, and squeezed her hand. Supposing Lily wouldn't be able to cope with the occasion? She felt sick, her stomach was somersaulting, as though she was on a terrifying fairground ride.

Frank shot her a look. 'Are you OK?'

She swallowed and nodded. This was ridiculous. She wished she hadn't eaten two mince pies.

The curtains parted and Lily, wearing a dark blue dress with a cream lace collar, walked to the centre of the stage in front of the now silent orchestra. Her hands gripped some music sheets. Frank's body tightened against Laurel's. There was nothing they could do to help Lily. She looked vulnerable, alone.

The Head of Music, a small dynamic woman, rapped her baton on the podium. What little sound there was faded away.

The woman nodded to Lily and smiled. A smile that said: You can do it. I have every confidence you will perform well.

Lily took a deep breath and straightened her back. There was a pause. Laurel felt she was about to explode.

'Tonight, I am going to sing for you two songs from my favourite musical *Carousel*. The first song is "What's the Use of Wond'rin'". In the story Julie sings of her love for Billy, he's a rogue, and is always getting into trouble, but she can't help loving him.'

The orchestra played the opening refrain, Lily opened her arms, seeming to embrace the audience, and sang.

Laurel's heart melted as the beautiful young voice filled the hall. She bit her lip, trying to keep back tears. The words moved her. It was true, when you loved someone, it was immaterial who they were, or what they did, there was nothing you could do about it except love them.

Frank was astounded. What a great voice, and Lily looked terrific. She'd lost weight since the double tragedy; he could see in a few years, when time had given character to her face, she would be a beauty. *Carousel* wasn't his favourite musical, too whimsical, all about angels and stars. 'You'll Never Walk Alone' was incredible, but you needed the voice of The Kop to do it justice.

There was a moment's silence as the last thrilling words faded. Then the hall exploded into applause. Lily bowed to the audience, several times.

'Thank you,' she said, smiling and glowing as the handclaps finally stopped. 'The second song from *Carousel* is "If I Loved You". Julie and Billy sing a duet, but neither hears the other, as they sing of their love. Then they part, never to know they love each other. It's a beautiful but sad song.'

Again, her voice soared, filling the hall. He was amazed at the depths of emotion she was able to express. The words needled him. It was true, he'd never told Laurel he loved her. Did she love him?

318

Were they like Julie and Billy, wasting their love? Both afraid of what would happen if they declared they loved each other? Afraid of what? Rejection? Embarrassment? Uncertainty? How did she feel about him?

He looked at Laurel. She was staring at Lily, her mouth half-open, lips curled with joy and pride. Had she ever looked so happy? She turned to him and gave him a sweet, trusting smile, like that of a young child. She reached out and took hold of his hand. His heart was breaking. Was the smile for him? Or for the beauty of Lily's voice? Or for the realisation this is where she belonged, that this was her true metier? He returned the pressure of her fingers and smiled back at her.

Author's Note

I haven't yet met an author who doesn't like doing research. When asked how the next book is coming along, if it isn't, I say, 'I haven't quite completed the research yet.' I don't think I'm the only novelist who bends the truth a tad.

The highlight of this dreadful year was a week in September self-catering in a cottage in Aldeburgh, where this novel mainly takes place. The best part of the week was meeting local people who have helped me with research for *The Great Shroud* and also the previous novel, *The Ship of Death*.

Research involved sampling the products of the famous Aldeburgh Fish and Chip Shop and meeting the owner, Peter, and his partner, Sally, at their house for coffee and a chat. Peter started working for his parents in the shop as a teenager and continues to put in shifts as a fryer. He was able to answer all my questions about the shop in the 1970s and showed me photographs of himself as a young man, slim as now, but with more hair, wielding a giant metal net as he scooped out battered cod.

The next day I met Charles, the Lifeboat Operations Manager for the Aldeburgh RNLI (Royal National Lifeboat Institution) and his wife, Beryl. Charles had already answered many questions by email and he has continued to do this during the writing of the book. I can't thank him enough.

Lastly, I met David, a volunteer for the RSPB (Royal Society for the Protection of Birds) and his wife, Bonnie, for a thank you lunch for all the valuable information he gave me about Minsmere Bird Reserve in the 1970s: the setting for *The Ship of Death*.

This is the best kind of research, meeting kind and interesting people who give generously of their time and knowledge to this grateful writer.

Acknowledgements

My thanks to Simon and Gail for their love and support.

To all my friends who have helped me through a difficult year.

To the marvellous people at Headline: to my editor, Bea Grabowska, for her kindness and understanding when times have been challenging, and her continued efficiency and help with improving this book; to designer, Simon Michele, for his fantastic and evocative cover – just what I visualized; to eagle-eyed proofreader, Jill Cole, and all the other people at Headline for their hard work in making this novel a reality.

To my other editor, Jay Dixon, for her sympathetic and efficient editing of *The Great Shroud*. Such a good person to work with.

To Charles Walker, former Lifeboat Operations Manager of Aldeburgh RNLI, for his full and detailed answers to my numerous questions. His patience was incredible!

To Peter Cooney, owner of The Aldeburgh Fish and Chip Shop, for answering my questions about life in a chip shop in the 1970s.

All mistakes, both deliberate and unintentional, are mine.

**Discover more gripping mysteries from
Vera Morris . . .**

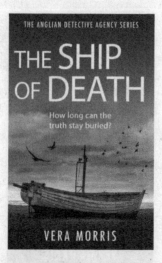

THE ANGLIAN DETECTIVE AGENCY SERIES

THE SHIP OF DEATH

How long can the
truth stay buried?

VERA MORRIS

**With a ruthless criminal loose on the Suffolk coast, life is
anything but peaceful for the Anglian Detective Agency . . .**

At Rooks Wood Farm, Rosalind Breen's twin sons grieve her death.
Daniel shoulders the burdens of running the farm and caring for
his brother, Caleb, who's shunned for his strange appearance.

Meanwhile, Minsmere Bird Reserve is suffering a spate of vandalism
and senior partners of the Anglican Detective Agency, Frank
Diamond and Laurel Bowman, are enlisted to find the culprits.
But shortly after taking the case, Laurel discovers the body
of a young man dumped in one of the meres and the
detectives are caught up in a murder enquiry.

All evidence points to one suspect but can the Anglian
Detective Agency catch the killer? Or will it take
another death for the truth to be finally set free?

Available to order

ACCENT

You can run but you can't hide . . .

Laurel Bowman has started a new life as a teacher on the isolated
Suffolk coast while she tries to get over the murder of her sister.
But it seems she cannot escape from death.

When the headmaster's wife is murdered, the detective in charge,
idiosyncratic DI Frank Diamond, soon has a list of suspects.
He is no stranger to Laurel, but despite their troubled past,
together they start to unravel the truth.

Then the murderer strikes again and Laurel must fight,
not just for justice, but for her life.

Available to order

ACCENT

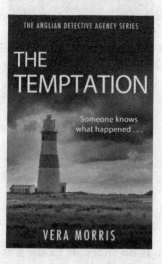

THE ANGLIAN DETECTIVE AGENCY SERIES

THE TEMPTATION

Someone knows
what happened . . .

VERA MORRIS

Someone knows what happened . . .

1971. David was thirteen when he went missing two years ago.
It's now up to Laurel Bowman and Frank Diamond, partners in
the newly formed Anglian Detective Agency, to find him.

But how do you solve a cold case with no leads? Could it have
anything to do with the brutal deaths of three local residents?

As their first big case unravels, they uncover a circle of temptations,
destruction and deceit. But the closer they get to solving
the case, the more exposed they are to danger. And now
both Laurel and Frank's lives are at risk . . .

Available to order

ACCENT

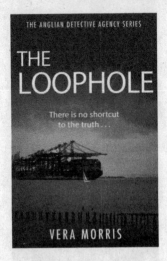

THE ANGLIAN DETECTIVE AGENCY SERIES

THE LOOPHOLE

There is no shortcut
to the truth . . .

VERA MORRIS

There is no shortcut to the truth . . .

On the hunt for two missing persons, Laurel Bowman and Frank
Diamond find they have another complex and dangerous case on their
hands as they go undercover at a holiday camp near Orford in Suffolk.

Using illicit searches, they uncover incriminating evidence about
several members of staff. Then two people are brutally murdered
and their missing persons case takes an even darker turn.

Does the answer lie in the past, with the long-ago murder of a young
mother and her baby son? What part does Orford Ness, a forbidden
and dangerous spit of land, play in this spine-chilling mystery?

Laurel and Frank uncover a web of deceit and cruelty as they
try to stop an ingenious sadist from murdering again.

Available to order

ACCENT